THE BREATHS WE TAKE

Seasons of Chadham High, Book Three

Huston Piner

A NineStar Press Publication

Published by NineStar Press
P.O. Box 91792,
Albuquerque, New Mexico, 87199 USA.
www.ninestarpress.com

The Breaths We Take

Printed in the USA
First Edition
November, 2018

Print ISBN: 978-1-949909-35-7

Also available in eBook, ISBN: 978-1-949909-28-9

Warning: This book contains homophobic language, underage drinking, and the death of a character.

A glossary of Yiddish and Hebrew terms can be found at the end of the book.

It's 1992, and seventeen-year-old Ben Carpenter has everything all figured out. He's gay, with a supportive family; he makes decent grades; and in Ted, Hope, and Doris, he's got three great friends he can always depend on. If he only had a boyfriend, life would be perfect, and he's working on that.

But things are getting complicated. First, Doris drags him into an ill-fated matchmaking scheme that could destroy their friendship with Ted and Hope. Then, Grandpa Marty moves in, throwing the whole Carpenter household into a total uproar. If that's not enough, the only way for Ben to get in his community service hours is to volunteer at the senior center, even though old people give him the creeps. And then there's that little matter of his feelings for Ted's brother Adrian that confuse him and threaten to expose a secret Ted must never know.

Ben's journey is littered with misunderstandings, tender moments, and unexpected ghosts from the past that reveal a two-decades-old mystery. As events unfold, Ben is forced to reevaluate what friendship, family, and love are really all about, and he discovers that, sometimes, there's more to life than a happy ending.

Seasons of Chadham High explores the evolving experience of gay teenagers in different eras—from the psychedelic sixties, through the me generation seventies and eighties, to the nihilistic nineties and beyond.

Eternal thanks to Raevyn, Elizabetta, & Natasha, to Kim Harnes & Michael Bowler, and to all the young people in love being themselves despite what others want them to be.

Love is like the air we breathe; it isn't always seen,

but it is heard, felt, and needed. ~Justin Martyr

Chapter One

SEPTEMBER 1992

There are certain days when everything just seems to come together. Then there are those days when things all fly apart. Well, there's also the kind when things begin to change. For me, a sunny day at the start of my junior year of high school was such a day. It began like any other, but before it was over, my life had taken a turn, and soon, everything—from my relationships with friends and family to what I thought I knew about love—would be changed forever.

So there we were, at one of the tables outside the lunchroom, just back from Labor Day weekend. Doris and I were sitting across from Hope and Ted, all of us soaking up the sunshine. The wind was a little gusty, but nobody was complaining. At least it drove the stench off. (Only Chadham High would put the dumpsters right around the corner from the school's one outdoor eating area.)

"Hey Ben, pass the salt."

I cut Ted a reproachful glance. The only shaker was two tables away.

"Why am I always the one who has to get the salt?"

"Don't be such a whiner. It's like social contract theory. You do little things for us, and we all do little things for you."

"Such as...?"

Hope flicked sandy-brown bangs out of her face. "Such as making sure you find the right guy to hook up with."

"The right guy?" I said, depositing the shaker just out of Ted's reach. "What do you mean the right guy?"

"Oh come on, Ben. You know when the right guy comes along, we'll all chip in to help you get him."

"Yeah, yeah, like that's ever going to happen. Here. At Chadham High. In this lifetime."

Doris nudged me in the side. "You've just got to be patient."

"Patient? My high school career's already halfway over, and I've got nothing to show for it. 'The right guy.' At this point, I'd be happy to have *any* guy show even a hint of interest in me."

I hadn't even finished speaking when Grant Framingham shuffled past us. Doris raised a sarcastic eyebrow and snickered, watching me grimace at his weasel-like nose and mousy brown hair.

"Really? *Any* guy?"

"Uh, no. On second thought, I'll wait for the right guy."

"You mean Colby Ryder," Hope said in a playful, mocking tone.

As if on cue, Colby emerged from the lunchroom, that luxurious ebony hair of his floating in the breeze, those dark-chocolate eyes gleaming in the sunlight. My heartbeat quickened, and my skin tingled at the very sight of him. He was so hot you could get burned by just touching him—not that I'd ever had that opportunity.

I watched him pass us, my shoulders slumping, while various fantasy images danced through my head.

"Oh God, what I could do to that boy. Why oh why couldn't he be gay?"

"Benjie," Doris chirped in a singsong voice. "Whining."

"It's just not fair," I said peevishly. "And I'm *not* a whiner."

They all laughed.

Okay. The truth was, maybe I *did* whine a bit—every now and then. But whining just came with the territory when you were seventeen years old, gay, and devilishly handsome, *and* you had about as much chance of finding a boyfriend as winning the lottery.

My problem was a question of demographics. Chadham High was one of those places where everybody fit into neat little boxes. We had the snotty *I'm Involved in Everything and All the Teachers Love Me* association. Then there was the *I'm a Jock and I'll Punch Your Face if I Want To* crew. We had the obligatory *I'm Smart and You're Not* guild, the *My Religion Says You're Going to Hell* congregation, and any number of the *I'm a* (fill in the demographic group of your choice) *and I'm Better Than You* societies. And of course, what self-respecting high school would be complete without the *Dude, Pass that Joint* tribe? As for the rest, they all fell into the *Please God, Just Let Me Live Long Enough to Get Out of Here* nation. That's the box Ted, Doris, Hope, and I were all in.

But what we *didn't* seem to have at good old Chadham High, at least as far as I'd been able to tell over the past two years, was more than the one lone gay student—me. Now, they say statistically, at least five percent of any given population will be homosexual. That meant there should have been about a hundred or so young gay people running around, and therefore, at least a few of them should have been healthy gay males. But if there were any other queers at Chadham High besides me, I'd long since come to the conclusion they were masters of disguise. I mean, sheesh. Talk about keeping a low profile.

I plopped my elbow on the table and cupped my chin in my hand. "Why can't any of the beautiful guys around here be gay?"

"Well," Ted said, "good looks are God's compensation for not giving us straight guys a good sense of fashion."

Doris leaned back in her chair with her mouth hanging open and stared at him.

"Oh Ted, I'm so sorry, and you lost out on *both*."

She burst into a fit of laughter, and Hope and I snickered.

Ted ignored her, stretched for the shaker, and sighed when he had to half stand to reach it. Then he unceremoniously dumped an ungodly large mountain of salt on his food.

Doris scowled.

"Ted, I swear you're going to give yourself a coronary."

He raised a sodium-laden fork to his mouth. "It's the only way I can stand to eat this crap."

She shook her head as Hope picked up the shaker and poured a liberal mound of salt onto her own plate.

"You know, you *could* just get an apple or an orange."

"Even the fruit here stinks," he said through a mouthful of whatever it was he was eating.

He was right. I glanced at the orange peel lying in my tray. There's sour, and then there's sour, but the sour in that orange had just been plain off.

Doris twiddled a strand of wavy black hair. "Has anybody had any luck finding something for their community service project?"

"I was hoping to do the Y," Hope said, "but they told me all their volunteer openings were already filled weeks ago, and they've got a waiting list a mile long."

"Yeah," Ted said. "I got the same answer when I called the city park service Friday afternoon. Apparently, the school board didn't take into consideration there are only so many volunteer positions available in Chadham County. Adding juniors and seniors to the number of underclassmen already required to do CS was an idea bound to fail."

"Well," Doris said with a grin, "I've got *mine* all set and ready. I talked with my priest, and she said I could help out preparing the Saturday meals-on-wheels plates."

"Hey," Hope said, "do you think I could help out there too?"

"I can ask. I don't know how much help they need though. She told me they've got a pretty large group of people working it. But yeah, I'm sure they'll let you. And even if they don't, if I drive you there Saturday, they've at least got to give you credit for the time you're there with me."

Hope smiled. "Cool. What about you, Ben? Are you having any luck?"

I folded my arms and sighed. "Oh yeah, I'm having great luck—all of it bad. Last week, I went to city hall, and they said no to everything, even the neighborhood beautification program. Apparently, you've got to have some kind of advanced degree in agriculture just to pull up weeds around here. And Saturday, I even checked out the library. Nothing."

"Well," Doris said, "you'd better come up with something. Two hundred hours is a lot of time to fill, especially if you've got to limit it to weekends and after school."

"Don't rub it in," Ted said.

Hope patted him on the wrist. "Aw, I'm sure you'll both find something."

I scoffed. "Tell me something, Hope. Your middle name wouldn't happen to be 'Springs Eternal' by any chance, would it?"

THE BELL RANG. We went inside, dumped our leftover food in the trash, and tossed our trays on the pile in the pickup window. While Ted and Doris disappeared among the people swarming down the front hall, Hope and I crossed the lobby to the back hall intersection. The clatter of locker doors being slammed, shoes scuffling, and the chaos of chattering voices buzzed all around us.

While Hope stopped off at the restroom for her traditional after-lunch visit, I leaned back against the wall for an after-lunch tradition of my own—surveying the guys passing by. I already knew most of the sophomores, juniors, and seniors, and I was always on the lookout for any of my favorites. But my main amusement that early in the semester was scoping out any good-looking freshmen.

So far, it looked like the majority of the ninth graders had second lunch, making my investigation much more haphazard. But the small herd of freshmen boys shuffling along on their way to PE that day seemed to represent a good cross-section. Most of them hadn't got the memo about skincare, and by the look of them, none believed in dressing to impress. But from what I was seeing, we definitely had a few really cute new guys that year. First, I noticed a solid-bodied little redhead who was absolutely drool-worthy. Next, a dark chocolate hottie passed by who could melt in my mouth any time. Then a tall kid with curly blond hair and rosy cheeks caught my attention. I watched them all disappear around the corner and wondered what they'd look like in decent clothes—or out of them.

"Oh to be young again," I said, remembering how innocent I was back when I was fourteen.

Hope emerged from the restroom, popped her traditional post-lunch breath mint, and checked the strap on her bag. She toddled over, shoulder bumped me in the direction of our creative writing class, and we began threading our way through the sea of zombies lumbering along to fifth period. It was like being part of a slow-motion stampede as people bumped, shoved, and tried to squeeze their way around us.

"Are you going to watch that Peter Sellers movie on TV tonight?"

She cast me a sidelong glance. "Pff, I wish. No, we're going to church—again. It's our parish feast day. We've got rosary, followed by mass, followed by a stupid reception."

"Your folks really are into church, aren't they?"

"You have no idea. They're driving me crazy. I wouldn't mind, if they didn't insist on dragging me along every single time they go. I mean, Sunday mass is okay, and things like Christmas and Easter are nice. But they're fanatics over the Virgin Mary, and it's like we've got to go to every freaking service for her on the calendar."

"I guess you haven't told them how much you like The Jesus and Mary Chain, huh?"

She laughed. "Are you kidding? They'd break my CD player and send for the exorcist."

Turning the corner to the English and Language Arts Department, we were just in time to see Patrick Frost leaving one of the classrooms. He was a long-legged basketball player I'd had a terrible crush on back when I was a freshman. As usual, he ignored the less-than-discreet once-over I always gave him.

Hope sniggered and elbowed me in the ribs. "I thought Colby Ryder was the only one you wanted to plug your socket."

"He is, but as a connoisseur, I can appreciate a thing of beauty when I see it, now can't I?"

"We've really got to find you a boyfriend before you start sucking the lug nuts off fire hydrants."

"Ha! Good luck. If there are any other homos in this school, they're so far in the closet they're behind Aunt Ginny's corsets."

After casting one last look at Patrick, I followed Hope inside Ms. Kiri's room and took my seat. Creative Writing was my favorite class. If you were like me, and you wanted to be a writer one day, what could be more fun than a class where you got to let your imagination run wild, write it all down, and then get graded for it?

It also didn't hurt that Colby Ryder was in the class too. Unfortunately, he sat on the opposite side of the room from Hope and me. But at least his seat was positioned so I had a perfect view of him the whole time.

I kept hoping that one day Ms. Kiri would team us up in pairs, and I'd get to work with Colby, although my idea of being creative with him had nothing to do with pencils and paper.

The assignment of the day was to write a short story based on any one of a series of headlines she'd brought in and projected on the board. The only stipulation was that we couldn't pick one we knew anything about. We had to use our imagination.

That was easy enough for me because A—I had an excellent imagination, and B—the only news I followed was about my favorite TV shows, a couple of movie stars, and that hot boy band that was all over MTV.

I chose a headline about two teenagers who had disappeared, and imagined a scenario. The headline hinted they might have been kidnapped, but I suspected it was more likely they'd eventually just turn out to be runaways. Anyway, it would do.

As news of the Missing Person Alert made its way throughout Backwater County, local police spread out, searching for the two Podunk Town teenagers. The pair had been reported missing after Friday night's Redneck Celebration Square Dance, held at the Benevolent Order of the Possum social hall. The two youths, identified as Chuck "Hotbody" Heartthrob and Wally "Puppylove" Wantaman were last seen leaving the hall at about ten o'clock. Witnesses reported seeing the teenagers walking side by side on

This Way Out Street, with Wantaman drooling over Heartthrob, the star high school quarterback. Police believed the two were likely picked up by person or persons unknown, and the boys' parents feared for the worst, believing them to have been kidnapped.

But what no one knew, and what their families would forever refuse to acknowledge, was that the two boys had in fact run away together.

Puppylove first fell for the raven-haired Hotbody back when they were both freshmen. For three years, he had grown ever more heartbroken and lovesick for the beautiful athlete. Desperate to confess his love before senior graduation and Hotbody's departure for Jocksaplenty University, Puppylove finally enacted his plan and asked the teenage super-stud to meet him at the Possum Hall event. To his delight, Hotbody agreed.

On the night of their disappearance, standing together in a quiet corner of the hall, Puppylove came close and hesitantly revealed his total devotion and deep passion for the handsome football hero. Then, while everyone else was distracted watching the square dance competition finalists, Hotbody surprised Puppylove with a quick kiss and his own declaration of love.

Being all too familiar with the abject ignorance and prejudice of their families, and the people of Podunk Town in general, both boys knew they had to be careful. So they snuck to the exit in search of a location where they could be alone and suck Slurpees in private.

It was when they nearly got caught playing tonsil hockey by sophomore student Alan Alwaysgossiping that they made their fateful decision. They would choose the path of love and make the commitment to spend the rest of their lives together.

Hotbody suggested they steal away to his mansion on the coast where they could live off the vast wealth he had recently inherited from his uncle, Mike "Moneybags" McCallum. And with that, the couple departed, never to be seen in Podunk Town again.

And so, while the missing teenagers mystery was never solved by the local officials, Puppylove and Hotbody lived happily ever after in the exclusive Better World Villas resort.

Okay, so the quarterback in my story just *might* have borne a striking resemblance to Colby. And the lanky Puppylove just might have shared some features with me. So what? It was just a coincidence. Could I help it if Puppylove dreamed of Hotbody for years and burned for the chance to lock lips with him? And so what if they fell in love? I mean, that kind of thing happens all the time in real life. Just not to me.

When the bell rang, I took my time packing my things so I could watch Colby lay his half-page effort on Ms. Kiri's desk. I even delayed turning in my own effort for a second or two longer so I could enjoy the full view as he walked out of the room.

Once he'd gone, I laid my story on the desk. Ms. Kiri immediately picked it up, gave it a glance, smiled, and shook her head. She'd always been a fan of my writing.

Hope was waiting for me as I rounded the corner.

"Let me guess. You wrote about the two missing teenagers."

"Yeah...so?"

She grinned. "I knew it. You've got to get over this Colby Ryder fixation. What was he this time? No, don't tell me. Let me guess. He was the policeman who saved the hapless missing homo and fell in love with him."

"Don't be ridiculous," I retorted. "He was the star high school quarterback who fell in love with the hapless homo and ran away with him."

"You're hopeless."

"Of course I'm hopeless. It's not like I can spend my time dreaming about my real life boyfriend. In case you haven't noticed, I don't have one."

"You've just got to be patient. You can't be the only gay boy here. Sooner or later, one of them is bound to stumble out of the closet."

"Right, and in the meantime, I'm the starving orphan outside the donut shop. The least you could do is let me dream about the one I want the most, even if I can't have it."

We stopped outside the Spanish classroom, and I turned to her with a melodramatic whimper. "I'm so alone, and nobody loves me."

Smiling, she tilted her head and gave me a quick hug and peck on the cheek.

"Aw. *I* love you."

I sighed and laid a hand on her shoulder. "I'd be the luckiest boy in Chadham High if that did it for me."

She smiled and slapped my side, spun around, bumped into an underclassman, and ricocheted into Mrs. Burnett's room for Spanish. Then I took a deep breath and continued on for my physics class with Mr. Ferguson.

THE LAST BELL of the day rang. I rummaged through my locker, grabbed yet another book, and sighed. I hated having so much homework to take home, but it was my own fault. I could have gotten some of it done in study hall, but I'd spent most of the period gossiping with Ted about one of the cheerleaders instead.

I slammed the locker door closed, gave the lock a quick spin, and plunged into the stream of teenage traffic surging shoulder-to-shoulder towards the parking lot. Emerging from the building into hot afternoon sunshine, I stepped out of everyone's way, dropped my bag, and stretched. People scurried past me, frantic to get away from Chadham High as fast as they could.

I cooled my heels near the building, waiting for Ted. He tended to be one of the last people out, and I always waited to walk with him to his car, a dilapidated old Honda he affectionately called "Baby." He needed me to. I was kind of like his bodyguard, and the body I was guarding him from was Vickie Parker. Just a glimpse of her with her boyfriend Barry Evers was enough to guarantee Ted would sulk the whole drive home. He'd been crushing on her, like, forever. It was really pathetic, especially since as far as she was concerned, he might as well have not existed.

"Hey, Ben."

Ted's brother Adrian and his friend Tyler Haynes were passing by me.

"Hey, Squirt. Hey, Tyler."

Tyler nodded, and Adrian said, "See you back at the ranch."

"Try to stay out of trouble between now and then," I said.

He looked over his shoulder, stuck out his tongue, and smiled.

Adrian always caught a ride home with Tyler—or more precisely, Tyler's brother Toby—instead of with Ted and me. After Toby got his license, he volunteered to pick Tyler up from middle school, which would save Mrs. Haynes the trouble, and just happened to guarantee Mr. Haynes would buy him that old clunker he wanted. It also meant Adrian got a ride home in the process. Nowadays, because he and Tyler were on the soccer team and often had practice after school, he still rode with them, which was fine with Ted. As far as he was concerned, Adrian was insufferable. But that was more out of jealousy than anything Adrian actually did. Good grades didn't come as easy for Ted as it did for Adrian.

I, on the other hand, thought Adrian was nice. He could be stubborn if he really wanted his way about something, but that didn't happen too often. And he made up for it by being as smart as a whip and having a great sense of humor. He was one of those kids who seemed to be able to do it all. He'd placed out of two freshman classes and was taking biology instead of earth science, and psychology on top of that. Smart kid.

As he and Tyler melded in with the crowd of departing students, I gave them the obligatory once-over and sighed. *No doubt about it, we've definitely got some cute guys in the freshman crop this year.*

Adrian had the same sandy-brown hair as Ted, but he wore it longer and shaggier, like a skater. I'd always thought he was cute, and that was before he'd hit that growth spurt over the past summer. Now, he was almost as tall as Ted, and thanks to soccer, he was really filling out quite nicely.

Tyler was barely taller than Adrian and gangling, with close-cropped wiry black hair. He was kind of cute in a kiddie sort of way. But while Tyler looked cute, Adrian was just plain hot. With that solid build, that beautiful face, and those rich brown eyes with the distinctive green ring in the irises, he could have hypnotized the dead.

"One of these days, that boy's going to make some lucky girl *very* happy."

As I lost sight of Adrian and Tyler, Ted came marching towards me, stuffing a history book in his bag. He flung the bag over his shoulder, barely missing some poor sophomore, and stormed off to his car. I gave the kid an apologetic smile before running off after him.

"I can't believe old Boone's given us *another* paper to write."

"Well, I did warn you," I said, falling in next to him. "You should have taken something else. Like you could have signed up for Humanities. You'd have as many papers, but at least they'd be about interesting things."

"Yeah, interesting to someone like *you* maybe."

We were passing the last bus waiting to pull out onto the access road when I spied her.

Uh-oh. Better think quick. But it was already too late. At that same moment, Ted looked up to see Vickie Parker standing next to Barry Evers in front of his car—a flashy import. They were having a very serious conversation, and Ted looked up just in time to see them hug each other...and to see Vickie give Barry a kiss.

Ted jerked his head away, glued his eyes on the pavement in front of him, and quickened his pace.

I rolled my eyes and shook my head. *So much for a pleasant ride home.*

If not for the grunge song that came over the radio halfway to Ted's house, the trip would have been even more miserable than it was. But you could always count on Nirvana to distract Ted. On the other hand, it came at a price—Ted trying to mimic Kurt Cobain's raspy voice on songs he didn't know the words to.

The Honda came to a stop in front of the Douglas house. Ted waited for two cars to pass, and turned into the driveway. I followed him inside, and we wandered through the living room to the kitchen.

"Hi, Mom."

"Hi, Mrs. Douglas."

"Hello, boys; there are muffins on the counter."

Ted grabbed one.

"Thank you, Mrs. Douglas," I said, "but I'm going to have to pass. I'm trying to watch my weight."

I had always liked Ted's mom, partly because she'd always been nice to me. From the beginning, she kind of figured out I was, shall we say, "different" from Ted's other friends, but she was supportive of our friendship anyway. She also had the same brown eyes with green rings that Adrian alone had been lucky enough to inherit. Ted and his older brother Eric had the plain old garden-variety brown ones like their father. Now, he—Mr. Douglas, that is—didn't share his wife's generous view of me at all. He had picked up on the fact that I was different too, and he clearly didn't approve. But other than a few random homophobic comments, he liked to pretend I didn't exist. I guess he thought if he ignored me long enough, I'd go away.

I followed Ted upstairs to his room. It still felt strange not going further down the hall to the room he used to share with Adrian. But when Eric left for college, it was agreed Ted would take his old room, and Eric would double up with Adrian on the rare occasions when he came home.

Ted dropped his book bag on the bed and put on a Pixies CD. We pulled out our copies of *Huckleberry Finn*, which we were reading for Literature, the one class we shared with Hope and Doris.

We hadn't been at it long when the phone rang. Ted started to reach for it, but it shut off in mid-ring, so we continued reading. A moment later, there was a double knock, and the door opened just far enough for Adrian to stick his head in.

"Ben, your mom called. She wants you to go home."

I checked the time—three forty-five—and wondered what was up. It was unusual for Mom to be home that early. Normally, I hung out with Ted until about five o'clock and got home just before she did.

Gathering my things, I said goodbye to Ted and closed the door on my way out.

Adrian's door was open, and the strains of the Divinyls' "I Touch Myself" were drifting out into the hall. The stairs were in the opposite direction, but I couldn't resist the temptation to double back and rib him over listening to such sexy music.

I came to the doorway and was about to make a sarcastic remark but stopped, completely thunderstruck by what I saw. Adrian was swaying to the music, swiveling his hips, and lip-synching. And except for the towel wrapped around his waist, he was totally naked. The sight of his broad solid pecs, firm abs, and smooth but muscular legs was mesmerizing.

In less than a second, my cheeks were on fire, and I was tingling all over. The whole display was taking me, emotionally and physically, to a place I knew I shouldn't go. But I was helpless to stop what it was doing to me. All I could do was stand there and gawk, while my hormones shifted into overdrive.

As the song got to the part where Chrissy Amphlett just recites the lyrics, Adrian turned and caught sight of me practically drooling over him. He froze in place and looked down at the floor, his cheeks glowing as bright as mine must have been. But after a second, he straightened up, looked into my eyes with a timid smile, and cleared his throat.

"You...uh...don't want to keep your mother waiting, Ben. You better get home."

Still blushing, but also still smiling, he sauntered past me to the bathroom. Then he turned back, made a kissy face at me, and closed the door. It took me a couple of seconds to come down, and I had to take a deep, slow breath before turning to go.

A five-block walk separated my house from the Douglas's, and right then, I needed every inch of it. That little show had left me really...uh...moved. It had just been *so* hot. And that particular song—wow! Let's just say if Colby Ryder ever danced around and lip-synched to a song like that, I'd have been ready to do anything he wanted—not that I wouldn't have anyway.

But Colby hadn't been the one who'd just sent my hormones stampeding; Adrian had. I'd never have dreamed seeing him dance like that would have affected me so...hard. I'd known this kid since he was six, and the last time I'd seen him without a shirt on, he'd been as skinny as a rake. But the boy I'd just seen—the *young man* I found dancing so seductively— could have passed for a junior, or even a senior. And seeing him with nothing on but a towel—he was so hot. His body was guaranteed to get a reaction. And he obviously saw the reaction he was getting from me.

But the way he smiled after he noticed me watching him—it was so innocent and coy, but somehow suggestive and teasing too. It was almost like he liked the idea of me perving over him.

No, he was probably just trying to downplay an awkward situation. He didn't want to admit I embarrassed him. And boy, it *had* to be embarrassing for him—it certainly was for me. If anybody had ever caught me like that, I'd have dug a hole to hide in and never come out.

The whole situation had been so awkward. I mean, I'd known Adrian so long he was almost like a little brother to me, but seeing him dancing had been so hot. The way he looked, the way he'd made me feel, the kind of thoughts I was still trying not to think—I really needed to put it all out of my mind.

But it wasn't going to be easy.

AFTER CROSSING THE final street, I walked around the house to the back door as usual. Mom was at the counter scribbling something on a notepad. Her bag was on the table, and she was still wearing her office clothes. Her lips were pursed, which usually meant something was bothering her.

"Hey, Mom."

"Ben, we've got a problem."

"What'd I do?"

She sighed. "*You* didn't do anything. No, I've got to go to Petersburg. Your grandfather's in the hospital again."

"Grandpa Marty?" I said, grabbing a chair. "What's happened?"

"He had another fall." She peeked inside one of the cabinets and added a note to the pad. "Luckily, he didn't break a hip this time, but he did manage to knock his head and crack a couple of ribs."

"That sounds serious."

"Well, it is, but I won't know how serious until I get there. The doctor said he's okay, but she wanted me to come down to discuss things."

"When are you leaving?"

"In the morning. I'm making a list of things you'll need to get for meals while I'm away. And, Ben, I'm depending on you to do the cooking. Let's not tempt fate and let your father try to cook again. And make sure he stays on his diet."

"How long are you going to be gone?"

"I don't know. But something's got to be done. Your grandfather can't keep going on like this. We've got to make some kind of long-term arrangements for him."

She jotted down one more addition to her list, went to her bag, fetched her credit card, and grabbed the spare keys to her car from a hook on the bulletin board.

"Here. Go to the store and pick these things up. Tonight, we'll order Chinese, but you'll need these other things for later. I'll make up a menu schedule while you're out."

BY THE TIME I got back, my father was home. He and Mom were in deep conversation when I brought in the first couple of sacks. It took me several more trips to bring everything in, so I only picked up bits and pieces of the exchange.

"I just don't know what I'm going to do with him..."

"He's a proud man. The very notion's going to be hard on him..."

"Things can't keep going on like this..."

"We've got to do something..."

"Stick to the menu, and no snitching, now. I mean it."

They both helped me put the groceries and supplies away, and we ordered dinner.

While we ate, they discussed different options they thought might have to be considered, but it was all hypothetical since, until Mom talked with the doctors, we didn't know what might be out of the question. One thing was clear though: Mom didn't want Grandpa living alone much longer.

Chapter Two

I GLANCED AT the calendar. Thursday, October eighth. It was hard to believe, but Mom had been in Petersburg for a whole month, and tomorrow would mark the beginning of a second. At first, we'd assumed she'd only be gone for a few days. But complications in Grandpa's recovery had kept him in the hospital. His cracked ribs were taking longer to heal than the doctors had anticipated, and Mom mentioned something about him showing symptoms they couldn't diagnose with confidence until his fall was ruled out as the cause. Each time she called, I could tell by the tone of her voice the stress was really getting to her.

She wasn't the only one.

A whole month had slipped by, and there I was again, staring at the dinner schedule on the refrigerator door. It had become a routine: Come home from school, check the menu, get out anything that needed defrosting, and set the table. And like every other day since Mom left, I dreamed of hearing the phone ring and her saying she'd be coming home soon.

My life had turned into a real drudge, and after a month of playing Feed the Daddy, I was more than ready for that little chore to be over. Don't get me wrong. I may not have been anywhere near a world-class chef, but I wasn't that bad either. I'd certainly not given Dad any reason to complain about the quality of his suppers in Mom's absence. But it seemed like every other day he tried to talk me into cooking things he wasn't supposed to have.

And not only did I have to cook the meals and try to keep him on his diet, but there was also the little issue of household chores to deal with. Technically, Dad and I were sharing them—which effectively meant *I* was doing everything. It made me feel guilty, but I couldn't help being jealous of my sister Eliana who was off enjoying the freedom of her first year at Dickerson University. Meanwhile, there I was, stuck keeping house.

I pulled a couple of fish filets from the freezer. The night's menu called for baking them in butter—a surefire winner with my father. And since it was such an easy recipe, I decided I had enough time to kick back and watch a little music on TV.

I flopped down on the living room couch, hit the remote, and immediately cheered. The first video to come up was Annie Lennox. I really liked her.

As the video played, my mind began to drift, and before I knew it, my thoughts had turned to Adrian—again. There I was, remembering every second of him dancing so seductively the night before Mom left for Petersburg.

On that particular evening, the news about Grandpa had temporarily put the incident out of my mind—at least until bedtime. But the next morning, when I showed up for my ride with Ted, the sight of Adrian decked out in a pullover and soccer shorts greeted me. He looked so good in them it took my breath away. His good-morning was friendly and innocent, but my body reacted as if it was a sexy come-on. There was no way I could avoid being, and looking, obviously turned on. And it didn't help that I couldn't stop myself from staring at those firm thighs and the way his knee socks accentuated the curve of his calves. His smile was bashful, but those hypnotic eyes had a teasing, almost seductive glint that had me totally bewitched. Luckily, the Toby-mobile pulled up at that moment, giving me a few minutes to compose myself before Ted came out.

But later that morning, Adrian passed me in the hall and winked. It was especially embarrassing because Hope and Ted were with me. Ted missed it entirely, which wasn't surprising—he liked to pretend Adrian didn't exist at school. I wasn't sure about Hope though. She may not have caught the wink, but she definitely noticed me blushing soon after it happened and flashed me an amused grin. Then that afternoon, I was on my way to Humanities when Adrian passed me again, smiling and nodding, which convinced me he was doing it on purpose to tease me.

As the week progressed, it seemed every time I saw Adrian, he smiled or winked in a way almost calculated to remind me of that night. But by Monday of the following week, the novelty must have worn off for him because he was back to acting normal, like it was all forgotten. For me, on the other hand, it took a month to stop focusing on how hot he looked every time I saw him. It hadn't been easy. But lying there watching music videos, I congratulated myself that I'd finally put the whole thing behind me...except for the fact that, once again, there I was, rock hard and thinking about him. *No doubt about it, I've got to find a boyfriend.*

THE THUD OF a car door closing told me Dad was home. I turned off the TV and met him just as he was coming in through the kitchen door.

"Hey, Dad. How was your day?"

"Not bad," he said, going to the sink to wash his hands. "You have a good day?"

"Ugh. It was school. What do you think?" (He always smiled when I said things like that. I guess in his day, school was a lot less stressful.)

I had just set the oven to preheat, when the phone rang.

"Hello?"

"Hey, Ben, it's me."

"Hey, Mom. How's Grandpa Marty doing?"

"It's complicated. Is your father home yet?"

"Yeah, he's right here."

"Let me talk to him."

I gave Dad the phone.

"Hey, Sweetheart, what's up? How's Marty?" He listened for a few seconds.

"Well, that's good news. Ben, your grandfather's being discharged."

Dad and I shared a high five. (For me, it was a double cause to celebrate. It meant Mom would be coming home soon and my kitchen duties would be over.)

But then he frowned. "I see. Well, what do the doctors recommend?"

There was a long pause before he spoke again.

"There's no way Marty would go for that. What's the other option?"

A *very* long pause followed that question.

"Margot, you don't have to convince me... No, of course I don't mind. Under the circumstances, I'm sure he'll do a *lot* better... Right, the senior center would be perfect, lots of people around his age."

Senior center? I had a mental image of Grandpa being sentenced to life in some old folks prison. Not only would it be horrible for him, but sooner or later, I'd have to go with Mom and Dad to visit him there—something I didn't want to even think about.

"Okay, Sweetheart. Take care. I'll talk to you Sunday."

Dad hung up the phone and turned to me.

"Well, it looks like Grandpa Marty's got some health issues that mean he can't live alone any longer."

"What kind of health issues?

"First, he's got emphysema—"

"That's a kind of lung cancer, isn't it?"

"Not exactly, but it does affect the lungs, and there's no cure for it. Second, according to the doctors, he's showing the early signs of Alzheimer's disease. That means his forgetfulness will get worse over time."

"So...he's going to an old folks' home?"

"That was the original idea, but when the doctors suggested it, he flat out refused, and you know your grandfather—next to your mother, he's the most stubborn person I've ever met. But if he can't stay on his own, and he won't go to a home, there's only one other option. He's going to come live with us. We'll set him up in the guest room—it'll be almost like having his own little apartment since it's got its own bathroom."

I put a stick of butter in the casserole dish and shoved it in the oven while Dad went to take a shower before supper.

The idea of Grandpa living with us made me apprehensive. Because my grandparents lived in Petersburg, I'd never been very close to them. Except for my mother, I didn't have a thing in common with them. It also didn't help that Grandpa was always grousing that I wasn't into sports. And for as long as I could remember, he seemed obsessed with the idea that I should have a girlfriend—two or three actually. When Doris and Hope came to my Bar Mitzvah, he totally embarrassed me by asking which one was my girlfriend—in front of them.

I would have told him I was gay, but Mom was certain he'd blow his top if he ever found out. Whenever we were around him, she always reminded me to keep quiet about it. So having him live with us could make my life complicated, especially if he started asking why I never dated any girls. And God forbid, if I ever did find a boyfriend, he'd be bound to put two and two together eventually. On the other hand, I figured with my luck, I'd probably be middle-aged before I even got a boyfriend for him to find out about.

THE NEXT MORNING, Doris and I were sitting in our U.S. government class first period, supposedly working on a presentation. But it was way too early in the day to even think about the Senate's filibuster rules.

"Have you heard from your mother, Ben?"

"Yeah, she called last night. The good news is my Grandpa's being discharged next week. The bad news is the doctors strongly advise against him continuing to live alone. My mom said from what she's seen of his house, she agrees. Apparently, ever since Grandma died, he's really let the place go. We thought he had a cleaning service come in a couple of times a month, but my mom said it doesn't look like that's happened in a long time, if it ever did at all. And she says he's getting to be kind of forgetful."

Doris shook her head. "That's too bad. My grandmother got so forgetful that, in the end, she didn't even know who I was."

"Wow. Was she still living at home?"

"No, she was in the old folks' home by then."

Our conversation was cut short by Mr. Kormany, who'd snuck up behind us. "How are you coming along on that filibuster presentation?"

We showed him what we had so far, and he harrumphed.

"I suggest the two of you put more effort into *researching* the topic than in practicing it."

(The man was always talking in riddles.)

We went back to taking notes, but my mind stayed on Grandpa Marty. As nervous as I was about him moving in with us, I was glad he wasn't going to an old folks' home. From the things Doris had told me, the one her grandmother had gone to didn't do much to help her. Plus, if he went to an old folks' home, I'd eventually have to visit him there, surrounded by all those creepy old people.

When class ended, we wound our way to the Math and Business wing. I had Economics. Doris had Pre-Calc. (*I* had Pre-Calc third period.) About halfway there, we crossed paths with Hope. She was on her way to the M-B wing too, for study hall.

I don't know which I'd have hated worse, having study hall second period, or having it anytime with Ms. Antallen. I had suffered through two years running of both Algebra *and* Geometry with her, and that was enough for anybody.

We stopped off at Doris's locker so she could get her book, and while we were waiting, Ted came walking up to us. He was on his way to Chemistry from Pre-Calc, and he was smiling—a rarity for a man coming out of Pre-Calc.

(That's right. The three of us had the *same* course at *three* different times—with *three* different teachers, which made studying together impossible. Thanks for nothing, Chadham High.)

"Well, look at you," Hope said, smiling up at Ted. "What did you do, ace a pop quiz or something?"

"Nope, even better," he said, beaming. "I aced a chapter test."

"Woohoo"—she high fived him—"congratulations."

Doris scoffed at her. "You didn't congratulate me like that when I aced *my* pre-calc test Wednesday."

"That's not true. You know I did."

But in fact, she hadn't. Over the last month or so, I'd noticed that Hope had started paying a lot more attention to anything Ted said or did than me or Doris. She'd also started sharing his enthusiasm for just about everything—except Vickie Parker, that is. I was beginning to suspect she was getting a crush on him.

For the next two hours, I suffered through one of Ms. Penger's boring economics lectures and a pre-calc test that left me with a headache so bad I could barely see straight. On the way to Lit, I asked Doris for an aspirin. While she rummaged through her bag, I squeezed my eyes shut and rubbed the bridge of my nose. She handed me a pill and followed me to the water fountain where I washed it down.

No sooner had I swallowed the pill than she started grinning.

"What's so funny?"

"That wasn't an aspirin."

"What was it?"

"It's for PMS symptoms," she said, snickering so hard she was almost cackling.

"Very funny, very funny."

Nevertheless, within ten or fifteen minutes, my headache was gone, and I was able to take part in a lively classroom debate about *Huckleberry Finn*. Later, on the way to the lunchroom, I mentioned how quick my headache had gone away, and Doris confessed that the PMS pill was essentially just aspirin and caffeine. Hope and Doris sniggered, and Ted found the thought of a "gay boy" taking a PMS pill hilarious.

We ended up eating in the lunchroom—not that we wanted to, but it had been drizzling on and off all morning, and the patio was soaked.

The gloomy weather outside, the low roar of all the people around us, and the unsavory odors emanating from the kitchen made for a depressing lunch period. Hope and Ted were going on and on about how much business homework they always had. After a full fifteen minutes of it, Doris rolled her eyes and jumped in to change the subject.

"We should go see a movie this weekend."

"Great idea," Ted said, straightening up. "The new Galactic Battleship movie is opening tonight—*Galactic Battleships Under Siege*. It's going to be fantastic."

She moaned. "Ugh, not another one. Those Galactic Battleship movies are so dull."

"Hey, wait a minute," I said. "They're not *that* dull. And that guy who plays General Sterman is hot."

"Yeah, well maybe," she said with a shrug. "But it'll be too crowded. We should wait and go some other time."

"We can go tomorrow night," Ted said, dumping salt all over his food.

Doris rolled her eyes. "Really?"

"Okay then, what do *you* want to do, Doris?" Ted wasn't ready to give up on *Galactic Battleships* so easily.

"We could hang out at the mall."

"Awe, no," Ted said. "I'd rather hang out with my aunt Mary."

"I wouldn't mind seeing *Galactic Battleships* even if it is crowded," Hope said, flicking her hair to one side. "Adventure movies are always more fun in a full house."

Doris looked to me for support.

"I don't really care either way."

"So *Galactic Battleships* it is," Ted said with a triumphant grin.

Doris rolled her eyes. "Okay, but at least let's wait and go tomorrow night, and *you're* springing for wings at Chicken Feathers."

"I'm so tired of Chicken Feathers," Ted whined. "Couldn't we go to Tino's instead? I hear this weekend, they're running a special on spaghetti, with endless breadsticks."

I groaned. "Everything at Tino's is so greasy, and the salad bar sucks."

"Chicken Feathers it is," Doris said smugly.

The important matters settled, Ted and Hope went back to complaining about homework.

AROUND ELEVEN THIRTY Saturday, we emerged from the theater into the chilly night air along with two hundred or so other people. So much for our idea to skip opening night in the hope of a smaller crowd. Doris and Ted's cars were parked at the far end of the lot, but I didn't care. At least the walk gave our clothes time to air out. The maxed-out theater had been hot and stuffy, and it took a while to get the smell of popcorn and body odor out of my nostrils.

As for the movie itself, I suppose it had its moments, but overall, it was a letdown for me—hardly any General Sterman, and zero *shirtless* General

Sterman. Doris didn't seem to have been very impressed either. She fidgeted in her seat the whole time and bolted to the exit the second it was over. I guess it could have been worse though. We could have had to sit through *Captain Ron* again. I doubted she'd ever forgive Ted for talking us into seeing that one.

She and I were lagging behind Ted and Hope who were already about halfway to the cars. It had gone without question that Ted would love the movie no matter what. That Hope would love it almost as much as he did was the surprise of the evening. There she was, weaving her way next to him, shoulder bumping him every now and then, and happy as a clam, comparing notes on their favorite scenes.

A guy sprinted past Doris and me and banged on the trunk of a car inching to the street with music blaring. Someone opened one of the back seat doors, and he jumped in.

Doris smiled. "Nice ass."

"I'd certainly give it a nine."

"You've got to be kidding. That was a solid ten if it was anything."

"It was good all right, but I've seen better."

"You've seen better? Where?"

"Around."

"Oh, I forgot. The sun rises and sets on Colby Ryder's ass, doesn't it?"

"Doris, believe me—the sight of Colby Ryder in the locker room is proof positive there is a God."

She laughed, and we kept walking. But not three steps later, she grabbed my arm and pulled me to one side.

"Ben, do you see that?"

"See what?"

She nodded her head to one side. "That."

I followed her nod to where Hope and Ted were leaning against the hood of Doris's car.

"Look at them. I knew it. They're falling in love."

I'd always suspected that underneath Doris's down-to-earth, take-charge shell lurked a hopeless romantic.

"Doris..."

"Listen, listen. Think up an excuse for you and me to stay out so Ted will have to give her a ride home."

"Are you crazy? I'm ready for bed now. And what if the two of them decide they want to stay out with us? It's ridiculous."

"Oh, come on."

"No."

"Oh pooh," she said, stomping her foot before following me to the cars. But knowing her like I did, I was certain I'd not heard the end of this.

AT QUARTER AFTER three, Sunday afternoon, I was staring at the freezer, debating what to set out to thaw, when I heard cars coming to a stop in the driveway. I went to the door. Mom was getting out of her car, and Dad's car was pulling to a stop next to it. They were early. I hadn't expected them until much closer to six. My plan had been to decide on something for supper, set things in motion, and be ready to treat everyone once they arrived.

Mom and Dad had talked on the phone for nearly a half hour the day before, and when Dad hung up, he shook his head.

"Ben, I've got to go to Petersburg tomorrow morning. Your mother's having a hard time convincing your grandfather to come live with us. She needs me to help talk him into it."

"You're not going to be gone for a month too, are you?"

"No," he said with a chuckle. "One way or the other, we'll be home by dinner time tomorrow night at the latest—*with* Grandpa Marty."

"You want me to look around for some rope and handcuffs?"

"Let's hope it won't come to that. Marty's just going to have to face reality."

And so Dad had left for Petersburg early that morning, and true to his word, here they all were. From the look of Mom's creased brow and less than happy expression as she shut the car door, I could tell it had been a hard sell.

Grandpa Marty got out of the car and stretched. It had been almost a year since I'd last seen him, and time had taken its toll. He couldn't have been much over five foot six—barely taller than Doris—but he looked even smaller now. His hairline sat higher on his pate than I remembered, and what hair he did have was much grayer. But at seventy-three, I figured that kind of thing came with the territory.

I stepped outside.

"Hey, Mom, Dad. Hey, Grandpa."

Grandpa Marty looked at me with a puzzled expression like he didn't recognize me—but then again, I'd had a pretty good growth spurt since the last time he'd seen me.

"Benjie," he said in a half-questioning tone.

I smiled and nodded.

"Look at you," he said, squeezing my arm before giving me a full hug. "My little boy's all grown up now. And I bet the girls can't keep their eyes off you—or their hands, eh?"

Mom rolled her eyes and said, "Ben, why don't you show Grandpa to the guest room?"

He turned to pick up a suitcase, but I stepped forward.

"That's okay, Grandpa, I got it."

I threw one suitcase under my arm and grabbed two more. From the number of them, it looked like Mom and Dad had gotten most, if not all, of his clothes.

"Did you have a nice drive down, Grandpa?"

He looked over at me like he'd forgotten I was there. Then he kind of snapped out of it and waved his hand contemptuously.

"A nice drive? It took forever, and the roads are horrible these days. And your mother hit every single pothole between Petersburg and Chadham."

Mom cut me a pained look that told me the trip wouldn't have gone fast enough for her if they'd flown home from Petersburg.

"Come on in, Grandpa."

I walked to the kitchen steps, set down a suitcase and opened the door, grabbed the suitcase again and went inside. Grandpa followed me.

We passed through the dining and living rooms, turned up the side hall, and came to the guest room. I'd put fresh sheets on the bed and given everything a good dusting the day before. The little living area was arranged in a neat and tidy layout, and I had made sure to give it a good spraying with air freshener.

Grandpa came in and looked around.

"You guys must have made real good time," I said, setting the suitcases down near the closet. "I didn't expect you for at least another couple of hours,"

Dad came in, lugging three more suitcases.

"Your mother had things all packed by the time I got there."

He gave me a quick glance and cut his eyes back to the hallway.

"I'll be right back, Grandpa," I said, sidestepping him and my father.

As I started down the hall, Dad said, "Marty, how do you like the room? We had it painted since the last time you and Ilana were here."

Ilana was my grandma. My sister Eliana was named after her. I was fourteen when Grandma died. The last time she and Grandpa Marty had stayed with us was the year before that.

When I reached the kitchen, I found the door propped open, the rest of the suitcases lined up to one side, and a couple of boxes on the table. Mom came in toting a couple of bags. She set them down next to the boxes and leaned back against the counter stiffly. Her eyes were tired and bloodshot. Her hair hung loose, missing the attention she usually gave it. She looked like she could use a good nap, or maybe a stiff drink. It had clearly been a difficult month for her.

My mother had a will of steel and the ability to stay calm under even the most trying circumstances—like that time I scraped my knee when I was a kid. The trouble was Grandpa had a will of steel too, and on more than a few occasions over the years, they'd been known to, shall we say, "disagree." It also didn't help that he was very conservative, and the two of them could really get into it. Sometimes, I wondered how a man like Marty Blackburn could ever have ended up with a daughter as liberal as my mother.

"Ben," she said, taking a final check outside, "I wanted to talk to you before you spend much time with Grandpa. Your father and I discussed it this morning, and we think, for the time being, we should all avoid saying anything about the fact that he's not just visiting."

"Why?"

"He really dug in his heels about moving in with us. You know how stubborn he can be. Your father had to convince him that we were only bringing him here for a visit."

"But Dad said you had everything packed by the time he got there."

Mom looked at me with sad eyes and took a slow breath, her shoulders slumping a little.

"I did. That's the thing. In a lot of ways, your grandfather's the same cantankerous old fool he's always been—" She sighed. "But in some ways, he's...just not all there anymore. I argued with him for days about moving in with us, and he wouldn't hear of it. But I spent part of Friday and all day yesterday packing up his clothes and personal things, and it didn't even register on him what I was doing. Then, your father showed up this morning and invited him to come visit us for the holiday, and Grandpa agreed with no problem."

"You mean Columbus Day?"

"For all I know, he could have thought he meant Passover. The point is, we want him to get used to staying with us before we have to remind him he's not going back."

She glanced to the dining room. "What's he doing now?"

"He's in his—um, in the guest room, talking with Dad."

"Good. Thank God for your father. He has a way of calming him down and—"

"Well, it's been a nice visit, and I've thoroughly enjoyed it," Grandpa said, walking into the room rubbing his hands together. "But all good things must come to an end, and I think I'd best be getting back."

Dad followed him in, his lips pursed in an apologetic smile.

Mom sighed.

TED AND I strolled through the mall, slowly wending our way to the food court. For a holiday, it was surprisingly less busy than I'd thought it would be. Those Columbus Day sales just weren't drawing them in like they used to.

We hadn't been to the mall in a while because Ted, and sometimes Doris, found it boring. It was true that if you weren't shopping, just hanging out in the food court could be as tedious as all get out, especially if you didn't like the vendors' food—and most of it *was* pure crap. I, on the other hand, didn't mind spending time in the mall. It was an ideal location for scouting out good-looking guys.

We stopped at the Asian food stand and placed our orders.

"You have no idea how weird it is having my grandfather living with us. It's surreal."

"Really changes the old family dynamic, huh?"

"Yeah, it's like suddenly having an extra parent and a little brother all rolled into one."

We paid the woman, picked up our trays, and grabbed a nearby table. Ted proceeded to dump salt onto a pile of fried rice that he'd already drowned with a half gallon of soy sauce at the counter. I fully expected him to turn into a pillar of salt with the first mouthful.

"So he's really out of it, huh?" Ted said through a forkful of rice.

"Well, not out of it exactly. It's strange. You can talk with him, and he makes perfect sense. I mean, at least he's not calling it in from the twilight zone or anything. But, like, he'd only been there about twenty minutes when he announced he was ready to go back home."

"So what did you guys do?"

"Okay, here's the really creepy part. My dad says, 'Marty, we're ordering Chinese for dinner—your favorite.' See, he's hated Chinese like forever. But Dad says that, and he's absolutely delighted. He forgets about wanting to leave, spends, like, a half hour looking over the delivery menu, and then chows down like he grew up in Hunan province."

"And that was the end of him wanting to go home?"

"Oh no, not a chance. After we ate, he mentioned going home again. So my father, quote, unquote, *reminded him* that he'd promised to stay and help him out with a project. And just like that, he was as happy as a clam the rest of the night."

"What's the project?"

"There isn't one. Dad took him out to the garage for about a half hour and they just puttered around. He plans to do it every day after he gets home from work from now on."

"You think that will work?"

"It did last night. Like I said, it's surreal."

Ted took a big gulp of his soda. "Sounds like life is becoming interesting at the Carpenter house."

"You're telling me."

I leaned back and idly looked around.

An old man at a table some twenty feet from us was sitting by himself eating, and he was letting the food dribble down his chin. I shivered a little and looked away.

Then I saw him.

On the other side of the food court, a totally mackable guy chewing on a chicken nugget was making for a table. I guessed he went to South Chadham High since I was certain I'd never seen him before—and believe me, I'd have remembered if I had. Tall, lanky, with that Colby-Ryder-like way of carrying himself, he made even the simple act of fingering a nugget totally ooze with sexual power. His eyes were the most amazing shade of blue I'd ever seen—really, even from forty feet away, they sparkled like they were glowing. And he was wearing skintight jeans and a stylish lavender pullover that just screamed, "Come and get me, boys; I'm gay as hell."

"Ted, I think I've finally found the one to take my mind off Colby."

"Oh yeah?"

"Yeah, over there. See him?" I said, nodding in Adonis's direction.

Ted squinted. "You mean the guy with the purple pullover?"

"Could there be anyone else? I think I'm in love. And it's not purple—it's lavender."

"Whatever. Okay, you've found him, but what are you going to do about it? It's not like you'd ever really go over there and talk to him."

"You never know. I just might."

"No way."

"Bet?"

"What are we betting?"

"I bet you I'll go over there and talk to him. And if I do, you have to call Vickie Parker up and ask her for a date."

"And if you don't?"

"And if I don't, I'll buy you the soundtrack CD for *Galactic Battleships*. Bet?"

He leaned back in his seat. "Okay, it's a bet."

Of course, making a bet and getting up the nerve to carry it out were two different things. For a few seconds, I just stared at the guy, rapping my fingers on the table. I pushed the chair out a few inches, but it took me another couple of seconds to bring myself to my feet. Meanwhile, Ted started snickering, certain I was going to chicken out at the last second.

Swallowing hard, I picked up my tray and walked it over to a trash can about ten feet from the guy. I glanced back at Ted, who was watching me with an amused smile.

Taking a deep breath, I forced myself to approach Mr. Swankalishous, stopped in front of him, and cleared my throat.

"Hi. My name is Ben, and I was just—"

"Whoa, there you are. You know, I've been waiting all day for someone like you to come along. Why don't you sit right down here and give me a kiss?"

A pale redheaded girl with pneumatic boobs flopped down next to my blue-eyed Adonis and planted the most sloppy, pornographic kiss on him I'd ever witnessed in a public setting. And from the way he was pawing all over her, it was totally clear that A—he was definitely *not* gay, and B—he wasn't the least bit afraid of open displays of affection.

My cheeks were burning so bad I was surprised they didn't set off the water sprinklers, and I could hear the faint echo of Ted laughing his ass off back at our table.

As Adonis came up for air, he looked at me.

"Did you want something?"

"Uh… Sorry, I thought you were somebody else."

I turned tail and retreated back to the table. Ted was snickering so hard he had to wipe the tears from his eyes.

"Mighty smooth, gay boy," he said between giggles.

"Let's just get out of here."

Ted got up and took his tray to a trash can, grinning from ear to ear.

"I've got to hand it to you. You picked a winner—at least, I bet that's what his *girlfriend* thinks."

"Please, don't rub it in. That was humiliating enough."

He clapped me on the back. "Come on, Romeo. I tell you what; I'll buy you an orange mango smoothie."

Five minutes later, I was sucking on my smoothie, fighting back a brain freeze.

Ted was still smiling. "Well, I may not have gotten that *Galactic Battleships* soundtrack, but watching that little scene was almost as good."

"Speaking of which, you lost the bet. So tell me— When are you calling Vickie? I hope you didn't think buying me a smoothie would let you off the hook?"

A tiny hint of anxiety passed over his face, but Ted was one of those guys who believed a bet's a bet no matter what, and it would just be too shameful for him to not honor his word.

"I'll call her this evening."

I grinned and gave him a wink. "I'll want full details first thing in the morning."

Chapter Three

TUESDAY MORNING WAS cold, and the walk to Ted's house seemed to take forever. At least Columbus Day had been radiantly sunny. Now, a mere day later, the air was damp and smelled stale, and the sky was one great big gray shroud, which made the chill worse.

I crossed the last intersection in time to see Adrian jumping into the backseat of the Toby-mobile before it sped off. Then Ted sprang out the front door, waved my way, and jumped in his car. He started the engine and Baby was humming by the time I got in, which meant we might have a chance of heat by the time we got halfway to Chadham High.

"How'd things go with your grandfather last night?" he asked, pulling out of his driveway.

"Not too bad. My father kept him busy all afternoon, so he was in a good mood during supper. He only complained about Mom's cooking twice."

"Uh-oh, you mean he's a complainer?"

"According to my mother, Grandpa Marty is not just a complainer; he invented complaining. But anyway, by the time Mom and I finished the dishes, he was quite happy. He was in the living room watching TV—football, which unfortunately meant that Mom missed *Murphy Brown*, but at least he wasn't complaining. Oh, by the way, I think she and Dad are planning to get him his own TV for his room."

"Sounds like a good idea."

I cut Ted a sidelong glance and shook my head. He wasn't fooling anyone. He was trying to distract me to avoid the question he knew was coming.

"So how was your talk with Vickie last night?"

"Oh," he said offhandedly, like it was a trifling matter he'd quite forgotten about. "I, uh, didn't get to speak to her."

"You chickened out."

"No, I called her—I did, but she wasn't home."

"So you left a message?"

"Not exactly. Her mother asked me if I wanted to, but I said I'd see Vickie today anyway."

"You mean you're going to ask her out to her face?"

He nodded.

"Wow, I'm impressed. I didn't think you had it in you."

"Well, you know me. When I set my mind on something..."

He trailed off, and I let the conversation drop. If he really was going to ask Vickie out at school—with the high likelihood that other people would be around to see, and hear, her answer—the last thing he needed was me needling him. I did hope I'd be there when he asked her though. If she said yes, I wanted to be the first to congratulate him, and if she said no, he'd need me for sympathy.

HALFWAY TO FIRST period, I crossed paths with Doris. As soon as she saw me, she grabbed me by the arm, practically dragging me the rest of the way to Mr. Kormany's room. I didn't have to wait long to find out what was on her mind.

"I've got a plan to hook Hope and Ted up. You saw how they were talking Saturday night."

"Doris, they were *just* talking—you know, something normal people do."

"They're perfect for each other. All they need is a little nudge, and they'll fall right over the cliff of love. Come on, Ben. It's just a little matchmaking, and between the two of us it'll be easy as pie."

"Whoa, Doris. Look, there's another word for matchmaking. It's called 'meddling,' and nine times out of ten, it backfires. All you're going to accomplish is getting them both pissed at you. And note, I emphasize the words *at you*—I don't want any part of it. The last thing I need is to get mixed up in some crazy matchmaking scheme."

She tsked. "All we have to do is get them to open up about their feelings. Once they realize what they already feel deep down inside, they'll take it from there."

"You're crazy."

She waived a dismissive hand. "Don't worry. I'll do all the work. You just follow my lead. We'll be so subtle they won't even realize we played a part in it."

"Doris, I'm serious. I don't want anything to do with it. And it's pointless anyway because Ted's finally going to ask Vickie Parker out. Today."

Doris froze in her tracks. Her eyes went wide, and her mouth dropped open.

"No. You're kidding. "

I nodded solemnly. "I convinced him to do it while we were at the mall yesterday."

"How did you do that?"

"Let's just say I appealed to his sporting nature." There was no way I was going to tell her how I had totally humiliated myself in front of Adonis and Raggedy Anne.

AS THE MORNING progressed, we kept our eyes open for any sign from Ted that he'd popped Vickie the question. I thought his best chance of asking her out before lunch was during morning break, but he and Hope used the time to cram for a business test.

After third period, Ted, Hope, and I trekked from the M-B wing to the Language Arts wing. We each stopped off at our lockers, but I was quicker exchanging my pre-calc book for *Huckleberry Finn* and moved on without them, keeping my eye out for Vickie. But by the time I got to Mrs. Barsanas's room, the only thing of note I'd seen was Adrian walking next to a very pretty girl. He noticed me passing by and nodded, while I wondered if she was the girl lucky enough to have nabbed him.

Doris was already sitting in her desk when I came in. I slid into the seat next to her, and she leaned over.

"Any luck?"

"No," I said, opening my notebook. "I don't know what Vickie's schedule is, but the only time I've ever seen her in the morning was before first period."

She tapped her pencil on her desk a couple of times. "That means he'll ask her during lunch."

"Possibly. That would seem like his best chance."

But when the four of us got to the lunchroom, Vickie was already sitting at a table, surrounded by her girlfriends. Now Ted might have been brave, but not even Superman would dare ask a girl out under those circumstances. So, instead, he spent the whole period taking little peeks in her direction while Doris and I wondered if he'd get a chance to make his move before lunch was over. Clueless about the waiting game going on around her, Hope spent the period chattering on about *Galactic Battleships*.

By the time the bell rang, Ted was no closer to asking Vickie out than he was before. Doris glanced at me and shrugged a shoulder before heading for the front hall, while I waited for Hope to finish her after-lunch restroom break, taking up my usual position for a few minutes of boy-watching.

In Creative Writing, Ms. Kiri gave us back our news reports—mine got an *A*. She now instructed us to use the report as the basis for a fuller narrative that included dialogue and more exposition. I decided to expand on the scene where Puppylove and Hotbody confessed their love for each other. It was romantic and erotic, and I naturally used Colby as the basis for a very detailed description of Hotbody.

My eyes wandered over to him. He looked especially sexy that day in super-tight jeans and a baggy pullover, exposing a little more of that collarbone I wanted to spend all afternoon chewing on. But more than that, there was something about the way he was sitting. His back was straight, and he had a contented, cocky expression on his face that was so stimulating I needed the whole of my next class to come back down to earth.

During study hall, Ted and I went to the library and grabbed a couple of the cushioned chairs near the newspaper rack.

"So what's the plan? Are you going to ask Vickie out or what? You're not welching out on the bet, are you?"

"No, I'm not backing out. I'm going to catch her after school."

"You mean in the parking lot?"

"Sure. Why not?"

I had to admire his bravery. Ted might not have been willing to risk embarrassing himself in front of a tableful of Vickie's friends, but he *was* willing to risk it in front of whoever might be passing by after school. On the other hand, as I thought about it, I decided maybe he was right. With everybody so focused on getting away from Chadham High as soon as humanly possible, they probably wouldn't even notice if Vickie laughed in his face.

Still, I wanted to be near enough to see it, and to catch him if necessary. If she turned him down, he'd be totally crushed and need all the sympathy he could get. So, I planned to be out in the parking lot early. On the way to my last class, I stopped by my locker to make sure I'd have everything I needed after last bell.

Time seemed to stand still, and the wait for three o'clock became almost unbearable. It didn't help that I had to suffer through Mr. Ember giving what had to be the most boring lecture in the history of humanities. It also didn't help that I sat up front, meaning I couldn't goof off—or avoid Mr. Ember's breath. "What on earth does that man eat for lunch?" I muttered to myself.

At last, the bell rang, and I bolted to get out of the building before the halls began filling up.

After such a chilly, gray morning, it had turned into a pleasantly cloudless afternoon. I moved to a spot where I could keep an eye out for Ted—and Vickie—as well as soak up some of that sunshine. Grant Framingham trudged past me, his mousy brown hair flopping in the breeze. Adrian and Tyler waved.

Doris and Hope yelled their good-byes. Hope was in a good mood. While swinging her arm up to wave at me, she scuffed her shoe against something, lost her balance, and staggered to one side. But she straightened up, laughing it off, and kept walking. Doris shot me a quizzical look, and mouthed the words *Did he do it?* I shook my head and pointed to the ground. Her eyes went wide as she turned to follow Hope. I knew she'd have preferred to hang around for the big event, but Hope rode home with her, and I was certain Doris wouldn't want her to see Ted talking to Vickie.

Ted bounded out the door, spied me, and came over.

"She hasn't left yet has she?"

"Nope, I've not seen hide nor hair of her."

We stood there for a few minutes, watching people hopping on buses or rushing off to this or that car. Colby emerged from the building, that luscious wavy hair floating and bobbing. I couldn't stop a very audible sigh escaping as he passed me, but if he heard it, he didn't show it. Not that it stopped me from watching him walk away.

Definitely a ten.

Meanwhile, Ted's attention was glued to the building, his eyes bouncing between the two exits on either end. He wasn't acting nervous per se, but he was bobbing on one heel. All at once, a group of about fifteen people spilled out of the exit at the far end of the building. By the time we caught sight of Vickie, she had almost reached the parking lot.

As Ted took a step forward, a burgundy Toyota Camry pulled to a stop in front of her, and my mouth dropped open. Colby Ryder jumped out, went around to the passenger side, and opened the door for Vickie. Then he pulled her into an embrace and kissed her, helped her get inside, and gingerly closed the door before racing back around to the driver's side.

Totally slack-jawed, we watched the Camry pull onto the service road.

A sting of envy pierced my heart, and the image of her in his arms was burning a hole in it. I wished I could trade bodies with her just for a second so I could taste those lips that had just kissed hers. My stomach felt hollow and uneasy as depression settled over me like a pall.

But my own disappointment was overshadowed by the groan of despair coming from Ted. His shoulders slumped, and his cheeks were ashen. I'd seen pictures of defeated soldiers who didn't look as devastated.

We barely spoke on the drive home, too upset to do much more than sulk. When we pulled up in front of Ted's house, he threw the stick to park and flung open the door. We got out and faced each other.

"I'm going on home," I said.

"See ya," he mumbled.

Five blocks later, I entered the kitchen to the boom of the TV.

"Hey, Grandpa. How was your day?" I shouted, walking into the living room.

But he wasn't there.

I grabbed the remote, turned the volume down, and glanced down the hallway. His bedroom door was closed.

I knew I should go and say hello, but I was just too depressed. So, turning in the opposite direction, I went to my room, dropped my book bag, and flopped down on the bed. *Okay, so Colby was kissing Vickie... I shouldn't let myself get this upset over it. It's not like I ever had a chance with him anyway.* But seeing them together brought home how romantically challenged my life really was. So I lay on the bed sulking over my nonexistent love life, lost track of time, and drifted off.

Until...

"Ben, where's your grandfather?"

My mother was standing in my doorway with wide, alarmed eyes.

"Isn't he in his room?"

"No. Was he in there when you got home?"

"I thought so. When I came in, the TV was on real loud, and his door was closed, so I just came here."

"What time did you get home?"

"I came straight home after school."

"You didn't stop off at Ted's?"

"Not today. I...had a headache."

She turned on her heels and rushed back to the living room with me right behind her.

"Where could he be?"

"How should I know," she snapped.

She went to the kitchen and grabbed the phone. I doubled back to Grandpa's room and looked around. His things were all still there, so he hadn't run away. After checking his bathroom just to make sure he wasn't in there, I returned to the kitchen.

Mom was on the phone talking to Dad.

"I'm worried, Ethan. He could be anywhere. Ben got here around three thirty or so, and he was gone then... No, he said the TV was on loud, and his room's door was closed, so he just assumed he was in there... Okay. Drive safe."

"I'm sorry, Mom. I should have checked on him."

"It's not your fault. I just can't believe he'd—" she broke off and went to the refrigerator. A piece of paper with large irregular script was dangling from a magnet. She pulled it off and read it.

"It's from Grandpa. It says, 'I'm going to the bookstore.' Bookstore? What bookstore?"

"Maybe he meant the mall."

She grabbed the spare keys from the bulletin board. "Here, take my car and drive around the neighborhood, then go to the mall and look for him. And take your time when you're looking in the neighborhood. Be thorough. If he's confused, he might be wandering around in circles."

I raced back to my room, grabbed my license off the desk, ran outside, and jumped in the car. Working my way through the neighborhood, I methodically looped around to leave no block unchecked. While I threaded my way through the streets, I tried to make sense out of what was happening.

Grandpa seemed normal enough for the most part, and if he'd just gone out for a walk, there'd be nothing to be concerned about. But the mall...? He'd only visited us a few times in the previous five years, and I couldn't believe he knew Chadham well enough to find his way to the mall. Plus, the mall was on the other side of town. It would take him a couple of hours on foot just to get there. It didn't make sense.

Almost fifteen blocks away from the house, I turned onto Franklin Street. It was a wide thoroughfare with sidewalks on either side. The houses were a mixture of middle-class dwellings, more or less like ours, and a few very well-to-do homes. Here and there, stately trees dotted the front lawns. Temple Beth Israel was up ahead, at the end of the block.

Technically, my family was Jewish, but Dad was the only one who ever showed any interest in actually practicing the faith—which wasn't saying much given his cravings for decidedly *un*-Kosher foods. Mom had already given up on the whole God thing by the time she was in college. She said it was enough to lead a good life and be nice to people. As for me, I guess I was kind of in the middle on the topic. I'd let God know I could use some convincing, and I was still waiting to hear back from him. I hadn't darkened the door of Temple Beth Israel since my Bar Mitzvah, partly because of God's lack of communication, but mainly because of the Beth Israel Community Center and Home for Seniors next door.

The center was a nice enough place, I suppose. It had a large hall for receptions and things on weekends. But the seniors' home, attached to it by a connector, made me very uncomfortable. Between the people who lived in the home and the programs for the elderly held in the center during the week, the place was always packed with old people, and they gave me the creeps. They dressed funny, they were all wrinkled, and some of them smelled.

As I got nearer, I could see the center was still pretty busy for five thirty on a Tuesday. Then it occurred to me that the center had a bookstore—or did have the last time I was there. *Could that be the bookstore Grandpa was talking about?* It was a crazy idea, but a lot less crazy than the thought of him trying to walk all the way across town to the mall.

I pulled up, went inside, and stopped. The main hall, with doors leading off in several directions, was dotted with cushioned chairs and tables. Numerous conversations buzzed all around me. Old people were sitting in little groups talking and playing cards or backgammon. The aroma of chicken cacciatore drifted through the air, reminding my stomach I hadn't eaten anything since lunch.

A large sign on the right indicated the bookstore's location. The door was open, so I walked over. A few people were milling about. Behind the counter, a guy looking to be in his mid-thirties was chatting with an elderly woman wearing glasses as thick as soda bottle bottoms. As middle-aged people go, the guy wasn't bad looking. He was a couple of inches shorter than me, clean-shaven, with nicely cropped almost white-blond hair parted on one side, and he had the greenest eyes I'd ever seen. As I approached, the old lady picked up a book from the counter and said goodbye.

"Uh, excuse me," I said. "I'm looking for an old man."

The guy laughed. "Well, you've come to the right place. We've got a fairly large selection to choose from, and I'm sure we can find one in your price range."

I chuckled and shook my head. "No, see, I'm looking for my grandfather. He just moved in with us, and when we got home today, we discovered a note saying he had gone to a bookstore. It's kind of a long shot, but he was here a few years ago, and I just thought maybe this was the bookstore he was talking about."

"Oh, you must be Benjamin," the guy said.

I gawked at him like he'd just made a rabbit appear out of thin air.

"Yeah," he continued. "Marty's here—or at least somewhere here in the center."

"Oh, thank God," I said with a sigh.

"He came in a couple of hours ago looking for a large-print copy of *Spies and Counter Spies* by Benjamin Simon. He's quite the talker, your grandfather. Among other things, he said he's in town visiting his daughter's family, and, oh yes, he just happened to mention that his grandson is also named Benjamin. By the way, you can call me Artie—everybody here does."

"Okay. Artie, can I use your phone? My mother's worried sick. Grandpa's got old-timer's disease, and we were afraid he'd wandered off."

"Sure," he said, passing me the phone.

I called home, and from the tone of her voice, Mom was relieved if highly ticked off. She told me to find Grandpa and to "put his sorry hide in the car and bring him home."

I thanked the guy for using the phone and wandered around the center for a few minutes. Then I spotted Grandpa over in a corner, reading his book.

"Hey, Grandpa."

"Benjie," he said, looking up. "What a nice surprise seeing you here."

"Yeah, Mom sent me to pick you up. It's time to go home."

He folded down the corner of a page, got up, and followed me. As we passed the bookstore, the blond guy was just locking up.

Grandpa stopped and shook his hand. "Artie, thanks so much for having this book. I've been dying to read it. Oh, and this is my grandson, Benjie—the one I was telling you about."

"Nice to meet you, Benjie," Artie said with a wink. "Hope you guys will visit again."

"Well, I don't know how much longer I'll be in town, but I'll try to pop back in if I can."

"Oh, I think you'll have time, Grandpa," I said dryly, and Artie smiled.

We walked back to the car, and Grandpa looked around at the facility.

"It's a nice center. We don't have anything near this nice back in Petersburg."

"Really? What do you like about it?"

As he rattled off a few things, I made a mental note to pass the information along to Mom and Dad.

After a few blocks, I switched the radio to a station that played crap like Big Band music and Mel Tormé. Personally, I could barely stomach it, but I knew it was the kind of music Grandpa liked. Speaking of things like my stomach, while he hummed along with whatever song they were playing, I wondered what we'd be having for supper—and when, since I was sure Mom had been too preoccupied to start anything.

No doubt about it, it was going to be a miserable evening.

I'D BARELY STEPPED outside homeroom the next morning before Doris grabbed me by the arm and started marching me along to Mr. Kormany's room.

"Did Ted do it? Did he ask her out? What did she say?"

I heaved a sigh and told her about the cosmic injustice that was Vickie Parker dating Colby Ryder—and the mortal wounds Ted and I were both suffering because of it.

If I had expected any sympathy from Doris, I'd have been sadly disappointed. You'd have thought I'd just told her she won the lottery. She practically squealed with delight.

"Wonderful. That means it's the perfect time for us to get him and Hope together."

"You really are out of your mind, Doris. This is the worst time to try and hook Hope and Ted up. Do you think Ted's going to stop wanting Vickie just because she's dating Colby? He needs time to get over her."

She scoffed. "That's just infatuation. The only thing he has in common with Vickie Parker is he almost thinks she's as beautiful as *she* does. Now, he and Hope, on the other hand—they've got lots of things in common. They've got common interests, mutual friends, and, most importantly, they've already got a history together. All we need to do is point them in the right direction, add a little heat, and they'll be tearing each other's clothes off in no time."

"Doris, Ted's in a vulnerable emotional state. He needs time to get over Vickie. He's on the rebound."

"Silly, all he needs is a little distraction—like Hope—and trust me, he'll forget all about Vickie."

"Well, I don't want anything to do with it. I told you before. Matchmaking almost always goes bad, and when it does, the matchmaker's the one who gets blamed."

She waved a dismissive hand. "Oh pooh, you've got nothing to worry about. I'll do all the work. You just follow my lead."

She kept going on and on about it right up until the first-period bell rang. All my attempts to talk her out of it, or at least to keep *me* out of it, fell on deaf ears. She wasn't even listening to me. But why should I have thought otherwise? Doris Whitfield was absolutely the most headstrong person I knew.

Forty-five minutes later, we were on our way to the M-B wing, and she was still spinning plans.

"Doris, for the last time, this is a terrible idea."

"Oh, you're just jealous because I thought it up first."

I rolled my eyes. "You really are whack; you know that, Doris?"

"We'll just be helping them along. You know they're made for each other."

"Doris—"

"Now relax and follow my lead," she said as we turned the corner, and Hope came bouncing up in our direction.

She was wearing her black cotton pullover with spaghetti straps and a patterned knee-length skirt featuring multilayered hemlines. The tightness of the top and the way the skirt hugged her hips nicely accentuated her figure. She and I exchanged the usual good-mornings while Doris stopped at her locker.

Right on cue, Ted sidled up to us. He had on a plaid shirt and faded black pleated jeans that gave his bony frame a meatier look.

Doris shot a quick smile in my direction and launched headlong into her campaign.

"Good morning, Ted."

"Hey, Ted," Hope said cheerfully, standing a little straighter.

"Morning," he said in a flat tone.

"Oh my, Ted, but don't you look handsome this morning," Doris said, giving him an exaggerated once-over. "Don't you think so, Hope?"

"As always," she said sheepishly.

"Thanks," he said and was about to say something else, but Doris continued, glancing my way and nodding in Ted's general direction.

"And Hope looks quite fetching today too, doesn't she, Ben?"

"Oh yeah, nice"—Doris elbowed me in the ribs—"I mean, yeah. She, uh, she could be on the cover of *Seventeen*."

"She sure could, couldn't she, Ted?"

"Uh, yeah," he said while Hope blushed at the sudden bombardment of flattery.

I rolled my eyes and broke free to cover the last leg to Economics, grumbling to myself the whole way. *Doris has got to realize how uncomfortable that whole conversation was, but does she care? No, she doesn't care. She's achieved her goal. She's forced Ted and Hope to compliment each other. And despite all my efforts to the contrary, she's pulled me right into the middle of it all.*

There was no way this was going to end well.

THURSDAY MORNING OF the following week had started out chilly, and it was still cool by midday as Hope and I fought the crowd on our way to Creative Writing. People were being extra rude, pushing and shoving like there was a prize for getting to fifth period first. Somebody must have bumped into Hope hard because she stumbled into me and it was all I could do to keep us both from crashing to the floor. She giggled and waved it all off like it was a joke, but it irritated me the way some people could nearly knock somebody down and just keep walking.

Then again, I was already in a bad mood. The past seven days had been miserable. How miserable? Let me count the ways.

First, there was the fact that my would-be fantasy boyfriend, Colby Ryder, was still going with Vickie Parker. And if the fact that they were dating wasn't bad enough, it was worse because they obviously had no problem being seen doing the most sickening things in public—like holding hands and kissing. Really, it was way disgusting.

Then, there was Doris. It was a full week into her campaign to hook Ted and Hope up, and she showed no signs of slacking off. That morning, we'd already seen two of her little engineered compliment exchanges between them. And then during lunch, she kept steering the conversation to things she knew they both liked, like music and movies, to emphasize how much they had in common. It was awkward, and it was embarrassing, and the worst thing about it was Ted was as oblivious to it as ever.

What worried me though was that Hope was showing every sign of falling right into line with Doris's scheme. That very morning, she'd barely needed any prompting before she told Ted how nice his hair looked. And at lunch, her eyes stayed fixed on him with the kind of puppy-like devotion he usually had for Vickie.

For seven days, I tried to stay out of it, but Doris was as determined I be her assistant matchmaker as she was to play cupid herself. Every time she got me out of earshot from the two of them, she went right back at it, needling me to do my part—as if I didn't have enough to deal with already.

Which brought us to Grandpa Marty.

The adjustment to having Grandpa live with us wasn't going as smoothly as we had hoped it would. It wasn't that he was hostile to living with us *per se*, although he still seemed to think of it as just an extended visit. No, the problem was us having to get used to him being around, and the complications it caused.

For instance, Mom enforced a very healthy diet on Dad to help him reach his goal of losing ten pounds and keeping them off. In Grandpa Marty though, my father had found a natural ally for his decidedly unbalanced nutritional cravings. Old Marty Blackburn might have been solidly in the lox and cream cheese bagels camp when it came to kosher foods, which was bad enough in my book, but that didn't stop him from also being one of those guys who couldn't imagine a Reuben without a ton of Swiss cheese *and* a gallon of Russian dressing. And just the previous night, Mom really lost it when she came home from working late at the office to find Dad and Grandpa pigging out on a quite un-kosher pepperoni and sausage pizza.

Grandpa was also really into those real-life mysteries and police TV shows, and at least one seemed to be on every night. That meant I missed all three of my favorite teen-focused programs. As far as I was concerned, that TV for his bedroom couldn't come fast enough.

And if Colby dating Vickie, Doris's matchmaking, and Grandpa being in the house weren't enough, there was the little issue of schoolwork. Because I was taking literature, creative writing, *and* humanities, my eleventh grade year had turned out to be a very reading and writing–intensive one. On top of everything else I was dealing with, it was just too much. I needed a break.

Ms. Kiri had just taken roll when I got an idea. We'd been working on another narrative assignment, one taking a couple of days to finish, and it was due the next day. I'd already finished working on mine, but there was no way I was going to tell Ms. Kiri that. She was notorious for rewarding people who got their work done early with more work to fill in the gap.

I gave it a minute and raised my hand. "Ms. Kiri, may I go to the library? I need to check a couple of things for my narrative."

Luckily, she didn't ask me what I might need to check since I intended to use the time to finish *Huckleberry Finn*.

Hope glared at me as I got up to leave. She'd already finished her narrative too and probably would have loved to go to the library herself. But Ms. Kiri knew us too well to let us both go at the same time. We'd been kicked out more than once because we were bound to crack each other up, especially since Hope was very prone to outbursts of giggling in the afternoon.

In fact, Hope and I both got kicked out of a library the very first time I got to know her—and Doris too for that matter. It was back in the seventh grade at the public library.

THERE I WAS, on a Saturday afternoon, doing some serious research on the Greco-Roman period. Okay, if you want to get technical about it, I was specifically interested in Greco-Roman art and pottery. See, for guys like me, the seventh grade is about the time you first start becoming aware of some of the more *physical* aspects of your attraction to boys. And the one thing I knew about Greek art was that it included lots of naked men and boys. But the pictures in the books in the middle school library somehow all stopped at the waistline. So, I'd gone to the one place where I knew I'd find books featuring better views—er, um—more detailed information for my research.

Yup. That was me—just a young man in pursuit of scholarly enrichment, ogling over a picture of a Greek urn that featured a young man sporting a rather large erection. And this book had lots more pictures like that too. "Oh, for the intellectual life."

Suddenly, a decidedly female snicker erupted right behind me. I swung around to find a short raven-haired girl peeping over my shoulder.

I slammed the book closed with a loud bang. People at the other tables jumped and glared at us.

"No, don't do that," she said. "I want to see too."

She leaned over me and grabbed at the book. I tried to slide it out of her reach, but a slightly taller, skinny girl with sandy-brown hair leaned over my other side, the two of them effectively pinning me down in the process. The taller girl snatched the book, flipped through it to the page I'd been on, and the two of them burst into a fit of giggles.

They say laughter is infectious, especially if you're really into the subject people are laughing about, so it didn't take long before I was giggling right along with them. With every page, and each picture, we snickered harder, and louder. The sandy-haired girl had a sort of hissing giggle, and believe me, it was a sound that really traveled. Between that and the raven-haired girl and me snickering, we were making a lot of noise and completely absorbed in each of the images we were looking at.

Which was probably why none of us noticed the librarian coming up behind us. She wasn't happy about all the noise we were making, and when she got a good look at *what* we were giggling at, she was livid. She slammed the book shut and glowered down at us.

"You ought to be ashamed of yourselves," she said in an angry whisper. "Now get out of here, and don't you dare come back until you're ready to act civilized."

Red-faced and feeling very self-conscious of all the eyes watching us, I slouched my way to the door with the two girls right behind me.

As soon as we were outside, the sandy-haired girl said, "What a bitch."

The short girl stomped her foot. "Yeah, and I wanted to check that book out."

At that point, all *I* wanted to do was get away from them, but they each wrapped an arm around one of mine and started pulling me along with them.

"You're in our social studies class," the short girl said. "I'm Doris. This is Hope."

"Hi. I'm Ben, Ben Carpenter."

"We know who you are," Hope said saucily. "You're the only boy in class who ever knows the *right* answer when Mrs. Harte calls on him."

I smiled and relaxed, deciding I should get to know them better.

Okay, so back then, I found it more than flattering to have anyone pay attention to me. But the more remarkable thing was that for the first time in my life, two girls were talking to me like I was a regular person and not pond scum, *one of them* almost. So we ended up going to the park and spent the rest of the afternoon talking.

Come Monday, the two of them slipped into desks next to mine in Social Studies, and within a day or two, I got the first of what would become thousands of after-school and weekend phone calls from one or the other of them. By the end of the week, they'd met Ted and pronounced him acceptable for friendship too.

And the four of us had been fast friends ever since.

From the beginning, we just seemed to have that symbiotic kind of relationship thing going on. Guys didn't pick on me as much or call me queer as often when I was around Doris and Hope (although I was still fair game when alone). And because people saw Ted hanging out with two pretty girls, his standing with the other straight guys definitely rose, as did his potential for dates—Vickie Parker notwithstanding. And because Hope and Doris were seen with Ted and me so often, they had a lot less trouble from the gropers and other sleazebags.

Yup, the four of us had always made a pretty good team together. The benefits were reciprocal, and our respect and affection for each other had been mutual.

If only Doris wasn't so determined to mess it all up.

I WALKED INTO the library thinking, "Why on earth has she got to play *shadchan* with Ted and Hope?" Then I realized I'd used the Yiddish word for matchmaker, and I thought, "Chalk up another one for having Grandpa Marty in the house. The next thing you know, I'll be saying *Oy vey!*"

I presented my pass to a sophomore sitting near the door, who barely looked at it before nodding me in. Then I crossed over to the periodicals section, grabbed one of the comfortable chairs, and opened my book.

Huckleberry Finn had just decided to dress up in drag so he could sneak into town to get information. It was a funny scene, leaving me grinning. Then the image of Huckleberry slowly morphed into a vision of Adrian wearing a skirt no longer than the towel he'd had wrapped around him that day in his room. My cheeks burned a little at the thought, but even so, my smile turned into a chuckle.

Then a voice somewhere near me whispered, "Hey, Ben."

I looked over to one side and was surprised to find Adrian actually sitting cross-legged on the floor just a few feet away from me. He was resting against the end of a bookcase with a magazine spread over his lap.

"Hi, Adrian. I didn't know you had study hall this period."

"No, I had it last period, but I didn't finish reading this—" He held up the magazine. "—so I'm skipping lunch,"

I slid out of the chair to join him on the floor as he shifted position to face me. He paused for a second, looking at me, bit his lip, and leaned forward.

"Say, I was wondering—what are you guys doing this weekend?"

"I'm not sure. We've not really discussed it yet, but we'll probably just end up hanging out or take in a movie or something."

"Oh, then could I maybe…uh…ask a favor?"

"Sure, Adrian, what can I do for you?"

"Well, you know the old Pitt Theater down in The District?"

"Yeah, more or less. Didn't it go out of business?"

"No, not exactly, but it doesn't play new releases anymore. Nowadays, they just show special features—you know, like foreign films and that kind of thing. Anyway, Saturday night they're showing this movie I'd kind of like to see, but it's rated *R*, and they'd never let me in."

"Yeah, I know what you mean. I've missed several movies over the years just because I wasn't seventeen."

"But you *are* seventeen now though, right?"

"Yeah."

"Well, see, that's the thing. I'm too young to get in on my own, but if I had someone with me who *is* seventeen, they'd probably let me in. So, I was…uh…wondering"—he pretended to examine a shoelace—"if you might consider going with me."

I blinked and said, "I'm flattered, but why don't you ask Ted to take you?"

"No, I wouldn't want to go with Ted. In fact, I'd appreciate it if you wouldn't mention it around him. You know what an ass he can be sometimes."

I leaned back and thought it over.

"It's a foreign film, you said?"

"Sort of. A lot of it was filmed in Italy. If you'll go with me, I'll pay your way, and if they don't let me in, I'll wait outside so at least you get to see it."

"Don't be silly. I'll pay my own way, and if they don't let you in, we'll go do something else."

"You mean you'll do it? You'll really go with me?"

He was smiling broadly, and those emerald encircled brown eyes almost seemed to glow.

"Sure, squirt."

"But you won't let Ted know?"

"I promise. It'll be our little secret. I'll just tell Ted I've got family business to deal with."

"Ahem."

We looked up to see Mrs. Becker looking down over her reading glasses at us.

"The library is for study, research, and reading—not chattering. Do you have passes?"

"Yes, I have a pass from Ms. Kiri."

She examined it closely before turning her attention to Adrian.

"I have second lunch."

"Well, I suggest you go to the lunchroom then.

He nodded to the magazine in his lap. "Can't I finish reading this?"

"I'll give you five minutes, but you better spend the time reading, not talking."

She walked away, and Adrian whispered, "The movie starts at eight."

"Okay, we'll meet at my house at seven. That way we can grab a bite to eat first."

"Thanks, Ben, I really appreciate it," he said with a shy smile.

Then he looked over at Mrs. Becker and said, "I guess I'd better go."

As he left, she frowned at him and eyeballed me a final time as I returned to my chair and Huck Finn.

Chapter Four

FRIDAY MORNING PROVED even chillier than Thursday had been. Doris and I were shivering as we made our way to the M-B wing. When we turned the corner, Hope fell into step beside us. She was sporting a long-sleeved pullover with broad horizontal black and white stripes, a short denim skirt, and knee-high boots with flat heels.

"Hi, Ben."

Before I could reply, Doris cut in. "Have you seen Ted this morning?"

"*I* have," I said dryly.

"I know *you* have. I was asking Hope."

"No, I haven't seen him yet today. Why?"

"He's wearing that beige pullover you like so much. You know, the one you said makes him look hot."

Hope looked down with a self-conscious smile. I shot Doris a disapproving glare. But I did have to admit she was right. That particular pullover did cling to Ted in all the right places.

As he walked up to us, Doris closed her locker door and grinned.

"Woohoo! Good morning, sexy. Hope and I were just talking about how good that shirt looks on you."

"Oh?" he said, surprised.

But before Doris could prompt her, Hope said, "Well, you look good in just about everything, but yeah, that shirt really does look nice on you."

They smiled at each other for a second before Ted said he'd see us later and left for Chemistry. As soon as Hope disappeared inside Ms. Antallen's room, Doris poked me in the side, grinning from ear to ear.

"What did I tell you? Our work's halfway done," she said and ambled off to Pre-Calc.

Okay, maybe her little ploy was halfway working, but it was the other half that was going to be the hard part. Ted was no Einstein, but as straight guys go, he was intelligent enough. The trouble was, he was also one of those guys who were almost impossible to derail once he got something in his head—and Vickie had been in his head for well over a year. On the other hand, he was up against Doris, and once she set her mind to something, nothing could stop her. *Jeez, talk about your unstoppable force versus the immovable object.*

WE ALL GROANED when we walked into the lunchroom. The menu board proclaimed pizza as the main dish of the day. It wouldn't have been so bad if Chadham High pizza just tasted bland, but it looked like something you'd more likely throw out than actually dare to eat. Since when was mozzarella cheese supposed to be green?

As always, Friday lunchtime conversation focused on planning our traditional Saturday night out.

"We should go to the mall," Doris announced, throwing me a conspiratorial glance.

Ted groaned. "Why on earth should we go to the mall?"

"It'll be a nice change"—she paused—"And I did happen to see a dress at Hot Miss Fashions and Accessories that would be perfect for Hope."

Hope blinked and stared at Doris, while I rolled my eyes.

Ted's response was predictable.

"Doris Day Whitfield," he said through a mouthful of pizza while Doris bristled at the mention of her middle name. "If you think me and Ben are going to follow you two around shopping all night, you're crazy."

"Not *shopping*," she retorted. "I just think Hope should have a look at that one dress and maybe try it on, that's all."

"Phew, that's a relief. Ben and I can hang out in the food court while you check it out."

"No, silly. You've got to come with us."

Ted almost choked on his milk. "What—why?"

"For your opinions."

"Our opinions?"

"Of course. Yours because you're a straight guy, and Ben's because he's got a *good* fashion sense."

I cleared my throat. "Uh, actually, I can't go with you tomorrow night. Family stuff—you know, my grandfather."

Ted stared at me like I was abandoning him to some unimaginable torture.

"That cinches it," Doris said. "You've got to come with us, Ted. We've got to have *some* male feedback."

Ted glanced over at Hope, who was making a pouty face and flashing him puppy dog eyes.

"Well, let's not take forever. *Reservoir Dogs* is playing, and I really want to see it."

"Me too," Hope said, sitting up straight. "And we can skip the mall, if you want. Doris and I can go to Hot Miss another time."

Doris opened her mouth, but before she could speak, Ted smiled.

"No, I want to see this dress, although you're bound to look good in it. You look good in everything."

For a moment, their eyes locked.

"If you're sure you really want to go," Hope said, blushing.

Ted tilted his head and sighed, grinning. "I'm sure."

Doris looked my way, cocked an eyebrow, and broke into a triumphant grin.

IT DIDN'T TAKE long before Grandpa Marty brought more than a few changes in my family's domestic routines. It wasn't just the occasional recurring discussion about when his "visit" would be ending. He also forced us into a sort of reacquaintance with our heritage.

After his arrival the previous week, he'd come to the Friday night dinner table wearing a tie and jacket, wanting to know why we weren't eating in the dining room and where the Sabbath candles, bread, and wine were. Then he started going on and on about how important it was to keep the Sabbath dinner as a family. Now, it had been years since we'd kept the Sabbath. Because Mom didn't believe in God, she didn't see much point in lighting candles and reciting prayers. Then, Grandpa said if we weren't going to keep the Sabbath, he was ready to go back to Petersburg. Dad jumped in and promised him we'd do it up right this week. He rummaged around, found a couple of candles, and recited the prayers over them when Mom refused to do it.

So that evening, as our second Friday night Sabbath together approached, the candles were out, the bread and wine were waiting, and Dad was wearing a tie. Mom had asked me to start the roast early to make sure it would be ready on time, and she and I had just finished setting the dining room table.

Grandpa walked to the kitchen wearing a jacket, tie, and a *kippah* on his head. We waited as he washed his hands. He came to the table, stood in front of his chair, and looked over at Mom. She glanced his way and turned to Dad. He and I stood up, and after a second, she rolled her eyes and tsked before standing too.

Dad lit the candles, said the prayer, and recited a blessing for my sister Eliana and me. Then he covered the bread with a cloth, recited a blessing over the wine, and we all took a sip. Finally, he said a prayer over the bread, broke off a piece for each of us, and we were ready to start dinner proper.

"Now *this* is how families should celebrate the Sabbath," Grandpa said.

Dad nodded, while Mom ducked her head and dished spinach onto her plate.

"Benjie, will you drive me to the synagogue after dinner? I want to attend the service."

I'd never been to a Friday evening Sabbath service, but the morning service took almost two hours, and I really didn't want to spend all night listening to people singing in a language I didn't understand. But when I gave Dad my don't-make-me-do-this face, he shot his own version of it right back at me.

"Sure, Grandpa," I said with a sigh. "I'll drive you."

WHEN WE GOT to the synagogue, the parking lot was about half full, and all the lights were on at the center, so we walked over. A buzz of conversations greeted us. Along with the expected numbers of old folks, groups of middle-aged people, and even a few kids my age, were milling around, slowly moving towards the hall that led to the synagogue.

"Grandpa, you wouldn't mind if I just hung out here, would you? I'm not really interested in attending the service."

"No, that's fine. The service should only take an hour or so, and then we can go home. I know you've probably got things you want to do—chat with the girls, maybe," he said, poking me in the side.

I grabbed a chair near the main door while Grandpa adjusted his *kippah* and joined the others filing into the synagogue for the service.

"Back again, I see," Artie said, walking towards me. "It's *Ben*, isn't it?"

"Hi. Yeah, Ben. And you're Artie."

"Yup. So I'm guessing you're here with Marty."

"Yeah, he wanted to attend the Friday night service."

"Not your kind of thing?"

"Not really—" I squirmed in the chair a little. "You must keep late hours at the bookstore."

"Oh, I just take turns running the bookstore. I'm really a counselor on staff."

"A counselor?"

"Yeah, I talk to the clients and residents."

"Mm-hmm."

"Sometimes, they have issues or problems, and I try to help them deal with them."

"Sounds scary."

"Well, it can be difficult at times, but it's also rewarding to know you're helping people, especially people your grandfather's age. By the time they come to a place like this, they've got a lifetime of things they've been through, plus whatever issues they're dealing with now, like their health and all."

"I think my mother wants to enroll my grandfather in your weekday program. See, he used to live in Petersburg, but the doctors told my mother he shouldn't live alone anymore because of the old-timer's disease. So, anyway, he's here living with us, but he doesn't know it's permanent yet, and we're afraid he'll take it hard when he finds out."

"Those kinds of transitions can be difficult for the elderly, especially if they've got Alzheimer's."

"Yeah. And he really scared us last week when he took off and came here by himself."

"Your parents both work?"

"Uh-huh. That's part of why Mom wants to enroll him here, so he won't be home alone all day. We're hoping if he likes coming here, it'll be easier for him to get used to living with us."

"Yeah, well, I think he'll like it here. We've got lots of activities and things for people his age. And we can keep an eye on his condition and report back to your mother if we see anything serious. Tell her to give our director a call."

"Thanks. I will."

"Okay, well I've got to go. Take care."

Artie smiled and shook my hand before leaving.

As I watched him walk out the door, I thought, "He's a nice guy. I like him. I bet he was cute back when he was a kid."

THE PARENTAL UNITS and Grandpa Marty were just finishing dinner Saturday night when Adrian arrived—seven o'clock on the dot. Mom and Dad were used to me going out on Saturday night, so the only surprise was Adrian showing up instead of Ted.

"Good evening, Mr. and Mrs. Carpenter."

"Good evening, Adrian," Mom said.

I stepped forward. "Grandpa, this is Adrian Douglas. Adrian, this is my Grandpa Marty. Grandpa, Adrian is my friend Ted's brother. You remember Ted."

He nodded, although from the look in his eyes I doubted he had a clue who Ted was.

"What are you kids planning tonight?" Dad said.

"Adrian and I are taking in a movie."

"Just the two of you?" Mom said.

"Yeah. Ted and the girls weren't interested in this one, so it's just Adrian and me."

"I'm surprised at you, Benjie," Grandpa said, sitting back in his chair. "I'd certainly choose doing what the girls wanted to do over going to a movie without them."

"He's doing it as a favor for me, sir," Adrian said. "It's one I really want to see."

"Yeah, Pop," Mom said, "you know, doing a good deed."

More than ready to get out of there before Grandpa said anything else embarrassing, Adrian and I said our goodbyes and went outside.

As we walked to the car, he said, "I guess your grandfather doesn't know you're gay, huh?"

"Nope, and he'll probably have a fit when he finds out."

"Awkward."

I settled down behind the wheel and took in how Adrian was dressed. He had on a loose-fitting pullover with large horizontal stripes and skintight jeans that accentuated his muscular thighs. He looked so hot, if we encountered any girls that night, I had no doubt who they'd be staring at."

"Where'd you like to eat?"

"I don't know," I said, starting the car. "Do you have any preferences?"

"I was thinking about this café in The District. It's a few blocks past The Pitt, and I hear the food is really good—and cheap."

"Sounds like a plan."

We backed out to the street and were on our way.

At one time, The District had been the vibrant heart of Chadham, home to dozens of shops, businesses, and various clubs, restaurants, and theaters. But over the years, the city had expanded outward with new neighborhoods, leading to the rise of shopping centers, and eventually, the mall. Nowadays, The District was no more than a shadow of its former self. Empty shops, buildings long past their prime, and businesses catering to select clienteles lined both sides of each street as we approached our destination.

When we came to The Pitt Theatre, I saw the title on the marquee and did a double take.

"*My Own Private Idaho*? Adrian, you do know what that movie's about, don't you?"

"Yeah, I know. But I...uh...I like Keanu Reeves, and I heard he's really good in it."

I nodded. "Now I know why you didn't want Ted to know. He may not have a problem with his best friend being gay, but I somehow doubt he'd be pleased if he knew I was taking you to see a movie about two gay teenage street hustlers."

"Are you mad at me?"

He was looking at me with such a timid expression I couldn't help but smile.

"No, I'm not mad at you. Come on, let's find that café."

We parked near a dilapidated old bar a couple of blocks down from the theater. The Beat Cave—what a hokey name—had probably been a popular hangout back when the world was new, but now, it looked like the kind of place only old hippies would hang out in, if anybody besides winos went there at all.

We turned the corner, and "Layla's Café" loomed before us, the smoky aroma of sizzling meat beckoning to us.

"Smells good," I said. "What kind of food do they serve?"

"Middle Eastern. Lebanese, I think."

"Interesting."

Large windows framing a central glass door revealed a bar with a row of stools facing the right-hand wall. Four or five booths stood in a row at the opposite back corner. Tables and chairs littered the rest of the café. A family with three kids was eating at a table near the booths. Swinging doors and a serving window led to what looked to be a small but efficient kitchen.

A middle-aged raven-haired woman greeted us.

"Good evening," she said in a heavy Middle Eastern accent. "How many tonight?"

"Just the two of us," I said.

She smiled, offered us one of the tables near the front windows, and gave us menus. I recognized falafels and ordered that with a salad. Adrian ordered shawarma.

"Ben, I can't thank you enough for taking me to see *My Own Private Idaho*," Adrian said as the waitress took our orders to the serving window. "There's no way Ted would ever take me to see it. I hope you don't mind going with me."

"No, it's my pleasure. To tell you the truth, I've wanted to see it since last year myself. I hear it's really trippy."

We chatted, and it wasn't long before the waitress brought our food.

I tasted one of the falafels. "Wow, delicious. Reminds me of the ones my grandma used to make."

Adrian took a bite of his shawarma and nodded approvingly.

"This is good too. Have you ever tried one?"

"No, what does it taste like?"

"It's similar to a gyro." He held it out to me. "Have a bite."

I smiled and shook my head. "No, I might contaminate it."

"I'm not worried," he said, grinning. "I've had all my shots."

"Okay. But only if you try the falafels."

He passed me the shawarma, and I took a bite while he cut off a piece of falafel with his fork.

"Not bad."

"Mmm," he said, chewing the falafel.

"We'll definitely have to come here again."

"I'd like that."

He took a sip from his glass, sat back, and studied me with his head tilted to one side.

"You know, I've always liked you, Ben."

"Thank you," I said, my cheeks feeling warm. "I've always liked you too. You're smart and friendly, and you're not the kind of pain most younger brothers are."

"That's because I'm not *your* brother. I think Ted would probably have a different take on that."

"Maybe, but don't sell Ted short. He can surprise when he wants to."

For a second, we fell silent. Adrian was still studying me with a soft smile. His eyes were mesmerizing.

Reluctantly, I broke eye contact to glance at the clock above the serving window.

"We better eat up. Don't want to miss the start of the movie."

His smile broadened, and he took another bite of his shawarma.

AS PREDICTED, AFTER carding me to be sure I was seventeen, the staff at The Pitt had no problem letting Adrian in with me. The movie was beautiful, and we were both moved by River Phoenix and Keanu Reeves's performances. We started for home sometime near eleven.

"It was so haunting," Adrian said, staring into the distance. "And I felt so sorry for River Phoenix."

"I felt sorry for both of them. In the end, Keanu Reeves may have gotten what he wanted in terms of position, but he looked terribly lost and lonely to me."

"Maybe he'd really been lost all along."

"Could be," I said.

We came to the corner of the block, and I pulled over to the curb.

"But River Phoenix is the one I really felt sorry for," Adrian said. "I mean, they literally left him on the side of the road like a piece of trash. That's so sad."

"Yeah, it wasn't much of a life."

"And being gay too—" He paused for a second and turned to face me. "Is it hard for you—I mean, being gay and all?"

"Well," I said slowly, "I don't know. I suppose everybody's life has difficulties, but to them, it's normal. It's all they know. And we don't *all* have it as hard as River Phoenix's character in the movie. That guy had some other pretty serious issues too."

"Yeah, I guess so."

"On the other hand," I said, "I guess I'm lucky. My folks were very supportive when I came out. So, for me, being gay hasn't been something I've had to struggle with, and other than a few jerks here and there over the years, I haven't had to deal with too much flack at school. Of course, it also helps to have friends like Ted who accept my orientation without so much as a blink. That kind of surprised me at the time."

"Yeah, it surprised me too."

He paused for a second before continuing.

"So you always knew you were gay, like from the beginning?"

I cleared my throat. "More or less. I think all gay guys do on some level. You might not understand it at first or be one hundred percent sure, but you know, then the old hormones kick in and *boom*, there's no doubt about it."

"So when did that happen for you?"

I shifted position. "Well, it all started to come together for me when I was thirteen or fourteen, but I'd say by early tenth grade, I definitely knew it for certain.

"Hmm."

He looked around and realized I'd stopped at his block.

"Hey, you didn't have to drive me home, Ben. You already did enough tonight just taking me to see the movie. I could have walked home from your place."

"Let it never be said that Benjamin Carpenter doesn't carry out his duty to the very end, especially on a date."

He broke into the kind of smile that could make a guy's heart skip a beat and leaned forward.

Then, in a hushed voice, he said, "Can I share something with you before I go?"

"Sure. What?"

He looked around and curled a finger.

I leaned over, assuming he wanted to whisper something in my ear.

He hesitated for a second. Then he wrapped his arm around me and pulled me close.

"I want to thank you for a wonderful night, Ben. It was really special."

His lips collided with mine.

All my life long, I had dreamed about a boy kissing me. Now here I was being kissed, and it beat the hell out of the one Amy Hyde had given me back in third grade. It was warm and moist, and it possessed a lustiness I couldn't have imagined possible, even in my wildest Colby Ryder fantasies.

I surrendered to the hunger suddenly overwhelming me. My hand, as if under its own power, found his neck, and I ran my fingers through his hair. In that moment, nothing else on earth existed. The touch of his lips and the sensation of his tongue, searching, teasing, tasting mine, consumed me.

After what seemed like an eternity, but one ending all too quickly, he slowly pulled away. We both sat back, staring into each other's eyes. My heart was racing, and my chest felt so light I could have floated up to the sky if I hadn't had my seatbelt on.

"Well, I better get inside," he said in a whisper. "Thanks again for a wonderful evening, Ben."

He squeezed my knee, got out, and walked up the block to his house, stopping at the door to wave at me before going inside. I cleared my throat, started the car, and drove home, the sensation of his kiss lingering on my lips.

How I got to sleep that night, I'll never know. I switched on the receiver while I got undressed for bed, and the first thing I heard was Sophie Hawkins singing "Damn, I Wish I Was Your Lover"—like I needed a song to put my feelings into words.

They say you never forget your first kiss, and there was no way I'd ever forget the one Adrian had planted on me. I lay in bed totally pitched and unable to shake its effect. It had been passionate, powerful, and masterful, and it had grown in intensity the longer it went on. When it ended, I was left breathless, ready to beg for more.

Lying there in bed, it was all I could do to keep my hands away from myself.

I had known in passing that Adrian dated a few girls over the last year or so. I'd even seen him with one or two in the hall at school. So, I'd just assumed he was straight. But he'd wanted to see *My Own Private Idaho.* And he asked me to go with him—probably the only gay person he knew. And he had all those questions about being gay. And that kiss... It all made sense now. He was questioning his orientation.

But if he was questioning his orientation, I had to be careful. Between that kiss and seeing him nearly naked that time, it would be so easy for me to get carried away. I could wind up making a fool out of myself, or worse, Adrian could end up getting hurt.

"No doubt about it," I said, rolling over. "I've got to find a boyfriend— and soon."

I SLEPT IN Sunday morning and then lay in bed for another hour. If there was one thing I liked, it was a nice lazy day. Waking up to warm sheets and a soft pillow on a day with nothing to do—the best part of any weekend—was just so delicious, and the prospect of a quiet, peaceful day so precious, that it almost seemed like too much to ask for.

And it turned out, it was. When I eventually dragged my butt out of bed and went in search of breakfast, I was greeted by loud, tense voices coming from the kitchen as I snuck in to pour myself a cup of coffee.

Mom and Dad were sitting at the kitchen table trying to reason with Grandpa.

"Pop, it's not a question of whether it's something you *want* to do or not, it's something you *need* to do. The doctors—"

He waved his hand. "The doctors— Doctors are like auto mechanics, go to three of them, and you'll get three different opinions."

Mom scoffed and turned to my dad.

"Marty, that fall was bad, and it could have been a lot worse if Mr. Guttmann hadn't found you as soon as he did. Living here ensures that if something happens—"

Grandpa shook his head. "Nothing's going to happen."

"Come on, Marty; let's just go and talk to the lawyer. He's a good man— a real... uh...*mensch*. If nothing else, it'll give you the chance to make sure you've got everything set up the way you want it if something else does happen in the future."

"Ugh! You fall one time and people act like—"

Mom tsked. "Pop, it wasn't just *one* time. It was the *third* time, and the second time it happened you broke your hip, remember?"

Grandpa's eyes widened at that, and I wondered if he'd forgotten about the three months it had taken him to recover.

"Let's just meet with Frank Brady," Dad said, "and afterwards, we can stop at the senior center and see what new books they've got in."

While they continued to squabble, I grabbed a Pop-Tart and beat a hasty retreat.

Back in my room, I sipped the coffee and munched on the Pop-Tart, thinking.

Over the past couple of weeks, I'd had plenty of opportunities to observe the dynamics of my mother's relationship with Grandpa. They were definitely father and daughter all right. They clearly loved each other very much, but they also irritated the living crap out of each other. Grandpa Marty was set in his ways, cantankerous, and he seemed to take a devilish delight in being obstinate just to annoy my mother. For her part, Mom had very limited patience when it came to foolishness, and when the mood hit him, Grandpa could be worse than a little kid. And the fact that Mom reacted to his shenanigans like he *was* a little kid irritated him to no end.

Switching on the receiver, I had no doubt the "discussion" would probably still be going on by suppertime.

Sometime after two, I was listening to k.d. lang singing "Constant Craving" when the phone rang. I sighed and picked up. It was Doris.

"So how did things go last night? I assume that by now Ted and Hope are engaged and planning the wedding."

"Ha, ha, not quite. But Ted *is* finally falling into line. When we got to Hot Miss, he couldn't have done any better if I'd told him what to do."

"You mean you didn't?"

"Hush. He was perfect. He was patient while Hope tried on the dress, and when she came out, he was so complimentary he had her blushing."

"You must be so pleased."

"I know, right?" she said, a giggle in her voice. "He even had her try on another one. Me too. So listen—tomorrow, you ask him about it on the way to school, and you and I can compare notes during first period. At this rate, it won't be long before they really *are* ready to get engaged."

"I can hardly wait," I said.

Doris missed the sarcasm completely and continued planning out Ted and Hope's future of domestic bliss for another twenty minutes.

As predicted, supper featured more grumbling from Grandpa. Over the course of the afternoon, they had apparently talked him into at least meeting with the lawyer, but he was making it crystal clear that he was only going under protest and expected to return to Petersburg all the sooner now that he knew my mother was "trying to kidnap" him. By that point, Dad was doing most of the talking, running interference for Mom, trying to answer Grandpa's objections, and casting the situation in a less drastic light. Good thing—Mom's jaw was so tight, I expected her to bite her fork off any second.

When everyone had finished eating, Dad suggested he and Grandpa go out to the garage to work on their mythical project, and as usual, Grandpa's mood instantly lightened.

As soon as Dad shut the door on their way out, Mom let out a weary sigh and started scraping food into the disposal.

"That man will be the death of me," she said with a snort.

"Mom, I'm sure he'll chill out after he gets used to the idea of living with us."

She cut me a sidelong glance. "Oh, he'll quit griping about Petersburg all right, but mark my words; he'll find something else to complain about."

As I covered a bowl with plastic wrap, I thought about it and decided she was probably right.

Chapter Five

"WHAT A WAY to start a Monday," I grumbled to myself. It was one of those mornings where you wake up about five minutes before the alarm is supposed to go off, and all you want to do is go back to sleep, but you can't. So you end up lying there with your hand on the alarm, waiting to hit it the second it goes off. And the whole time, you're hoping if you play your cards right, you can hit the snooze button and drop back off for a few more minutes.

At least, that's what I was hoping to do.

A sharp knock on my door put an end to that.

"Yes?" I said, dragging the word out to let my frustration at being forced to speak before I'd had my first sip of coffee come through in all its whiny glory.

"Ben, I need to talk to you."

"Sure, Mom. Come on in." When a parent says they need to talk to you like that, especially one like my mother, it's best to offer no resistance.

As she closed the door behind her, Mom said, "Ben, I need you to do me a favor."

"Okay, sure. What can I do?"

"I need you to come with me when I take Grandpa to the lawyer's office."

"But I've got school."

"I've already written a note asking them to excuse you for being late because you were helping me with a family emergency."

"I thought Dad was going with you?"

"He *was*, but he got a call from work. Something's come up, and he had to go in."

I stared at her blank-faced, not quite getting the big picture yet.

She tsked. "You know your grandfather. If I take him alone, he'll act up a storm."

I sighed. "Do I have time to shower?"

"Don't take too long. We need to be there by nine."

I sat up and stretched. The idea of spending a whole morning in some dusty lawyer's office was about as appealing as watching paint dry. But on the other hand, I *was* getting out of my two least favorite classes, and if we didn't have to meet the lawyer until nine, I had plenty of time for a nice, slow, luxurious shower. So I grabbed a towel, headed for the bathroom, and after a short pause to take care of the usual pressing morning business, I relaxed under the hot, steamy spray.

A half hour later, I was dry, neatly dressed with my hair combed, sitting in the kitchen enjoying a hot cup of coffee when Mom came marching into the room, her arms crossed tight.

"So," she said, rolling her eyes and leaning on the counter, "now that it's almost time to go, he's decided he's not going. Typical,"

"Should I talk to him?"

"You can try. Maybe he'll listen to you. God knows he won't listen to me."

After taking a final large gulp of coffee, I went to Grandpa's room and knocked on the door. "Grandpa, can I talk with you?"

He was sitting at his table, dealing out a game of Solitaire.

"What can I do for you?"

"Well, Mom and I are ready to leave, and she just told me you've decided you're not going."

"I told her from the beginning I wasn't going to talk to no lawyer. I only agreed to a short visit so she'd stop nagging me. Well, now I've visited for a while, and I'm ready to go home. And I'll tell you another thing—the very idea of having your mother take over my affairs is not only ridiculous, it's insulting. No sir, I'm not having it."

I sat across from him and sighed.

"I understand how you feel, Grandpa. I don't like it sometimes when Mom and Dad make decisions for me. Nobody likes it when other people are in charge. But it's not that Mom wants to boss you around. We love you, Grandpa, and when we heard that you fell and were in the hospital, it really scared us—especially Mom. What could it hurt to just talk to the lawyer? And after we're done there, we can stop at the center to see what kind of new books they've got."

He tsked and put down the cards.

"All right. I'll go talk to this lawyer of yours and see what he says. But I'm telling you now, if I don't like what I hear, I'll tell him to his face right then and there."

"That's fair. Come on, Grandpa. Let's tell Mom we're ready to go."

Mom was waiting in the kitchen. When we walked in, it was hard to tell if she was relieved that Grandpa had decided to go along with the meeting, or if she was still concerned about what he might say or do once we got there. In any case, it wouldn't take us long to find out.

We found a parking space on a side street in The District and walked a block and a half. I noticed that although Grandpa didn't seem to have a problem keeping up with Mom and me, he was wheezing. I don't think Mom noticed, but it reminded me he had emphysema. I wondered how long a person with a disease like that had, but I quickly put it out of my mind.

We came to the Chadham Bank & Trust building, and I wondered whether Mom needed to stop off and do some business before we went to the lawyer's office. But she passed by the main doors and went to another door slightly farther along. We crossed a small landing to a staircase and began ascending.

Grandpa grumbled the whole way up.

"What?" he said, panting. "Couldn't you have found a lawyer with an office on a higher floor? I get nose bleeds at high altitudes, you know."

At the second floor, the stairs turned back to ascend to a third, and presumably a fourth floor, but Mom led us down the hall to a door at the end.

The plaque read Brady, Sawyer, Hartford, and Associates.

Grandpa read off the names and scoffed, "Lawyers."

Mahogany wall panels, dotted here and there with impressionist paintings, gave the room a professional but relaxed atmosphere, enhanced by the pleasant rosy aroma of a vase of flowers. Chairs and coffee tables with magazines lined two walls. A wraparound desk surmounted by a countertop-like ledge stood in one corner, with a hallway behind it.

A man with coarse dark hair sat at the desk. He appeared to be in his late twenties, clean-shaven with a strong chin. His dark gray suit, burgundy tie, and white shirt were stylish but subdued. I didn't usually go for older men, but he was strikingly handsome for a man his age, and when he looked up, rich hazel eyes greeted us.

"Good morning. May I help you?"

"Yes. I'm Margot Carpenter, this is my father Marty Blackburn, and this is my son Benjamin. Mr. Brady is expecting us."

"Ah, yes," the man said. "Please step this way."

He led us down the hall to a conference room. A large table surrounded by twelve or so chairs stood in the center of the room. The walls were lined with volume after volume on jurisprudence, state law, and courtroom precedents.

"If you'll have a seat, I'll tell Mr. Brady you're here. And would you like something to drink? A cup of coffee or water perhaps?"

"No, thank you," Mom said.

He glanced my way.

"Water, please."

Grandpa just shook his head.

The man stepped back out, closing the door behind him.

Grandpa looked around at all the law books. "I'll bet this is going to cost a pretty penny. How else do you think he could afford all those books and that expensive paneling? Lawyers."

Mom sighed. "Pop, please. Uncle Albert was a lawyer. And Mr. Brady and Gabriel are doing this as a favor. Now, behave."

Grandpa rolled his eyes and scowled

The door opened, and a tall, very thin man came in, looking almost as old as Grandpa. He was wearing a dark suit and tie, and he was bald, with a fine ring of shortly cropped gray hair and thick glasses. The younger man followed him in, with a bottle of water, a coaster, and a napkin, all of which he handed to me.

The bald man picked up a thick file lying on the table.

"Kerry, would you mind giving this to Laura? Tell her I said it all looks fine to me."

"Sure," the young man said, taking the file and stepping out of the room.

The thin man smiled at us. "Now then, good morning, everyone. Allow me to introduce myself. I'm Frank Brady. And you must be Mrs. Carpenter."

Mom rose to shake his hand. "Pleased to meet you, Mr. Brady, I can't tell you how much Ethan and I appreciate you and Gabriel helping us out like this."

"Not at all," Mr. Brady said. "Please, call me Frank."

"Thank you," Mom said. "And call me Margot. This is my father, Marty Blackburn"—she motioned towards Grandpa, who didn't get up—"and this is my son Benjamin."

Mr. Brady walked over and shook Grandpa's hand, then mine, and went to the end of the table, where a couple of folders and a notepad awaited him.

Pulling up a chair, he said, "Gabriel gave me a basic summary of your situation, but perhaps you'd like to fill me in."

Mom cleared her throat. "My father here is coming to live with us. He's got a home and property in Petersburg that will need to be sold, and we'll need to arrange power of attorney so I can take care of it for him, as well as documents for down the road."

"I don't need you, or anyone else, to take care of me," Grandpa said testily, adding a curt nod. "And lawyers are useless."

Mom rolled her eyes, but before she could say anything, Mr. Brady interjected.

"I know what you mean, Mr. Blackburn. Sometimes, I think the only reason God created lawyers was so real estate agents could have someone to look down on."

Grandpa's eyes narrowed and he grinned. "So what do you think you can do for me?"

"We can set up several powers of attorney documents. One to allow your daughter to handle the selling of your house for you, one to act on your behalf if you become incapacitated, and one to authorize her to help look after your finances."

"And what if I decide I don't want her help?"

"That's up to you. All of these will be written up on a voluntary basis, and you'll have full rights to terminate any or all of them whenever you so desire."

"Okay, well, I want to terminate them all right now. There, that's saved everybody a lot of trouble. Now, when can I go back home to Petersburg?"

Mom sighed. "Pop, you can't go back. You need to stay with us."

Grandpa folded his arms and snorted. "You don't think I can take care of myself. Well, you're wrong. I can take care of myself just fine."

Mom leaned forward. "No, you can't. How long did you lie there with your forehead bleeding before Mr. Guttmann found you? How long would you have lain there if the two of you didn't have a regular date to play backgammon? Pop, you *need* to live with us."

"I don't need your help. I'm not some *fakakta* cripple."

Mom let her hand drop to the table and looked up at the ceiling, shaking her head.

"Grandpa, it's not just about you needing us," I said. "We need you too. *I* need you. It's kind of nice having you around these days. I never got to see you as much as I wanted when you lived in Petersburg. And Mom and Dad want you to stay with us too."

"Yeah, I'm not so certain about your mother."

"Of course she wants you here. She loves you. The only reason you two argue so much is because you're so much alike. But let me tell you, when she called after she'd seen you in the hospital, she's the one who said she wanted you to move in with us. I was there. Dad and I agreed with her, but she was the one who brought it up. And it wasn't out of pity. It was love."

Grandpa scratched his beard.

"Well, what if I don't like it here?"

"If there's something you don't like, tell us, and we'll work it out."

"What about my friends in Petersburg?"

"You can still talk to them on the phone, and I'm sure we'll be able to arrange for you to visit them every now and then."

He shook his head slowly. "I don't know, I don't know."

"Come on, Grandpa. We need you here. *I* need you here."

Mr. Brady leaned back in his chair with his fingers interlaced. "That's a powerful argument, Mr. Blackburn—a loving family, a grandson who tells you he needs you. I know a lot of men who'd give everything in the world for that. And wouldn't it be nice to have them around if something did happen and you really did need help?"

"That's right," Mom said.

Grandpa pursed his lips skeptically, and he didn't reply for a couple of seconds.

"Okay, okay," he said at last. "We'll try this out—for a while—for Benjie's sake. I can help him learn how to be a real man, a *mensch* like his grandfather."

Mr. Brady smiled. "I'm sure you can, Mr. Blackburn. And what a blessing for any young man to have a wise, caring grandfather to turn to for advice."

We spent another half hour or so with Mr. Brady asking questions and taking notes for important details in the documents he was going to draw up. Grandpa answered his questions and accepted Mom's corrections when his memory was fuzzy. By all appearances, he was ready to live with us. He even smiled at Mr. Brady's occasional jokes.

But I couldn't help noticing a certain wistfulness in his eyes. There was a sadness about him hiding just below the surface. He was putting on a good show, but I could tell he was just playing along, pretending to believe he was doing us a favor.

Suddenly, I began to understand, and I felt sorry for him. It wasn't so much that Grandpa didn't want to live with us; it was that for him, moving in with us was a defeat. It was something he had to do whether he wanted it or not. He had become an old man who couldn't look after himself anymore. He needed us, and he knew he'd only need us more and more as time went on. Time and aging were taking something from him—something he could never get back—and the fact that we all knew it too embarrassed him.

I wished I could say or do something to help. But I realized all I could do was make a commitment to be extra nice to him—and not take it too personally when he embarrassed me, or when he eventually found out that the grandson he so proudly wanted to make a *mensch* out of was a *fagalah*.

The ride from the District was quiet. Mom didn't turn the radio on, and no one said a word until we were back in our neighborhood.

"Don't forget," Grandpa said when Mom turned the corner onto Franklin Street, "Ethan promised to take me to the senior center bookstore if I agreed to meet that lawyer of yours."

"All right, Pop," Mom said with a sigh, but I caught her glancing back at me from the rearview mirror.

We pulled into the senior center parking lot. Each step Grandpa took seemed to cost him a little more energy. I held the door for him and Mom and followed them inside.

We were halfway to the bookstore entrance when a familiar voice greeted us.

"Why if it isn't my friends Marty and young Benjamin."

Grandpa faltered. "Hello there...uh..."

"Artie," he said, smiling. "And let me guess—" He turned to my mother. "—you must be Marty's daughter."

"Nice to meet you, Mister uh..."

"Please, call me Artie."

"Artie. Yes, I'm Old Troublemaker Blackburn's daughter. Call me Margot. My father wants to peruse your bookstore."

"Sure thing. You know the way, Marty," he said with a wave of his hand.

Grandpa went inside the bookstore, and Mom turned to Artie.

"And while he's browsing, I'd like to speak with your director if he's available."

"It's she," Artie said. "I'll see if I can locate her."

He turned and took no more than two steps away from us before turning back.

"Ah, there she is. Just a second."

He crossed over to where a middle-aged woman stood talking to an old man who was sitting at a table, holding a deck of playing cards. She had frizzy auburn hair, glasses, and was dressed in a pantsuit, a white lab coat, and sensible shoes. Artie approached them, waiting until the woman finished taking a note on a clipboard she was holding, and after a brief exchange, he led her over to us.

"Good morning. I'm Dinah Markov," she said, holding out her hand." I'm the center's director. Artie says you'd like to speak with me."

"Good morning. Yes, I'm Margot Carpenter. This is my son Benjamin. My father is in the bookstore at the moment. We'd like to enroll him in the weekday program for the elderly if you have an opening."

"Yes, we can accommodate him. Would you come with me please?"

"Ben, keep an eye on your grandfather while I'm away."

Artie turned to me. "So I'm guessing your parents worked out everything with Marty about living with you?"

"Yeah, we met with a lawyer this morning."

"I'm glad. And I'm sure once we get him involved in things here, he'll relax and feel more at home."

"I hope so."

A very old, frail-looking woman came over to us and wagged a finger at me.

"There you are, Seth. I've been looking all over for you."

I took a step back, a bit freaked out.

Artie took a step forward. "Mrs. Gilder, this isn't your son. This is Benjamin."

"Don't give me that," she said with a scoff. "Don't you think I can recognize my own son?"

"Uh, that's because Seth and I look so much alike," I said. "Everybody always says so."

The old woman stared at me doubtfully and fumbled in her pocket. She pulled out a thick pair of glasses, put them on, and looked me over suspiciously.

"You see?" Artie said. "Like Ben says, everybody's always mixing him and Seth up."

"Yes, well—" She paused and folded her glasses, putting them back in her pocket. "—when you see Seth, you tell him I said to get his little *tuchus* home. His dinner's waiting."

"Yes, ma'am, I will. I promise."

She gave me a curt case-closed nod and walked off.

"You handled that very well," Artie said.

"Really? I was kind of scared."

"No one would have guessed it. You dealt with her, and you did it without embarrassing her. I'm impressed."

"Thanks. It just came to me, and it seemed like a way to not upset her."

"Have you ever thought about going into social work?"

"No, I'm going to be a writer."

Artie smiled broadly. "A noble profession. Say, do you have your community service hours for school lined up?"

"Uh, no, I don't." It had been weeks since the last time I'd even thought about it.

"Why not volunteer here? You seem to have a knack for it, and we could always use more young people. Many of our residents and clients especially like interacting with young people."

"Oh, I don't know," I said, looking down. "Old people kind of give me the creeps."

"Hmm. How much experience have you had with the elderly?"

"Not much, I guess," I said, crossing my arms. "Most of the people in our neighborhood are middle-aged, and we didn't get to see my grandparents much when I was growing up."

"There you are. It's just nerves from lack of acquaintance. Why not give it a try? I'll be around to help if you need it. And if you don't feel more comfortable after a while, you can always drop out."

I had to admit it was a tempting offer. I really did need those community service hours, and the center was the only place to have anything to offer. Not to mention the fact that I was already a month behind. But being around all those old people...

"I'll...uh...have to talk it over with my folks."

"Sure. Tell them if they have any questions to give me a call. Now, if you'll excuse me, I better get back to work."

He walked to the other side of the room where three old guys were playing dominoes, pulled up a chair, and joined them.

"Wow," I thought, "if all you've got to do is play games with them, maybe it wouldn't be so bad after all." Then I saw Mrs. Gilder wandering around talking to herself, and my optimism collapsed.

I DIDN'T GET to school until halfway through my fourth-period class, Literature. Having to join a class already in progress is awkward in the extreme. First, just coming into the room interrupts things, which means all eyes are on you. Then you've got to stand there while the teacher reads the note and corrects her attendance book. Then you slump off to your seat, knowing you've totally irritated her. Meanwhile, half the class is wondering where you were, and the other half thinks you're stupid because you should have worked it out to miss the whole period.

As it was, I arrived in the middle of the final class discussion on *Huckleberry Finn*. The debate was on the book's racist setting and whether its racist language should disqualify it for teenage readers. While two people on the other side of the room were loudly disagreeing with each other, Ted leaned over.

"What was up this morning?"

"My mom needed me to help get my grandfather to the lawyer's office."

"Did everything go okay?"

"More or less. I'll fill you in later."

Mrs. Barsanas rapped her podium to end the escalating argument on the other side of the room, told everyone to pass our copies of *Huck Finn* forward, and began distributing copies of *Heart of Darkness*.

The bell rang at last, and we were on our way to the lunchroom.

"So where were you this morning, Ben?" Hope asked as, one by one, we dropped our books off in our lockers.

I explained, once again, what my morning dealing with my grandfather had been like. "So everything's all set for him?" Doris asked when I finished.

"Well, it was touch and go for a while, but he did finally agree to stay with us, so maybe it'll be all right."

"As long as he doesn't change his mind," Ted said.

"I think you know him almost as good as I do."

THE REMAINDER OF the school day was uneventful, except for one important thing. Hope and I were on the way to Creative Writing after lunch. When I stopped by my locker, I noticed a folded up piece of paper someone had slipped in through the air vent. I unfolded it and smiled as I stared down at Adrian's flowing cursive.

> *Dear Ben,*
>
> *Thanks for making Saturday night the best time of my life. You were so nice. I just can't believe how lucky I am to have you as a friend. Thanks for everything! I look forward to being with you again soon.*
>
> *Love,*
>
> *Adrian*

Hope noticed me folding the note and slipping it into my pocket.

"What's that? Don't tell me you've got a secret admirer? Or is it from a secret *boyfriend*?"

"Huh? Neither," I said, continuing on to Ms. Kiri's room.

Our assignment for the day was to write about something surprising. Ms. Kiri said it could be fictional or based on something that really happened, as long as we described it, and the reaction to it, realistically.

Normally, I'd have chosen a Colby-centered topic—my recent shock in finding out he was dating Vickie being a timely choice—but no matter how hard I tried, I just couldn't keep focused on it. After getting that note, Adrian was all I could think about. So, since I couldn't get him out of my head, I decided to start writing and see what happened.

Mark Lonelyboy had given up. Life wasn't just passing him by; it was constantly running him off the road. Whenever he got his hopes up, whenever he thought there might be the tiniest hope that the boy he dreamed about could show some interest in him, here would come life, barreling along, to trip him over and stomp on him before leaving him behind in a cloud of disappointment.

At last, desperation melted into hopelessness, and he despaired that he was destined to a life without love. Days stretched into weeks. Weeks stretched into months. The best he could say for it was that his heart no longer ached. It just sat in his chest like something heavy but empty. Often, he found himself walking in the park and staring at the river, debating whether to throw himself in, always chickening out until "next time."

One day, he was sitting on a bench, staring at the flowing waters. They were gray and churning. Watching them was so hypnotic that he didn't notice when someone sat down next to him. When he finally looked over, he was surprised to see Percy Goodlooking, a childhood friend he hadn't spoken to in ages.

Percy was watching him, his sandy-colored locks swaying in the gentle breeze.

"Percy! What are you doing here?"

Percy smiled at him. "I often come to the park. It's a nice place to think and clear my head. I see you here every now and then, but you always seem so preoccupied, I wasn't sure if I should disturb you."

"Oh, I'm sorry. I'm usually thinking about how lonely life can be when nobody loves you."

"I understand. But you know, sometimes you have to step outside of yourself."

"What do you mean?"

"You have to take a chance."

"What kind of chance?"

"Well, something like this."

Percy leaned over and kissed him. It was tender and passionate, and Mark's skin tingled from the emotional current rippling through him. It was everything he dreamed of in a kiss and more.

And it happened so fast that when it was over, he wasn't sure it had really happened. He stared at Percy, confused and uncertain, embarrassment fighting the excitement melting the icy void in his chest.

His mind raced, remembering all the times Percy had been around—never up close or imposing, but always nearby and always there with a kind word. Mark looked into Percy's eyes and realized he wasn't just good-looking. In fact, he wasn't good-looking at all. He was beautiful. And he had just kissed him.

Percy studied him and hesitantly asked, "Well, did you like it?"

"Like it? Yes, very much."

"Would you like more?"

Mark nodded.

When Percy kissed him again, a spark in Mark's chest ignited, and his heart burst into flames. And from that point on, he was known as Mark Lonelyboynolonger.

As soon as I set my paper on Ms. Kiri's desk, she picked it up to give it her usual once-over. After she scanned the page, she looked up at me, her eyebrows rising, and tilted her head to one side.

I shrugged and mumbled, "Variety," before leaving to catch up with Hope.

"So what was Colby this time?" she said, bumping into me.

"He...uh...wasn't in this one."

"Oh? What did you write about then? That surprise birthday party we threw for you back in eighth grade?"

"No, I wrote about a surprise kiss."

"Ooo, I'm intrigued. Who kissed you? Do I know him?"

"Nobody kissed me. It was just fiction."

"Oh, yeah? I'll bet it was the guy who wrote that note. It was, wasn't it?"

"You're crazy."

"Oh, am I?" she said, flicking her bangs aside. "Then why are you blushing?"

"I'm not," I said, quickening my pace.

"You are, and you're lucky you're not Catholic. You'd have to go to confession big time for telling a lie like that. Come on; tell me. What's the story? Who is it? Who's sending you love notes?"

"It wasn't a love note. If you must know, it was a thank-you note. I just did a favor for somebody, and they wrote me a thank-you note, that's all. It was just a thank-you note."

"Uh-huh. Well, either way, sooner or later, you'll have to tell me all about who kissed you."

She broke into an impudent grin, and as she turned to go to her next class, she crashed into a girl. The girl glared, but Hope continued on her way.

I reflected on the certainty that Hope would demand a more detailed explanation for my story. So, I decided the next time she brought it up, I'd tell her it was based on a fantasy—she'd buy that.

I'D JUST FINISHED cutting up tomatoes and onions for a salad when Mom walked in, set her bag down, and leaned back against the counter. After dealing with Grandpa all morning, she had gone into the office for the afternoon and ended up working an hour later than her usual quit time.

"Hey, Mom."

"Hey."

"How was the office this afternoon?"

"It was okay," she said, munching on a piece of carrot. "Where's your grandfather?"

"He's in the living room watching the news. You never did say—did you get everything set for him to start going to the center?"

"Yeah. I was going to tell him he'll be starting tomorrow, but I wanted your father to run interference when I broke the news. So, of course, he called and won't be home for dinner—wonderful."

"Grandpa might not give you as much trouble about the center as you think," I said, scraping the cut vegetables into a large bowl with the other fixings. "He seems to like the place, and he's definitely friendly with that Artie guy."

That reminded me about Artie's community service offer. I couldn't risk my folks finding out I'd not even given it a try, so I cleared my throat.

"Speaking of which," I said, slowly, "you know I've got that community service requirement, and I still haven't found anything, and—"

"Benjamin, you've known about that since the end of August," she said, crossing her arms.

"I know, Mom, but that's not the point. See...uh...Artie suggested I could volunteer at the center for my community service hours."

"You thanked him, I hope."

"Well, not exactly. I told him I'd think about it."

Mom stood up straight with her hands on her hips.

"Why didn't you just say yes?"

"Well...see...it's just...I'm not totally comfortable with the idea of volunteering there."

"Not totally comfortable? What's there to be not totally comfortable about?"

"Well, being around all those old people," I said, sprinkling sesame seeds over the salad. "They kind of freak me out."

Mom laughed. "Well, if old people freak you out, then, yes, the senior center would definitely be a challenge."

"Yeah, I *told* Artie that." I slid my hands into my pockets. "But he said I probably feel that way because I haven't had a lot of experience with them, and I'd feel better when I got to know them. But I don't know... So anyway, I was...uh...thinking that maybe I'd...uh... just tell him I can't do it."

"Ben, it's your decision. Just remember you do need those service hours. And even if you're there for only a couple of hours in the afternoon, it might make it easier for your grandfather to adjust."

"But what if I can't handle it?"

"Whether you can handle it or not ultimately depends on you. You'll either face your fears or you won't—the choice will be yours."

"I don't know. Do you really think I should try it?"

"I'm not going to tell you what to do. You're seventeen years old, and you ought to be mature enough to decide something like this on your own."

I nodded and went to the fridge to get some cheese, feeling like a coward.

"Okay. I'll call Artie tomorrow after school and tell him I'll do it," I said, getting out the grater.

"Here, give me that," she said, taking it from me. "If you're going to do it, go call him now. The number's on that magnet on the fridge. And be sure to thank him for helping you out."

"Mom, he's probably already gone home by now."

"If he already left for the day, ask them to take a message."

My mother knew it was best to get me to commit before I had a chance to change my mind. And she *was* right. I really did need those community service hours. So, I called and left a message with my name and number for Artie. The man on the other end was very nice. He welcomed me aboard and assured me I'd have a lot of fun. I wasn't so sure but guessed I'd find out soon enough.

A half hour later, the three of us were eating supper. Grandpa had been unusually quiet ever since our meeting with Frank Brady that morning. He was so quiet, it made me worry how he'd take it when Mom spilled the beans about enrolling him at the center.

I didn't have to wait long to find out.

Mom glanced my way and cleared her throat.

"Pop, while we were at the senior center today, I spoke with Dr. Markov about enrolling you in their weekday program."

He stared at her with furrowed brows and scoffed defiantly. "You mean that *daycare* program for senile old babies who need their diapers changed twice a day? No thank you."

Mom broke into a sarcastic grin. "Oh, come on, Pop. You know better than that. If you were that bad off, we'd commit you as a resident, not enroll you in the weekday program. No, it's just activities and classes and things to keep you from getting bored."

"And what if I like being bored?"—he waved his arms around and pointed a finger at her—"I'm not going to let some pencil-necked goon in a lab coat try to force me into some stupid basket-weaving class. I do things because *I* want to, not because it's on some damn schedule."

"Dr. Markov said the programs and activities are strictly voluntary, and participation is up to the clients. Some people go there to play cards or backgammon or dominos. Some people just socialize. Really, what you do there will be up to you."

He threw his fork onto his plate and crossed his arms.

"I'm not going, and that's final."

Mom looked at me with imploring eyes.

"Gee, Grandpa, I'm sorry you're not going to be there. See, Artie asked me if I'd be a volunteer as part of my school's community service program. I'll be there after school every day, but I'm kind of nervous about it. I'd feel a lot better if you were there."

He pursed his lips and glared at me, but after a few seconds, he snorted.

"Well, maybe I'll try it out for a few days—just until you get settled in."

"Thanks, Grandpa. I really appreciate it."

He stabbed a forkful of salad, and Mom heaved a sigh of relief and mouthed *thank you* to me.

Chapter Six

I CAME TO the Douglas's house just as the Toby-mobile pulled up. Adrian came bounding out the front door, dashed across the yard, and pulled open the rear passenger-side door. But before he got in, he looked my way with a sheepish smile.

I was still standing there with flushed cheeks when Ted came out. The two of us got into Baby, he revved the engine to encourage the heater, and we backed out of the driveway.

"My grandfather is starting the day program at the Beth Israel Community Center today," I said.

"Glad you guys have finally got that all worked out. I know it's been a problem."

"Yeah. And by the way, I've finally found something for my community service hours. I'll be volunteering there."

"You lucky dog. The way things are going, I'll have to do mine over the summer."

"Wait—I didn't know that was an option."

"Technically, it's not. But if you don't get your hours in during the school year, they threaten to hold you back *unless* you make it up over the summer. So, in fact, it actually is an option after all, just one they don't advertise. Not that you've got to worry about it now."

"Still, I'm going to keep that in mind in case things don't work out at the center. Say, would you mind dropping me off there after school today? In fact, I'll probably need a lift there every day from now on. I'll reimburse you for the gas of course."

"Don't worry about it. We'll find some way to work it out. Maybe you'll buy me a burger every now and then or something."

"Thanks, Ted."

IN CREATIVE WRITING, Ms. Kiri gave us back our papers, and when she handed me mine, Hope snatched it. She gave it a quick read and looked up at me, wide-eyed and smiling.

As soon as class was over, she started grilling me.

"Someone really did kiss you," she said, shoulder bumping me. "Who was it?"

"No one kissed me. I just made it up."

"Are you kidding? I read what you wrote. That kiss happened, and it must have been *way* good to stop you drooling over Colby, because that clearly wasn't him in the story. Come on; tell me. You know I tell *you* everything."

"Look, as far as Colby's concerned, I just finally realized that he's a lost cause, and as for the story, it was just pure fantasy—two completely separate things."

"Okay, don't tell me if you don't want to. But I'll find out sooner or later."

"Seriously, if you must know, it was based on a fantasy I had once about kissing Jon Bon Jovi."

"Uh-huh, says you."

She turned to go, plowed head on into a passing student, and offered him a sniggering apology. I went on to the Science wing and had no sooner walked into the physics room than Mr. Ferguson waved me over.

"A note for you from the office."

I set my books down on the desk and unfolded it.

> *Art called. Don't come to the center today. Unexpected business. Will devote full time to your orientation tomorrow. Welcome aboard.*

That certainly freed things up, for that day anyway. I just hoped Grandpa wouldn't look for me too hard that afternoon.

TED AND I took what would be the last of our traditional rides home. The days of stopping off at the Douglas house with Ted to do homework—and goof off—were coming to an end.

We got out of the car, and I flung my book bag over my shoulder.

"You coming in?"

"I really shouldn't. I've got a ton of homework, and I need to call my mother to let her know not to look for me when she goes to pick up my grandfather. But, hey, can I borrow that R.E.M. CD of yours? I want to add one of the songs to a mixtape I'm making."

"Sure, come on up."

We went inside, and I said hello to Mrs. Douglas, who asked about my grandfather and said to tell Mom we were all in her prayers. Ted grabbed a cookie, and I followed him upstairs to his room. After searching through his shelves, he handed me the CD, and I thanked him for the loan, stuffing it in my book bag. "Would you close the door on your way out?"

"Sure," I said, while the opening chords of "Smells Like Teen Spirit" filled the room.

When I stepped into the hall, I couldn't help glancing towards Adrian's room. Thanks to my raging hormones, I was tempted to "drop by" for a quick hello—and whatever else might happen. But my head told me I should go home. I was reading too much into that kiss. He was probably straight and just experimenting. All I'd accomplish by "dropping in" would be an awkward exchange in which I'd come off looking like a fool. So, I did the mature thing and turned to go.

I'd almost reached the head of the stairs when I met Adrian on his way up. Our eyes met, and the hair on my neck prickled. A slow, soft smile played over his lips.

"Hey, Ben," he said in a hushed voice. "Got a minute?"

I licked my lips and swallowed. "No, I...uh...need to be getting home."

"Please?" he said, coming close. "Just for a second or two. I promise I won't keep you long."

"Okay."

His smile broadened as he stepped to one side and went to his room. I hesitated for a second but followed him. It was like I was being pulled forward, rock hard and magnetically drawn to him.

He laid his book bag on his desk and held a hand out to take mine.

"Adrian, I really can't stay...long."

Those beautiful eyes locked onto mine, and he tilted his head, lips pouty, still holding out his hand. I let the strap slide down my arm and offered it to him. When he took it, his fingers brushed against mine for an instant, sending a shiver traveling up my arm.

He set my bag down next to his and took a hesitant step closer to me.

"I just wanted to thank you again for Saturday night. I really wanted to see that movie, and seeing it with you made it so much more special."

He took another step closer, wrapped one arm around my waist and the other around my neck, and then we were kissing. He pulled me tight against him, removing any doubt whether he was experiencing the same yearning I felt. I ran my fingers through his hair, and when he nibbled on my neck, a soft groan escaped that I barely recognized as coming from me. Our lips united again for another fiery moment. Then he looked into my eyes.

"Adrian," I whispered, "we shouldn't be doing this."

My voice didn't sound very convincing, even to me.

He wiggled against me and smiled. "Why? Don't you like it? It sure seems like you do. And *I* like it." He hesitated and his expression turned serious. "And I like you. I want you, Ben."

My cheeks were growing hotter than lava.

"But what if this is just a phase? What if you're really straight?"

"It's not a phase. I'm gay—and I'm attracted to you."

"But if Ted saw us, he'd freak out."

"Well, let's just keep it between us then. I could come over to your house sometimes, and we could hang out together, and maybe we could even visit that café again."

"Adrian—"

He cut me off with another kiss, his tongue conquering my failing resistance.

"I could even come over later tonight," he purred.

"No, not tonight," I said, breathless. "We're dealing with my grandfather tonight."

"Tomorrow after school?"

"Starting tomorrow, I'll be volunteering after school at the senior center on Franklin."

"Okay, tomorrow night then. I'll drop by after dinner."

He took a slow step back and squeezed my hands before releasing me. My heart was racing. He broke into a smile so innocent and yet so captivating I wanted to spend the rest of my life just drinking it in.

"I've got to go," I said, fumbling for my book bag and barely managing to hike it over my shoulder.

"Okay. See you tomorrow."

Despite telling myself not to do it, I leaned forward for a final kiss, this one brief but just as robust as the ones before it. The sight of his blushing cheeks was so enticing I had to stop myself from going in for another.

How I made it down the stairs without collapsing, I'll never know. Closing the front door behind me, I heaved a sigh that was almost a pant and started for home, my mind awash in a confusing jumble of guilt, contentment, and outright teenage horniness. "How Will I Know" was running through my mind.

Maybe this wasn't all just some passing phase. Adrian said he was gay, and he wanted me. And God help me, I wanted him too; I couldn't help it.

But what about Ted? What if he found out?

I shook my head. It was all pointless. I was being ridiculous. What I needed to do was to think this through logically.

Was I attracted to Adrian? Obviously. Was he attracted to me? It certainly seemed that way. But it was dangerous. I was on the way to being eighteen—mature, almost an adult—while Adrian was still a kid, vulnerable. He could well end up getting hurt.

No, I was the older one, and I needed to act responsibly for both of us. Adrian and I couldn't be in a relationship.

By the time I got home, I had it all figured out. I'd let Adrian come over tomorrow night. I'd sit him down and tell him that as much of a turn-on as kissing him was—*and* touching him, *and* feeling his arms wrapped around me—despite all that, we couldn't do it again. I'd break it to him gently, and I'd promise to be there for him, but I'd be firm. It was for his own good. We just couldn't be in a relationship. Period.

I GOT HOME and called Mom to let her know I wouldn't be at the center when she picked up Grandpa. Then I went to my room, put on some music, and tried to do my economics homework. But after about fifteen minutes, I realized it was futile until I took care of some...uh...business. So even though it would make it harder for me to tell Adrian we couldn't be in a relationship, I stripped down, grabbed a towel and my bathrobe, and took a slow, hot shower. Afterward, I went back to my homework, finished it, and worked on my mixtape until Mom and Grandpa got home.

I met them in the kitchen. Grandpa didn't seem any the worse for wear from his first day at the center. He asked me why I hadn't shown up, and I explained the call from Artie and assured him I'd be there the next day.

Mom asked me to keep Grandpa company while she took care of dinner. He and I watched TV until my father's voice alerted us that supper was ready.

The conversation initially focused on Grandpa's day at the senior center, and I was happy to note he seemed much more alert than he had been recently. He told us about beating a guy at backgammon three times in a row and participating in a lively game of dominos with four other guys. He also mentioned that aside from the bookstore, the center had a well-stocked reading room he planned to take full advantage of.

Talk then shifted to the logistics of transportation.

The basic plan called for Mom or Dad to drive Grandpa to the center every morning.

Then Mom glanced at Dad and said, "The only thing left to work out is arrangements for the end of the day."

"Yeah, and that's going to be a problem," Dad said. "Marty, I can't be the one picking you up every day. I've got to stay late and deal with contractor issues too often."

"Well you know I can't do it," Mom said. "I've got too many clients who can only meet after work."

Grandpa tsked. "So I'll walk home from the center."

Mom shook her head. "Oh no, I don't think so. You know how unpredictable the weather around here can be in winter. No, Pop, that's completely out of the question."

"I absolutely agree," Dad said. "Nope, the only solution is to get an old secondhand car and have Ben drive you home."

For a couple of seconds, I just stared at him, the expression on my face apparently so comical he and Mom started laughing.

Then Grandpa said, "If anyone's going to buy him a car, it's going to be me."

Dad shook his head. "Marty, no, we'll take care of it."

"It's the least I can do if the poor kid has to cart me home every day."

"How about if Margot and I pay half?"

Grandpa paused, then he nodded and turned to me. "Of course, you won't just use it to drive me home. You'll use it for other things too—like taking a girl out, eh, Beryl?"

"Benjamin," Mom said.

"Right. Sorry, I was thinking about an old friend."

Dad said, "Ben, if this sounds okay, you and Grandpa and I can go car shopping this weekend. What do you say?"

What did they think I was going to say? I couldn't thank them enough.

It was hard to believe. I was getting a car! This was a boon I hadn't expected until after I graduated, got a job, and saved up the money. And suddenly, thanks to Grandpa Marty living with us, I was actually going to have one.

THE SECOND I stepped foot in the Douglas family yard the next morning, Adrian came out and made straight for me. The maroon Henley pullover he was wearing highlighted his amber-brown locks and made the green rings in his eyes stand out even more than usual. He was so gorgeous, it was all I could do to control the urge to take him in my arms and kiss him.

He broke into a coy smile. "You're early today."

"I wanted to get here before the bottom fell out."

"Yeah," he said, looking at the sky. "It's supposed to be rainy all day."

"That's what they say."

"So," he said, glancing down before locking eyes with me, "will eight o'clock be okay for tonight?"

"Yeah...about that. We need to talk. Adrian, I'm really flattered by all this, and—" I cleared my throat. "—you are...uh...very attractive. But I don't want you to get hurt."

"Then don't hurt me," he said, his smile turning sultry.

"Adrian—"

He sniggered. "I'm joking, Ben. But look, I'm not fragile. I won't break."

"I know but—"

"Let's wait and talk about it tonight."

Before I could say anything else, Toby and Tyler pulled up. Adrian bounded over and threw open the door.

"Hey, Ben," Toby shouted.

"Morning, Toby, Tyler."

"See ya later," Adrian said before jumping in.

As they drove off, Ted came out.

"You should have come inside," he said, walking over to Baby.

"I just got here."

"So are you still on for the center today?"

"So far as I know. But, hey, guess what? My folks are buying me a car so I can drive my grandfather home from the center. As soon as we get it, you'll be off the hook dropping me off."

"Congratulations, man. That's fantastic—" He paused and grinned. "—I guess I better get that burger fast before you get your own wheels and no longer need me, huh?"

"Don't worry. You'll get your hamburger. I promise."

On the way to school, I filled Ted in on the sneaky way my folks told me about the car and the plans to go looking for one that weekend. Then we talked about the different cars I might end up with and which ones Ted would recommend.

We got to school, parked Baby, and had just passed the big engraved Chadham High School marquee, when Ted stopped.

"Well, once again, congratulations," he said, offering me his hand. "I'm going to miss the company on the drive back and forth."

"Yeah, me too," I said shaking it.

WHEN I RAN into Doris on the way to first period, I was all ready to tell her about the car, but before I could even say hello, she cut me off.

"Hope says you've found yourself a boyfriend. Who is it?"

"Hope's crazy. I just wrote something about an imaginary surprise kiss for a creative writing assignment, that's all. It was just fiction."

"Oh pooh, and I was hoping we could set you and your beau up on a double date with Hope and Ted. But don't worry. Once we seal the deal on the two of them, we'll start working on getting you hitched too."

"You know, Doris, you should really work on getting *yourself* a boyfriend. Maybe then you'd have less time for trying to fix everybody else up."

"Don't you worry about me. I've already got someone I'm interested in."

I turned to look at her. "Oh? And does he know you like him?"

She twiddled a strand of hair and smiled, "Uh-huh."

"Really? So don't just stand there—tell me. Who is it?"

"Never you mind. You'll find out when the time's right."

I couldn't pass up the opportunity to needle Doris about her secret heartthrob. Besides, she was having as much fun as I was despite pretending to be annoyed by it. So, I decided to wait to tell her about the car when we met up with Hope before second period. That way, I could kill two birds with one stone.

We ran into her at the usual intersection on our way to the M-B wing.

"Hope, guess what?" I said as soon as we saw her.

She ignored me completely and said to Doris, "Did you get Ben to tell you about his secret boyfriend?"

"I don't have a boyfriend."

"So you keep saying."

Doris tsked. "Don't be silly, Hope. He told me all about it. He was just using his imagination."

"You didn't read it. No one's imagination is *that* good. To write something like that you've got to have had some serious gum swapping experience."

"Moving right along," I said. "Guess what? My folks are getting me a car. See, I finally found a community service project. I'll be volunteering at the senior center my grandfather's going to. So, in exchange for driving him home, I get a car. Can you believe it?"

"That *is* great news," Hope said, "and it'll make it so much more convenient for you and your squeeze when you want to be alone."

I rolled my eyes but didn't answer—it would just encourage her. And at that moment, Ted showed up. As soon as Hope laid eyes on him, I knew I could rest easy that she was done trying to find out who my imaginary boyfriend was—at least for now. As she looked at Ted, her face couldn't have revealed more longing if she'd had "kiss me" written on her forehead.

Later, Hope and Ted and I had just turned the corner to the Language Arts wing when I caught sight of Adrian. He came right up to me. It was a lucky thing Hope and Ted were so wrapped up talking about an episode of the previous night's TV lineup that they didn't even notice I'd stopped walking with them.

"Hey, Ben," he whispered.

"Hi, Adrian."

"How's your day going so far?"

"Fine. How's yours?"

"Oh, it's going okay," he said, blushing, "but it'll be a lot better tonight—say about eight o'clock. See you later."

He walked away, and as I continued on to Mrs. Barsanas's room, I kept reminding myself I had to be firm and tell him we couldn't be in a relationship. And I'd have to do it quick because if I didn't, I wasn't sure I'd ever be able to.

STANDING JUST INSIDE the center's main doorway, I looked around, my stomach filled with butterflies. Somewhere between fifty and sixty people were spread out here and there. Several tables of old women playing cards balanced a near-equal number of old men either also playing cards, or playing dominos, or backgammon. Small groups engaged in conversations also dotted the landscape. Artie waved to me from the other side of the room, and I walked over.

"Hey, Ben. Once again, welcome aboard. First things first, let's get you a name tag, and then we'll stop off and visit with Dr. Markov. Now, do you want your tag to say Ben or Benjamin?"

"Ben, I guess."

"Ben it is. You don't know how lucky you are. Before Dr. Markov took over, they used to be very formal around here."

Five minutes later, the two of us were sitting in Dr. Markov's office while she explained that my job was simply to mingle with the old folks—clients and residents, she called them. If I saw someone alone, not participating, I was to say hello. If I got the idea something was bothering them, I was to alert Artie or one of the staff members. Other than that, I could join in games with them or just chat. It seemed simple enough.

I thanked Dr. Markov for the opportunity to help out, and Artie and I went back to the main hall.

"So, how are you feeling about all this?"

"Still a little nervous. What am I going to talk to them about? I don't have anything in common with them. And I somehow don't think they'd be interested in the kinds of things I like."

"Don't worry. Just start out by asking them how they're doing. Believe me, for some of them, that'll be enough to keep them talking for a half hour or more. Another thing you can do is ask them where they're from. You might be surprised to find that some of the people here have led very interesting lives. You'll learn a lot, you'll find out you've got more in common with them than you think, and I bet you'll make some friends along the way too. Just remember, if anything comes up that bothers you, come to me."

I took a deep breath and, surveying the hall, caught sight of Grandpa talking with a couple of guys near the bookstore. He was broadly gesturing while he spoke, something I'd noticed he often did. His companions seemed to be listening closely, one of them holding a hand cocked to his ear. I decided I'd wait and say hello to them later.

Strolling to the other side of the room, I spied a short, bald-headed man with a salt-and-pepper beard and bushy brows sitting alone at a table. Although he didn't look particularly sad or upset, I decided to check in on him. Taking a slow deep breath, I walked over.

"Hi, my name is Ben. I'm a new volunteer here."

He looked up at me and frowned.

"What?" he said in a heavy accent. "You have to speak up. My ears aren't as good as they used to be."

I cleared my throat. "I said, my name is Benjamin, and I'm a new volunteer here."

"Hello, Benjamin. My name is Herman, Herman Topolski."

"Would you mind if I joined you, Mr. Topolski?"

He rapped his fingers on the table. "It's a free country, so sit."

"Thank you," I said, pulling up a chair.

The problem was I didn't have a clue what to say. After a few seconds, he rolled his eyes.

"There, so we've introduced ourselves, you're sitting down—now tell me, what do you want with me?"

"What do I...? Nothing. I—I just noticed you didn't seem to have any company today, so I—"

"You know, sometimes a man needs to be alone with his thoughts."

"I—I'm sorry—" I started to get up. "—I didn't mean to disturb you. I— I just thought we might talk for a while."

He tsked and waved a hand.

"Sit down, sit down. I said *sometimes* a man needs to be alone with his thoughts. Sometimes, a man needs company to *distract* him from his thoughts."

I sat back down, and Mr. Topolski stared at me, pursing his lips and rapping his fingers again.

"So what do you want to talk about?"

After a couple of very uncomfortable seconds, I cleared my throat and tried to start with something I thought would be easy.

"Uh, are you a resident?"

"A resident?"

"I mean do you live here, or are you here for the day program?"

He paused for a second before scoffing.

"Do I live here? What are you, some kind of *meshugeneh*? Look at me. Yes, I live here, if you can call it living."

"D-don't you...uh...like it here? Why?"

"Why do you think? I'm old, the only relatives I have never visit, and the people here that aren't *shmendriks* are a bunch of *kolboynicks*."

"Oh, I'm...I'm sorry you feel that way. But it's a nice enough place to live, isn't it?"

He scoffed again. "Well, look around. It's not exactly Regency Park, is it?" He shrugged his shoulder and continued, "But on the other hand, I suppose I have lived in worse places."

"How long have you...uh...been a resident here, Mr. Topolski?"

"Well, if you must know—five years. And you can call me Herman."

"That's a long time to live in a place like this."

"Oh, I don't know."

"Where are you from?"

He waved his hand. "Let's not talk about that. You tell me about yourself. How old are you, Benjamin?"

I told him and spent some time talking about my family and my friends. He listened and nodded every now and then, and after a while, he seemed to feel more relaxed. He asked me about school, and when I mentioned the disgusting food they served in the lunchroom, he leaned back in his chair and chuckled.

"Believe me. You don't know how good you've got it. I've been in places where they didn't feed you at all, and if they did, it really *was* rotten."

"Yeah, I guess you're right. I suppose I'm just a complainer."

At that, he laughed out loud. "Trust me. If you're a complainer, you'll fit right in with the *kvetches* in this place. It's lousy with them."

Melvin, one of the staff members, came over.

"Mr. Topolski? Mr. Shalit, Mr. Melnik, and Mr. Levine asked me to invite you to join them for a game of Rummy."

Herman rolled his eyes and leaned towards me.

"Shalit cheats. The other two need me to play because their eyes aren't good enough to catch him."

He stood up and shook my hand.

"It was nice talking to you, Benjamin. You're a good boy."

"Thank you. I enjoyed talking with you too. See you later, Herman."

My success with Herman bolstered my courage, so I started introducing myself to people. I spent a few minutes with Grandpa so he could introduce me to his friends. Turns out, most of their time together focused on "discussing" politics—something that would bore me to death. As soon as I could, I politely said I needed to mingle and left them to their arguments.

Before I knew it, it was running for six. A woman came out of the dining hall, rang a bell, and announced that dinner would be served in fifteen minutes. People began putting away their dominos and cards, and little groups shuffled to the dining hall, some leaving on their own or talking with each other as they went. The nonresidents milled around, waiting to be picked up.

I looked for Grandpa Marty, but before I could spot him, Artie waved me over.

"How was your first day?"

"It was all right. I was kind of nervous at first, but I chilled out after a while."

"Mm-hmm," he said, crossing his arms. "Melvin tells me you had a nice chat with Herman Topolski."

"Yeah, he's a nice guy. Very funny."

Artie nodded. "Ben, you impress me more and more. Herman Topolski rarely talks to anyone. The only way we can get him to be sociable at all is to get him to play cards or backgammon, and when he does, he accuses the other players of cheating."

"Really? He didn't seem very antisocial to me."

"Like I said, Ben. You seem to have a knack for working with these people. Getting Topolski to talk is quite an achievement. Did he tell you much about himself?"

"No, mostly he asked about me and my folks and school and all."

"Not surprising. Well, congratulations on pulling off a minor miracle on your very first day. See you tomorrow?"

"Yes, sir."

"Have a good evening."

He gave me a pat on the back and walked away.

I turned back to the entrance just as Mom came in. Grandpa Marty and I got to her at about the same time. When she asked us how our day had been, Grandpa told her his friends—"people he knew," he called them—had been impressed by me.

I'D JUST FINISHED loading the last plate from supper in the dishwasher when a light rap on the kitchen door drew my attention. Adrian smiled at me from the other side of the window, and I waved him to come on in. His hoodie was zipped up to his neck with the hood pulled over his head. His clothes were damp from the intermittent drizzle that had been going on since early in the afternoon.

"Hey," he said, wiping his face.

I pulled a dishtowel from a drawer and threw it to him.

"Here, use this. And give me your hoodie. I'll throw it in the dryer so it'll be dry on your way home."

He unzipped the hoodie to reveal a black crewneck pullover. It looked good on him and highlighted his complexion.

"Why hello, Adrian," Mom said, walking in from the living room. "I didn't expect to see you—or anyone else—on a night like this."

"Hi, Mrs. Carpenter. It's not raining too bad, and I wanted to listen to music with Ben."

"Well, all the same, when you start home, have Ben lend you an umbrella. You know where they are, Ben."

"Yes, Mom."

We went to my room. I closed the door and switched on the receiver. The sounds of soft rock filled the air. Adrian was watching me with a bashful expression. He took a slow step forward. Then he pulled me into his arms and kissed me.

"Adrian, we need to talk," I said, even though my lips had other ideas.

"Okay," he said, but he kissed me again.

"Adrian, I'm serious."

He sat on my bed, and I pulled my chair over to face him.

"Adrian, we can't be doing this."

His face fell and he whispered, "You don't like me?"

"Of course, I like you."

"You think I'm ugly."

"Are you kidding? You're not only beautiful. You're damn hot."

"But you don't like me."

"I just don't want you to get hurt. I'm seventeen, and you're what? Fourteen?"

"Fifteen."

"Okay, fifteen. But how can you be sure a relationship with me—or any other guy—is what you really want? What if you're just not sure about your sexuality yet? What if you're just confused?"

He pouted for a few seconds as the music drifted around us. Then he said, "I'm not a little kid, you know."

"I know you're not."

"And I'm not confused about my sexuality. I really am attracted to you. Nobody has a problem with a fifteen-year-old girl dating a seventeen-year-old boy. Why should it be any different for us?"

"It's not that simple; it's complicated."

He stared deep into my eyes. "It doesn't have to be."

Those emerald-enclosed brown orbs summoned a new voice in my head. It reminded me how I'd always thought he was cute, how truly hot he was now, and how I'd been more than ready to be in a relationship when I was his age. In less than a second, my resolve to be the strong one, the mature one, the big brother, melted into unreserved desire.

"I—I don't know, Adrian..."

"Ben, I'm not confused. I've liked some girls in the past, and I've liked a few boys too. I liked the girls okay, but it was the boys I was really attracted to...just like I'm attracted to you now. This isn't some phase I'm going to grow out of. I know who I am. I'm me, and I'm gay...and I'm attracted to you."

"I—"

"The only question is, are you attracted to me?"

"It's not that simple. What about Ted?"

"Ted won't find out."

"What if he does?"

"If he does, he'll eventually get over it."

"You don't think he'd tell your father?"

"It wouldn't matter if he did. Dad would just do what he always does with things he doesn't like. He may gripe about stuff, but every time he's confronted by something he doesn't like, he ignores it and hopes it'll go away. He caught me wearing nail polish once, and he didn't say a word. He just pretended he didn't see it. Uh-uh, my dad finding out is one thing we don't have to worry about."

He leaned forward, took my hand, and pulled me onto the bed next to him.

"Come on, Ben, there's nothing to worry about."

He had me. The only things that worried me were him not really knowing what he was doing and his father finding out about us. And he had answers for both.

He wanted me. And I couldn't deny it; I did so want him. How much more careful would we have to be than if he were any other boy? If that five percent of the population thing was true, all the other gay teenagers at

Chadham High were out there being careful, and they were pulling it off. Why couldn't two more do it too?

I looked into his eyes and surrendered.

"All right. But let's take things slow, okay?"

"It's a deal. So, how about we seal the deal with a nice—" He gave me a peck on the cheek. "—slow" He brushed his lips over mine. "—kiss?"

I took him in my arms and pulled him close. What started out as a tentative kiss grew in intensity. Toad the Wet Sprocket came on, singing "All I Want."

After a moment, Adrian sighed. "I can so identify with that song right now."

"You do know it's a breakup song."

"All I know is I want to spend the rest of my life feeling like I do right now in your arms."

He pulled me down to lie on the bed. We French-kissed, and he nibbled on my ear, making me rock hard. When I returned the favor and nibbled on his neck, he ground his hips against mine, revealing he was as pitched as I was. We ran our fingers through each other's hair, and I caressed him, delighting in every curve of his arms and shoulders.

The minutes slipped away. We could have gone on necking all night, but a radio station newsbreak reminded us of the time. I gave him my brush, and after attending to his own hair, he brushed mine. We kissed one final time and then went to the kitchen. I got his hoodie out of the dryer and found him an umbrella.

"Maybe I should drive you home," I said, looking at the rain.

"I'll be all right. I told you before, I won't break."

"Well, don't get a cold."

"I won't," he said and snuck in a quick kiss before adding, "See you tomorrow."

I wandered back to my bedroom in a kind of daze. I had a boyfriend—a hot, handsome boyfriend. Adrian was everything a guy could want. He was beautiful. He was smart. And he wanted me. I felt giddy; it was like I'd never really been alive before.

We just had to keep it between us. That would be easy enough.

Chapter Seven

THE REST OF the week seemed to fly by. Ted dropped me off at the senior center after school each day, and I got to know a few more of the residents and clients. The more interaction I had with them, the more my uneasiness around old people began to fade. They weren't as creepy as I used to think—except for Mrs. Gilder (but she was harmless). Some of them had health issues that made them cranky, but overall, they were really just like everybody else—regular people.

Thursday, Artie told me that because Herman had warmed to me so quickly, it would be nice if I could spend a few minutes with him every day. It didn't take me long to figure out that, with Herman, a few minutes meant at least a half hour. But I didn't mind. Despite his gruff exterior, he was a nice guy. He liked to joke, and he enjoyed listening to me talk about my folks, my friends, and the goings-on at school. Spending time with him quickly became something I looked forward to. Of course, Herman was just one of the many old folks I was getting to know and enjoy being around, and I was flattered when Artie told me I was fast becoming everybody's favorite.

The real highlight of the week for me, though, had nothing to do with the center. Friday night, Adrian and I spent a couple of hours in my room blissfully lip-locked while "listening to music." At one point, we were lying on my bed. He was on his back, and I was running my fingers through his hair—something I found so fascinating I could have made it my life's profession.

"—and Randy Parker is so immature," he was saying. "He actually thought I'd be jealous because he's going out with Alexis—like I care. I only dated her the one time, and that was just to shut Tyler up. But Randy thinks everything is a competition, and he can't stand that any girl might find me—or anybody else—more attractive than him."

"Well, you *are* very attractive," I said, pulling him closer. "I bet a lot of girls would rather go out with you."

"Thanks, but I wasn't fishing. And it doesn't matter how many girls—or boys—want to go out with me. There's only one person I want to be with, and I'm kissing him now."

He kissed me, and we stared into each other's eyes.

"You know," I said, "you really took a risk kissing me after the movie that night. What if I'd gotten angry?"

"That wasn't going to happen," he said with a half smile. "I knew you'd like it."

"Oh? And how did you know that?"

"By the way you looked at me that day you walked in on me getting ready for my shower. It was so obvious you were attracted to me. I could have pushed you over the edge then and there. But just to be sure, I did spend a few days testing you, and the look in your eyes every time you saw me said that if I kissed you, you'd like it even if you told me to stop. All I had to do was find an excuse to get you someplace alone."

"You evil boy; you mean you consciously set out to seduce me?"

"Hey, you can't seduce the willing," he said with an impish grin before leaning in for another kiss.

When I walked him to the door that night, I surprised myself by saying, "I love you."

He turned back and said, "I love you too."

We looked into each other's eyes and both knew those words reflected a reality far greater than their dictionary definition. It was one of those shared moments people always talk about. I touched Adrian's arm for a mere second, but the touch of his skin sent a rippling current all through me.

The rest of my night was filled with relived random moments—the remembrance of how he looked on different occasions, his face, his hair, even how he smelled. Falling asleep was easy because I knew I'd be dreaming about him.

SATURDAY EVENING WAS Halloween. Grandpa and Dad were manning the front door for trick-or-treaters, and no doubt sneaking in a few select noshes. Mom was splitting her time between cooking supper and warning them to keep their hands out of the candy bowl.

Trick-or-treating was the last thing on my mind. I had begged off hanging out with Doris, Hope, and Ted—Grandpa Marty provided a ready-made excuse for any occasion. Instead, Adrian and I planned to visit Layla's Café for the one-week anniversary of our first kiss. I could barely believe that only one week before, I'd been totally unaware of the sweet taste of his lips, and I wondered how I'd survived so long without it.

About five o'clock, I found Mom in the kitchen.

"Hey Mom, can I use the car tonight? Oh, and I won't be home for supper."

"Pretty soon you won't have to ask that question anymore," she said, turning to face me.

"Yeah, I still can't quite believe it. I thought I'd be an old man in my twenties before I'd ever have my own car."

She laughed and pointed to the spare keys. "So what are you up to tonight? Meeting up with Ted and the girls to go trick-or-treating?"

"Uh, no," I said. "Actually, Adrian and I are hanging out."

"You and Adrian have gotten quite chummy recently. You better be careful or Ted will get jealous."

My mother had the eyes of a hawk, and she caught my guilty blink.

"Ben, you want to tell me what's going on between you and Adrian?"

It was one of those uncomfortable moments when it's hard for a kid to look his parent in the eye.

"We...uh...we just realized we have a lot in common."

Mom wasn't buying it. "Ben..."

"Promise you won't get mad, and promise you won't say anything?"

"That depends on what you tell me. And let me say right now, if the two of you are robbing convenience stores or doing drugs, you're in big trouble."

"No, no, nothing like that." I cleared my throat. "Adrian and I...we're kind of dating. But Ted can't find out because if he does, he'll blow his top."

She nodded like she'd suspected it all along. "Are you having sex?"

With that, the moment officially went from uncomfortable to embarrassing.

"No, of course not."

"Well if you do," she said, crossing her arms, "one of you better use a condom."

"Mom," I whined, totally mortified. "Please, do we have to talk about things like that?"

She leaned forward with her hands on her hips. "With all the diseases going around these days, not to mention HIV, you better believe we have to talk about it."

"We aren't having sex, okay? I don't think either of us is even ready for it. I mean, Adrian's only fifteen."

She went to her bag and pulled out a twenty. "All the same, use this to buy condoms—just in case."

I suppose I should have been grateful to have parents who accepted my orientation, but some conversations are just too cringeworthy to contemplate, and this was one I never wanted to think about again.

I looked up to see Adrian coming to the door. Before I could try to stop him from knocking, Mom saw him and waved him in.

"Hi, Mrs. Carpenter," he said.

"Hello, Adrian. Ben tells me the two of you have a date tonight," she said, emphasizing the word *date*.

He glanced my way and saw how obviously uncomfortable I was.

"Uh, yeah. Just hanging out."

"I see. Well, the two of you have fun. Just be careful."

"Uh, sure," he said while I crossed the room as fast as humanly possible.

"And Ben? Remember what I told you."

"Yes, Mom."

"Have a good time." Her smile was both genuine and thoroughly embarrassing.

"Come on, Adrian," I said, hustling him out the door.

"Bye, Mrs. Carpenter."

"Bye, Adrian. Drive safe, Ben."

"What was that all about?" he asked as we got in the car.

"Nothing."

"Nothing?"

I sighed. "Okay. She knows about us."

His eyes went wide. "Sh–she knows? How did she find out?"

"She dragged it out of me. But she's okay with it, and she won't say anything around Ted, so we're safe. She...uh...even gave me money to buy condoms."

He laughed out loud. "Oh my God. And for a minute there, you had me worried. Condoms—it must have been so weird to be talking with your mother about condoms."

"You have no idea—it was awkward beyond belief."

"Here, let me make you feel better." He leaned over and kissed me.

For a second, I forgot the whole embarrassing exchange with my mother—until I glanced at the kitchen door while starting the engine. She was standing there, watching us through the window with an amused grin on her face.

I threw the car in reverse and backed out of the driveway.

The drive across town to The District gave me time to relax and focus on Adrian. Even just chatting with him and holding hands was magic. After parking the car, we shared an "end of journey" kiss and walked up the street to the café. The raven-haired woman who had greeted us before smiled when we came in. It was early enough that we were the only customers, and she told us to sit wherever we wanted. Adrian didn't hesitate to head for one of the booths near the back. She gave us menus and went to fetch water and flatware.

After I decided what I wanted, I watched Adrian looking over his menu. I took note of the contours of his cheeks and jawline—strong, yet somehow delicate. His neck was solid and alluring. His brows were lush, and the sandy-brown bangs overhanging them gave his complexion a rich glow.

He set his menu down, noticed me watching him, and smiled, blushing. My own cheeks were warm as I smiled back. The waitress took our orders and went to the kitchen.

"You really are a heartbreaker," I said.

"So are you."

I let out a laugh. "Yeah, sure."

He took my hand in his. "Don't underestimate your own appeal. You've got good skin, and you're damn handsome with that nose and those dark chocolate eyes."

"I always thought my nose was my least attractive feature."

"Ben, you don't have a least attractive feature."

"I could say the same about you."

He tilted his head to one side and took my hand. "Happy anniversary, Ben."

"Happy anniversary," I said as the waitress brought our food. She noticed our clasped hands and blushing cheeks, and smiled.

We spent the meal talking about school, TV shows, and music we liked. It was a pleasant surprise to discover we both loved "How Do You Do!" by Roxette even though it didn't fit with the kind of music we usually listened to. It was such a happy and contented feeling to know we had so much in common.

An hour later, we stepped out into the chilly evening air. It was so beautiful, and I felt so happy being with him that I took his hand in mine almost without thinking. Impulsively, I pulled him close and gave him a quick kiss. Why not? The street was empty and we were out of sight from the café.

Still holding him in my arms, I sighed and took in how stunning he looked in the glow of the streetlight. His bangs were fluttering in the breeze, and his eyes seemed to glow as they looked into mine. We caressed each other, and he pushed up against me when my fingers brushed over his behind. I should have resisted the temptation, but I kissed him again.

Too late, I spied a car that had just turned onto the street. It looked familiar, and my breath caught in my throat when I realized why. Mr. and Mrs. Murphy must have gone to Saturday evening church services at the cathedral downtown. They didn't know me all that well, so I hoped all they'd remember was the "scandal" of two teenage boys in each other's arms, kissing. But as the car passed, I saw Hope sitting in the backseat staring wide-eyed at us, her mouth open in an amused smile.

"Adrian, we've got to get out of here fast. That was Hope in that car. I've got to talk to her before she does something stupid like calling Doris, or worse, Ted."

We both took off at a trot for the car. In less than a minute, we were racing back to our neighborhood as fast as I dared to go. Time seemed to slow down when we turned onto Franklyn. Groups of costume-clad children were wandering from house to house and crossing streets with little concern for their safety. The weary adults escorting them were vainly trying to keep them organized and on the sidewalks, but it was a lost cause. Navigating around them made the last few blocks a protracted nightmare.

Finally, we turned up the street I lived on and closed the distance to my house. I sprinted into the kitchen with Adrian right on my heels.

Mom was putting the last glass in the dishwasher.

"You're back early," she said as we rushed across the room.

"Yeah," I said over my shoulder. "I need to use the phone."

"Ben, hold up. What's going on?"

Reluctantly, I turned back, sidestepping Adrian.

"Hope saw us. We were in The District...uh...holding hands, and she saw us. I've got to call her before she tells anyone."

"You mean Ted."

"Right."

"Ben, you and Adrian need to tell Ted."

"Mom, I need to call Hope *now*. We can't even think about telling Ted or not if she tells him first."

"Go," she said, sweeping her hand up to point towards the hallway.

I gave Adrian a pained smile. He was positively cherry-faced, trying to look anywhere but at my mother. I guess it was one thing to know my mother was onto us, but something else entirely to hear her talk about it. I pulled him along, and we dashed to my room. He closed the door and sat close to me to listen in while I grabbed the phone.

"Hello?"

"Hope, it's me," I said.

"I got it, Mom. It's for me—" She lowered her voice. "—you guys must have raced home. We only just got here."

"Hope, you can't say anything to Doris about this. And especially not to Ted."

"So little Adrian is your secret boyfriend," she said with a snicker. "Wow, who'd a thunk it. And I thought he was a little ladies' man."

Adrian rolled his eyes and muttered, "Little."

I brought the handset closer, clutching it. "Hope, listen to me. If Ted finds out, he'll kill me, and God only knows what he'll do to Adrian. You've got to keep this a secret. Please."

She was silent for a couple of seconds, and I was ready to scream before she finally tsked.

"Well, you've always been there for me, so yeah. It'll be just between us. I suppose you two deserve your own bit of happiness just like everybody else."

I threw my head back and closed my eyes as Adrian and I both let out sighs of relief.

"Thanks, Hope. I owe you."

"Yeah, well, just thank your lucky stars my folks didn't recognize you. Let me tell you, they talked about the two of you the whole way home. Personally, I thought you looked cute together, but they were definitely not amused. Hey, I've got to go. But Ben? You've got to tell me how you two hooked up."

"Later, Hope."

"Okay, bye."

"Whew! That was a close one," Adrian said and broke into a grin. "What are you going to tell her about how we got together?"

"What am I going to tell her? I'll just say I hypnotized you and seduced you before you could resist it."

"Well that is kind of the truth. I mean, you *are* irresistible."

"Yeah, but the real truth is you had me the moment you kissed me. Well, that, and that dance."

"Ooo. You liked the dance that much? Well, we'll have to arrange a little reenactment sometime."

We were about to kiss when a knock on my door startled us.

"Are you boys hungry?" Mom said. "Do you two want anything to eat?"

"Thanks, but we've already eaten," I said.

"Okay, well, play nice."

We both blushed knowing she had a pretty good idea what kind of playing we'd be doing. But it didn't stop us from sharing a passionate kiss before I switched on the receiver. Then we really got into some serious lip action.

SUNDAY MORNING, DAD and Grandpa spent an hour or so looking through car ads in the newspaper, circling ones they viewed as possibilities. After lunch, Dad called a few, and he, Grandpa, and I drove around to check them out. Within two hours, we settled on a respectable gray Plymouth four-door hatchback. Between Dad and Grandpa, the owner didn't stand a chance and ended up agreeing to sell it to us for a thousand dollars less than he'd been asking. They shook hands on the deal, and Dad arranged to meet him the next morning to sign the contract. Of course, in the midst of all of this, I had to suffer through the obligatory embarrassing experience of Grandpa ribbing me to be careful where I parked when a girl and I wanted to use the back seat. However, it did give me a few creative ideas about new ways Adrian and I could spend time together.

Since Adrian had soccer practice, I thought I might as well get my literature assignment out of the way after we got home. Despite its low page count, *Heart of Darkness* was turning out to be a much deeper read than I had anticipated. I thought it would be easy because I'd heard it was the source of *Apocalypse Now*. Maybe so, but it was a lot different from the movie. In the book, this guy Marlow tells about his time in Africa and the enigmatic Mr. Kurtz. It's a compelling—if kind of racist—account. But the more I read it, the more I realized that Marlow wasn't very reliable in telling his story. He kind of misjudged a lot of the things he witnessed. When I finally put the book down, I thanked God I was more objective about things than he was.

That night, I went to bed early because I wanted to get to Ted's house early the next morning. Dad would finish up buying the car sometime during the day, so tomorrow would be the last time I'd ride to and from school with Ted. Of course, the real reason I wanted to get there early was so I could see Adrian and maybe have a chance for the two of us to sneak in some quick necking.

But despite setting an early alarm, I still didn't get up until almost the usual time and had to rush through my morning routine. To save time, I grabbed a Pop-Tart to eat on the way over to Ted's house.

Once I got there, I stood around, hoping Adrian would sense I was near and come outside. After a minute or two, when he still hadn't appeared to reward me with a good morning kiss, I went to the door and knocked. Mrs. Douglas greeted me.

"Why, good morning, Ben. You're early."

"Yes, ma'am. I wanted to get here early because this is the last time I'll be riding to school with Ted. My folks are buying me a car today so I can pick up my grandfather at the senior center."

"Congratulations," she said, patting my shoulder. "I know Ted's going to miss having you with him."

"Me too."

Then she said the words I was waiting for.

"He's upstairs getting ready. Go on up."

"Thank you."

I started up the stairs at a casual pace, but as soon as she was out of sight, I took them two at a time. I had almost reached Ted's room when footsteps came scampering up the stairs behind me.

"Hey, you're early," Adrian whispered.

"I wanted to see you before taking my last ride to school with Ted."

"He's in the shower. Come on. We don't have much time."

We raced to his room, and he closed the door, locking it behind us. It took less than a second for my book bag to land on his bed and for us to be in each other's arms. His skin was still moist from his own shower, and the spicy aroma of his cologne was titillating.

"Your lips taste like blueberries," he said, giggling.

"Breakfast," I said, hugging him tighter.

We kissed again, and he nibbled on my ear, sending shivers down my spine. All too soon, we heard the shower being shut off. After a final kiss, Adrian crept over to unlock and open the door while I took a quick look in the mirror, ran a comb through my hair, and picked up my book bag.

"Ah, here comes his majesty now," he said distinctly enough to draw Ted's attention as he came out of the bathroom. He stopped at the door, a pair of boxers hugging his hips, a towel draped over his shoulder.

"Hey, Ben. You're early."

"Yeah, well, I thought we could share a little time before our last ride to school together. Little did I know, you take longer in the shower than my mother."

"Ha, ha. Come on."

I followed him into his room, and we chatted while he finished dressing. Adrian joined us as we went downstairs and out to the car. While Ted walked around to the driver's side, Adrian gave me a discreet smile, and I mouthed the words *I love you.*

Then Ted and I were off on our last-ever drive to Chadham High.

HOPE SHOT ME a quick smile and batted her eyes when she met Doris and me on our way to second period. I tilted my head and whispered, "You promised." Pursing her lips into a tight grin, she blinked and nodded. But I knew it was only a matter of time before she'd have to say something.

Fortunately, she chose to bring it up during morning break. Doris had left to get her French book, and Hope and I were leaning against a wall, killing time until Ted showed up from his chemistry class.

"So you and Adrian are, like, really a couple?" she said under her breath. "How did it all happen?"

"He asked me to help him get into an R-rated movie, and one thing led to another."

"I never would have pegged him for being queer."

"What do you mean?"

"Well, he never acted girly. He's always acted kind of straight. Although it certainly did look like he was into you Saturday—big time."

"Just because he's gay doesn't mean he has to be effeminate. *I* don't act girly, you know."

"No, but you do have your prissy moments every now and then."

I furrowed my eyebrows and scoffed, but she nudged me in the side.

"Just kidding. And you two really do make a nice pair. But you know you're never going to keep it from Ted. You'll screw up some time or other, and he'll find out for sure."

"Not if we're careful."

"Yeah, well, you weren't very careful Saturday. It could have been Ted just as easily as me and my folks."

"I doubt that. Ted's not Catholic. He wouldn't be going to The District for church on a Saturday evening."

"You get the point," she said, sniggering.

"Yeah, yeah, I get it. We'll be careful."

She squeezed my arm. "And Ben, I really am happy for you."

I sighed and said, "Thanks," just as we saw Ted rounding the corner, which effectively ended the conversation.

The rest of break was taken up with her making doe eyes at Ted while he complained about the stench in Mr. Ferguson's room. I just hoped the stink would have dissipated by the time I had him for Physics that afternoon.

TED AND I shared our last ride from school together, and as soon as we got to his house, I raced home, excited to see my car parked in the driveway. I let myself in and found a note from Dad on the kitchen counter next to a set of keys. The note said to take it easy and be careful—the kind of thing you'd expect from any parent under the circumstances. But it ended with a happy face. I got in the car, so excited I was giggling, and even more so when I noticed the radio had a built-in cassette player—how cool was that?—and proudly began my first drive in it.

By the time I got to the center, I was feeling good about life. Things were good at home, I had my own car, I had great friends, and I had the most amazing boyfriend a guy could ever want. And volunteering at the center was a breeze. Artie had been right. The more time I spent around the old folks, the more I liked being there. It might not necessarily be something I'd want to do for a living, but I was beginning to think I could see myself volunteering with the elderly for the rest of my life.

I'd just finished spending time with Mrs. Kadelburg, a chubby little woman with a great sense of humor, when Jamal, one of the staff members, beckoned to me.

"Benjamin, would you mind taking over in the bookstore for a few minutes?"

Taking a turn in the bookstore was by far the easiest part of volunteering at the center. You just parked yourself on a stool near the register and waited to ring up any sales. Given the time of day I was volunteering, that meant it was basically time spent reading or daydreaming. And to think they actually gave you community service credit for it. *Wow.*

I'd been there only a few minutes when a man came in. He appeared to be in his thirties, had stylishly cropped brown hair, and was wearing a very fashionable suit and tie. He looked around and came over to me.

"Excuse me. I'm looking for Bobby Warren. Would you know where I could find him?"

"Bobby Warren? I don't think I know him. Is he a client or a resident?"

"No, no. Bobby's one of the staff, or that's what his brother told me."

"I'm kind of new here, but so far, I haven't met anyone named Bobby. Are you sure you're in the right place?"

"Yes, this is the right place—" He sighed and shook his head. "—unless Oscar didn't really want to help me. I guess I should have known."

He looked so sad that I felt sorry for him.

"He still might work here, Mister. I just might not have met him yet. You should probably ask some of the other staff members."

"No, if he was here, I'm sure you'd have heard of him. This just turned out to be a wild goose chase. I don't know why I thought Oscar would help me anyway."

"Really, sir, don't take my word for it. I've only been volunteering since Wednesday."

"No, I'd better go."

"Wait, what if it turns out he does work here? Where can he reach you?"

He pulled a card out and jotted down a number.

"Here, I'll be at that number while I'm in town. If you do find him, tell him to please give me a call."

I grabbed a pencil.

"You said his name is Bobby Warren, right?" I said, scribbling on the back of the card.

"Right. Thanks."

I turned the card back over and glanced at the name—*Vincent Marcel.*

Opening the register, I pulled out the cash drawer and dropped the card underneath. Whoever counted the money would find it and contact that Warren guy, if he did work there.

It wasn't long before Jamal came back, and I went out into the hall. Herman Topolski was wagging a finger at a thin bearded man with a high forehead.

"Cheat! Cheat! You're a cheater, you old *fershtinkiner*!"

The bearded man raised his hands and looked up at the ceiling.

"Why oh why do I have to put up with such a *shmo*?"

Melvin was trying to calm them down, but they were only getting louder.

I hurried over.

"Hi, Herman. What's the matter?"

"What's the matter? I'll tell you what's the matter. This old *shnorrer* is nothing but a lowdown *yentzer*!"

"Who are you calling *yentzer*, you *nudnik*?"

"Mr. Lehmann, why don't you come with me," Melvin said, giving me a nod to Mr. Topolski.

"What were you playing, Herman?"

"Backgammon, but he cheated. He's always cheating."

"Backgammon? Is that a good game?"

He stopped and looked at me with wide eyes. "You never played backgammon before?"

"No. Is it hard to learn?"

He broke into a grin. "Are you kidding? It's easy."

Actually, I'd been playing backgammon since middle school, but I let him explain the rules, and then we played a couple of matches. I made sure to make just enough blunders so he always came out on top. Under the circumstances, I thought it best.

Before I knew it, it was getting near time to go. Herman shook my hand.

"Benjamin," he said, speaking loud enough for people at the tables near us to hear, "it was a pleasure to play with someone who's *not* a cheater for once. And don't worry. You'll get better at backgammon over time. You're a real *boytchik*."

I thanked him, although I wasn't sure whether he was complimenting me or calling me a chick. (Mom later explained that "*boytchik*" more or less meant "a nice boy.")

Then I looked for Grandpa and didn't see him. I wandered around for a few minutes and was beginning to get worried. So, I stepped outside to see if there was any sign of him in the parking lot.

And that's where I found him. Grandpa was standing next to another old man, talking—both of them with cigarettes hanging out of their mouths!

"Grandpa! What are you doing?"

He dropped the cigarette and stepped on it.

"It's my grandson. I better go, Isaac."

"Ishmael," the man mumbled.

Grandpa came towards me, hands in his pockets, looking very sheepish.

"Grandpa, you know you shouldn't smoke—nobody should. And don't you have emphysema?"

"I was just being sociable. Isaac doesn't have anyone to smoke with."

"Ishmael," the man said again.

I tilted my head, with skeptical eyebrows. Grandpa looked away with a guilty frown.

"It was just one. Don't tell your mother."

"Only if you promise me you won't do it again."

"I promise. You'll never see me with a cigarette again."

"Okay. Come on in while I check with Jamal if it's okay for us to go."

He followed me inside, looking like the kid who just got caught with his hand in the cookie jar.

Chapter Eight

ADRIAN AND I had been going together for a little over two weeks, and we'd developed a kind of routine. He'd come by every couple of days after we had our suppers, and we also spent Sunday afternoons together. Any more often and we risked Ted getting suspicious.

The minutes Adrian and I spent alone together were magical. They were never enough, but in them, my whole world was transformed. My feelings for him were becoming much stronger—and not just the sensual ones. I loved holding him in my arms, not just because of the physical sensation, but because it was *him* I was holding.

And knowing he wanted *me* changed everything. Monday afternoon, when I saw Colby with his arm around Vickie's waist, I realized that the sense of apocalyptic disaster I always used to get whenever I saw them together had completely vanished. Now, because I had Adrian, Colby didn't even look hot anymore. When I thought of words like beauty, handsome, and sexy, Adrian was the only image that came to mind.

Veterans Day was approaching. It fell on a Wednesday that year, which was nice because we got the day off from school, making it almost like getting an additional weekend right in the middle of the week.

And I had everything worked out.

My plan was simple. First, I told Ted and the girls I'd be getting in some extra community service hours at the center—which wasn't a complete lie. I did plan to go in early that afternoon, but Adrian and I were going to spend some quality time necking in my room and then pay another visit to Layla's Café first.

The day began almost like a regular school day, except I was to drive Grandpa to the center while Mom and Dad got ready for work. Neither Dad's construction company nor Mom's investment office were taking the day off. All the better for my plan.

At the appropriate time, Grandpa and I left for the center. We stepped out to a cool but sunny morning that promised to be perfect for cuddling with Adrian later.

On the way to the car, I noticed Grandpa was walking a little slower than normal.

"Are you feeling all right this morning?"

"Just a little stiff." His words came out kind of wheezy.

We pulled into the center's parking lot. One of the things Artie had told me on my first day was that staff parking was at the far end of the lot, and clients who still drove and visitors got the spaces close to the building. So, even though I was only dropping Grandpa off, I parked in my usual spot.

About halfway to the door, he suddenly staggered to one side. I grabbed his arm to steady him.

"Are you okay, Grandpa?"

"Yeah, yeah. I just tripped."

I kept a close eye on him the rest of the way in and suggested he sit down for a few minutes once we got inside. He pulled up a chair to sit with some of his buddies while I went over to the nearest staff member.

"Rosalita, would you keep an eye on my grandfather this morning?"

"Sure, is there something wrong?"

"I don't know. He's wheezing more than usual and moving kind of slow, and he nearly fell down in the parking lot."

"Okay. I'll pass the word to Jamal, and I'll mention it to Dinah."

"Thanks. I appreciate it."

I checked on him before leaving. Other than looking tired, he was chatting with his friends just like he always did. I told him I'd be back that afternoon and left.

I had arranged for Adrian to come by around nine thirty, so I had plenty of time to get back home and spruce up before he arrived. The prospect of spending a whole morning making out with him was getting more exciting by the minute. It was like the very act of breathing was intoxicating. Each breath took me closer to being with him again.

Then I turned the corner. Mom's car was still in the driveway. I sighed and pulled up next to it, hoping against hope she'd ridden in with Dad. But one quick glance at the kitchen door confirmed that not only was she still home, she was in the kitchen, watching me pull up.

"I thought you were going to be at the center today," she said as I came inside.

"I am," I said, not wanting to look her in the eye.

"So why are you back? What did you do, forget your *yarmulke*?"

"No. See, Adrian and I are going to spend some time together this morning, and then we're going out for lunch. And *then* I'm spending the rest of the afternoon at the center."

"Uh-huh," she said, crossing her arms. "And just what were the two of you planning on doing alone in the house all morning long?"

"Nothing. We're just going to listen to music and hang out. That's all."

"Did you buy those condoms I told you to get?"

My mouth fell open. "Mom! We won't *need* condoms. We won't be doing anything like that, I promise. Jeez."

"Uh-huh," she said. "Well, I've got to get to the office. But just in case something does...come up, there are a few condoms in your father's bedside table."

If I could have turned any more red-faced, I'd have blended in with a brick wall.

"Oh my God, Mom, stop it, you're embarrassing me! We won't be having sex. Really. And can we please stop talking about this?"

"Okay," she said. "I've got to go. Be good."

At that point, she really didn't have anything to worry about. The thought that my father kept condoms in his bedside table was enough to ensure I'd probably never undress again before I was thirty.

DESPITE THE AWKWARD conversation with my mother, I did manage to work up enough enthusiasm to spend a good hour and a half necking with Adrian. We chatted and listened to music, and lay on my bed, savoring each other's caress. Adrian was such a good kisser; the taste of his lips was like a drug I couldn't get enough of.

We left for the café around eleven, wanting to get there early in case they were busy with lunchtime business, even though it was a holiday. As we navigated our way through The District, it looked like we had nothing to worry about. The streets were mostly empty.

"I'm glad you're my boyfriend," Adrian said as I pulled up to a stoplight.

"I'm glad you're mine."

"I liked you for a long time, you know."

"Really?"

"Yeah. You were always nice to me, and I thought you were good-looking the first time you came over."

"I was only nine the first time I visited you guys, and you were what? Six?"

"I was seven. And don't underestimate yourself. Those dark brown eyes of yours were enough to steal a kid's heart even then."

The light changed and we pulled forward.

"You're the one with the beautiful eyes. I'd never seen anybody with green rings circling brown irises until I met you."

"My mother has them too."

"Yeah, but you were cute enough to begin with, and with those eyes to die for—"

"You thought I was cute?" he said with a satisfied smile.

"Well, yeah, of course I did. At the time, I remember thinking how I wished I had a cute little brother like you. Then I'd be able to look at you every day."

"Do you think I'm cute now?"

"You're beyond cute. You're beautiful, and hot—damn hot."

I pulled into a parking space, shut off the engine, and looked at him. He was smiling and blushing

"I love you, Ben."

"I love you too, Adrian."

And then it hit me. I really was in love with him. We'd fallen into the habit of saying we loved each other, like all people who are dating do. It was kind of the automatic thing to say when one of us had to leave. But what I felt for him had grown into so much more. I didn't just love him; I'd fallen in love with him. How had I gone so long with this beautiful boy so close and not let myself want him? And how lucky could a guy be that someone as warm and wonderful as Adrian would fall in love with him?

The street was as empty as ever, so we held hands during the half block walk to the café. The cool autumn air tickled my neck and filled my lungs. The smell of searing meat wafted from the café, and I realized that aroma would now forever remind me of being with Adrian and realizing for the first time I was in love with him.

I squeezed his hand and smiled when he squeezed mine back. When we came to the mouth of an alley, I pulled him over so we were more or less out of sight from the street, took him in my arms, and kissed him. He was so beautiful, and I felt so alive holding him tight. The dance our tongues engaged in was a delicate waltz of tender passion. At that moment, I knew loving him was my destiny.

When we entered the café, the raven-haired waitress smiled. We were practically regular customers by now. This time, she didn't ask whether we wanted a table or a booth. She just grabbed a couple of rolled-up forks and knives and walked us straight to the last booth in the row. Then she looked over her shoulder at us, smiled again, and arranged both settings on the same side of the table.

"Young people should have their privacy," she said, setting two menus before us.

I slid into the booth with Adrian following me while the waitress went to fetch glasses of water. As soon as she was out of sight, we were kissing and didn't stop until she pointedly cleared her throat just before returning with our water. I decided to leave a big tip.

We enjoyed the meal and chatted about the *Young Indiana Jones* show on TV. I was amused and flattered when Adrian said he thought Sean Patrick Flanery was cute and quickly added not as cute as me though.

Later, we strolled down the street holding hands and stopped at the alley for another round of kissing before going to the car. It was tempting to go back to my house and spend the rest of the day snuggled up together. But the thought that, with my luck, Mom would come home early and think I'd lied to her convinced me to do my duty. So, I dropped Adrian off and doubled back to the center, arriving at about one o'clock.

As I pulled into the parking lot, I was startled to see an ambulance standing near the front door. I raced inside and looked around, praying that Grandpa wasn't the reason it was there. The paramedics were crowded around a table about twenty feet from where I was standing. My mouth was dry, and invisible fingers were tightening their grip on my throat. But to my relief, I spied Grandpa sitting at a table near the bookstore playing dominos. The invisible fingers released me from their grip.

Then I looked back and realized the man the paramedics were attending to was Herman. He was very pale and wasn't so much sitting in the chair as kind of slumped into it, like someone had put him there. One of the ambulance guys was shining a little light in his eyes while another rolled up his sleeve to check his blood pressure. Dr. Markov stood nearby talking with a third.

I didn't want to get in the way, and frankly, I was afraid I might upset Herman. But I did want to know what was happening, so I crept a few steps closer.

"Mr. Topolski," Dr. Markov said, "you've got to take your medicine, and I mean *swallow* it—not just take it from the staff and throw it away."

"Bah," he said weakly. "I've just been a little faint ever since that black cat crossed my path."

The paramedic examining his eyes said, "Black cat? What black cat? Surely, they don't let cats in here."

Herman scoffed. "Young man, given enough time and distance, a black cat crosses everybody's path eventually."

Dr. Markov tsked and said, "Mr. Topolski, be serious. Your glucose level is through the roof. You've got to take your pills."

"Ack, they make me feel sick, and at my age, I don't need sick."

As the guy removed the blood pressure cuff, I noticed a series of numbers tattooed on Herman's forearm. It reminded me of something, but I couldn't remember what.

Despite his protests, the paramedics brought over a wheelchair and wheeled him out.

I walked over to Dr. Markov.

"Is Herman going to be all right?"

"If we can actually get him to take his medicine, he should be fine. But he's one tough old bird when he makes up his mind."

"Sounds like my grandfather. Dr. Markov, what was that funny tattoo on his arm?"

"I thought you'd know that. It's from his time in Birkenau. Herman's a Holocaust survivor. In some camps, they tattooed the prisoners with numbers so they could be identified after they'd been stripped of their clothes and sent to the gas chambers."

"Oh God. My grandfather once mentioned a cousin who'd been tattooed like that during the war. I was too young to know what it meant then and wanted to know more, but he wouldn't talk about it. Now I know why. Poor Herman."

"Yes, he's been through a lot in his life. He's the only one of his immediate family to survive."

"He told me he has relatives."

"Distant ones—a few cousins and their children who got out before the war started."

The thought that anyone could lose their whole family in such a terrible massacre made me queasy, and I shook my head. Dr. Markov patted my arm and walked away.

DORIS AND I had just got out of second period Thursday morning and were threading our way through the crowds. Everyone was moving even slower than normal thanks to having had Veterans Day off.

"I've been thinking," she said. "It's high time Hope and Ted go out on a date."

"Shouldn't that be something *they* decide—when, and if, they *do* decide?"

"They should have gone out last week. I don't know why Ted hasn't asked her yet."

"Maybe he's not ready. Maybe they aren't as into each other as you think."

"Oh, they're into each other. Have you talked with Hope on the phone recently? Ted's just about all she talks about."

"Because it's all you ever *let* her talk about."

"Nun-uh. She does it on her own."

"Only because you've got her trained. Jeez, Doris, it's like you're some kind of teenage Pavlov."

"Well, today, we're going to get them together once and for all. Just one more little push, and our job's done."

Hope came towards us, with Ted not far behind. Doris spent the rest of morning break working to lure him in. But the bell rang before she could manipulate him into it.

She tried again at lunch, but Ted spent the entire walk to the lunchroom complaining about *Great Expectations*—how long it was and how boring he found it.

As soon as we sat down at the table, Hope started telling Doris and me about an exchange that happened in their business class earlier that morning. It involved a student who was well known for quick comebacks.

"So Ms. Penger is going on and on about the benefits of competition, and she says convenience stores drive down local food prices and increase quality. And then Wyatt Roberts says, 'Ms. Penger, that might be how it works in *your* neighborhood, but over on the east side, if it ain't from Chicken Feathers or Royal Burgers, the food's gonna be expensive *and* crappy no matter how many Stop 'n' Steals the neighborhood's got.' And the whole class totally loses it."

We all started laughing...and then it happened.

Vickie Parker and Colby passed our table. Ted's smile faded, and his eyes took on that same misty faraway look they always did when he saw her.

Doris glared at him, and I would have laughed and said "I told you so," but then I noticed Hope. She was staring at her plate, her cheeks burning.

In one quick movement, she grabbed her tray and bolted for the trash can.

Doris scowled at Ted and slammed a hand on the table.

"Charles Edmund Douglas, you are without a doubt the most infuriating idiot on earth. You spend all your time pining for a girl who doesn't even know you exist when there's been someone right here the whole time who thinks the world of you."

"What are you talking about?"

"Ugh! Don't you have eyes? I know you've not got any brains."

With that, she grabbed her tray and stalked off.

"What was that all about?"

"Ted, she was trying to tell you something."

"What?"

"Think about it."

He stared at her chasing after Hope and shrugged a shoulder.

I heaved a sigh. "Ted, have you noticed a...let's call it a pattern recently between you and Doris and Hope?"

"Like what?"

I rolled my eyes. "Well, think about it. For example, maybe something's been happening a lot recently?"

He stared at me blankly.

I tsked. "Think in terms of compliments."

"Well, yeah. Doris has been complimenting me a lot recently. She says something nice, and then she asks Hope if she agrees."

"Right. And then she prompts *you* to return the compliment. Now think about all that in the context of what just happened and what it might mean."

Slowly, confusion gave way to recognition. His eyes opened a little wider, his jaw hung loose, and his cheeks flushed.

"You mean, she..."

I pursed my lips, raised an eyebrow, and nodded. "Yeah, I'm pretty sure."

"Oh God," he mumbled, staring at the table. "Now it all makes sense. How could I have been so stupid?"

I scoffed. "We don't have enough time to answer that one."

"But, Ben, seriously, I don't know what to do. I mean, I never dreamed something like this would ever happen."

"Okay. So you didn't think it would happen, but it has. The question now is how do you feel about it?"

"Well, I don't know. I'm kind of in shock."

"Duh. And besides that…? Are you *interested*?"

"Well, yeah, I'm interested. I mean she *is* hot."

I rolled my eyes. "So are you going to ask her out? I mean, Doris and I certainly won't mind."

"I should think you of all people wouldn't mind me going out with *any* girl," he said and paused. "I guess I should talk to her about it."

"Okay—when?"

"I'll call her tonight."

WHEN LUNCH ENDED, I didn't spend much time looking for Hope and Doris before going on to Creative Writing. I figured Hope needed some space, and it would just make it more embarrassing if Doris and I were both hovering over her. I also decided that when I did see her, unless Hope brought up Ted—which I thought highly unlikely—I'd pretend the whole lunchroom incident never happened. No need to steal Ted's thunder before he called her that evening.

She finally showed up at Ms. Kiri's room just before the bell rang. One quick look was all I needed to know I'd made the right decision. Her face was flushed, and she walked with a nervous, uneven gait, clutching her books tightly to her chest. She stayed totally quiet the whole period, and as soon as class was over, she pulled herself to her feet and walked away without so much as a glance in my direction.

Later, after the final bell had rung, I'd just thrown my economics textbook in my book bag and was heading for the parking lot when Ted called to me. I stopped and waited as he walked over.

He stopped and shifted his weight onto one foot. "How long do you think she's liked me?"

"I don't know exactly, but the first time Doris and I talked about it was after the Galactic Battleships movie. At first, I wasn't so sure about it, but she was absolutely certain. From then on, she was determined to get the two of you together. And you know Doris—once she makes up her mind, nothing on earth can stop her."

"Yeah," he said with a smirk. "She's got to have her way or die trying."

I watched him walk away, a swagger in his step. If things worked out, he'd soon be the one driving Hope home instead of Doris.

A minute or so later, I inched the Plymouth closer to the utility road, rapping the fingers of one hand on the wheel while scrolling through the FM stations with the other, looking for anyone playing decent music. Before I found anything, I spied Hope and Doris heading to her car. Doris saw me and handed her keys to Hope. I rolled down the window.

"How's she doing?" I said, nodding towards Hope.

"How do you think?"

"Well, I did tell you these things have a way of blowing up in your face."

"Yeah, yeah."

"But the good news is I had a talk with Ted after the two of you left—"

"And?"

"And I think things just might work out after all. At least, he's going to call her tonight."

Doris broke into a wide grin. "You see, I told you we'd get them together. I just didn't think we'd have to hit Ted over the head with a two-by-four to get his attention."

"Yeah, well, let's hope things go smoothly from here on out. For a while there, I was really afraid you were going to mess things up for all of us."

"I told you they were made for each other. It was bound to happen."

"More like you got lucky."

The girl behind me honked her horn, and I pulled forward.

WHEN I GOT to the center, I walked in and looked around. Grandpa was at a table with his political coffee klatch buddies. For once, he wasn't doing most of the talking, so I decided not to interrupt them. Jamal caught my eye and nodded to one side. Herman was sitting at a table by himself again. He had a little more color in his cheeks, no doubt thanks to having taken his medicine for a change. I walked over.

"Hey, Herman. How are you feeling today?"

"How am I feeling he says. I'll tell you how I'm feeling. I'm feeling terrible. I had to have a little nosh just to settle my stomach, and now I've been belching for over an hour."

"Oh. Well, do you feel up to a game of backgammon?"

His mood changed instantly.

"So, you want to try your luck again, eh? Okay, just remember, no cheating."

"I promise," I said, grinning. "Besides, you'd probably beat me anyway."

"You know, you're right about that. Come on."

He let out a long sonorous burp and led me over to another table set up with a backgammon board.

While we played, Herman asked me about my day at school, so I told him about Doris "the *shadchan*," and how things nearly blew up in our faces.

"That's why those kinds of things need to be left to the professionals," he said. "Now if you're smart, you won't let her try the same *mishegaas* on you."

"Not a chance."

"So tell me, *bubbela*. Do you have a girlfriend already?"

"Well, sort of, but promise me you won't tell my grandfather."

"What's the matter? Is she a *shiksa*?"

"Something like that. Just don't say anything to my grandfather."

"Is he here?"

"Yeah, that's him over there," I said, pointing. "His name is Marty."

Herman squinted. "Oh him—not to worry. You can't get a word in edgewise around him anyway."

After engineering a striking defeat for myself, I congratulated Herman and moved on to visit with some of the others. Mrs. Gilder, again confusing me with her son, gave me a finger-wagging lecture, Mr. Shalit commended my patience for being able to "stand spending so much time" with Herman, and I sat a few minutes listening to Mrs. Kadelburg gossiping about some of the others.

Time flew by, and the next thing I knew, one of the kitchen staff was announcing it was suppertime. I walked over to the table where Grandpa and his buddies were sitting.

"Hey, Grandpa, you ready to go?"

He looked up at me with a blank stare. "Go? Go where?"

"Home. Mom and Dad will be waiting for us."

He stood up, and I turned to go. I was halfway to the door when I looked over to realize he was still standing at the table with a blank stare.

I walked over to Rosalita who was standing a few yards away.

"Rosalita, has my Grandpa Marty been all right today?"

"He's been a little quiet—for him, that is. But other than that, I haven't noticed anything. Why?"

"I don't know. But I told him it was time to go, and he stood up. But he didn't follow me to the car, and he's still just standing there."

We went up to him, and Rosalita gave him a quick once over. "How are we feeling, Mr. Blackburn?"

"I—I'm fine. I just got a little dizzy when I stood up. But I'm fine now."

"Are you sure?"

"Yes, yes, I'm sure. Come on...Benjie. Let's go."

He turned and started to walk off in the wrong direction.

"This way, Grandpa," I said, motioning to the door.

Rosalita and I shared a glance, and she nodded. I knew she'd be having a word with Dr. Markov and Artie before the evening was over.

Grandpa was quiet the whole way home, and I was becoming worried. When we came in, he went to his room. I told Mom what had happened.

She sighed and rested her hands on the back of one of the chairs.

"It's probably nothing, but I'm glad you told the staff. They seem like good people. They'll keep an eye on him."

I stopped off at the bathroom to wash my face and had just gone to my room when the phone rang. I sat on the bed and answered it.

"Hello?"

"Ben, you did say you talked to Ted about Hope today, right?"

"Yeah."

"And he understands about Hope."

"Yup. I talked with him right after you and she left the lunchroom. It took him long enough, but I finally got him to put two and two together. He said, quote, she's hot, unquote, and he's going to call her tonight. So, devil's due, I have to hand it to you, Doris. Despite all my misgivings, and that little hiccough today, it looks like you've actually pulled this whole matchmaking thing off."

"I'm not so sure."

"Why?"

Doris hesitated for a couple of seconds before replying.

"Well, he called *me*. It was really weird. He told me he'd been thinking, and he'd come to a decision—a decision he said I'd be very happy to hear."

"Okay, so what did he say?"

"That's the thing. He said if I didn't mind, he wanted to announce it tomorrow at lunch. Why would he think I'd mind?"

"Oh, okay, I get it," I said, leaning back against a pillow. "Don't worry. When he and I were talking, I told him to go for it with Hope, and that you and I wouldn't have a problem with it—you know, that it won't upset us if they become a couple. He must have decided to make sure you really are okay with it too before he asks her out tomorrow."

"Whew, that's a relief. For a second there, I thought he'd got it all wrong."

"Doris," I said, chuckling, "I know it's hard, but you'll just have to deal with the fact that your scheme actually worked. So, accept my congratulations, be happy, and shut up about it."

"Thanks," she said dryly.

"You know, Ted never ceases to amaze me. After being such an idiot and upsetting Hope so bad today, asking her out in the lunchroom, in front of us, is kind of a classy way to make it up to her."

"Yeah, I guess so."

"So what about Hope? How did your talk with her go?"

"Not as well as your talk with Ted. I waited until we were on the way home, played dumb, and asked what upset her at lunch. Of course, at first, she denied everything. So, I point-blank said I thought maybe she got upset because Ted was going all shiny-rock over Vickie and that maybe she liked him herself."

I sat up straight. "And? Did she admit it?"

"Kind of. At least she didn't outright deny it. So I told her to just chill and things would work out for the best."

"Yeah, she'll forget all about that little incident after he asks her out."

THE ALARM WOKE me from a dream in which Adrian and I were grown up, out of school, and living in our own home. Okay, the house looked suspiciously like the one I already lived in, neither of us looked any older than our current ages, and we weren't doing anything in the dream all that noteworthy. But it was sexy and romantic just the same, and right then, all I wanted to do was go back to sleep so I could continue dreaming about it.

But duty called, and while dreaming about Adrian had its attractions, knowing I'd see him at school—and more importantly, after dinner that night—was reason enough to get out of bed.

As soon as I walked into the kitchen, I knew something was wrong. The coffeemaker was over half empty, there were two mugs with cold dregs in them sitting on the counter, and no sign of Mom and Dad. I peeked out the window. Both of their cars were in the driveway. I'd just turned to go look around the house for them when Dad came into the kitchen.

"Dad, what's going on?" I asked as I poured myself a cup of coffee.

"Your grandfather had some kind of spell last night," he said, collapsing in a chair.

"A spell? What do you mean?"

"He wandered into our bedroom in the middle of the night looking for your grandmother."

A chill ran through me.

"Grandma?" I said, sliding into a chair across from him.

"We had to remind him she's gone."

"How'd he take it?"

"It didn't faze him—at least he didn't seem to get upset when we told him."

"Is he all right now?"

"I don't know. He's asleep. Your mother and I are taking him in to see the doctor later this morning, and then your mother's going to speak with Dr. Markov about things."

"What can I do?"

"Go to school, and put all this out of your mind."

"Should I skip going to the center today?"

"No. For all I know, he might be there by the time you get out of school. Right now, we're kind of playing everything by ear."

After news like that, I really wasn't hungry, but I forced myself to eat some toast and had a glass of orange juice. Looking out the window at the overcast skies, I shook my head. "On a morning like this, I could have used a bit of sunshine—I really need the vitamin D."

The drive to Chadham High was somber. I didn't understand what was happening to Grandpa Marty, but I knew whatever it was, it wasn't good. I had visions of getting called out of class for some undefined bad news, which made me feel worse because I didn't want to think about what that bad news could be.

Taking a deep breath, I decided Dad was right and turned on the radio to have something else to focus on. Natalie Merchant's voice came drifting through the speakers. Of course, why play the new single "These are the Days" when they could play "Like the Weather?" Yup, playing a song about rain and depression was a great joke on a morning like that.

As fate would have it, Ted and I arrived at the same time and found spaces next to each other on the far side of the lot. At least it had stopped raining.

As soon as Ted got out of Baby and I saw what he was wearing, I knew we were all going to be in for quite a ride. He had on his black cross trainers, a pair of faded jeans that clung to his curves in *all* the right places, and a skintight striped pullover that revealed a very attractive chest and slim abdomen, over which a loose denim jacket made his shoulders appear almost as broad as Adrian's. He looked hot, and he knew it. As I got out of my car, a puff of wind revealed he had also chosen a cologne to complete the ensemble. And I was amazed; it actually didn't stink—a first for Ted.

We exchanged greetings, and I looked over at him. His expression was eager, yet assured. The way he carried himself betrayed a kind of quiet confidence. Add it all up, and I had to admit the boy came off sexy—something I was sure Hope would appreciate on sight, and even more so when he asked her out.

"So, did you, uh, make that call last night?" I asked, watching him out of the corner of my eye.

"Yup. But I kept it short. See, I decided that asking her out, and making this sort of official, was something that needs to be done in person."

"Good thinking."

"I'm going to do it at lunch. That way you guys can share in the moment."

"I'm flattered. And let me be the first to say congratulations."

"Thanks."

After stopping off at my locker, I was on my way to homeroom when I ran into Doris.

"How's Ted this morning?"

"Dressed to impress and raring to go."

"Ooo, excellent."

"What about Hope?"

"She's dressed okay, but she was kind of sullen when she got in the car, so I decided to try and boost her spirits a little. I told her that I just had a feeling today was going to be a day none of us will ever forget."

"That should get her curiosity up at the least."

"I thought so, but she still seemed a little uneasy, so I told her I was confident that by the end of the day, she'd realize sometimes things work out exactly the way they should."

Doris gave a thumbs-up and crossed her fingers. I nodded and left for homeroom.

WHEN DORIS AND I met up with Hope on the way to second period, it was obvious she was still hurting from the previous day's lunchroom incident. Her hair wasn't as neat and orderly as she normally wore it, and her eyes were puffy, like she hadn't slept well.

"Hey, Hope," I said while Doris shuffled books in and out of her locker. "How are you today?"

"Oh, it's just another happy day at Chadham High," she said in exaggerated sarcastic tones.

Doris scoffed. "I told you in the car, I've got a feeling today's going to be special. Ben had a long talk with Ted yesterday."

"Yup, we straightened out a few things," I said.

Doris closed her locker and turned to face us.

"Trust me, Hope. Everything's going to work out perfectly. You'll see—" Ted rounded the corner and sidled up to us. "—and look who's here."

"Hi, Hope. Good morning, Doris," he said grinning from ear to ear. "Hey, nice dress, Doris."

"Thank you. And how about Hope this morning?"

"Oh, yeah. You look nice too. Hey, if it's not raining, let's eat lunch on the patio."

"The patio?" Doris said. "Sure, but what makes you mention it now?"

"Oh, no special reason," he said, giving her a wink. "And you know, it'll be so much quieter out there. Too many distractions and too much noise in the lunchroom. Well, got to run. Chemistry's waiting."

He strutted off. Hope clutched her books to her chest and walked away to study hall.

When morning break rolled around, I found Ted and Hope waiting for their third-period classes in the M-B wing. Ted was still in full got-the-world-on-a-string mode, leaning against a wall with one foot crossed in front of the other. Hope didn't seem quite as defeated as she had earlier. Her shoulders were no longer slumped, and her hair seemed to have gotten a little of its bounce back.

"There you are," he said as I approached them. "Where have you been?"

"I left my pre-calc homework in my locker and had to go back and get it."

"Did you see Doris?"

"Yeah. Doris has a French test this morning and needed to study for it."

Ted smiled and shook his head. Hope was quiet, watching him. The bell rang, and we hurried off to our respective classes.

Chapter Nine

I'D BEEN SITTING in Mrs. Barsanas's room for only a couple of seconds when Hope came in and took her seat. She was frowning, and her eyes were glassy.

"Where's Ted?"

"He stopped to wait and talk to Doris when she got out of French." Her tone was flat and bitter.

I glanced over to the door and leaned closer to her. "Uh, Hope, listen. I had a long talk with Ted after you and Doris left the table yesterday, and…well, even a straight guy like Ted can have a brain spark and get something right every once in a while."

She scrutinized me with doubting eyes. "Really?"

"Trust me," I said, giving her my most reassuring smile. "Everything's going to work out exactly the way it should, and let me just say I couldn't be happier."

Doris and Ted arrived as the bell rang, and Mrs. Barsanas started calling the roll.

When class let out, we headed for the lunchroom, stopping at our lockers on the way. It was one of those rare occasions where the weather actually seemed to be cooperating. Most of the clouds had drifted away, and the patio was dry. The air was unseasonably pleasant, with a light refreshing breeze.

Grabbing the nearest table, we all sat down, with me next to Doris and Ted across from me next to Hope. The three of us were all on the edge of our seats, waiting for Ted to get down to business. But he was playing it cool, taking his time. He sat there eating his lunch, totally oblivious to our increasing suspense.

Finally, he put down his fork, wiped his mouth, and broke into a sly smile.

"You know, sometimes I can be pretty dense."

Doris scoffed. "You can say that again."

"Like, I was stupid to be hung up on Vickie for so long when the girl I really should have wanted was right here all along."

Hope took a slow deep breath.

"That's why, here and now, I want to say I'm sorry, and I want to make things right." He glanced from me to Doris to Hope. "I've been a fool, and I really want to make it up to you. Doris, will you go out with me?"

Doris's mouth fell open, Hope's head spun around to stare at him, and I dropped my fork.

Ted's eyes were still glued on Doris, his face a shy, childlike image of innocence.

"Like I said, I know I've been kind of stupid, going on and on about Vickie recently, but the truth is, I really do like you. So what do you say?"

Doris's face turned fire-engine red, and she practically flew away from the table. Hope's face was ashen gray. Ted watched Doris march off with a bewildered expression on his face and turned to me.

"I guess she's shy about that kind of thing. Maybe I should have waited until the two of us were alone, huh?"

"Yeah, well maybe that would have been a better idea," I said.

"I guess you're right, but we'll have plenty of private time when we go out."

Hope was still staring at him. What was going through her mind was anybody's guess, but I was fairly certain it had something to do with whips, chains, and a red-hot poker.

Then, just when I thought things couldn't get any worse, Ted held out his hand.

"And Ben, I can't thank you enough for all you did to help me see the light."

Hope shot me such a fierce glare I was half expecting laser beams to shoot out of her eyes. She jumped up, turned on her heels, and stormed out.

Ted stared after her stupidly.

"What's up with her?"

I looked up at the sky and sighed. "Ted, you are unbelievable."

"Well, anyway, I need to go find Doris."

"No, Ted. I think you should wait and talk to her later, maybe after school—or better yet, tonight. You can call her."

"You really think so?"

"Trust me on this one."

"Yeah, I guess your kind knows how girls think."

After that, the two of us sat there in silence until the bell for fifth period rang. We stacked Doris and Hope's trays on top of our own, dropped them off, and Ted joined the crowd shuffling down the front hall. I looked around and decided Hope and Doris were probably in the girls' restroom. So, I leaned against a wall and waited for them.

There were only a few people still rushing off to this or that classroom when they finally came out. Doris caught sight of me and waved me to join them.

Hope's face was flushed, and she was swaying a little while rummaging through her bag. Her expression was eerily calm, almost tranquil.

Doris was frowning.

By the time I got to them, Hope had finally found her breath mints. She fumbled with the dispenser until Doris grabbed it and retrieved a couple. As Hope took them from her, she looked up at me. Her face glistened with a dewy sheen, like she was ready to burst into a sweat.

"Hi, traitor," she said. Then she popped the mints in her mouth and continued rummaging through her bag.

The smell that hit my nostrils was unmistakable, and my eyes practically popped out of my head.

"Hope? Have you been drinking?"

She straightened up to look my way with unfocused eyes.

"Well, I'm not a rocket scientist, but based on my calculations, I'd say I'm shit-faced."

I turned to Doris, who was glaring at her with pursed lips.

"Damn it," Hope said pulling her hand from her bag. "I must have dropped them in the stall."

She wheeled around and staggered to one side. Doris and I both grabbed an arm to steady her. She glared at us and pulled away.

"Be right back," she said, taking uneven steps in the general direction of the restroom.

Doris watched her go, and then she stomped her foot and turned to me.

"I can't believe she would do something as stupid as this."

"Where the hell did she get vodka from?"

"Apparently, she had it in her bag. I was waiting for Ted to come in so I could give him a piece of my mind when I saw her running to the girl's room. By the time I caught up with her, she was already in one of the stalls. At first, she was crying. And I told her to get ahold of herself. I said, 'Ted's an idiot. He's just got it all wrong.' She actually accused me of stalking him.

I told her she was crazy, and I didn't want a thing to do with him. Then she got real quiet. And I thought that maybe she was calming down. But when she opened the stall door, I knew something was wrong. She had this silly look on her face, almost like she was satisfied about something. That's when I got a whiff of her breath. Whatever possessed her to bring alcohol on campus, and today of all days?"

Hope emerged from the restroom, grinning, and staggering even worse than before. She was twirling a key ring around her finger.

"Found them," she said and leaned forward, giggling. "They were in my bag the whole time."

Doris stamped her foot. "Hope, where did you get the vodka from?"

"My folks—they've always got loads, and you know what? It's a really great thing to round off a meal with."

Doris turned to me. "What are we going to do?"

I shrugged my shoulders. "I don't know. She needs time to sober up."

Hope staggered to one side again, but when I reached out to help steady her, she slapped at my hand.

"Don't you touch me, you traitor. You're the one behind this. You knew I liked him, and you set him up with Doris, didn't you? You knew I liked him, and you worked to make him fall in love with her—" Her eyes brimmed with tears. "I trusted you. Why do you hate me so much?"

"Hope, I don't hate you. Listen, Doris and I were trying to hook Ted up with *you*. He just got the wrong end of the stick as usual. But once he—"

She scoffed. "Don't lie to me."

"I'm not lying."

"Oh, yes you are. You lie all the time. You even wanted me to lie about you passing love notes and getting it on with Adrian—" Doris gave me a startled look. "—but now all your lies are coming out, aren't they. And to think I thought you were my friend."

Hope's eyes overflowed with tears. She swung around and stumbled off to the restroom again. Doris turned to me.

"You better go on to class. I'll try and talk to her."

She took a step but stopped. "You and Adrian?"

"I'll explain later. But whatever you do, don't breathe a word about it to Ted."

I grumbled to myself the whole way to Ms. Kiri's room. This had turned into exactly the disaster I'd predicted it would be.

Ms. Kiri was returning graded papers when Hope finally came in.

"Hope, you need to work on your punctuality," she said, holding out a paper to her.

Hope swayed a little but regained her balance and took it. Chantal Rodriguez, always quick on the uptake, cut me a sidelong glance and grinned.

Then, to my horror, instead of turning up the aisle to her seat, Hope went directly over to Colby. He looked up at her swaying in front of him with a quizzical expression on his face.

"Colby, you and Vickie look so nice together," she said a bit too loud and with the slightest slur. "Whatever you do, don't let anyone—" She made a deliberate look in my direction. "—*anyone* sabotage things."

"Hope, take your seat, please," Ms. Kiri said.

She spun around unsteadily, and I nodded towards her seat and mouthed the words *Please, come here.* She leaned forward like she was bracing against a gale-force headwind and marched over, a grinning Chantal and the bemused Colby watching as she fell into the seat next to mine.

"And I thought you were my friend," she mumbled.

The next forty-five minutes were stressful beyond belief. Luckily, Ms. Kiri gave us a surprise pop quiz that took up most of the period, so other than the burning heat of Hope's rising hostility not two feet from me, the time passed without any more drunken outbursts. But now that she was just sitting, the alcohol was beginning to wear her out. Every once in a while, her head drooped forward, only for her to jerk it back upright. Her complexion was slowly going from flushed red to sickly green, and I expected her to puke any minute. She didn't, but when the bell rang, she coughed and quickly swallowed like she had almost upchucked. Then, slumped shouldered, she aimed for the door, and I followed her out of the room.

Doris met us so quickly she must have run from her chemistry class.

"How is she?"

"So-so. Doris, those PMS pills of yours—didn't you say they have caffeine in them?"

"Yes, of course."

"I think Hope could use one right now, or maybe two."

She fished one out, gave it to Hope, and pointed her in the direction of the water fountain.

"Do you think she's going to be all right?"

I shifted my weight to one foot and thought about it.

"Well, she didn't make too much of a scene in Creative Writing, although it was touch and go there for a while. And on the positive side, she didn't throw up, so maybe we're past the worst of it."

"I hope so," Doris said, watching Hope lap away at the fountain.

"Do you want me to help you get her to her next class?"

She looked her over. "No, I think I can get her there. Besides, sooner or later, she'll be needing to talk about this, and no offense, hun, but with what she said about you earlier, she'll not want you around when she does."

"Yeah, and when you two talk, straighten her out about that."

"Speaking of which, you better talk to Ted and straighten *him* out."

"Me?" I said, staring at her.

"Yes, this is all your fault anyway."

My mouth dropped open. "My fault? You've got to be kidding. I didn't want anything to do with this from the start."

"Exactly. And that's why everything went wrong. You didn't do your part. If you had, Ted and Hope would be together right now. Ben, how will you ever be able to live with yourself knowing you're responsible for breaking up such a wonderful couple?"

"Doris, you're the one responsible for messing things up, not me."

"Projection is so ugly, Ben, and it really doesn't suit your sweet, caring nature."

I scoffed. "I can't believe you."

"You've got to act fast. Now, what are you going to do?"

I flinched. "I—I don't know, damn it. I'll have to think about it."

"Well, you better hurry."

With that, she turned and went over to Hope, who was still swilling water from the fountain.

BY THE TIME study hall rolled around, I had made a plan. Once Mr. Delvecchio had taken roll, I suggested to Ted that we go to the library. That gave us the walk there and—if Mrs. Becker would cooperate and leave us alone—the majority of the period to talk uninterrupted.

"Ted, I think we should discuss a couple of things," I said as we approached the library.

"What things?"

"Well, you and Doris for example."

"Yeah, I'm going to call her as soon as I get home so we can set up our first date."

I sighed. "Ted, you remember how Doris has been fishing for compliments from you for a while now."

"Yeah?"

We stopped to show our passes to the girl at the door.

"Well," I said, "didn't you notice that she was always getting you to say nice things about Hope?"

We found a couple of seats.

"Yeah, that was so cool, the way she got me to notice her by pointing to Hope."

I shook my head. "No, she really *did* want you to notice Hope. Doris isn't interested in you; Hope is."

Ted tsked. "Oh come on. You should have heard her on the phone last night. Doris likes me all right."

"No, Ted. She doesn't. Trust me. Doris spent over a month trying to hook you and Hope up. She thought if she got you guys to start complimenting each other, eventually you'd fall in love. And it worked, at least as far as Hope goes. She's the one in love with you."

"You sat right there and told me Doris liked me," he said with noticeable irritation.

"No, I was trying to tell you Hope likes you. You got it all wrong."

He turned to face me. "Benjamin Isaac Carpenter, I don't know what kind of game you're playing, but it's not funny. What do you think I am—stupid?"

"Well, I don't know what else you'd call it after you humiliated the one girl in Chadham High who loves you."

He snorted, and his expression hardened.

"Well, if that's your opinion of me, you can just butt out. I know what I'm doing."

To my shock, he got up and marched out the door. I sat there shaking my head.

"This is hopeless. The whole world has lost its mind. Well fine, Doris can straighten him out."

I spent all of my last class and the whole drive from school to the center reliving all the stupid things Doris had done that resulted in our lunchtime fiasco. When I pulled into the center parking lot, I took a deep breath. I needed to focus. On the way from the car to the entrance, I made the commitment to put Doris, Hope, and Ted out of my mind.

When I walked in, I spied Grandpa sitting with his buddies. He was talking and gesturing, which was a good sign, so I decided not to interrupt him and went looking for Artie.

He was huddled in a group, talking with Jamal, Melvin, and Rosalita. The expression on his face made me jittery. He tended to be upbeat, but his usual smile was missing. Melvin saw me coming, nudged him, and nodded my way. Artie said something, and the other three walked away, which made me even more jittery.

"Benjamin, got a minute?"

"Sure, Artie."

I followed him to the room next to the bookstore that the staff used for breaks. He went to the table and pulled up a chair.

"Have a seat."

"What's up? Is anything wrong?"

"I know you've been getting close to Herman Topolski, so I wanted to tell you up front. Herman had a heart attack last night. The doctors think he's going to be okay, but at his age, it's going to take time."

"I want to visit him," I said.

"He's in the cardiac intensive care unit and can't have visitors, but I'll let you know as soon as he can. I'm sure he'd appreciate a visit from you."

"Thanks," I said and paused for a moment before continuing. "Artie, did my mom say anything about my Grandpa when she brought him in today? He had some kind of fit or something last night, and she was going to take him in to see the doctor."

"Yes, she did, but it might be better for you to talk about it with her when you get home."

"I've been worrying about him all day, and now with the news about Herman, I really don't want to wait until six o'clock to find out what the doctor told her."

Artie looked down and rapped his fingers on the table.

"Okay. She said the doctor told them the episode last night was a sign Marty's Alzheimer's is getting worse. It tends to hit people in fits and starts, and things can get worse without warning. The good news, though, is since midday, he seems to have come out of it. Other than being low energy, he's been pretty much back to his old self."

"So what does it mean?"

"I wish I could tell you, Ben. It could mean that the episode last night was nothing more than an isolated incident and may not happen again, or at least not happen again for a while. Or it may be a sign that things are going to get worse from here on out. At this point, there's no way to tell. Unfortunately, with Alzheimer's, beyond knowing the general pattern of the disease, the only way to know how it's progressing is through observation."

I glanced at the calendar on the wall. It was Friday the thirteenth—didn't that just fit? They say when it rains, it pours. My day had already seen enough trouble at school, and then the news about Herman, and now this news about Grandpa. It all made me feel kind of like I was drowning. I leaned back in the chair and took a slow breath.

Artie studied me for a second.

"Ben, if you want to take the day off, no one will hold it against you."

"No, I need the community service credits."

"You know, you're part of the community too. Part of learning to care for others is learning to take care of yourself. And don't worry about the credits. I'll give you full credit for the day."

"No, if I went home early, I'd have to take Grandpa with me, and that might make things worse. The routine is good for him."

"Are you sure you weren't a gerontologist in a past life?"

"What's that mean?"

"It means you're insightful. Okay, get out there and mingle, but if you decide you need a break, take it."

"Thanks, Artie."

I went back to the main hall. Mr. Melnik shuffled over to me.

"You heard about poor Topolski?"

"Yes, sir."

He shook his head. "The poor man—he's his own worst enemy, you know. The number of times I told him, I said, 'Topolski, you've got to take care of yourself. Your health comes first; you can kill yourself later.' And now there he is, lying in a hospital bed. That he should suffer so much in his life and now be all alone with no one to comfort him."

"Artie told me he's not allowed visitors."

"I don't mean people like you or me. I mean family."

"I thought he had a few cousins and relatives."

"Pshaw, relatives. He told me about those so-called relatives. They don't know him from Adam, and believe me, they could care less. The only way they'd ever care about him would be if he was dead and he left them something—the poor man. His family, his real family, all died in

Auschwitz—his parents, his brother, his sisters. And then after the war, his wife, God rest her soul, she died without giving him children. You know, he told me he always wanted a son. That's part of why he likes you. And another thing, he said to me the other day, 'Melnik,' he said, 'that Benjamin is a good man. He doesn't cheat, and he reminds me of my brother.' That's a big compliment coming from him. He told me he and his brother had been very close before the *Shoah*."

I couldn't help it. I almost broke down. Mr. Melnik patted me on the arm and walked away, giving me an opportunity to retreat to the break room where I spent a few minutes composing myself and washing my face with cold water.

AFTER SUPPER, I went to my room and had just switched on the receiver, when my phone rang.

"Hey," Adrian said in a hushed voice. "What's going on with Ted? He's in a really weird mood. Mom asked him how you were doing these days, and he said you were meddling in things you ought to leave alone. And I mean he was being *really* crappy about it."

I plopped down on the bed. "Oh, Adrian, it's all a big mess. Doris has been trying to hook him up with Hope, but he got things all wrong, and now he thinks Doris is in love with him. And when I tried to talk some sense into him, he got mad and told me to butt out."

"I always wondered if he got dropped on his head when he was a baby. I guess I can stop wondering."

"It's not just Ted; everybody's acting crazy. Hope's mad at me because she thinks I tried to hook him up with Doris."

"Do you want me to come over early?"

"Better not come at all tonight. With my luck, Ted would show up and catch us kissing, and that's all I need after a day like I've had today."

"But I want to see you," he whispered, and I smiled.

"Believe me; I want to see you too. After what I've been through today, all I want is to feel your arms around me and let you kiss all my cares away."

"Maybe we could sneak out for a ride and park somewhere nice and private."

"No, I need to hang around the house tonight. But I've got a better idea. Why don't we make tomorrow a special date night? We can eat at Layla's and take in a movie. Maybe find a cozy spot in the back."

"That sounds nice… And you know," he said slowly, "if you want, I could tell my mom I'm spending tomorrow night at Tyler's, and you could sneak me in after the movie."

"You mean stay the night?"

"Well, yeah. Ever since you told me about your mother giving you money for condoms, I've been thinking about it…and I…I want to make love with you."

"Adrian, I don't think that's a good idea. I'm not sure either of us is ready for something like that yet."

"Well," he purred in his most seductive tone. "We could cuddle up tomorrow night and talk it over."

"It's too soon to even think of something like that. What say we just plan on dinner and a movie first, okay?"

"Okay," he said in an I'm-only-playing-along voice. "Say I come over about six tomorrow night?"

"Sure, that sounds great."

"I can hardly wait."

"Me too."

I hung up and sat there for a few minutes mulling things over. If I knew Adrian, he'd tell his mother he was staying at Tyler's and show up ready to spend the night, regardless of what I said. But if he did wind up sleeping over, at least I didn't have to worry about us doing anything serious. I'd never bought the condoms, and as long as he didn't show up with any, things would stay G rated.

About eight thirty, the phone rang again. This time, it was Doris.

"Ben, this has been a Friday the thirteenth for the books."

"You're telling me?"

"You don't know the half of it."

"What else is there to know? You spent a month and a half playing matchmaker, and now, Ted thinks he's supposed to be with you, and Hope's humiliated. Oh, and to top it all off, she thinks I'm the one behind it all. Great job."

"There's more. Hope's mad at me too. She's not talking to me. She was getting hostile when I walked her to her sixth-period class. Then I waited for her for over a half hour after school. So, after I gave up and went home, I called her, and come to find out, she'd taken the bus. She said she'd seen you and me always whispering, and now she knows why—we were plotting against her. Then she told me she hated me and hung up. She hung up on me, Ben. We've got to do something."

"Like what? Until you get Ted straightened out, Hope's a lost cause."

"I thought you were going to talk to him."

I lay back on the bed and tsked. "I did talk to him, and you know what? He got pissed and told me he knows what he's doing and to stay out of it. I honestly thought he was going to slug me, Doris. Can you imagine? No, you're the only one who can sit him down and get him to listen."

She sighed, and after a few seconds, said, "I guess you're right. I'll call him tomorrow."

"As much as I hate to say it—Doris, this is something you've got to do in person."

"Oh, no. If I suggest getting together with him, he'll think it's a date for sure. If it has to be in person, you've got to be there."

"Are you kidding? Me being there will only convince him I'm trying to break you two up."

"We can meet him at the mall."

I thought it over for a second. "Hmm, that might work. He wouldn't dare try to kill me in front of all those witnesses."

"I'll call him in the morning and set something up for tomorrow afternoon."

"Uh, no, not tomorrow," I said, sitting up. "I'm...uh...going to be busy all day tomorrow—my grandfather, you know. Set it up for Sunday afternoon."

"Okay, Sunday afternoon then."

I hung up and shook my head. I wasn't one to be superstitious, and I'd always thought that whole Friday the thirteenth business was just some silly Christian thing, but after a day like the one I'd been through, I was beginning to have my doubts. I rubbed the bridge of my nose and pulled open the drawer of my bedside table for an aspirin.

Conspicuously front and center was an unopened box of condoms. I sighed and shook my head.

THERE'S ONE DAY a year called Yom Kippur when Jews are supposed to really think about all the things they've done wrong and the people they've hurt in one way or another—in short, all the things when we've not been as good to each other as we could be and should be. The idea is that through such a self-assessment, we can resolve to become kinder, more generous, better people. That year, Yom Kippur had come and gone over a month before, but the day after Friday the thirteenth might as well have been it for me.

Other than a call from Doris saying we were to meet Ted in the mall food court Sunday at one thirty, I spent most of the day in my room thinking things over. After all the years I'd known Ted, Hope, and Doris, I'd failed them as a friend. I'd let Doris drag me into her matchmaking scheme even though I knew from the start it would backfire. I didn't assert myself to make her stop it. I didn't say anything to warn Hope and Ted about what she was doing. I didn't do anything; I just went along and watched it blow up in all our faces. It was ridiculous, it was sad, and it was as much my fault as anyone else's.

And then there was Adrian. It was a mighty struggle for me to decide what to do if he did end up staying the night, which, knowing him, seemed likely to happen. By the time we'd seen a movie, it would be late enough that sneaking him into my bedroom would be easy. But that would be like encouraging him to lie to his folks. It was one thing for him to not tell them he was gay, but it was something else to let them think he'd be sleeping at Tyler's house when he planned to be with me all along. And not just *be* with me. He wanted to do a lot more than just spoon together.

But what if Adrian wasn't as ready for sex as he thought he was? What if the experience turned into something he regretted, or worse, something that traumatized him?

The trouble was, if he really did want it, I couldn't deny that, despite myself, it was something I so wanted too. And that was the heart of my dilemma. Could I be enough of a *mensch*, as Grandpa would put it, to do the right thing and say no, or would I give in and let my emotions and physical desires take over? It was like a test.

And the worst part of it all was that it was like Mom expected me to fail the test. She'd bought the condoms and put them where she knew I'd find them. It was like when push came to shove—oh God, the very thought—she knew I'd abandon all caution.

And that brought me to the crucial question: If Adrian did end up sleeping with me, could I keep it at just that—sleeping? I was seventeen years old, almost an adult, but was I mature enough to do the right thing, even if I wanted to do something else?

The funny thing, though, was that through it all, I never once seriously entertained the thought of putting the condoms in the trash so they wouldn't be there to tempt me. Maybe on some level, I saw it as part of the test. I remembered some proverb to the effect that it's easy to be honest when there's no other option.

And there it was. It all became clear to me. I had a duty to myself and, more importantly, to Adrian. I had to make a mature decision and stand by it. So, I resolved to be gentle and supportive, but not let things get out of hand. Whether he wanted it or not, whether *I* wanted it or not, we wouldn't be having sex—at least not that night.

Little did I know at the time, I had nothing to worry about.

Chapter Ten

AS SIX O'CLOCK approached, I kept an eye on my front window and caught sight of Adrian crossing our front yard for the driveway and kitchen door. As predicted, his knapsack was slung over his shoulder. He saw me and smiled. I jumped up and raced through the house, slowing down only as I approached the kitchen, where Mom was chopping up cabbage.

"See you later, Mom," I said as I attempted to cross the room without looking guilty.

Adrian knocked on the door, but I motioned for him to wait outside.

"Going out with Adrian again?" Mom said, looking over her shoulder.

"Uh, yeah, we're going to have dinner and take in a movie."

"Oh? What are you going to see?"

"I don't know. We'll have to talk it over."

"Okay, well, have fun and drive safe."

"I will. Thanks, Mom."

I went outside, unlocked the passenger door, and walked around to the driver's side. Adrian threw his knapsack in the back before getting in. It was a cold, overcast evening, so I gave the engine a little time to warm up. While we sat there with the engine idling, I took in how he was dressed. The whole time, he sat watching me with come-hither eyes.

I had to give him credit. An off-the-cuff glance would see just another casually dressed teenager. But closer examination revealed a teenager on a mission. His jeans may have covered his lower half, but the denim concealed nothing. Every curve, each muscular inch was perfectly outlined. He was wearing an olive-colored pullover that also accentuated his chest and abdomen. Even the winter jacket over it couldn't deflect from the overall impression his outfit made: he was a guy with youthful good looks and virility, dressed to arouse sexual interest.

And it was working. My resolve from earlier in the day was being reduced to a minor skirmish in a war against my hormones I was predestined to lose.

"Adrian, I told you staying over was a bad idea," I said.

"But you didn't say no to the idea."

"I said let's just plan on dinner and a movie."

"Actually, no. You said, 'let's plan on dinner and a movie *first*'—that wasn't a no."

The kid's got the makings of a great lawyer in him.

I sighed and backed out of the driveway.

"Which movie do you want to see tonight?" I said.

"Let's see the new Dracula movie. From what I hear, it should be good."

"Okay."

We drove to The District and followed our now regular routine. We held hands as we walked down the street, stopping off for a couple of minutes at the mouth of what we now referred to as *Smackers Alley* before going on to Layla's.

The waitress smiled as we came in, grabbed two menus, and walked us straight back to "our booth." The second she left with our orders, our arms were around each other and our lips fully engaged. Adrian's kisses were more aggressive than they'd ever been, and his hands roamed farther afield.

I knew what he was doing. He was priming the pump. He wanted to get me on edge and keep me there. He wanted to weaken my defenses for the final conquest to come after we got home. With each caress, he was also proving that my fears he might later regret having sex were ludicrous. This boy knew exactly who he was and exactly what he wanted. And what he was doing to me was getting exactly the reaction he intended.

He didn't stop pressing his advantage until the now familiar cough told us the waitress was approaching with our orders.

The food, as always, was delicious, and after we calmed down from our pre-dinner workout, we spent the time chatting and flirting. The movie didn't start until eight o'clock, so we took our time and enjoyed ourselves. I still tried to convince myself that when we got back to my room, there would be no sexual activity beyond kissing and cuddling, but by that point, with Adrian more than willing, I was as ready to lose my virginity as I'd ever be.

At about a quarter to eight, we paid for our meal and emerged into the now very chilly night air, walking hand in hand.

"I hope the movie's good," I said. "The last Dracula movie I saw was a horrible comedy that really sucked."

"So far, it's got good reviews. But for me, the main attraction's coming *after* the movie."

When we got to the car, I went to unlock the door for him, but he pulled me close and held me in his arms. I wrapped my arms around him and brought a hand up to cradle his head, my fingers lost in his sandy locks. Our lips came together, I held him tight, and the warmth of his body radiated through me.

We were out in the open, where any passing car would see us. Yet the danger of being seen kissing in public only enhanced the moment. I wanted to take him straight home and jump into bed with him. He had unleashed a hunger inside me only he could satisfy. I was in love with him and wanted nothing more than to please him, to find my own fulfillment in our shared passion, and to spend the rest of my life with him.

The world around us dissolved. The only sounds that existed were the rustle of our embrace and the beating of our hearts. All I could sense was the fragrance of his body. All I could feel was the strength of his arms around me.

Until a hand grabbed my shoulder and spun me around.

"What the hell do you think you're doing?"

Ted was standing there glaring at me with a fury I never would have imagined possible. His fists were clenched. He was scowling, red-faced, and his eyes were positively blazing.

"I didn't believe it when Hope called and said I'd probably find the two of you here, but here you are, just like she told me you'd be. Man, did she peg you right, you queer traitor. What kind of sick pervert are you, trying to corrupt my kid brother?"

"Ted, you don't—"

He shoved me back with both hands. "You listen to me. You can be queer if you want. That's up to you. I don't care. But go find yourself another cocksucker to screw. There's no way in hell I'm letting you turn my little brother into a faggot like you."

Adrian stepped forward. "Get the hell out of here, Ted."

"Shut up, Adrian," he seethed. "I'm parked down the street. Go get in the car."

"Like hell, I will. Come on, Ben."

He snatched the keys from my hand and unlocked the door. I turned back just in time to catch a fleeting glimpse of Ted's fist coming at my face. I dodged it, barely, and backed away from him.

"Ted, calm down. We should have told you about this earlier, but believe me; you've got it all wrong."

He lunged at me. Adrian jumped between us. They scuffled and swayed, both shouting at each other. Adrian grabbed him from behind. Ted struggled to throw him off. I just stood there like an idiot, shocked that after all those years of Ted being my best friend, he'd just called me a faggot.

Ted spun around, finally throwing Adrian off, and took another swing at me. Adrian kicked him in the knee pit and sent him crashing to the sidewalk. Then, as Ted rose up, Adrian locked his arms from behind.

"God damn it—let go, and go get in the car like I told you."

"Go to Hell. This is none of your business."

"Like hell, it's not. I saw everything. I'm not going to let this queer molest you."

"If you saw everything, then you must have seen that it was me molesting him. *I* was the one kissing him. Guess that makes *me* the queer."

"Shut up, Adrian. You don't know what you're talking about."

A police siren wailed in our ears.

"What's going on here?" the cop said getting out of the patrol car. "Let go of him."

"Officer, he tried to pick a fight with him," Adrian said, pointing from Ted to me.

Ted took a step towards me, but the officer stuck out a warning arm that he'd better not try anything.

"What do you say?"

"He was molesting my little brother," Ted spat, cocking his head in my direction.

Visions of public humiliation, yelling adults, and ham-fisted teenage knuckles pounding my face flashed in my head. I could already see the handcuffs coming out for me.

"We're gay, officer," Adrian announced, wrapping his arm around mine. "He's my boyfriend, and—" He shot a finger in Ted's direction. "—*he's* just jealous."

The officer took a step away from Ted and looked him up and down with a raised eyebrow.

Crimson-faced, Ted stared round-eyed at Adrian. His knuckles were white, but his hands were shaking. He was snorting like a bull.

"Look," the officer said. "I don't care who's whose boyfriend, or who's jealous of who. I want the three of you to get out of here. And if I catch any of you trying anything else stupid tonight, I'll put all three of you in jail and let your folks settle it. Now get out of here."

"Yes, officer," I said, my hands shaking.

Adrian marched past Ted and got into my car. I cleared my throat and tried to look casual as I walked around to the driver door and got in. Ted's eyes, glowing with hostility, followed my every move. I started the car and inched down the street, turning at the corner, and driving a couple of blocks before pulling into a parking lot.

My heart was still pounding. I closed my eyes, took a deep slow breath, and tried to calm my nerves. I had never seen Ted so enraged, and the shock continued to build inside me.

I remembered when we first met back in the third grade after his family moved to Chadham. We were a case study in opposites. I was mousy and shy, while Ted was outgoing and full of confidence. But the thing was, he wasn't as snotty as most of the other boys. He was always nice to me and took time to talk and play with me during recess. It didn't take us long to become fast friends, and until that night, the closest thing to a test of our friendship had been the first time he invited me over to play one Saturday.

Back then, his family lived across town, and I'd never had to have a parent drive me to a friend's house to play before. The whole idea had me more than a bit anxious. What if he got mad at me and told me to get out? What if I had to walk home alone? And if I did, what if I got lost? I was so nervous about it I almost backed out. But in the end, I summoned up what courage I could and had Mom drop me off.

A reassuring smile greeted me when Ted opened the door. He showed me around the house, and I met his mother. She was very nice, and I was beginning to feel better about being there. But then I met his older brother Eric, who at thirteen was already a real dick. Ted had warned me about him, and it didn't take me long to decide Ted was a good judge of character. Eric made it clear he didn't like me at all. And Mr. Douglas was no better. He sized me up first thing, was clearly unimpressed, and proceeded to ignore me. Between him and Eric, I wasn't sure I wanted to stay. In fact, I'd started to rethink that whole walking-home-alone option.

But then I met Adrian and decided to stay. At the time, he was a cute little seven-year-old and nowhere near as pesky as Ted had made him out to be. His hair was long and shaggy, he was skinny, and those green rings in his eyes fascinated me. Despite the age difference, he was someone I'd have wanted to be friends with even if I'd never met Ted. He was sweet, and he was the kind of kid you just wanted to be around.

My guided tour ended in Ted's bedroom. I was surprised to see posters of Hall & Oates, Dexys Midnight Runners, Joan Jett, and, significantly, no baseball posters. We spent a few minutes talking, and I was finally relaxing when he suggested we go outside to play catch. I said sure but knew it was going to be a lost cause.

We went outside, and he tossed a baseball my way. It was a light, well-directed pitch, and it hit me square in the chest. When I fumbled around after it and tried to throw it back, it flew wildly to the left, sending Ted chasing after it. With each toss, he threw the ball slowly and more gently in the vain hope I might at least catch one. But I kept on missing them, and the one time I halfway threw it straight proved to be an accident never to be repeated.

Things went on like that for a half hour or so, and, eventually, patient though he was, Ted gave up and suggested we go inside and play a video game.

"I'm sorry," I said as we walked back inside. "I should have told you I'm no good at ball."

"That's okay," he said cheerily. "Ball's not for everyone."

We played the video game for a couple of hours, and despite the fact I was no better at it than at playing catch, I laughed my head off. The best part was no matter how lousy I was, it didn't seem to make a bit of difference to Ted. In fact, I was shocked to find he actually liked me in spite of it. And I discovered that although he liked sports and video games, he wasn't a fanatic, and didn't mind that I wasn't into them.

From that day on, he'd not only been my friend, he'd been my best friend. For eight years, he never once questioned why I never got interested in girls the way he did. And when I confessed to him that I thought I might be gay, he didn't even bat an eye and continued to be my best friend. He knew me almost better than anyone and accepted me for who I was. And I loved him for it.

But seeing me kissing Adrian had brought out his true colors. He'd called me a queer and a faggot, and he wanted to beat me up. It was like he'd accepted me being gay until he had to deal with the reality of what that meant about me. I felt like I'd been stabbed in the back. I was hurt. I was angry. And I was beginning to be afraid.

The touch of Adrian's hand on my arm brought me out of my trance. Our eyes met, mine filled with fear and worry about what the next twenty-four hours might bring, his gazing at me with a calmness that was almost surreal given the impending maelstrom I was certain was heading our way.

"This was just what I was afraid of all along," I said, panic building inside me. "And it's exactly what I didn't want for you. Who knows what Ted will do now?"

"Ben, he won't do anything."

"What if he tells your father? I don't care about myself, but I don't want you to get hurt."

He took my hand.

"Ben, I told you before, Ted won't say a word to my father. And even if he does, Dad will assume he's exaggerating, or he'll just pretend he didn't hear it."

"Didn't you see how pissed he was?"

"Yeah, I saw. Okay, so Ted's pissed. We both knew if he found out, he would be. But believe me; it's nothing to worry about."

I turned back to him and studied his face. His jaw was set, and his eyes were shining.

"Come on," he said, caressing my cheek. "Let's just go on and see the movie. Then we'll go home like we planned."

"Adrian, don't you realize what all this means?" We can't go to the movie. I've got to take you home, *your* home, now."

His mouth fell open. "What? Home? Why?"

"Look, Ted might not say anything about us, but all he needs to do is hint that you're not at Tyler's, and when your folks check it out, you'll be in big trouble and—"

"No, I don't want to go home," he said, crossing his arms. "I want to spend the night with you."

"I want to spend the night with you too. But we can't. Not tonight. Not after what just happened. Come on. Let's go."

I started the car. Adrian glared straight ahead and pouted the whole way. When we came to the block he lived on, I pulled over at the corner. The sight of Baby parked outside confirmed that Ted had gone straight home. Adrian was still glaring into the distance, frowning. I touched his arm, and he turned towards me. The shadows couldn't hide the disappointment in his eyes. I brushed my fingers along the edge of his chin.

"Look, if Ted does come to terms with this, fine. But right now, tonight, I don't want to take the chance of you getting in trouble. Just go in there, and if anyone asks why you're not at Tyler's, you can tell them you felt sick and wanted to come home."

He rolled his eyes and snorted.

"I wanted to spend the night with you," he said in a petulant tone.

"I know. And I wanted it too, even if I did say it wasn't a good idea. But we can't, not tonight."

Adrian scoffed. "I'll never forgive Ted for screwing this up."

We hugged each other and shared a slow, passionate good-night kiss. Reluctantly, he pulled away, got out, and moped across the yard to the front door and went inside. I waited for a minute, but no yelling or loud crashes exploded from inside the Douglas house, so I started the car and drove home.

When I went inside, I felt jumpy. My father barely glanced my way as I passed the living room, and Grandpa didn't notice me at all. But Mom eyed me curiously.

I'd been sitting in my room staring at nothing for maybe five minutes when a light rapping on the door brought me back to the real world.

"Come in," I said.

"You're home early," Mom said, closing the door behind her. "Is everything all right?"

"Yeah, sure," I said, rolling my eyes.

"Did you and Adrian have a fight?"

"A fight?" I said with a sad chuckle. "You could say that. We ran into Ted. Hope told him about us and where to look for us."

"Why would she do that?" she asked, crossing her arms.

"It's a long story."

"So what happened?"

"Ted found us. He wanted to punch me out, but he and Adrian got into a fight, and ..." I looked down.

"And what?"

I sighed. "And a policeman broke it up and told us to get out of there. So, I dropped Adrian off and came home."

Mom pursed her lips and looked away for a moment.

"Ben, I hope you realize how much trouble the three of you could have gotten into. Fighting in the streets...You could have all ended up in jail."

I bowed my head. "Yeah, the officer kind of mentioned that."

"And if you had, you can bet the news would have picked up on it."

"Believe me, Mom. I wanted them to stop, but Ted was pissed from the get-go, and that pissed Adrian off. It all happened so fast, and then the officer was there."

"Okay, so you took Adrian home..."

"Yeah."

"And Ted?"

"He went home too. He got there before us."

"What do you think he'll do?"

"I don't know. Adrian says he won't say anything to his father."

"Do you believe him?"

I shrugged. "For all I know, he could have told him already."

"Oh, I don't think so. In fact, I'd say you can be sure he hasn't said anything yet."

"Why?"

"Because I would think that if Franklyn Douglas knew his son was dating another boy, he'd be on the phone screaming his head off by now, if not pounding on the front door."

"Adrian says he'd just pretend he didn't know about it."

"Well, even if that's so—" She paused and looked me in the eye. "Ben, I told you before that you and Adrian needed to talk this out with Ted, and if he couldn't accept the two of you dating, you should break it off. It's wrong to come between a boy and his brother."

"I know. It's just..." I couldn't tell her how much in love I was with Adrian. She'd think I was being childish.

"...it's hard."

"I know it is."

She came over, kissed me on the cheek, and stopped at the door before leaving.

"Well, I've given you my thoughts on the matter. But ultimately, it's up to you. Once again, Ben, you're seventeen. You need to think this through and make a mature decision."

I sat there for hours, waiting and worrying, expecting the phone to ring or to hear angry fists pounding on the front door any minute. But time passed and nothing happened.

Finally, sometime after eleven, I brushed my teeth, got in bed, and lay there brooding.

I couldn't believe Hope would be so vindictive as to rat Adrian and me out to Ted like that. And him calling me a faggot hurt so bad I couldn't see how our friendship would ever recover. And I was so worried for Adrian. What if his father didn't just pretend he didn't know about us? What if he got violent? What if he beat him?

I switched on the receiver just in time to hear Suzanne Vega singing "Luka," and a vision popped inside my head of Adrian blaming a black eye on walking into a door. I shut the receiver off, turned off the light, and rolled over.

I SPENT MOST of Sunday in my room. I wanted to call Adrian and make sure he was okay but didn't try in case Ted answered the phone. So, I listened to music, spent a couple of hours reading, and played a couple of games of dominos with my dad and Grandpa. After supper, I watched TV for a while and went to bed early.

Monday morning was sunny, but it was literally freezing. I bundled up in my coat and pulled the hood up before jumping in the car. It took forever for the heater to overpower the cold, and I was still chilled to the bone when I got to Chadham High.

Grateful for the warm, if stuffy, air in the hall, I put my coat and book bag in the locker and had just got out my U.S. government textbook when my eyes fell on Adrian. I was so relieved to see no bruises on that beautiful face. He looked miserable, but his expression softened when he caught sight of me, and he quickened his step.

"Thank God you're all right," he said before I could speak. "After Ted got home yesterday, I was afraid you and he'd had a fight. I wanted to call you or come over, but thanks to him, I didn't dare."

"What happened? Did he tell your folks about us?"

"No, Ted didn't say a word, just like I told you. In fact, he ended up having his own explaining to do—" He looked past me. "Uh-oh, here he comes. Talk to you later."

He turned and walked away.

I looked over and saw Ted marching towards me. I'd expected him to still be angry, but what I didn't expect was to see the shining black eye he was sporting.

"What the hell happened to you?"

Instead of answering, he pushed me against my locker, glaring at me and gritting his teeth, a hand on each of my shoulders.

"You listen to me, and you listen good, you pervert," he growled, louder than I'd have liked. "You keep your damn hands off my brother."

"First off," I said, breaking free of him, "keep your voice down unless you want Adrian to get a bad reputation."

Ted looked over at the two or three people close enough to be curious about whatever was going on.

"What are you looking at?" he snarled, and they all shuffled off.

"Now tell me," I said. "Who did that to you? Your father?"

"What? No."

"Adrian didn't do it, did he?"

"No... If you must know, it was Doris. Doris punched me."

"Doris?"

"Yeah, she called me Saturday and asked me to meet her at the mall yesterday. When I got there, I told her I'd always thought she was hot, but never thought I had a chance with her until you told me she was in love with me. Then she called me an idiot and said she'd never date me in a million years. She said Hope was the one in love with me, but she didn't think she'd ever speak to me again now. So I said, if Hope wasn't speaking to me, why did she call and tell me about you trying to convert Adrian. That's when she hit me and said *she* didn't want to speak to me again either."

He was still looming over me like he was ready to beat the crap out of me any second. But his drooping shoulders and sad expression made me sorry for him.

"Ted, I should have told you what Doris was up to weeks ago."

"Right now, I don't give a damn about Doris *or* Hope," he said, drawing himself up to his full height. "I just want you to keep your hands off Adrian. He's straight, and I'm not going to let you recruit him to your disgusting lifestyle."

I ran my fingers through my hair and stared at the ceiling before replying.

"Ted, let's get a couple of things straight, okay? First off, I'm not recruiting Adrian to anything. Second, you've got no right to call me names or put me down for who I am."

"Uh-huh. Like I said, you leave my brother alone. And by the way, don't ever speak to me again."

He pushed me against the locker and walked away while I stood there gawking after him. What happened to the guy I'd known for so long? I shook my head and started for homeroom. Sadly, I realized it was easier for him to believe I was trying to recruit Adrian than to accept the possibility that he just might be gay.

Then I realized how right Mom had been. If I kept seeing Adrian, Ted would eventually tell his father, who, for all I knew, would beat the crap out of him—after killing me. And even if Adrian was right and his father just pretended he wasn't gay, I'd already become a wedge between him and Ted. If Adrian and I stayed together, it would only get worse, and one way or the other, Adrian would end up getting hurt. And it would be my fault.

As the reality of what I had to do sank in, a vision played out in my mind—Adrian and me staying together, me going to Dickerson, him following in a couple of years, and the two of us growing old together. It was a bitter image because it could never be. I had to break up with him. It was the only mature thing to do. But it was already breaking my heart, and I suddenly felt sadder than I had ever been in my life.

WHEN I MET up with Doris for first period, she fell into step beside me, but neither of us spoke until we were halfway to Mr. Kormany's room.

I cleared my throat. "I hear you talked with Ted yesterday."

She glared at me. "The least you could have done was call me to tell me you weren't coming. I had to face him all alone."

"Doris, I was so depressed after what happened Saturday night, I didn't even remember that I was supposed to meet you. And you weren't exactly alone in the middle of the mall food court."

"That's not the point. Anyway, it doesn't matter. I think he finally got the message."

"Oh, he got the message all right. The trouble is, thanks to Hope, he thinks I'm trying to turn Adrian queer."

"Yeah, he was blathering something about that yesterday. What exactly happened Saturday night?"

We stopped and I lowered my voice. "He caught the two of us kissing on the way to my car and tried to beat me up. The two of them got into a fight, and a policeman nearly arrested all three of us. Then Adrian left with me."

"Oh, my God. Do you think he'll get over it?"

"I don't really care. He called me a faggot and a pervert. As far as I'm concerned, Ted and I are through."

"Well, if he's going to be such an ass, you're better off. I'd have thought he'd rather have Adrian with you than some dip-wad."

"Doris, he doesn't want Adrian with a guy at all. He doesn't want to admit his brother's gay."

She shook her head. "What are you going to do?"

"What *can* I do? I can't come between the two of them—they're brothers. I've got to break it off with Adrian. What about you and Hope?"

"I called her Saturday afternoon and told her you and I were trying to get her together with Ted. But she said she knew what we were trying to do, that we were trying to humiliate her. And then she hung up on me. She's as crazy as Ted. Ugh. This is all his fault."

I had to say it. "Well...technically, Doris, this isn't Ted's fault; it's *your* fault. If you hadn't stuck your nose in and played matchmaker, none of this would have happened."

"*My* fault?" she retorted. "It's not my fault that Ted's too stupid to put two and two together."

"Instead of just suggesting he ask Hope out, you went through all that...that *fakakta* 'Doesn't Hope look nice this morning?' crap. That's what led to all this. "

She stopped and faced me with her hand on her hip. "If you'd done your part, they'd be together now."

"I told you from the beginning to leave me out of it. It's because of you that Hope thinks I was plotting against her. And now that I think about it, it's your fault she called Ted and told him about Adrian and me."

Doris stamped her foot and stormed off to Mr. Kormany's room. She ignored me the whole class, and when it was over, she got up and left without saying so much as a word. I picked up my book and shuffled out to the hall by myself.

It was a strange new existence. Doris was mad at me and avoiding Ted. Ted was mad at me and avoiding Doris. And Hope was mad and avoiding all of us. I didn't bother looking for any of them on the way to second period, although I did catch a fleeting glimpse of Hope going into Ms. Antallen's room for study hall. Her step was unsteady, and I wondered if she'd been drinking.

During break, I wandered around looking for Adrian but didn't find him.

As luck would have it, the next time I did see him was on my way to fourth period. It wasn't the best timing. Ted was just a couple of yards ahead of me, and Hope was a few yards behind me, muttering under her breath.

Adrian bypassed Ted completely and came right up to me.

"Are you all right? What did he say?"

"We need to talk.'

"Are you okay?"

"I'm fine, Adrian. We just need to talk."

"Can you drop me off after school? We can talk then."

"Okay, sure."

As she passed us, Hope bumped against me, hard, but then she staggered a bit before regaining her balance.

Adrian squeezed my arm before walking away. I turned to watch him go and sighed.

Literature was a nightmare. Our assigned seats had Ted and me on either side of Doris, with Hope sitting directly behind her. Doris kept her eyes firmly on Mrs. Barsanas. Ted split his attention between Mrs. Barsanas and shooting icy looks in my direction. And as for Hope, I couldn't see what she was doing, but every now and then, a whispered grumble reminded us she was there.

Lunch was just as surreal. Doris grabbed a seat at a table that was mostly full to make sure neither Ted nor I could sit near her. Hope picked a spot at the far end of the lunchroom as if daring any one of us to try and get close. Ted and I ended up at the same table but ignored each other the whole time.

Then came Creative Writing. I'd gone straight to Ms. Kiri's room as soon as I finished eating and cooled my heels in the hall until the bell rang. When Hope came in, I knew in an instant she'd had an after-lunch drink— a big one, judging by the way she swayed as she crossed the room to her chair. Chantal Rodriguez cut a knowing glance in my direction and smirked.

Hope was so out of it even Ms. Kiri noticed and asked her if she was all right. She mumbled something about lunchroom food and her time of the month. At that, Ms. Kiri dropped the matter.

The day's writing assignment was to write a fairy tale. I needed no time to think up something and started writing.

Once upon a time, there was a lonely boy named Harold. Harold lived in a land where if a boy was found to be in love with another boy, one of them was put to death. But Harold could never fall in love with a girl. He had tried and tried, but to no avail. So, years passed, and Harold languished alone and unloved. He had been blessed with friends, but he craved the kind of intimacy other people enjoyed and he could only dream about.

Then it happened—he met the boy of his dreams, Noah. Harold was immediately smitten by Noah and ecstatic that someone so handsome, smart, and caring actually wanted him. The two of them fell in love, even though society's ignorance and bigotry demanded they keep their love a secret. They were careful and discreet and found lonely places where they could spend time together and see in each other's eyes the fiery glow of true devotion. And for the first time in his life, Harold was happy.

But the wicked witch Desdemona had discovered Harold and Noah's secret. She appeared before Harold and cackled that she would expose them and ensure that Noah would be the one put to death. Harold begged her not to do so and offered to do anything to save Noah's life. So, the demonic Desdemona gave Harold a choice: he could accept exile, leaving Noah to believe he had abandoned him, or else Desdemona would ensure that Noah was the one to die when their love was exposed. It was a painful choice but one Harold made immediately. He would accept exile to save Noah's life.

Harold was taken to a distant tower from which he could never escape, and he thought, in his grief, he would at least have the consolation of knowing that Noah would be free. But the evil Desdemona had one more trick to play. In the heart of the tower, Harold found a crystal ball that revealed Noah's life after Harold's disappearance. Day after day, Harold watched Noah and prayed he would find some measure of happiness. But as time passed, Noah's pining turned to bitterness, and then to anger, and finally, to depression. To his horror, Harold watched as Noah killed himself in despair.

Desdemona's cruelty completed, she opened the gate of the tower and told Harold he was now free to leave. Life without Noah, once unthinkable, then tolerable only in the belief that Noah would live and find happiness without him, was now a reality that crushed Harold's heart. And so, instead of leaving the tower, he climbed to the top and threw himself out of a window, and the only sound as he fell was the low whimper of his weeping.

It was a sad ending for a fairy tale, but, given my mood and what I had to do, it was the only one I could write.

THE AFTERNOON DRAGGED on. With each passing minute, I grew more depressed, and when the final bell rang, I heaved a sigh and walked to the car feeling like a condemned man. Adrian was waiting when I got there. I unlocked the door for him and went around to the driver's side.

There were cars on either side of us, and as soon as I got in, he leaned over and kissed me. This wasn't getting any easier.

"So, did Ted tell you what happened? Of course, he acted pissy all Saturday night because I left with you instead of him, and then he goes out yesterday afternoon and comes home with a black eye—" He paused. "I was so glad this morning when I saw he hadn't been fighting with you. Anyway, he comes home with a black eye, and my parents are, like, yelling at him about getting into a fight, and then he says a girl hit him. And my mom's like, 'What did you do to her?' and he says, 'Nothing,' but she won't believe him. It went on for hours. He stuck to his story, but they still don't believe him."

"He was telling the truth."

"What?"

"Remember I told you about Doris trying to fix him up with Hope and how he got it all wrong and thought Doris was in love with him? Well, she met with him to straighten things out. I was supposed to be there to help her, but after Saturday night, I totally forgot about it. So, anyway, he told her about catching us, and she hit him. But, hey, at least he finally figured out she isn't in love with him."

Adrian shook his head and sniggered.

"Man, oh man, Ted's as dumb as a conk."

"Adrian, he thinks I'm trying to recruit you to my 'disgusting lifestyle.'"

"Then maybe we should let him see me throw my arms around you and kiss you."

"He'd just think I've got you trained."

"Like I said, dumb as a conk. I bet if you got up close to his ear, you could hear the ocean."

I let him continue chattering on about Ted. It was the typical kind of "my brother's an idiot" talk all siblings engage in, but in the context of what was going on, it just drove home the point that what I had to do was for the best.

We pulled into the driveway at my house, and I turned off the engine. Adrian broke into a half smile and licked his lips.

"Mmm, got a few minutes for us to go inside?"

I took a deep breath. "Adrian, we've got to stop seeing each other."

The color drained from his face.

"What? Why?"

"Ted's your brother. If he can't accept us, we've got to break up."

He shook his head, his eyes starting to get glassy. "No. I don't want to break up. Ted's got no right to decide who I can see. It's none of his business. He can't run my life."

"It's not a question of him running your life. It's that he's your brother. I shouldn't come between the two of you."

"*He* shouldn't come between us," Adrian said, getting louder, the words coming out faster with each sentence. "Ben, we don't have to do this. We don't have to break up. We can stay together, and if he doesn't like it, he can just lump it."

"If we don't break up, he'll end up telling your father. Then what?"

"I told you before; my dad won't do a thing."

"So you keep saying, but what if you're wrong? And even if he doesn't, it doesn't change things. We've *got* to stop seeing each other."

"But I don't *want* to stop seeing you. I don't want to stop seeing you. I want to be with you, Ben."

"I know, but this can't go on. We have to break up. That's just the way it's got to be. I'm sorry."

His eyes were glistening, searching mine, and his lower lip began to tremble. He seemed smaller somehow, and as the emotion overwhelmed him, he started crying.

Invisible fingers squeezed my throat, and a rock fell into the pit of my stomach. I wanted to hold him and tell him everything was going to be all right. I wanted to kiss his tears away and make him smile again. But I couldn't. All I could do was hold back my own tears and watch him break down in front of me.

Then humiliation became too much for him, and he grabbed his book bag, flung the door open, and ran off.

I heaved a ragged sigh and started the car. Paul Young was singing "Every Time You Go Away." I groaned, leaned my arms and head on the steering wheel, and let my own tears flow.

Chapter Eleven

I GOT TO the center, exhausted and feeling defeated. "Why is it," I wondered, "that doing the right thing so often feels bad?" I went into the men's room, splashed cold water on my face, and looked in the mirror. The boy who looked back at me had sad, bloodshot eyes. I ran a little more water over my fingers and wiped them, straightened up, and threw my shoulders back. I had a job to do, and no matter how bad my day had been, I was going to do it.

The door hadn't closed behind me before I saw Mrs. Gilder coming my way.

"Seth, you bad boy. I've been looking for you all afternoon. You are grounded, young man. Do you hear me? Grounded."

I really wasn't in the mood for it.

"Mrs. Gilder, I'm not your son. I'm Benjamin. You know, the one who looks like your son?"

As always, she stared at me for a few seconds, but right at the point when I expected her to tell me to let Seth know such and such, she glowered at me and raised a hand.

"Don't you use that tone with me."

I recoiled and just missed being slapped in the face. Melvin and Rosalita came trotting over and got between her and me. She continued trying to slap me, insisting I was her son and calling me a liar, getting louder by the second. Dr. Markov rushed over and started talking to her.

I backed away and found Artie standing next to me.

"She's getting worse, I'm afraid," he said, and then he took in my face. "Hey, Ben, are you all right?"

We started walking to the break room.

"I'm just a little shaken, I guess. I've had a rough couple of days, and I wasn't as ready for that as I should have been."

"Under the circumstances, I think you handled it as well as could be expected. We can't be at our best one hundred percent of the time. You know, you—"

"Ben?" a voice rang out.

Adrian was standing inside the entrance, looking around.

I gave Artie an apologetic glance. "Uh, I've got to...uh—excuse me."

Adrian caught sight of me and marched up. We met in the middle of the room.

"Adrian, what are you doing here?"

"Ben, I won't let you break up with me. You can't just throw me away like that."

He was loud and angry, but his eyes were red.

"I'm not throwing you away. I'm trying to protect you."

"I don't need protecting. And I'm not letting Ted run my life. Why are you?"

"I can't let myself become a wedge between you and him."

"*He's* the wedge, Ben. He's the wedge," he said, the urgency in his voice mounting. "And you've got to stand up to him. Why should we have to break up just because he doesn't approve? It wouldn't be right if you were a girl. Why should it be right just because you're a boy?"

"It's not that simple. It—"

"It's exactly that simple. Look, I'm in love with you, and you're in love with me, right?"

Most of the old people were either too deaf or not close enough to hear us. The staff, however, was a different story, and discussing my love life out in the open made me very uncomfortable.

"Adrian, I...I don't think this is the—"

"You do love me, don't you? You said you did... You do, don't you?"

He stared at me, waiting for me to say something.

But I didn't say anything. I just stood there, too self-conscious of all the people around us to speak. And in that silence, the hope in Adrian's eyes gave way to doubt. Suddenly, he wasn't the equal I'd come to see him as. He was a wounded fifteen-year-old boy, a child, vulnerable, fragile, and afraid. His lip was quivering, and a tear slid down his cheek.

"Ben, please," he said in an imploring whisper. "Please...don't throw me away... Please."

And then he was openly crying. I'd thought it was bad in the car, but there, in front of all those people, it was as pathetic a sight as I could ever imagine. I had wanted to protect him, but instead, I'd broken him, and seeing what I'd done was breaking my heart.

He turned on his heels and bolted. I hesitated in shock for a second and then chased after him, but by the time I got to the door, he was out of sight.

I came back in. A few of the old people were looking at me. The staff, on the other hand, were all doing a perfect job of *not* looking at me, which made it worse.

Artie walked over and put a hand on my shoulder.

"You weren't kidding about having a tough day, were you? Come on."

He led me to the break room and pulled up a chair.

"Romance troubles?"

"I...uh..."

"You know, it's okay to be gay, Ben. And it's okay to be young and in love. And for the record, all relationships hit a bump in the road every now and then."

"I broke up with him today after school," I said, and tears started streaming down my cheeks.

He nodded and waited a second.

"Do you want to tell me about it?"

I heaved a sigh and tried to control myself. "I didn't want to do it. It was something I had to do."

"Why is that?"

"His brother is—was—my best friend...and he...he found out about us. That can't be fixed, but I don't want to drive a wedge between him and Adrian."

"Adrian is your boyfriend?"

"He was. I broke up with him to protect him. I don't want him to get hurt."

"Uh-huh. Can I tell you a secret?"

"What?"

"I'm gay too."

That wasn't what I was expecting him to say, and I blinked.

He went on: "And I found myself in something of a similar situation back when I was in high school. See, we had some trouble—real trouble— and we each made some bad decisions when what we really needed to do was to talk things over. So, can I offer a word of advice? You said you broke up with Adrian because you want to protect him. Well, shouldn't he have some say in that? You say you don't want him to get hurt, but he looked pretty hurt out there to me. For that matter, so do you. What I'm saying is you might want to talk it out, not just announce it and leave him no say in the decision."

"But if we don't break up, what about Ted? He and Adrian are brothers."

"Ben, you're not responsible for Ted's decisions. You're only responsible for your own. And just as Ted should respect Adrian's choices in life, so should you. Look, I'm not saying you and he *should* stay together, I'm just saying the two of you might do better to talk things over. Otherwise, you might both wind up regretting it. I know I did."

"What happened?"

Artie sighed and looked away. "We were madly in love, and the whole school found out about us. You can't imagine how homophobic society was in those days. I got beaten up—bad. That's where I got this scar."

He pointed to a mark above his left eye that I'd never paid much attention to before.

"Artie, I'm so sorry."

"In those days, things like that used to happen to gay kids all the time. We've still got a long way to go, but at least things are a little better nowadays. Anyway, we didn't talk things out. And then we lost the chance. It was over, and he was gone from my life forever. "

He cleared his throat. "So what about you and Adrian?"

"I don't know. My mom keeps saying I need to make mature decisions, but every time I try to, it seems to backfire."

"Unfortunately, mistakes happen no matter how old or mature you are. What does your heart tell you?"

"I don't want to break up with Adrian. I'm in love with him."

He leaned back in his chair and sighed. "If I've learned anything in life, it's that there are some things we need at least as much as the air we breathe—some things even more. Take love for instance. A life without love can hardly be called living at all. We need love more than we need the breaths we take. So, if you really love Adrian, maybe you could begin by telling him that when the two of you talk things over."

He stood up, patted me on the shoulder, and smiled. "If that's what you decide to do, that is. It's up to you."

He walked to the door and paused. "Why don't you hang out in here for a while? We all need a little downtime every now and then."

I leaned back in the chair and crossed my arms. "Whoever it was who said things get easier when you get older was crazy."

AFTER SUCH A tense beginning, I felt skittish making the rounds the rest of the afternoon. Dr. Markov and Rosalita had taken Mrs. Gilder to her room, whether to counsel her or sedate her I wasn't sure. Even so, the memory of her scowling face, the outrage in her eyes, the way she'd swung at me—it both scared me and made me ashamed. She wasn't a big woman, but when she raised her hand to hit me, I'd been terrified.

On top of that, the incident with Adrian left me feeling embarrassed and incredibly guilty. No one who heard us could doubt we were both gay. Watching him cry, they all had to think I'd been heartless in hurting him so bad. And the fact that I was the reason he'd humiliated himself in public like that made me wish I could go back in time so it never would have happened.

The only bright side of it all was that Grandpa Marty apparently missed all the commotion entirely. On the trip home, he listened to the radio and hummed along with a couple of the tunes just like always. When an old Sinatra number came on, he started singing along. "A hundred years from today," he crooned, almost as flat as Sinatra, glancing my way like he thought I liked the tune.

That night, I only picked at supper and didn't pay attention to anything going on at the table. I was pretty much in my own little world. My mind ran through a dozen scenarios of finding Adrian and apologizing for hurting him. I even toyed with the idea of sneaking over to the Douglas house and throwing pebbles at his bedroom window like in some movie. But I figured with my luck, I'd bust the window, or Ted would take out the trash and catch me.

I tossed and turned all night. Images of Ted yelling at me, Doris walking away, Hope calling me a traitor, and, worst of all, Adrian crying made sleep nearly impossible.

I was exhausted Tuesday morning. The shower and extra coffee with breakfast only helped so much. I drove to school early in the hope of catching Adrian before homeroom. I had toyed with the idea of waiting for him outside, but it was almost as cold as the day before—and damp on top of it. If I'd known where his locker was, I'd have waited for him there, but beyond guessing it was somewhere on the far side of the building with all the other freshmen lockers, I didn't have a clue. All I could do was wander around before homeroom and hope to run into him, which didn't happen. That left me with only one option—looking for him between classes.

On top of that, dealing with my once closest friends was like picking my way through a minefield. The tone for the day was set before second period. Doris still wasn't talking to me, which made working on our latest U.S. government project next to impossible. I also saw Hope making for Ms. Antallen's room, weaving an unsteady zigzag path through the hall. If she was already drinking that early in the morning, I had no doubt she'd wind up being expelled by lunchtime. Even a Chadham High teacher would have to notice how drunk she was. Every time I passed Ted in the hall, he scowled at me as if I was evil incarnate. It was all too depressing for words.

During morning break, I finally got lucky. I spotted Adrian going into one of the boys' restrooms and went in after him. There were at least seven other guys milling about. He'd just finished taking care of business and was on his way to the lavatory. The second he laid eyes on me, he froze.

I stepped close and whispered, "Hey, got a minute?"

"I...uh..." The fear in his eyes was agonizing.

"How about I give you a ride after school?"

His eyes searched mine; he bit his lip and swallowed before answering.

"I—I can't."

"Well, can you come over tonight?"

He stared at me warily and ran his fingers through his hair.

"No, I don't think so."

"Can you call me?"

"W—why are you doing this?"

"Because I need to talk to you."

A big football player knocked against me on his way out.

"Jerk," Adrian said, but the jock either didn't hear him or didn't consider us worth the effort.

I leaned closer and whispered, "Can we at least find somewhere we can talk for a minute?"

He studied me for a second and nodded. We found a spot that was more or less private and leaned against the wall.

"I'm sorry about yesterday," I whispered. "I was wrong, and I don't want to break up. Let me give you that ride after school so we can really talk."

He looked down for a second, and when he looked up, his eyes were glassy.

"I—I've got to go," he said, turning away from me.

"Please let me give you that ride. I do love you," I said, not caring if anyone heard me.

THE DAY CONTINUED to be just as depressing as it had started out to be. The bad feelings and mutual avoidance by my now-former best friends was incredibly stressful. I shared one period with each of them, plus Literature and lunch. Einstein would have marveled at the bending of space and time in our lit class. Each minute felt like an hour. Spatially, the four of us were sitting in close proximity, but emotionally, we were as distant from one another as galaxies.

Lunchtime saw the four of us choosing strategically separate locations to eat. We did, however, pick spots where we could keep each other firmly in view.

Doris and I did have one area of common interest. We both positioned ourselves so we could keep an eye on Hope. What we saw wasn't encouraging. She ate next to nothing and left for the restroom a few minutes before the bell rang. Doris made eye contact with me, and we both got up to follow her. As predicted, she wound her way to the restroom. Instead of going in after her, Doris waited with me for her to come out, and when she did, her gait was unstable and somewhat aimless. All bad blood aside, the two of us rushed over to her.

"Hope, are you all right?" Doris asked.

Hope swayed in place and stared at her blankly before seeming to recognize her.

"I'm not talking to you," she said in a slow slurred voice.

"Hope," I said, "how much have you had to drink today?"

"Hi, traitor. I'm not talking to you either."

Doris grabbed Hope's arm, as much to steady her as to get her attention.

"Hope, how much have you had today?"

She broke into a sloppy smile and leaned in close to us.

"I left the janitor a present in the trash. Bad luck for him though—it's empty."

I gave Doris a nod, and she dashed to the restroom.

"Hope, you've got to stop doing this. And where are you getting the booze from? If your parents found out, they'd kill you."

She scoffed. "My parents? My parents are an enema to me."

"You mean enigma."

"No, I mean enema. They're a pain in my ass, and all I get from them is shit. They nag at me about my grades, and why don't I pray more, and why don't I hang out with the kids from church. They hate all my friends, especially you. They say you're a sexual deviant and going to Hell."

Doris came hurrying back to us.

"It was a pint of vodka. Hope, how full was that bottle when you started this morning?"

"It was full. But don't worry," she whispered conspiratorially, patting her bag, "I've got more right here."

She turned to walk away but spun around too fast and staggered to one side.

And to our horror, she stumbled straight into Mr. Allen, our principal. He grabbed her arm to steady her, and then he took a big sniff, and his eyes went wide.

"Uh-oh," Doris said as the two of us took a step back.

"You two, come over here."

He looked us over suspiciously, but after a few seconds, I guess he decided we looked sober enough.

"What do you know about this?"

"This?" I asked, like Hope wasn't falling down drunk not two feet in front of me.

"This girl is intoxicated. Now what do you know about it?"

"Nothing," Doris said. "We just noticed she seemed out of it, and came to ask her what was wrong."

He looked at me, and I nodded. Without another word, he took Hope by the arm and marched her off to the office.

"Oh God, is she in big trouble," Doris said. "Her parents really will kill her."

"Maybe it's a blessing in disguise. At least they'll be able to get her help. She needs help, Doris."

The bell rang, and we went our separate ways.

I SPENT THE rest of the day moping about how messed up everything was. The last thing Hope needed was getting caught drunk by Mr. Allen. Out of all of us, she was suffering the most. Her heart had been broken over Ted, and she thought Doris and I had betrayed her. Now her parents would put her through hell for embarrassing them, and they'd probably send her to St Dominic's, which wouldn't help at all. She already resented the way they forced her into churchy things. Going to a religious school would probably just make her drinking problem worse.

And poor Doris—she never said it, but I could tell it wounded her that Hope would think she'd tried to steal a boy from her. It also didn't help that the Murphys were certain to call the Whitfields and blame Doris for Hope's drinking. She would face a whole night of being cross-examined by her folks over something she had no part in, only adding to the sting of Hope's rejection.

In study hall, Ted continued his homophobic big brother routine, and I realized I could never see him as my best friend again. At that point, I wasn't sure I even wanted him as a friend at all.

Of course, none of us would ever be the friends we were before. Even if Hope came to believe that Doris really had been trying to hook her up with Ted, she'd never trust her again because of the way she'd gone about it. And I'd have a hard time ever trusting Hope again after she ratted me and Adrian out to Ted.

Adrian... As the school day drew to a close, all my focus turned to him. All I'd accomplished by my stupid attempt to be noble was to hurt him and make a fool of myself. I'd broken his heart, and my stupid attempt to apologize and move on like nothing ever happened that morning had been ridiculous. I'd screwed up the best thing that ever happened to me.

The last bell rang, and I shuffled off to my car in total despair, my eyes focused on the ground in front of me. About twenty feet from the car though, I looked up, and my heart skipped a beat. Adrian was leaning against the trunk, watching me. His eyes were wary and frightened.

"I'm glad you're here. Thanks," I said.

He gave the smallest nod, and I unlocked the door for him. We got in, joined the line on the service road leading to the highway, and didn't speak until I pulled into my driveway.

"Déjà vu," he said as the car came to a stop. "

I cleared my throat. "First, I want to apologize again. I didn't mean to hurt you."

"You have no idea how *bad* you hurt me. Ben, I've never loved anyone like I love you, and when you told me you were breaking up with me, I felt like my whole world was falling apart."

"I'm so sorry. I never should have said it. It wasn't even something I wanted to do."

"Then why did you do it? Ted keeps telling me you're only using me, and then out of the blue, you tell me you're breaking up with me and say it's because of him. But when I asked you if you loved me, you wouldn't even answer. Why?"

"Believe me; it wasn't because I don't love you. I do."

"Then why wouldn't you say it?"

"I was in shock. I didn't think breaking up would hurt you that bad. I never wanted to make you cry."

"Then why did you say we had to break up? Are you afraid of Ted?"

"No," I said, rather defensively, and then I sighed. "I thought I was being noble. Family is important. And I thought if I came between you and Ted, it would end up hurting you, and I didn't want that to happen. But then I turned out to be the one who hurt you instead, and I am so sorry. I was wrong, and like Artie said, I wasn't being fair to you because I wasn't letting you have a say in the decision."

"Who's Artie?"

"He works at the center—he's a counselor, and kind of a friend."

Adrian nodded and was quiet for a moment. Then he took my hand in his.

"Look, family *is* important, and Ted is my brother. But why should he get to decide who I can, or can't, fall in love with? If loving you comes between him and me, it's not your fault. It's his. The other night, I told him whether he likes it or not, I'm gay, and even if you and I never saw each other again, I'd still be gay, and he'd just have to get used to it."

"And he accepted that?"

"Of course not. He said you've got me brainwashed. So I told him how I got you to take me to the movies, and how I surprised you with a kiss. He actually had the gall to say you must have manipulated me into it somehow."

I sighed. "He'd rather think I'm seducing you than believe you're gay."

"Well, he's got to wake up to reality. Whether he likes it or not, I'm gay...and I love you."

"Then you forgive me?"

"Of course, I forgive you," he said, squeezing my hand.

I took him in my arms and kissed him. As our lips came together, the weight of the world fell from my shoulders.

We stared into each other's eyes for a moment, and then Adrian said, "But you've got to stand up to Ted. You've got to make him understand that you're not just playing me along, that we really are in love, that we're going to be together, and if he really wants me to be happy, he's got to accept it. But even if he doesn't, you and I are still going to build a life together."

"Sounds like you've got it all worked out."

"No, I haven't got it *all* worked out. That depends on you. Are you going to confront Ted?"

"I don't know. What if he jumps the gun on you and tells your parents? What if he decides to just beat the crap out of me instead?"

"I thought you weren't afraid of him. I mean, you said you love me."

"I do, but it'd be hard to kiss you with a broken jaw. And with Ted, that could be a real possibility."

"Ain't I worth the risk?"

Staring into those gorgeous eyes, there was only one answer to that question.

"You're worth everything on earth."

"Then stand up to Ted," he said, pulling me close and kissing me.

I wasn't confident that I could make Ted believe I truly was in love with Adrian, or whether it would change anything if he did. And maybe I *was* a little afraid he'd beat the crap out of me. But I knew in my heart it didn't matter. I was so in love with Adrian I really was willing to risk anything, even Ted beating me up.

I WAS ALMOST an hour late getting to the center. Artie noticed me as soon as I walked in and raised his eyebrows inquisitively. I smiled and nodded. He gave me a thumbs-up.

I mingled and worked my way around the hall, stopping to *kibitz* over a five-player domino tournament that I was told had been going on for hours. Mrs. Kadelburg spent a few minutes telling me about her son's visit earlier in the day, and I moved on to chat with Mr. Lehmann. He spent most of the time I was with him talking about Herman. Despite the number of times he and Herman had locked horns over his alleged cheating, he clearly missed him and said he hoped he would return soon. It struck me that as much as the two of them argued, for Mr. Lehmann, their exchanges were a vital, and on some level, even enjoyable part of his day.

It was nearly time for the dinner bell that announced the end of the day program. Melvin motioned from across the room for me to join him.

"I thought you might want to know that I caught Marty and Ishmael outside smoking after lunch today. Smoking's not allowed around the center, but Ishmael manages to get ahold of them somehow, and now it looks like he's made your grandfather a partner in crime."

"Thanks, Melvin. I'll let my folks know."

On the drive home, Grandpa was quiet and wheezing loudly. We walked into the kitchen, where my mother was preparing a fish for the oven.

She looked up. "Good evening, how was everybody's day?"

Grandpa didn't answer and kept walking. I leaned against the counter.

"My day had its ups and downs."

"Want to tell me about it?"

"Well, for one thing, Hope's probably been suspended. Mr. Allen caught her drunk."

Mom turned to fully face me.

"Hope? What was she doing drinking?"

"I don't know. Doris and I found out last week she's been sneaking in a drink after lunch for God knows how long. But it's gotten worse since then."

"Why?"

"Well, it's complicated," I said, walking over to stand next to her. "But it has to do with Ted. Anyway, she's in real trouble, and I'm worried about her."

"You should be. At her age, drinking's not a good sign. So, what good happened today?"

"Adrian and I got back together."

She blinked and raised an eyebrow. "Oh? When did you break up?"

"Yesterday."

One corner of Mom's mouth curled into a smile. "So you talked things out with Ted?"

"No—" I cleared my throat. "Actually, Adrian and I talked things over, and we decided being together is more important than pleasing Ted."

"Well, I hope that turns out to be the right decision."

"Thanks, Mom. Oh, one other thing—another bad one. Melvin told me he caught Grandpa smoking outside with a buddy of his."

She let a hand drop to the countertop and looked up.

"And," I said, "he's done it at least once before, because I caught him in the act last week."

"And why didn't you tell me?"

"He promised me he wouldn't do it again."

"The old fool! He's already got emphysema. And smoking outside on a day like today, what does he want to do? Add pneumonia on top of it?"

"So, are you going to talk to him about it?"

"You better believe I'm going to talk to him about it. Go in there and keep an eye on him until suppertime."

I went into the living room. The TV was way loud. Grandpa was grumbling about something someone had just said on the program he was watching. They paused for a commercial as I came in.

"Hey, Grandpa, what are you watching?"

"*The Blare Report.* They're doing an exposé on government mismanagement. You won't believe how much waste those liberals are getting away with."

"Probably not. Say, what's on that channel that shows old movies?"

"What? I don't know. I'm watching Jim Blare."

"Oh, I just thought they were running a Humphrey Bogart festival this week."

"Bogie? Well, I suppose it won't hurt to check during the commercial break."

I switched channels, and while the movie didn't feature Humphrey Bogart, it did have John Wayne, another of Grandpa's favorites, so we settled down to watch it.

"Now that was a man," Grandpa said after a few minutes, "a real *mensch*, and a staunch conservative all his life."

I nodded, happy he was a little more alert than he'd been recently.

"Yup, he was a real man, and a real ladies' man too."

We watched a few more minutes in silence, and then he gave me a sidelong glance.

"So tell me, who are you dating these days? One of those *shiksa* girls you hang out with?"

"Well...uh...no. They're just friends. I wouldn't date either of them."

"Why not? They're both pretty enough."

"I know. I think they're very pretty. But they're...uh...not my type."

"Oh, I see. What about your friend, the one you used to ride to school with?"

I said it before I could stop myself. "Ted? He's not my type either."

My cheeks began to burn, and I took a quick glance at Grandpa and turned back to the television, hoping he'd stay focused on John Wayne.

"You know, there's nothing wrong with being a *fagalah*," he said, matter-of-factly.

"I just—what?"

"I said there's nothing wrong with being a *fagalah*—you know, queer, homosexual, gay, or whatever they call it nowadays. That is what you are, right?"

"I...uh..."

"So, tell me—your parents, do they know?"

"Uh...yeah. Yeah, they do."

"And your sister, she knows?"

"Yeah, she knows I'm gay."

"And is she a dyke?"

I burst out laughing at the thought of what Eliana's reaction would be if he asked her that question.

"No, Grandpa, Eliana's straight. I'm the only gay kid in the house. And it's not polite to call them 'dykes.' They're called lesbians. But how did you figure out I'm gay?"

He waved a dismissive hand, "What? You think I'm so senile I don't know a lover's quarrel when I see one?"

I looked down. "Oh, I thought you'd missed all that yesterday."

"How could I miss it? There are three things in life that you can't hide—poverty, coughing, and love. And that *shegetz* boy with the long hair was very upset and very loud. I trust the two of you have made up since then."

"Uh...yeah, we did."

"Good."

"I'm sorry, Grandpa. That was a terrible way for you to find out about me. No wonder you were so quiet in the car yesterday."

He tsked. "What are you talking about? I figured out you were gay weeks ago."

"You did? How?"

"'How,' he says. You expect me to live here and not notice you never talk about girls? I figured either you must be gay or the girl you like is a

Democrat. And then the *shegetz* boy is always coming over, and I see the way you look at each other. That cinched it. What's the boy's name again?"

"Adrian."

He nodded. "He seems like a nice boy."

"You...you really don't mind that I'm gay?"

"Benjie, why should I mind? It's no skin off my teeth who you fall in love with. Like Einstein said, 'You can't blame gravity for falling in love.' When I was young, one of my friends was gay, and he was a nice enough guy. Tell me— Are there a lot of gays at your school?"

"I don't know. If there are, they're all keeping a low profile."

"Maybe they don't dress to impress. *You* certainly don't dress as flashy as the kids they showed on that news report about the BLT community."

"It's the *LGBT* community, and I dress okay," I said, turning to face him.

He tsked. "If you say so."

"I *do* dress okay. I just don't believe in showing off in front of people who wouldn't appreciate it."

Then, I caught the gleam in his eye. We both grinned and went back to John Wayne.

Given all the coming-out horror stories I'd read about, and the negative, even violent reactions some kids face from their families, I couldn't believe how lucky I was to have a family who actually accepted me.

"You know, Grandpa, I would never have thought you'd approve of homosexuality."

He seemed genuinely surprised. "And why shouldn't I? People have a right to live."

"Well, yeah, but I mean you being so conservative and all."

"Benjie, there's a big difference between believing in the Constitution and personal liberty, and being a nut. This isn't Nazi Germany, you know. Besides, I've got some pretty open-minded friends, and we talk."

"You mean at the center?"

"Where else? Believe it or not, a couple of those old *shmoes* are just as gay as you."

I was dumbfounded. "Really?"

"What? You thought it's something that just goes away when you get older, like losing your hair? My friend Jonah tells me there's even a gay bar around here somewhere."

"You're kidding. A gay bar in Chadham? That's almost too surreal to imagine."

"Well, that's what he says anyway. But don't you even think about trying to find it. You're way too young for any bar—gay or otherwise."

"Don't worry."

"Promise?"

"Promise."

We watched the movie for a few more minutes. John Wayne was in the middle of a big silly fight with ten or twelve other people when Dad came in.

"Good evening, Marty, Ben."

"Hi, Dad."

Grandpa nodded.

"Ben, your mother says supper's almost ready. Marty, do you need to clean up before we eat?"

"Clean up? No. Take care of a little business, yes."

He got up and left for his room while Dad made his own trip to the bathroom.

In the kitchen, Mom was setting a bowl down on the table.

"Well," I said, "the cat's out of the bag."

"What do you mean?"

"Grandpa knows I'm gay."

She straightened up with a startled expression on her face.

"How did he find out?"

"He...uh...said he guessed it weeks ago."

"And...?"

"And he said it's 'no skin off his teeth' who I fall in love with."

"Are you sure he understands that it means it'll be with a boy?"

"Mom, he even guessed Adrian's my boyfriend."

She pointed towards the dining room with her thumb. "And he said he's okay with it? That man, in there? My father, your grandfather?"

"That's what he said, and he seemed pretty sincere."

"As long as it's not just the Alzheimer's talking."

"I don't think so. He seems to be genuinely okay with it."

"Well, just the same, let's not push it. You know how he is."

"Yeah, if he finds out I'm not a Republican he'll probably write me out of his will."

"Oh, posh! That's nothing. He's disowned me ten or twelve times for that over the years. Wait until I confront him about smoking tonight and see what happens."

GRANDPA'S REACTION TO my being gay may have been low-key. Supper, however, proved to be anything but. At issue? Cigarettes. When Mom confronted Grandpa about sneaking out with Ishmael, he initially denied it. After a few minutes of them going back and forth over why Melvin would "make up" such a story, I asked him if he'd maybe gone out with "Isaac" to keep him company. He admitted that he had and said accepting the cigarette was just being sociable. That confession was followed by a lengthy lecture from Mom about his emphysema and the dangers of smoking, especially at his age. She laid the guilt on thick, and Dad jumped in every now and then to appeal to Grandpa's "good sense"—something Mom seriously doubted he had.

By the time I'd excused myself, rinsed my plate, and gone to my room, the discussion was still going strong. An hour or so later, when I went to take a shower, they were still at it. I wouldn't have been surprised if I'd come out for breakfast the next morning and found them still at it then. If there was one thing Grandpa and Mom shared, it was the joy of a good argument.

The drive to school the next morning was the gloomiest in over a month, but at least it wasn't as cold as it had been in the last few days. A light breeze revealed that the featured item on the day's lunchroom menu was to be meatloaf and rice. Chadham High was the only place I knew where you could stick a fork in a scoop of rice and eat it like a candied apple.

Doris was sullen when our paths crossed on the way to first period. Her eyes were tired and baggy, and she yawned before speaking.

"Hope got suspended—two weeks, followed by a week of in-school suspension."

"How'd you find out?"

"From her parents. They called to tell my parents it was all my fault that Hope got drunk. Apparently, they still think it was a one-time thing."

"What was your parents' reaction?"

Doris scoffed and rolled her eyes. "My mother actually searched my room, Ben. She searched my room *after* I told her I didn't have anything to do with Hope's alcohol problem. It would have been embarrassing if it didn't make me so mad I could spit."

"Did Hope's folks say anything about getting her some treatment?"

"They're going to talk to their priest and take it from there apparently. Oh, they're also thinking about making her finish out high school at St. Dominic's."

"That won't help her drinking any."

"You're telling me. They wanted to put her in St. Dominic's when we were freshmen, but she pitched a fit and said she'd had enough of religion as it was. They went around and around about it for a couple of weeks. Finally, their priest suggested it would be all right for her to continue in the public school system."

BY WEDNESDAY, IT became clear the only bright spot in Hope's suspension, if you could call it that, was that Doris and I were talking again. She was taking Hope's rejection hard and needed someone to confide in. But it was so awkward whenever we passed Ted in the hall or saw him in class. The grimace he always shot us made it clear any misguided lovesickness he might have harbored for Doris had ended the moment her fist made contact with his eye. And of course, as far as he was concerned, I was still Dracula, intent on sucking his brother's blood.

When I stepped outside after school, warm sunshine invigorated every inch of my body, giving me an emotional boost. Everyone felt it. People were smiling, and the way some people strutted to their cars, I half expected them to break into a dance. For me, the moment would have been perfect if I could have found a place to kiss Adrian.

I got out at the center feeling great and jogged inside. Grandpa was sitting with his politics buddies, listening intently to what one of them was saying. I saw Mrs. Gilder wandering around and gave her a wide berth. Mr. Lehmann chatted with me for a few minutes to update me on Herman's condition and the hope he'd be coming back soon. Time passed quickly, and before I knew it, the supper bell was ringing, and the daytime clients began congregating near the front door.

I found Grandpa still sitting at his political coffee klatch table.

"Hey, Grandpa, ready to go home for supper?"

He stood up, leaned forward with a hand resting on the table for support, and sighed.

"I'm a little tired tonight, Ben. Could you give me a hand?"

I flagged Jamal over and asked him to help Grandpa to the door while I brought the car around. When I pulled up, Jamal was standing next to a bench where Grandpa sat looking tired and winded. We bundled him into the car and got his seatbelt on him.

Every block or so, I glanced over to check how he was doing. He wasn't looking any better. Even in the dim streetlight, I could see that whatever was happening was getting worse. He looked so bad it began to frighten me.

We were two blocks away from home when he started coughing. It was a deep, throaty, congested cough, and I began to worry he was dying. I sped up, torn between going on home or taking him straight to the hospital. But the coughing lessened, so I decided to take him home and let my parents decide what to do. My hands were shaking, but I managed to cover the last block without being too reckless.

I honked the horn as we pulled into the driveway and then jumped out and ran around to the passenger door. Dad looked out the kitchen window and saw the panic on my face.

I unfastened Grandpa's seatbelt, but when he turned to get out, he leaned forward and started coughing again. I guessed Dad had called to Mom because the two of them came running.

"What's the matter?" Dad asked.

"I don't know. He said he felt a little weak, but then he had a coughing fit on the way home, and...look at him."

Grandpa's hands were on his knees. The cough took on a deeper sound. In the driveway light, his skin was a pale gray.

Then he choked and threw up.

I was no expert in vomit, but even I could see this puke was bad news. It was a dark brown, almost black color. He groaned and wretched and kept bringing more of it up.

Mom ran back to the kitchen. I could see her turning off the stove and moving a pot from the burner. She grabbed the telephone, dialed a number, and spoke a few hurried words.

Meanwhile, Dad was standing out of the line of fire, a hand under Grandpa's arm to steady him.

Mom came out with a damp towel and wiped Grandpa's chin, which was spattered with throw up.

"Ben, get in the car and help your father get him back in his seatbelt."

I ran to the driver's door and jumped in, picked up Grandpa's left leg, and set his foot down on the floorboard. Dad stepped around the puddle of vomit and did the same with his right leg, then he pulled the belt around him and passed it to me.

Mom ran into the kitchen and came back out, shoving a thick manila envelope in her bag and slamming the door behind her. She set a smallish trash can in Grandpa's lap.

"Pop, if you need to throw up again, do it in this."

To my shock, Mom and Dad both jumped in the backseat.

"Ben, put your seatbelt on. We're going to the emergency room. Don't speed, just move."

I started the engine, and the four of us began the trip to the hospital.

Chapter Twelve

WE PULLED UP at the emergency room. Dad jumped out and garnered two of the staff who ran over with a wheelchair and began carefully removing Grandpa from the car.

Mom leaned forward and said, "Ben, you park the car and join us inside."

It took me forever to find a parking space. When I raced inside, Mom was talking with one of the administrators, showing her power of attorney in dealing with Grandpa's medical issues and signing him in. Dad was standing near a doorway watching as doctors and nurses examined Grandpa.

"What's wrong with him?" I asked.

"That's what we're here to find out. But coughing up blood is not a good sign."

"That was blood?"

"I'm pretty sure so, yeah. Given his emphysema, it's not surprising."

We were there for over two hours before one of the doctors came out to us.

"You're Mr. Blackburn's family?"

"Yes, I'm his daughter Margot Carpenter. This is my husband Ethan and my son Ben. How is my father?"

"He's coughing up blood, which you already know— I understand he has emphysema."

Mom nodded.

"There are several possible causes for the hemoptysis. We'll need to do some tests and take an X-ray to narrow the possibilities."

"Marty also has Alzheimer's," Dad said.

"Good information. That'll help us interpret some of his symptoms. So, we're going to admit him and evacuate the congestion in his stomach and lungs overnight. Tomorrow, we'll have him X-rayed and begin running tests. My advice for you all is to go home. He's not in any immediate danger based on what we know so far. Get a good night's sleep and come back tomorrow. He'll be in ICU."

Mom and Dad thanked her. Mom got permission to peek in on Grandpa before we left, and the three of us stepped out to a cool, cloudless night with a crescent moon shining weakly above the city glow.

"Is Grandpa going to be all right?" I asked, leading them to the car.

"We can only hope," Mom said.

The drive home was quiet and depressing. No one voiced their fears, but we were all brooding over the dark possible outcomes looming on the horizon.

It was running for ten when we got home. Mom began resurrecting supper—spaghetti. None of us was very hungry, but we did eat some before putting everything away for leftovers.

I went to my room and lay on the bed staring at the ceiling. Before recent events changed everything for me at school, I'd have called Ted, or Doris, or Hope to unburden myself about the emotional strain I'd just gone through. Now, the only one I could even consider calling was Doris. On the other hand, she'd have probably been the one I'd have called anyway since she had experience dealing with her grandmother's illness. But somehow, the fact that she was now the only one I *could* call made things more depressing. So, instead of calling her, I moped around for an hour or so before getting undressed and going to bed

THE NEXT MORNING, after my shower, I joined Mom and Dad in the kitchen. They were both taking the day off to be at the hospital. I halfheartedly asked whether I should skip school and join them, but they both said absolutely not—I was to go to school and put in my time at the senior center. If anything serious came up, they'd call to let me know.

I didn't make a fuss. The truth was, I really didn't want to go anyway. The hospital smelled funny, and I didn't like being around all those sick people, not to mention there was nothing to do but sit around and wait.

The drive to school turned out to be the loneliest since I'd gotten my own car. I really missed having Ted to talk to. And if that wasn't depressing enough, right as I pulled onto the access road to Chadham High, a light rain began to fall—not enough to drench you, but enough to leave you damp and chilly the rest of the morning.

As soon as I saw Doris, I said, "Hey, my grandfather's in the hospital. He had some kind of fit and started coughing up blood last night."

"I'm so sorry. Is he going to be all right?"

"We don't know. They're going to X-ray him today and run some tests. We're pretty worried."

"No duh. It sounds serious, especially if they have to run tests to find out what's causing it. Is there anything I can do?"

"Just keep him in…in your thoughts."

She smiled and squeezed my arm. "Sure thing; I'll even pray for him. I don't suppose the God of Israel would turn away the prayer of a Christian."

"No, I guess not. Thanks, Doris."

We walked a little farther.

"Hey, have you heard anything from Hope?"

"No. And after that call from her parents the other night, I don't think they'd appreciate me checking in to see how she's doing."

I shook my head. "Mark my words—They're going to be no help to her at all. They'll just point their fingers at anybody and everybody because they're afraid someone might point the finger at them."

"Right."

I SPENT THE rest of the day feeling tired and listless. The only bright spot came when I saw Adrian during morning break. I filled him in on what had happened, and he said to let him know whatever I needed. He asked me if I wanted him to come over after supper, but I told him it probably wasn't a good idea since I didn't know what I'd find when I got home.

Of course, at the end of the school day, I found him waiting by my car.

"I missed my ride," he said, shrugging his shoulder.

"Oh? How did you manage to do that?"

"Easy—I told Tyler to go on home without me."

I couldn't help but smile. I really did want some time with him.

We drove to my house and parked the car. Then we spent a few minutes swapping spit before I had to drive on to the center. As I watched him waving at me from the rearview mirror, I sighed. It was funny. Nothing had changed. I'd still lost two of my best friends. Grandpa was still in the hospital, and no one knew what was going to happen. But, my God, being with Adrian made me feel like everything was going to work out—at least for the moment.

By the time I got to the center, however, I was back to worrying about Grandpa again. No sooner had I come inside than Artie walked over to me.

"Hey, Ben. I didn't expect you today. Your father called this morning and told me what happened to Marty. How are you holding up?"

"Frankly? I'm exhausted, and I still don't know what's going on because I haven't heard from my folks all day."

"Come on—let's go to the break room and call the hospital."

A Rolodex beside the phone had cards for a bunch of doctors and every unit at the hospital.

"They said he'd be in ICU," I said as Artie looked through the directory.

He dialed the number and waited.

"Hi, I'm calling from Temple Beth Israel Senior Center. I've got Marty Blackburn's grandson here. Would either of his parents, Mr. or Mrs. Carpenter, be able to come to the phone?" He paused for a bit and continued, "Yes, we'll wait. Thank you."

After a few minutes, he handed me the receiver.

"Hello?"

"Dad, it's me. I'm at the senior center. How's Grandpa?"

He hesitated for a second before answering.

"Ben, we don't have the full picture yet, but what we do know isn't good. The X-ray showed several spots on his lungs that weren't there when he was X-rayed in September. That means cancer. The lab tests will take a while before we know what kind."

I was stunned.

"I'm glad you went to the center, son," Dad said. "You don't need to be bumming around the house by yourself, and frankly, there's nothing you can do here. Finish out your time at the center, and by the time you get home, one or the other of us should be there or on the way. Can you put one of the staff on?"

I handed the phone back to Artie.

"Yes, Mr. Carpenter, this is Artie. If there's anything we can do, just name it... Yes... No, he seems to be holding up okay... I see... No, it's not a problem. Glad to... Yes...You're all in our prayers. Bye."

He hung up the phone and gave me an appraising glance.

"Your dad's worried about you. You didn't tell me how scary things were last night."

I looked away before answering, and when I did, it all came out in a rush. "It was kind of embarrassing. He started coughing in the car, and he looked so bad, and I thought he was dying. Then when we got home, he started throwing up this black stuff, and Dad said it was blood. He threw up. A lot. And they made me be the one to drive to the hospital. And I was so scared."

"That *does* sound scary. And yet you got him home and then got him to the hospital without panicking."

"Without panicking? Are you kidding? I felt like I was falling apart the whole time."

"That's a natural response in an emergency. The important thing though is that despite your fear, you held it all together. That shows maturity and fortitude."

"Yeah, but, Artie, sometimes I just wish I could be a kid again and not have to deal with mature things."

He smiled and gave me a hug.

"We all do, believe me. I'm proud of you, just the same. And your folks are too. As Marty would say, you're becoming a real *mensch*."

We both laughed.

SATURDAY MORNING, MOM and Dad had gone to the hospital to talk with the doctors. At about ten o'clock, they called me with the news. All of Grandpa's test results were in. He had an aggressive cancer, and treating it would be complicated because of his emphysema. In addition, the cancer would likely quicken the pace of his Alzheimer's. Therefore, the doctors recommended he should be admitted to a hospice. They'd mentioned a few, but Mom and Dad decided to talk things over with Dr. Markov first, as she'd told them the senior center was equipped to provide palliative care. Ultimately, it was decided Grandpa would come home for Thanksgiving and become a resident at the center soon afterward.

Since I had nothing else to do and didn't want to sit around all day worrying about Grandpa, I decided to put in some extra time at the center. While I drove, I mulled things over. On the one hand, thinking about Doris's grandmother, I found the whole idea of sending Grandpa to any center distressing. On the other hand, I didn't really know much about the place Doris's grandmother had gone to, but I was very familiar with the senior center by now, and I trusted the staff. In the end, I just didn't like the idea of Grandpa dying.

I'd finished a game of dominos with Mr. Levine when I noticed Melvin standing in the bookstore doorway. He waved me over and asked if I'd look after the place while he took a quick break. I said sure and perched myself on the stool behind the register.

It didn't take him long to return.

He flashed me an ironic smile as he came in. "How was business while I was gone? Booming?"

"Oh, yeah, I'm exhausted. I don't know how any one person can handle it on their own."

He laughed. "I'll have you know I'm a professional. It really did get busy in here a couple of hours ago though. I actually had *two* customers at the same time, and one of them bought an expensive hardback."

"Ooo."

"Say, that reminds me," Melvin said. "The guy gave me a fifty, and when I went to put it under the money tray, I found this." He held up the card Mr. Marcel had left with me. "Do you know anything about it?"

"Yeah, this guy came in a few weeks ago looking for somebody. I didn't recognize the name, but I told him I was new, and he left his card so I could ask around for him. Truth is, I clean forgot about it."

"That's funny."

"Why?"

"Because you didn't recognize the name, but you do know the man he was looking for."

"I do?"

"Yeah. Let me explain. Before Dr. Markov took over, the previous director was real formal. Our name tags listed our initials and last name—you know, like in the army or something. Mine was M. J. Goldstein. Anyway, that's how Artie became Artie. See, Artie isn't his name; it's a nickname. His real name is Robert Duncan Warren—R. D. Warren, get it? Since 'R. D.' sounds an awful lot like 'Artie,' that's what people here started calling him, and it's what he's gone by ever since."

He handed me the card. I looked at the name I'd jotted down and read it out loud.

"Bobby Warren."

"That's our Artie. I'll let you pass along the card to him."

"I haven't seen him today."

"He'll be here at two."

I stepped out the bookstore thinking about the man who'd left the card. I'd told him I would ask around for him, and then I forgot all about it like some untrustworthy kid. The least I could do was make it up to him.

I went to the break room, picked up the phone, and dialed the number.

"Hello?"

"Hi, Mr. Marcel? It's Benjamin Carpenter. You met me in the bookstore at Temple Beth Israel Senior Center a few weeks ago. Listen, I've found Bobby Warren for you."

Five seconds of dead silence followed.

"You...you're sure? Let me get a pencil."

"No need for that. If you can come to the senior center at say two o'clock this afternoon, I'll make sure you get to talk to him."

"You don't know what this means to me. I can't thank you enough."

"My pleasure. See you at two."

AT QUARTER TO two, Mr. Marcel came in. He was wearing a stylish pullover, pleated slacks, and polished shoes. I strutted up to him, all smiles.

"Mr. Marcel, hi. Bobby's not here yet, but if you'll come with me, I'll take you to where you and he can talk when he gets here."

We went into the break room where I pulled up a chair for him and told him I'd be back soon.

Artie arrived right at two o'clock on the dot. I was waiting for him only a few feet from the break room door and motioned for him to join me.

As he crossed the hall, I went inside.

"Mr. Marcel, he'll be here in just a second."

Artie leaned in through the doorway. "Hey, Ben, what's up? How's your—"

Mr. Marcel stood up and took a step forward.

"Bobby."

Artie stared at him with wide eyes, his mouth hanging loose, the color draining from his face.

"Nick...?" he whispered. "I thought you were dead."

Now I was confused. Who was Nick?

Artie covered the four steps that separated them in a flash. He brought his hands up, and at first, I thought he was going to hug him. But as soon as he reached him, he shoved him hard in the chest. I gasped in shock as Mr. Marcel staggered back from the blow but made no response.

Artie retreated a step, his fists in a clench, his chest heaving. "Do you have any idea what I went through for you?"

His voice was strained, his words a low hiss. "For four years, every time the phone rang, I prayed it was you."

He was shaking, his breaths coming in gulps as he tried to control himself. "And everyone said you were dead. But I kept hoping, and hoping. And nothing."

Mr. Marcel just stood there, listening, his focus zeroed in on Artie's eyes.

"Then after twenty-two years, you just show up like nothing ever happened?"

Artie raised his fists again, and I was certain he was going to hit him. But he threw them down, turned, and stormed out, slamming the door behind him.

After a moment of shock, Mr. Marcel ran after him, and I followed. Artie was already halfway out the entrance door when we emerged from the break room. By the time we got outside, his car was racing out of the parking lot.

"I'm so sorry, Mr. Marcel. I didn't know he'd react like that."

"How could you?" he said, straightening up. "Anyway, it went about as well as could have been expected."

As he walked away, Melvin came out and stood next to me.

"That's the guy who left the card? Who is he? Artie took off like a bat out of Hell."

"I'm not sure, but I think he's Artie's long-lost friend from high school."

"Not the happiest of reunions, I guess."

"That would be one way of putting it."

SUNDAY, MY PARENTS and I went to the hospital. When we arrived at ICU, they told us they were preparing to transfer Grandpa to a regular room. While the nurses were getting him ready, I noted a corridor marked CICU, so I walked over to the nurse's station where a nurse was writing a note in a ledger.

"Excuse me," I said. "I have a friend in CICU—Herman Topolski. I know visits are supposed to be limited to family members, but Herman doesn't have any family in the area. Would it be all right if I just said a brief hello and let him know all his friends are thinking about him?"

"That sounds like something I'm sure he'd appreciate. Come on."

He accompanied me down the CICU corridor, which had its own nurse's station, and after explaining things to them, they showed me to Herman's room.

He appeared to be dozing. His eyes were closed, and his interlaced hands were resting on his stomach. Several cords stuck out of his hospital gown leading to a heart monitor beeping away next to the bed. A table held a small bouquet of flowers and a single get-well card.

"Mr. Topolski, you have a visitor."

He didn't respond. The nurse cocked his head in Herman's direction.

I cleared my throat. "Herman? Are you asleep?"

"Am I asleep? No, I'm driving to Cleveland."

Then he opened his eyes. As soon as he saw me, he smiled.

"Why, if it isn't my old friend Benjamin. How are you, Benjamin?"

"I'm fine. How are you feeling?"

"I'm bored to death, and I'm exhausted. Every time a man tries to take a nap in here, they wake him up. Then they leave you with nothing but this *fakakta* torture machine"—he cocked his head in the direction of the heart monitor—"with its beep-beep-beep. I'm telling you, Benjamin, this is why people end up in the loony bin."

"Wow, I'm sorry, Herman. Would they let you read if you had a book?"

"How should I know? That's another thing—they don't tell you nothing about nothing."

I turned to the nurse, and he nodded.

"I'll see if I can find you something good to read. In the meantime, tell them they have to get you better soon because everybody at the center misses you."

Herman tsked and rolled his eyes.

"No, it's true. Mr. Lehmann especially told me he misses you."

"Lehmann? He misses trying to cheat is all he misses. I'm warning you, Benjamin. Don't play backgammon with him."

"He's not that bad."

"Suit yourself. Just remember, if you play with a cat, you can't complain when you get scratched."

"Maybe he just needs you there to help him stay honest."

Herman grinned.

The nurse quietly cleared his throat.

"I've got to go. But it's so nice to see you."

"Benjamin, it's good to see you too."

"I'd have come sooner, but they said visitors weren't allowed."

"Then how did you get in? What? Did you bribe the guard?"

"No, my grandfather's in ICU, and they're transferring him today. So I asked if they'd let me just say a quick hello."

"Your grandfather? Which one is he?"

"Marty, Marty Blackburn."

"Oh, yes. Well, tell him I hope he feels better soon."

"I will. And Herman, we all want you to get better soon too."

"Thank you, my friend."

He held out his hand, I shook it and started back to the main ICU unit with a smile on my face. It felt good to know I'd brightened Herman's day, if only for a few minutes. I made a mental note to ask around the center and get him a book he might like.

Dad noticed me coming out from CICU.

"Ben, what were you doing in there?"

"One of the guys at the center had a heart attack a few weeks ago. I just wanted to drop in and let him know everyone wants him to get better soon."

"Oh. Well, that's nice. Come on, they're ready to transfer your grandfather."

Grandpa was sitting in a wheelchair with an IV bag dripping into a tube sticking out of his arm. We followed as they wheeled him to an elevator, down a hallway, and into a more standard-sized room with a bed, large cushioned chair, TV, and a couple of visitors' chairs.

While they were helping him from the wheelchair to the cushioned chair, I looked him over. It was the first time I'd seen him since the night we'd taken him to the emergency room. His arms hung limply at his side. He was pale, and he appeared thinner and smaller.

Mom took a seat across from him.

"How's this, Pop? A step-up from ICU, huh?"

He looked at her and blinked, but he didn't say anything.

Dad perched himself at the foot of the bed.

"Marty, the doctor said if you behave yourself over the next couple of days, we can bring you home for Thanksgiving—turkey, stuffing, all the dishes you like."

Grandpa had turned to him when he started speaking but didn't react.

I got a sinking feeling in my stomach.

"Grandpa," I said. "Herman Topolski from the center is in here. I just saw him, and he said to tell you he hopes you feel better soon."

Grandpa nodded and spoke for the first time since I'd seen him.

"You mean Herman the hermit," he said.

His voice was weak and raspy, but I found it encouraging he remembered Herman at all. Then he sighed and looked at Mom.

"Where's Ilana? She should have been here an hour ago."

The sinking feeling in my stomach returned like a large rock crashing to earth.

"She's not coming today, Marty," Dad said.

Grandpa nodded.

We stayed with him for a half hour or so. When it became clear he was getting tired, Dad and I helped him get in bed, and the three of us said goodbye. Mom had some last-minute things to discuss with the nurses and told Dad and me she'd follow us out in a couple of minutes.

We took the elevator down and started walking to the car.

"Why does he keep asking about Grandma?"

"Alzheimer's doesn't just make someone forgetful. Sometimes, they get confused and kind of relive a memory. They can even talk to you and think they're talking to someone else."

"We have a lady at the center who confuses me with her son all the time."

"Sounds like she's got Alzheimer's too."

"Yeah. But Grandpa wasn't that bad Wednesday night. What happened?"

"The doctors said that physical trauma can sometimes make the Alzheimer's worse. When he had that spell Wednesday night, I guess it kicked it into high gear."

"So he won't get any better?"

"He might have moments when he's more clearheaded, but Ben, in the end, it's only going to get worse. I'm afraid it's only a matter of time before we lose him."

"I feel like I've only just started getting to know him."

Dad wrapped an arm around my shoulder and said, "Marty's always been quite a guy. Make the most of the time you have left with him. You'll get memories you'll treasure forever."

ADRIAN CAME OVER later after we got back home. He asked me about Grandpa, and I told him how weak and confused he was. When he asked how I was doing, I told him how bad the whole situation made me feel, and he gave me a hug. Lying there in his arms, listening to music and cuddling, the stress I'd been under melted away. Peaceful and whole now, it was like I wasn't complete when I was away from him. The touch of his lips on my cheek almost took my breath away.

We'd been quietly lying in each other's arms for a while when he spoke up.

"Hey, Ben, I've got an idea."

"Always a dangerous announcement."

He pretend swatted my arm.

"Silly. I want to start riding to school with you. That way, we'll be guaranteed a little time alone every day."

"Won't Tyler think it's odd for you to suddenly dump him for your brother's former best friend?"

"Nah, I'll just tell him that my mom said it wasn't right for me to ride with them since it's out of Toby's way."

"What about soccer?"

"That's different. I could still ride home with him on those days."

"And when he sees you riding with me instead of Ted?"

"Tyler won't think twice about it. He thinks Ted's as big a jerk as I do."

"Well, the idea of starting the day with a good morning kiss does have its appeal."

"Yes, it does. I'll tell Tyler tomorrow morning, and ride home with you after school."

"But you know, Ted will definitely find out, and it'll irritate him to no end."

"I don't care. All the better."

I grinned. "You are so devious, I should spank you."

He pulled me close. "Shut up and kiss me."

IT WAS THANKSGIVING week—only three days of school before that glorious four-day weekend—and the clock was ticking for that 3:00 PM Wednesday afternoon prize. For me, it was officially the slowest Monday in the history of the world, and I counted down the minutes to the end of the day. If not for the two brief encounters with Adrian in the hall I think I would have screamed. But just seeing him made me smile and wish we could be like other couples and hold hands or share a hug in public. Straight kids didn't know how good they had it.

When the bell finally rang, butterflies fluttered inside me. Adrian standing by my car was the most beautiful thing I'd ever seen. We held hands on the drive to my house and spent ten wonderful minutes necking before I had to leave for the center. Knowing I'd see him again in the morning made my whole body sizzle. I loved him so much it suddenly struck me to wonder if maybe he was the proof of God's existence I'd been waiting for.

But I was a little apprehensive about going to the center. I hadn't seen Artie since that disastrous meeting between him and Mr. Marcel and didn't know what to expect.

No sooner had I entered the building than Artie headed my way.

"Hey, Ben. Let's take a minute to chat in the break room."

As we crossed the hall, I was filled with anxiety. Would he ball me out? Was he going to terminate my community service? I'd be screwed academically if he did. And coming to the center had become such an essential part of my life that I'd miss it terribly if he banished me.

He closed the door behind us, grabbed a chair, and motioned for me to do the same. He sat, leaning forward, with his forearms and clasped hands on the table.

"Artie, about Saturday—"

"Ben, I want to apologize. I shouldn't have acted the way I did with Nick, and especially not in front of you. It was wrong, and I'm sure it upset you. I'm sorry."

"Artie, *I'm* sorry. The guy came in looking for you weeks ago, but I didn't know your real name then. He left his card, and I forgot all about it. Then, when Melvin explained things to me about your name, I thought instead of just giving you the card, I'd have the guy come in to meet with you. That was wrong. I didn't know why he wanted to see you, and it was wrong to take you by surprise like that. I should have just given you the card. I thought I was doing something nice, but it wasn't, and I'm sorry."

"Ben, you're not at fault. The truth is, Nick and I both put you in a bad spot. Again, I'm sorry."

"You keep calling him Nick, but the card he left gave his name as Vincent Marcel. I don't understand."

Artie shook his head. "'Vincent Marcel.' I should have known. Of course, he wouldn't know I'd recognize the name—which makes it all worse."

"I don't get it."

"Vincent Marcel is Nicholas Horton. Remember when I told you about someone I fell in love with in high school? That was Nick. After everybody found out about us, he disappeared, and people assumed he'd killed himself.

"Well, the night I graduated from Chadham High, his father gave me a journal he'd found that Nick had been keeping when we were together. In it, I found a picture he'd drawn of me—an unbelievably good one—and he'd signed it *Vincent Marcel.* I guess he thought a name like Nicholas Horton wasn't fitting for an artist. Do you still have that card?"

I pulled out my wallet and handed the card to him.

"I was right. 'Vincent Marcel—portrait artist and illustrator.' So that's how he survived all this time—by using his gift as an artist. Nicholas Horton disappears, and Vincent Marcel is born."

"So what are you going to do?"

"I don't know—" He leaned back in his chair. "I waited for him, Ben. I've waited for him since I was fifteen years old. I never met another man I could love like I loved Nicholas. And all that time, not a word from him—nothing. Okay, he wrote in his journal that he thought I blamed him for us being outed, but he should have known me better than that. If he'd just called me, I'd have told him I still cared. He *should* have called me. I've had a broken heart for him all these years, and now he just shows up out of the blue."

Artie hung his head and fell silent.

I cleared my throat. "Take some advice from a rank amateur?"

He looked up at me, his eyes misty.

"When I recently hit a rough spot with the one I love, a very wise man told me we should talk things out, and it was the best advice I ever got. Let me ask you something you once asked me. What does your heart tell you?"

He tilted his head to one side and smiled. "I need more time to process all of this."

"Then that's what you should do. Take your time, and don't make a hasty decision. I do have one question though."

"What's that?"

"Should I call you Artie or Bobby?"

He laughed. "Around here, the residents and clients call me Artie, so out there, I'm Artie. But my friends all call me Bobby, and you are my friend."

SOMETIME THAT AFTERNOON, my sister Eliana had arrived from college for Thanksgiving. I knew she was coming, but not exactly when, so it was a nice surprise to find her in the kitchen talking to Mom and Dad when I got home from the center.

"Eliana, you're home," I said, running over and hugging her. "Welcome home. I've missed you so much."

"I've missed you too."

Then she whispered in my ear, "You'll have to tell me all about the boy I saw you making out with in the car earlier."

I smiled, even if my cheeks did feel a little warm.

The joy of having Eliana home gave some balance to our sadness over Grandpa's condition. Having the four of us together again made us each feel a little better. We all took a hand in preparing supper—well, Mom, Eliana, and I did. We let Dad get the salad dressing from the fridge and grab the croutons from the cupboard.

Soon, we were enjoying our first meal together since Eliana had left for Dickerson. She answered all our questions about her life at college and told us about the friends she'd made and her classes. It all sounded so exciting, I imagined being there and doing all the things she told us about.

Then Eliana said, "Enough about me. How about you, Ben? How are things going at school?"

"Not great."

"Having trouble in one of your classes?"

"No. Hope got suspended."

Eliana's mouth fell open. "Suspended? What on earth would Hope be suspended for?"

"It turns out, she's got a drinking problem. They caught her totally wasted and gave her a two-week suspension. She doesn't come back until next week, if she comes back at all. Doris thinks her parents might send her to St. Dominic's."

"I never would have suspected Hope of having a drinking problem," Dad said.

"Us neither; it was a shock."

Eliana shook her head. "Poor Doris, I bet she's beside herself."

"She's devastated. It's not been easy for either of us."

Dad looked up. "Either of you? What about Ted?"

"He's not talking to us. It's complicated."

"Is that why you've been hanging out with Adrian so much recently?"

I glanced at my mother. She gave an encouraging nod. Eliana's eyes were gleaming as she began to put two and two together.

"Well...you see, Dad...it turns out Adrian's gay, and we're kind of seeing each other. Ted doesn't like that much."

"I see," Dad said, nodding his head. "I trust you boys are being smart enough to use protection."

I dropped my fork. "Oh my God! Is that all the two of you ever think about? We aren't doing anything to *need* protection."

Mom and Eliana started sniggering, and Dad smiled.

I turned to my sister. "Eliana, did they do this to you?"

She bobbed her head up and down. "Yup."

"You could have warned me. Why, oh why, couldn't I have the kind of parents who *don't* talk to their kids about sex?"

I took my plate to the sink and began scraping it. A knock sounded at the door, and my folks new fit of giggling told me Adrian was outside.

"I'm going for a drive," I said, rushing to finish cleaning up. "I'll be back later."

Adrian noticed my flushed cheeks as I hurried him to the car. He patted my leg as I backed out of the driveway.

"More open and honest communication with the parental units?"

"It's like my whole family is sex-obsessed."

He tsked. "My family acts like sex doesn't exist."

"You have no idea how lucky you are."

We drove to the park and found a quiet spot, and I took him in my arms. As I kissed him, Grandpa's remark about necking in the backseat ran through my mind, and I smiled.

We made out for the next twenty minutes or so, and would have stayed there longer, except for the cop car that pulled up beside us. The officer saw us in each other's arms kissing, honked the horn, and motioned for us to move along.

I was mortified, but Adrian laughed out loud.

"I bet he's thinking we're the sex-obsessed ones now," he said.

I rolled my eyes and turned onto the street. "If you weren't so cute, I'd pop you one."

He leaned over and kissed me below my ear. The car swerved.

"And if you keep that up, I'll wind up wrecking us."

He grinned and kissed me on the cheek, and we held hands the rest of the way home.

"WOW. SO MUCH drama."

Eliana and I were sitting on my bed. I'd just finished telling her about how my friendship with Hope, Ted, and Doris had been thrown into chaos.

"My friends and I never had that much drama when I was a junior."

I stared at a photo of the four of us and frowned. "I don't know if things will ever be the same again."

"They probably can't be. But that doesn't necessarily mean what comes out of it will have to be bad. People change as they get older, and sometimes these things have to happen for everybody to recognize the change. That's how relationships grow."

"Or end," I said.

"So, tell me. How did you hook Adrian? I didn't even recognize him. And when did he get so cute?"

"He's always been cute," I said. "And to tell you the truth, I didn't hook him. *He* hooked me."

"That little stud. You must feel very flattered."

"I just worry that he's so young, you know. I don't want him to get hurt, and Ted's a real problem. Adrian says if I stand up to him, he'll eventually accept us, but I'm not so sure."

"Oh my, are you falling in love with him?"

I looked down and shrugged a shoulder.

"You are, aren't you? Aw, Benjamin, that's so sweet."

"I've kind of dreamed about the two of us going to Dickerson and living together, but..."

"But what?"

"I'll be gone two years before he graduates."

"Are you worried about him missing you? Or are you worried he'll move on?"

"A little of both, I guess. Two years is a long time. Anything could happen."

"If you two really are in love—I mean not just going through some schoolboy crush—you'll survive those two years."

"Yeah, but a lot of things can change in two years."

"Yes they can, and if it's real love, those changes will only make your love grow stronger."

"Mom said if Ted doesn't accept us, we should break up. She said it's wrong to come between two brothers. I tried to do it, but it hurt Adrian so bad I couldn't."

Eliana leaned back and rested on her elbows.

"Ben, Mom's big on family. I don't know, maybe it's a Jewish thing or something. But you and Adrian have to do what's right for you. Like I said, if it's love, you'll survive it."

"And if we don't?"

She gave me a hug. "If you don't, you'll be hurt and feel really bad. But it won't last forever, and you'll grow because of it. And, hey, the fact that you're worried about it makes me think maybe you two really *are* in love."

We sat in silence for a few minutes, and then she looked at me with a half smile.

"So *have* you two done it yet?"

I rolled my eyes. "My God, my whole family is nothing but a bunch of sex maniacs. No. Adrian wants to, but I'm not sure he's old enough to handle it. The last thing I'd want would be for something like that to scar him."

She stood up and tousled my hair.

"No doubt about it, little brother. You are definitely smitten."

I WOKE UP the next morning to find Adrian on the bed next to me nibbling on my earlobe and sending my body into its highest state of arousal.

"How did you get in here?"

"Your sister. I thought college students were supposed to sleep in when they had time off."

"She's always been an early riser," I said, yawning.

He looked me over with a wry smile.

"Seems she's not the only one."

He started to move in for a kiss, but I held him off.

"You better wait until I brush my teeth. Dad says my morning breath can peel wallpaper."

With an exaggerated pout, he slowly got up, letting his hand accidentally brush against me.

"In the state I'm in, you're living dangerously," I said.

"Hey, danger is my middle name."

I tousled his hair and went to my dresser, grabbing a clean T-shirt and boxers. Then I rushed to the bathroom to take care of business.

When I came back in, drying my hair with a towel, he was sitting in my chair flipping through the pages of *US Weekly*.

He looked up and gave a wolf whistle.

"Ben, you should really wear shorts more often. You've got great legs."

"Sir, you flatter me. But I suspected all along you only wanted me for my looks."

"Well, I do have to admit that even if you weren't so lovable, those legs alone would be a mighty temptation."

I threw on some trousers, a long-sleeved shirt, and socks and shoes. After sharing a proper good-morning kiss, he followed me to the kitchen.

Dad was reading the paper and munching on a piece of toast. Mom was at the counter reviewing notes she had written on a pad. Eliana gave me a big wink from over her bowl of cereal.

"Good morning, Adrian," Dad said. "Can we get you anything? Something to eat? Juice? Coffee?"

"No, thank you, Mr. Carpenter."

"Well," Mom said, "now that Ben's here... Your father and I are going to meet with Dr. Markov later this morning and fill out the paperwork for Grandpa Marty to be admitted to the center."

Eliana frowned. "You mean he won't be home for Thanksgiving? I haven't even had a chance to see him yet."

"We're not going to admit him right away," Dad said after taking a sip of his coffee. "Dr. Markov told us we could leave the actual admission date open-ended. Doing it this way, everything at the center will be already arranged for when it becomes necessary. Until then, we go back to life as usual. So, Ben, you'll still be bringing him home from the center, except for days when he has to go in for treatments."

"How long will he be able to stay at home?" Eliana asked.

"Unfortunately, it won't be long," Mom said. "It all depends on the cancer treatments, his emphysema, and the Alzheimer's progression. Anyway, if things work out, I'll be bringing him home later today, or by tomorrow at the latest, so we'll all be together for Thanksgiving."

"Good," Eliana and I both said.

"And after Thanksgiving, we'll take things one day at a time."

I WAS SO preoccupied thinking about Grandpa that I wasn't much company for Adrian on his first ride to school with me. We were both quiet most of the way, but as we drew near Chadham High, he cleared his throat.

"So your grandfather's got cancer *and* emphysema."

"Yeah."

"I'm so sorry."

"Yeah, me too. When I first heard he was coming to live with us, I wasn't very happy about it. He's embarrassed me more times over the years than I can count. But...now that he's been here awhile, I've gotten used to him. Oh, he has his moments, but he can be funny, and he paid half for my car, and—oh, with everything going on, I forgot to tell you—he knows I'm gay and that you're my boyfriend, and he's okay with it. He even said you're a nice boy."

I heaved a sigh. "He's become a real part of my life, and I thought he'd be around for years. Then—boom—just like that, everything's going downhill."

We turned onto the service road to Chadham High, and I parked the car.

Adrian leaned over and hugged me.

"I know you're upset about what your grandfather's going through. Just remember that I'm here for you, whatever you need."

We'd no sooner started walking to the building than I saw Ted standing with his arms crossed, waiting for us just outside. Over the last week, his black eye had faded to a greenish yellow, making him look like some cheap hoodlum. Right then, the expression on his face made him look positively menacing.

I shook my head. "Adrian, I've got a feeling that it's going to be one of those days."

Chapter Thirteen

AS WE CAME up to him, Ted growled, "You're just damned and determined to turn my little brother queer, aren't you?"

"Damn it, Ted," Adrian said, "I told you before, he can't turn me queer because I've *been* queer all along."

"No, you haven't. You've never once acted like a sissy in your whole life."

I took a step forward, my temper rising.

"Oh, so now you're saying *I've* acted like a sissy all these years."

Ted shot me a condescending smirk.

"You may not swish, but you've never been very manly."

"You don't have to take that from him, Ben," Adrian said, scowling.

Ted glared directly at me in the old psych-them-out ploy.

"He's not going to do a damn thing, Adrian. And even if he tried, I'd just beat the crap out of him. He's not a real man."

Before either of us could see it coming, Adrian slapped Ted so hard he stumbled to one side.

"Ben's every bit as much a man as you are, Ted—more so, because he's got a brain."

Adrian stormed off. Ted stood there, rubbing his cheek, which already glowed with a hand-shaped red mark,

He pointed a finger at me. "This isn't over."

The next time I saw Ted, Doris and I were standing by her locker before second period. The slap mark Adrian had given him was visible a mile away.

"But why slap him? Why not punch the crap out of him?"

"Because if he punched him, one of three things would have happened. Ted would have spent the whole morning not answering Mr. Allen's questions about who punched him, which would piss him off and make things worse for us. Or it would have turned into a fight, and they'd have both been suspended. Or the three of us would have ended up fighting, and all three of us would have been suspended. On the other hand, anyone who sees that slap mark will assume a girl did it and that Ted had it coming. And *everybody's* going to see it."

And see it, everybody did. By morning break, about half of the people I passed in the hall were talking about it, wondering who'd done it, and making crude jokes about Ted.

Adrian and I had established a particular spot where we could spend a few minutes together and still get to our next classes on time. I felt a bit guilty not setting some time aside for Doris, but not enough to stop spending as much time with Adrian as possible. I was especially eager to see him again that morning. It had only been a little over two hours since he'd delivered the slap-marking blow to Ted, but it felt like an eternity had gone by since then. I smiled when I saw him waiting for me.

He saw me too, but he wasn't smiling.

"Ben, we have to talk."

"What'd I do?"

"You didn't *do* anything—that's the problem. Ted insulted your masculinity, and you just stood there. You should have beat the crap out of him or at least said something to shut him up."

"Adrian, an insult is only as effective as how much you let it bother you. At best, a punch would have meant he'd have to explain it—which he wouldn't do—and in the end, he'd have just been even more pissed off."

"That's not the point, Ben," he said, leaning towards me. "*I* stood up for you. Aren't you ever going to stand up for me?"

When I didn't respond, he shook his head. "Don't you get it? When he says you're turning me queer he's not just insulting you, he's insulting me too. He's saying what I feel for you isn't real. He's saying I don't know what I'm talking about when I say I love you. But believe me; I know exactly what I mean and exactly what I feel."

"Okay, I get the point," I said, nodding. "I didn't see it from that angle before, but I do now. I'll stand up to him—but not at school. It needs to be at a place and time where he and I can have it out. But I will—I'll stand up to him. I promise."

"Thank you. That's all I wanted to hear."

His expression softened, and he sighed.

"I'm sorry, but I just can't stand him denying the reality of our relationship."

"I understand, really. And one way or the other, Ted's going to have to accept that I really do love you with all my heart."

A girl passing us must have heard me because she glanced at us and sniggered.

"I love you too," Adrian said, and he squeezed my arm before heading off to his next class.

THE DOCTORS WANTED to keep Grandpa one more day, so Mom had to wait until Wednesday to bring him home. Eliana was to go along to help. I couldn't imagine what kind of day they were facing, but I didn't envy them.

On the other hand, my day began like the one before it, with me waking up to Adrian kissing me and nibbling on my ear.

"Mmm, if this is going to be a regular feature of the new routine, I love it."

Like the morning before, he waited while I brushed my teeth and showered. And he treated me to more wolf whistling and flattery while I dressed. It was the kind of attention a guy could really get used to.

But the table talk at breakfast again revolved around Grandpa's deteriorating health, leaving me in low spirits. So, Adrian let me vent and held my hand the whole way to Chadham High. When we got there, he gave me a firm hug and kissed me before we got out of the car. I felt so lucky to have him.

The school day seemed to drag on forever, but the last bell finally rang, and Adrian and I headed home. A mounting excitement built up inside me the closer we got, and I kept my fingers crossed, hoping Mom and Eliana would still be out. When we finally pulled into an empty driveway, I turned to him and smiled.

"Oh yeah, I forgot to tell you. I'm not going to the center today. Artie told me to take today and tomorrow off. So...would you uh...like to come inside for a while?"

Adrian's eyes lit up, and instead of answering, he broke into a smile, got out, and stood by the kitchen door waiting for me like a puppy.

Inside, I listened for any sign of someone being home. Then I yelled out a "Hello, anyone home?" and got no answer. We promptly went to my bedroom where I switched on the receiver, and we fell into each other's arms.

Adrian ran his fingers through my hair, sending shivers down my back—and elsewhere. My hands roamed under his pullover. He began unbuttoning my shirt. We looked into each other's eyes. The time was right, and we had the house to ourselves. We were in love, the bed was soft, and the condoms were within arm's reach. Prince was singing "Cream."

Then a rap on the door startled us.

"Ben, we're back from the hospital. Mom says come out and give us a hand with Grandpa."

"Be right there, Eliana."

"Oh, and hi, Adrian," she added with a giggle before the click of her footsteps faded away.

Adrian pulled me in tight for the most passionate kiss we'd yet shared. Our eyes met. He sighed, grabbed his jacket, and picked up his book bag. We moved through the house with sheepish faces, but when we got to the kitchen, we still hadn't met anybody.

"They must have taken him to his room," I said.

"I'll try to come by sometime tomorrow."

"Call first, just to make sure everything's okay."

"Sure. Well, see ya."

"Wait a minute."

I kissed him one last time, before he went to the door, and I turned to go to Grandpa's room.

When I saw him, I was taken aback. He hadn't even been in the hospital a full week, but in that short time, the change in him had been profound. He was sitting in a wheelchair, wearing what appeared to be the same clothes he'd worn the day he was admitted. But they hung on him now like they were at least a full size too big. His hair was disheveled. His cheeks were hallowed, and his lips seemed thinner. His skin was dry and ashen. But what really got to me were his eyes. They were bloodshot, and there was a milkiness in them that gave his whole face a cadaverous appearance.

Eliana was fixing an oxygen hose over his ears. It had two tiny appendages that fit under his nose. My mother was unpacking his things. She looked up and saw me standing there.

"Ben, there are a couple of oxygen tanks in the trunk of my car. Please bring them in. And be careful, they're heavy."

I went out and found the two green cylinders. They were about four feet long, with handles attached at the top end. A fold-up dolly lay on top of them. After setting it up, I pulled the first tank out—with some difficulty—and strapped it down. Except for the steps up to the kitchen door, it was easy to transport after that.

"Where do you want me to put this one?"

Mom pointed to one side of the doorway. I unstrapped it and turned to go get the other one.

SUPPER WAS AS strange an affair as I could remember. Eliana had baked a chicken, which was okay, but she'd also made a "mess" of collards, something she said she'd become quite fond of from the college cafeteria. Personally, I thought they were disgusting—almost as bad as kale. To my surprise though, Dad lapped them up like a hungry hound.

But the thing that kept getting to me was Grandpa's condition and how we were all ignoring it, like everything was normal. There he was sitting in the wheelchair, a tube around his head and up his nose, and a ginormous tank on wheels sitting in the corner. He looked so frail, and it seemed to take him more energy to chew his food than he could ever get from eating it. The knife and fork trembled in his hands, and he was extra slow in bringing the fork to his mouth.

And that wasn't all.

At one point, he looked at my mother and said, "Ilana, pass the kohlrabi, please."

His voice was soft and breathy.

"I'm Margot, Pop, not Momma. And it's collards, not kohlrabi."

"So Grandpa," Eliana said, "what are you most looking forward to for your Thanksgiving Day supper?"

He put his fork down and stared at his plate for a moment.

"Chopped liver," he said at last.

Eliana and I looked at each other and wrinkled our noses.

"Come on, Pop," Mom said. "It's Thanksgiving. We're going to have turkey and all those traditional side dishes. I'll make you chopped liver another time."

"Marty, I think what Eliana means is what *Thanksgiving* dish are you most looking forward to."

Without looking up, he said, "Latkes."

Mom rolled her eyes, but Eliana said, "No problem, Grandpa, I'll make you latkes."

After supper, Dad wheeled Grandpa into the living room. I followed with the oxygen tank Then Mom checked that his tube was positioned right while Dad turned on the TV.

Grandpa looked exhausted. He was panting, and he leaned to one side, using the armrest of the wheelchair to prop himself up.

"What do you want to watch, Marty?" Dad asked, aiming the remote.

He hesitated before speaking, his voice barely a whisper. "What day is it?"

"It's, uh, Wednesday."

"Turn it to *The Virginian*—Great show."

That thoroughly confused me.

"Marty, *The Virginian* isn't on tonight. How about we watch *Unsolved Mysteries*?"

Dad switched the channel.

"Would you like an after-supper coffee?"

Grandpa pondered the question for a moment before asking, "Are you having one?"

"I am if you are," Dad said.

"Okay, I suppose that would be nice."

As Dad started to the kitchen, my mother's voice rang out, "Ben? You've got company."

I caught up with Dad and whispered, "What was he talking about? I never heard of a show called *The Virginian*."

"It was on in the sixties. He's a little confused."

We got to the kitchen to find Adrian in an uncomfortable exchange with Eliana.

As I came into the room, she was saying, "And how long have you two been dating?"

"I...uh..."

"Adrian, hi. Want to listen to some music?"

"Sure," he said quickly.

"Come on."

We started through the living room, and Adrian leaned over to me, "You have the most awkward family on earth."

"You have no idea."

Grandpa noticed us as we crossed the room, so I stopped.

"Grandpa, you remember Adrian? This is my friend Adrian."

He stared at him for a long moment and turned back to the television.

The two of us continued on to my room and closed the door.

"He seems really out of it," Adrian said.

"Yeah, it's really freaking me out."

"I can tell. That's why I came over."

We cuddled and listened to music for an hour or so, and when he got up to go, I walked him to the door, ignoring Eliana's smirk as we passed through the living room. Pausing at the kitchen door, we shared a hug and a tender good-night kiss.

Adrian caressed my back, saying, "I'll give you a call tomorrow."

"Maybe we can go for a drive or something."

"I'd like that."

THE RAINY SEASON that seemed to define the word autumn in Chadham that year continued on Thanksgiving, and the threat of a chilly soaking drizzle overshadowed the parade down in The District. I felt sorry for the people who'd be marching, but not enough to risk standing in the rain in solidarity.

After two days of seeing Adrian's beautiful face first thing, waking up to an empty room on such a dark, chilly morning was a tremendous letdown. I wandered through the living room and found Grandpa watching the Macy's parade on TV. I said good morning to him, but he only glanced at me in response. In the silence between the program and a commercial, his labored breath was more pronounced than it had been the previous evening.

My parents and Eliana were in the kitchen. The smell of turkey roasting in the oven wafted through the room, reinforcing my readiness for breakfast. Mom was spooning pumpkin pudding into a casserole dish. Eliana was grating potatoes. Dad was sipping coffee and reading the newspaper.

"Good morning, son," he said cheerily.

"Morning," I said, pouring myself a cup of coffee and sitting down across from him.

"So what's on your agenda today?"

"Besides eating to excess, I don't have one," I said. "Well, eating to excess and regretting the two weeks it'll take me to work off the extra pounds I'll gain because of it."

"Not getting together with Adrian?" Eliana asked over her shoulder.

"I don't know, maybe. And can we quit with the amused comments and embarrassing questions whenever he's around? It weirds him out, and it's not fair."

"Can I help it if the two of you are just too cute for words?"

"If we're too cute for words, then knock off cross-examining him every time he comes over."

"My, someone woke up grumpy this morning, didn't they?"

"Eliana," Dad said before taking another sip of coffee.

She turned to me offering a genuine smile. "I'm just kidding. And I really am happy for you, Ben. Adrian is a very cute...uh...*nice* boy. I only hope I'll find a guy that nice one of these days."

"You will," I said, breaking into a grin. "He'll be the one running away from you screaming."

"Dad," she whined melodramatically, "are you going to let him get away with that?"

"Knock it off, both of you. Ben?"

"I'm sorry. I was just joking too."

The phone rang, and I jumped up to get it. To my disappointment though, it was Jim, one of the guys who worked for Dad's company.

"Dad, it's Jim."

He took the phone.

"Yeah, Jim, what's up?" He listened for a moment. "Uh-huh, I expected that. Listen, I appreciate you driving by there to check. If it's not there first thing in the morning, I'll get on the horn and raise hell with them... Okay, happy Thanksgiving. Bye."

He hung up and took his cup to the sink.

"What did Jim want on Thanksgiving?" Mom said.

"Oh, we were expecting a lumber delivery yesterday, but Ruckers called making excuses and promised they'd get it there today. Well, I knew that was bull the minute I heard it. So, I asked Jim to drive by the site, and lo and behold, no lumber. I'll straighten it out tomorrow."

"Ruckers sounds pretty unreliable," I said.

"No, they're usually quite dependable. But every now and then, I have to light a fire under them to keep them committed."

"Ben, what's your grandfather doing?" Mom asked.

I stepped into the living room and took a peek at him, then returned to the kitchen.

"He's watching TV," I said and added, "He's wheezing kind of hard."

"I noticed that too," Mom said. "We'll keep an eye on it and check in with the doctor if it gets worse."

The phone rang again. I was standing right next to it, so I grabbed it, hoping this time it would be Adrian.

"It's Stacy," I said, holding out the receiver.

Eliana practically leaped across the room.

"Stacy, hi. When did you get in?"

She spent a good ten minutes on the phone.

"Okay, see you soon. Bye, Stace."

"How's Stacy doing?" Mom said.

"She's good. She didn't get in until late last night. Her flight was delayed, and then she missed her train."

"Which school is she going to?" Dad said.

"Wheaton."

I scratched my chin. "Where's that?"

"It's just outside Chicago. She's coming over in a half hour. I better hurry up and finish prepping these latkes."

Mom said, "I told you, you don't need to make them. Your grandfather probably won't even remember saying he wanted them."

"I know, but it's no trouble, and even if he doesn't remember asking for them, he might like them."

Mom shook her head. "It's a good thing you're in college. You'd spoil him rotten if you were here all the time."

"Dad likes latkes too, don't you, Dad?"

"Well, I—"

"He likes them *too* much," Mom cut in. "You can have one tonight, Ethan. One."

Dad put on his pouty face. "Aw, come on, dear. It's Thanksgiving. And haven't I been doing good?"

"Well, yes. I guess you have," Mom said long-sufferingly. "Okay, two then."

He grinned from ear to ear. Eliana and I shared a moment, both knowing full well that if the latkes were anywhere on the table near Dad, he'd sneak as many as he could get away with.

The phone rang again, and I picked up, fully expecting it to be one of Mom's friends this time.

"Hey," Adrian said. "How are things going?"

"Hey. Okay. You want to come over? We can hang out or maybe go for a drive."

"I'll be over in a half hour."

"Great, see you then."

"I love you."

I glanced over at Eliana who was looking right at me.

"Yeah, me too. Bye."

My cheeks were warm. Eliana grinned, but she didn't say anything.

ABOUT A QUARTER to ten, Stacy pulled up outside. Eliana and Stacy had known each other since kindergarten. They'd been friends since at least middle school and best friends since their first year of high school. Eliana sprang out the door before Stacy even shut her engine off, and they hugged each other with the kind of joyful abandon two guys couldn't get away with if they'd survived a nuclear blast together.

The two of them came in, arm in arm, chattering away a mile a minute. Mom and Dad greeted Stacy like a beloved niece. Over the years, she'd spent almost as much time at our house as her own. Even I got a solid hug from her.

Adrian then appeared at the door, and Mom and Dad exchanged Thanksgiving greetings with him. Eliana introduced him to Stacy—without any teasing—and the two of them went to her room to continue catching up. In the meantime, I had a moment to take him in.

He looked so beautiful that morning that I wanted to jump him right then and there. His jeans gripped his thighs to a sexy perfection, and he was wearing his jacket over a gray-and-white striped shirt that was loose and just begging for a hand to sneak up under it. But it was his face that drew my attention. His cheeks were chill-blushed, and his hair was windblown and messy. I wondered how it was possible for him to get even more attractive each day.

"Want to go for a drive?" I asked, and he nodded.

"Drive safe," Mom said.

"Where do you want to go?" I asked as we got in the car.

"As long as I'm with you, I don't care where we go."

We wound up at the park, and since it had stopped raining, we strolled along the boardwalk. It looked like we were the only ones there.

"I dreamed about you last night," Adrian said, "well, actually, both of us."

"Was it a good dream?"

"So good, I didn't want to wake up. We were out of school and living together. It was wonderful. Have you ever dreamed about me?"

"I dream about you all the time. And yeah, I've dreamed about us living together, daydreamed about it too."

We stopped and leaned against the rail overlooking the river. The churning waters were beautiful to watch and soothing to the ear.

"Adrian, what do you want to do when you get out of Chadham High?"

He grinned. "Move in with you."

"I mean besides that, silly. Like, do you want to go to college?"

"I guess so."

"What do you want to study?"

"I don't know. I never really thought about it."

He noticed the surprise registering on my face and said, "Is that a bad thing?"

"No, I don't think so, at least not now. You've got the rest of high school to think about it, and even if you graduate and still haven't decided, that's what they have general college courses for—to help you consider the possibilities."

"Are you going to college?"

"I hope so. I'd like to go to Dickerson if I can get in—" I paused. "—I was kind of thinking that if you went to Dickerson too, once you got there, we could move in together."

He blinked and smiled. "So we both want the same thing."

"Yeah, I guess we do."

He pulled me in for a kiss. He didn't look around to check whether anyone would see us; he just did it. His arms were around my neck, and mine were around his waist. His lips were warm.

From somewhere in the distance, a voice rang out, "Faggots!"

We didn't break away. Adrian raised his arm in the air and shot the finger at whoever it was, and then we walked on down the boardwalk, our hands around each other's waist. Spending time with Adrian was just what I needed. Sharing our dreams about the future and knowing that we both saw ourselves together in it was exhilarating. And his audacity in kissing me in public and shooting the finger at our homophobic heckler somehow made the reality of our love all the more potent.

I dropped him off at the corner near his house and drove home, my body still humming with the buzz I always got from being with him. Mom was in the kitchen when I came in, so I asked her if she needed any help with the dinner preparations.

"No, but you can keep me company if you'd like."

I pulled up a chair at the table.

"How are things going with you and Adrian?"

I sighed and smiled. "They're going great."

She wiped her hands with a towel and sat down across from me.

"Mom, you'll think I'm crazy for saying this, but we're in love."

She smiled. "I would *never* have guessed. Tell me— What about Ted? Did the two of you work things out with him?"

"No. I *am* going to talk it out with him though. Adrian says Ted needs to respect his choices in life, including about me."

"Adrian's quite mature for his age," Mom said. "But remember, even though he may be mature, he is still young, and he still has a lot of growing up to do."

"I know," I said, looking at the table. "We talked about the future today, and he hadn't even thought about whether he wants to go to college. That kind of shocked me."

Mom leaned back in her chair with a half smile. "Ben, you didn't think about going to college until we drove up to Dickerson last year so Eliana could look it over. All I'm saying is be gentle with him. If you really love him, you've got to put his needs first."

"Mom, that's all I want."

She raised an eyebrow. "And what if he grows to not be in love with you anymore?"

The thought hit me like a punch in the gut.

"I...I hope that never happens. But if it did, as long as it was good for him, I'd accept it. It wouldn't be easy. It'd kill me inside, but if it was best for him, I'd accept it."

She took my hand. "You're a good man, Benjamin Isaac Carpenter. Adrian's lucky to have you. And I wouldn't worry too much about him dropping you anytime soon. It's obvious he's smitten with you."

"Eliana says I'm smitten with him."

"That's the way being in love tends to work," she said as she got up and went back to the counter.

I hung out with Mom until two o'clock when everything was ready. In our family, the big Thanksgiving meal could either be called a late lunch or an early supper. The only big difference from previous years was we didn't have candles lit at the table. Grandpa's oxygen tank made that dangerous.

The food was good, and everyone was in good spirits. As Mom predicted, Grandpa didn't remember asking for latkes at all, but he clearly enjoyed eating one. And Dad did manage to sneak a third latke onto his plate before Mom caught him and moved the rest out of his reach.

THE NEXT MORNING, I was chilled to the bone during my drive to the center. Between the cold, damp weather and the short distance to the center, by the time the Plymouth's heater really started kicking in, I was already parking. It felt strange being at the center without Grandpa there, and it was depressing to think that the next time he would be, it would likely be for keeps.

Because of the holiday, there were fewer clients for the day program, but their smaller numbers were balanced by the presence of more family visitors who came to spend time with the residents. The fewer clients and added visitors made my job easier. I joined Mr. Shalit, Mr. Melnik, and Mr. Levine for a round of hearts, and while no one cheated, I quickly saw why Herman found it frustrating to play with them. They didn't cheat, but they were absolutely ruthless.

I was only scheduled to be there for four hours, so at one o'clock, I said goodbye to Bobby, Melvin, and Rosalita and went outside. Halfway to the Plymouth, a car pulled into the parking lot and stopped near me. It was Nicholas Horton.

He rolled down the window.

"Hey, do you have a minute? I'd like to talk to you."

I wasn't sure I wanted to get in the middle of another emotional scene between him and Bobby.

"I, uh, don't have much time."

"I just need a couple of minutes—I promise."

I sighed. "Yeah, okay."

He parked the car, and I walked over to him.

He hesitated before speaking.

"About the other day, what you need to understand is that Bobby and I are—"

"It's okay. I already know Artie—I mean Bobby's gay. He told me after he found out I am too."

Mr. Horton let out a sigh of relief and glanced at the building.

"Is he in today?"

"Yeah, he's in there."

"I really need to talk to him, but I don't want to upset him again. Is he still mad at me?"

"Look, Mr. Marcel, or Horton—"

"Call me Nick. And you're Ben, right?"

"Yeah, Ben. Look, Nick, I don't want to get in the middle of something between the two of you."

"I know, and I'm not asking you to. I just want to know how Bobby's doing so I can decide what I need to do. Do I stay in town in the hope he'll talk to me? Or should I just give up and go home?"

"Where is home for you?"

"At the moment, I live in Toronto. So what do you think? Should I hang around?"

I stared off in the distance for a second before answering.

"Bobby told me what happened to the two of you when you were in school and how you disappeared. Why didn't you ever let him know you were alive?"

He leaned back on the hood of his car.

"He blamed me for us being outed, and he cut me off."

"Bobby didn't blame you for him being outed. He told me that himself. He couldn't contact you because he got beat up—bad."

Nick stared at me, his mouth hanging open.

"Beat up? Nobody told me."

It was obvious he was still in love with Bobby, and I knew I was treading dangerously close to playing *shadchan*, but he looked like he needed a little encouragement, so I said, "He also told me he's never loved anyone like he loves you. It just hurt him that you never contacted him. What changed your mind after all this time?"

Nick sighed and stared into the distance.

"Bobby was, and always will be, the love of my life. I remember the first time I met him. I hadn't figured out I was gay yet, but he was beautiful, and I couldn't take my eyes off him. I fell in love with him before I even realized it, and that love hasn't changed. Over the years, a couple of guys wanted to have relationships with me, but when they kissed me, all I could see was Bobby. Now, I've been offered a fellowship at the School of the Arts up in Lynchburg. It's only an hour by rail, so I had to try to see him. I just couldn't be so close and not even try."

He paused and sighed. "So should I try to talk to him again? What do you think?"

"Yeah, I definitely think you should talk to him. He told me he waited for you. That means he still loves you. Just tell him what you just told me."

A voice came from behind us. "He doesn't have to."

Nick and I turned our heads so fast it was a wonder we both didn't get whiplash. Bobby was standing not three feet behind us.

Nick sputtered, "Bobby, I— How long have you been standing there?"

"Long enough. Nick, I'm sorry I got so upset the other day. It was just a shock to see you like that after so much time."

"It's okay. I had it coming."

"How did you find me?"

"It wasn't easy. Your phone number must be unlisted. So, I tracked down Oscar in Charlottesville. He wouldn't put me in contact with you himself. He said if I wanted to talk to you, I had to make contact on my own. But he wouldn't tell me where you live, he only told me you work here. Until Benjamin called, I thought he'd just sent me on a wild-goose chase."

He glanced down before saying, "I've missed you so much."

"Yeah, me too."

They stared into each other's eyes so intently I could have nudged one of them and they'd be in each other's arms in less than a second. So, I scuffled my foot on the pavement and cleared my throat.

"You guys have a lot to talk about, and you could probably use some privacy, so I'm going to take off. I hope it works out for you; I really do."

"Thanks, Benjamin," Bobby said.

Nick nodded. "Yes, thanks. I hope I haven't made you too late for your appointment."

"Appointment? Uh, oh no, I'll be fine."

When I reached the Plymouth, I turned back to look at them. They were leaning on the hood of Nick's car, shoulder to shoulder, talking. Crossing my fingers, I unlocked the door and got in.

SATURDAY WAS COLD, but at least it wasn't raining. It would have been a perfect day for soft music and cuddling with Adrian on my bed, but he'd called the night before to tell me his folks were driving over to Roanoke to visit his mother's sister for the remainder of the holiday weekend. I don't know who was more disappointed, him, or me.

Since everything in the house now revolved around Grandpa and his health issues, staying at home, without Adrian to keep me distracted, was a depressing prospect. I wasn't scheduled to work at the center until Monday, which took that option off the table. So, I decided to go to the mall and see if Bug Out Books had anything Herman might be interested in.

When I got within sight of the mall, I was tempted to turn around and go back home. I'd forgotten how busy the place would be with all the after-Thanksgiving Christmas sales. But since I was already there, I scouted around, found a parking space, and hiked to the nearest entrance. The place was packed—not quite shoulder to shoulder, but close enough.

Bug Out Books was doing a booming business. With all the people crowding around and trying to squeeze by each other, checking out the two or three sections I usually frequented took me forever, first getting to them, and then actually being able to browse what they had once I got there. I did see a few titles I thought Herman might find interesting, but the checkout lines were so long I decided to wait and come back another time.

What I couldn't leave without doing though was getting an orange-mango smoothie. It must have taken me a good twenty minutes to get to the food court, and another ten in line to get one.

I'd just inserted a straw in the cap and turned around when I spotted Doris, and my eyes went wide. She was sitting at a table with none other than Patrick Frost. The way he was looking at her alone would have told me he was her secret admirer, and the two of them holding hands left no doubt. My lips curled into a smile just in time for her to look over. She didn't appear to be embarrassed, but she was definitely not expecting to see me. I shot her a quick thumbs-up before melting into the crowd. They didn't need me interrupting things.

Sunday, I hung around the house and spent some time with Grandpa. He seemed a little more clearheaded than he'd been since he got home from the hospital, so I tried to draw him out with a few questions about his childhood. As he talked, I envisioned a world with kids playing makeshift games on dingy streets beneath gray skies. It must have been a tough life, but for all the misery, I kind of wished I could have experienced it.

"It was a different world in those days," Grandpa said. "We didn't have none of your fancy-shmancy cable TV. We listened to the radio for news, music, dramas, and comedy shows. And we were lucky to have that. Nobody had any money in those days, and every penny was precious—no room for luxuries. I didn't even see a movie until I was eleven years old—the Marx Brothers. I laughed so hard my sides hurt. Anyway, that was the Depression, and after that, things slowly started getting better. That is, until the war came."

"Did you serve in the war?"

"The war? I enlisted in 1942. I was a little older, so they had me working in supplies, and I never saw a single day of battle. Not like my cousin Hiram. He saw fighting all right. The Nazis captured him and sent him to the concentration camps. Thank God, he survived. But he was never the same...never the same..."

He cleared his throat, and his eyes were beginning to look teary, so I changed the subject.

"Do you remember the first time you saw a television?"

"Television? Yeah, it was in a shop window. We thought it was like magic in those days. And everything—well, most everything—was live. It was a different world."

From television, the conversation drifted to other areas, including music (he hated Elvis Presley and despised the Beatles), and we talked about how things had changed over the years (none of the changes very good in his opinion), and politics (no one could compare with Barry Goldwater).

It was nice talking to him and more interesting than I'd have thought possible before I started volunteering at the center. I spaced out my questions so he didn't have to talk too much all at once. But although he seemed to be enjoying himself for the most part, the effort was clearly wearing him out, and his wheezing worried me. So, I asked him if he wanted to take a nap, and he nodded wearily.

I wheeled him to his room and helped him get into bed. Then I brought in the oxygen tank and made sure his tubes were set right.

"Have a good nap, Grandpa," I said, turning to go.

His eyes were already closed.

"Thank you...Oren."

I made a note to tell Mom he'd forgotten my name again.

"SO, TELL ME all about you and Patrick," I said when I met Doris on our way to first period, the Monday after Thanksgiving. "You've really lucked out. He's a cutie."

She was positively beaming.

"Luck had nothing to do with it. He's been working up the nerve to ask me out for a couple of months now. I noticed him looking at me sometimes when we passed each other in the hall, but none of our classes are near each other, and he has second lunch. So we never had a chance to talk. Anyway, Wednesday afternoon, I was on my way to the car, and he ran up to me in the parking lot. I don't know who was more nervous—him or me. After wishing me a happy Thanksgiving, he kind of blurted out would I like to get together with him sometime. Of course, I said yes, and he asked for my number. Then he called me Saturday and asked if I wanted to grab a bite with him at the mall."

"And you said, 'Are you crazy? With all this leftover Thanksgiving food?'"

"No, silly."

"How romantic—just the two of you and the four thousand other people crammed in there searching for Christmas bargains."

"Oh, hush," she said, elbowing me in the side but grinning from ear to ear.

Later, we passed Ted on our way to the Math and Business wing. As was the usual routine nowadays, he ignored her and scowled at me.

"He is such a baby," Doris said.

"Hey, you're lucky. He's just ignoring you. I get the hairy eyeball every time he sees me."

She sighed. "He needs to put his mind on Hope."

"Speaking of Hope…" I said.

She passed by us, clutching her books to her chest, walking at a clipped pace and ignoring us as completely as if she'd never met us. She looked thinner than the last time I saw her, but the color in her cheeks was brighter and healthier looking.

"Any chance you two will get to talk?"

Doris sighed. "About as much as you'll probably have. I'd kind of hoped that whatever therapy they've got her on, coupled with drying out, would help her see things more sensibly. But apparently, she still thinks Ted and I are together. Until we can get that notion out of her head, she'll not be in any mood to talk things out with anybody."

"You could tell her you're still willing to drive her home. After all, in the great balance of things, she'd have to prefer riding with you to taking the bus no matter how mad at you she is. And what other choice does she have?"

"Her folks could be picking her up."

"I hadn't thought of that."

I OPENED THE door at the center, remembering how uncomfortable I'd been that evening my mother sent me to look for Grandpa Marty. Now, it felt as natural as being in my own home. I'd really grown fond of a lot of the clients and residents; I counted the staff I worked with as good friends, and meeting Bobby turned out to be the best gift a gay teenager could have—a great role model. The way he worked with people, his quiet compassion that fostered trust and affirmed the dignity of others was something I wanted to cultivate in myself.

I walked over to Jamal for my routine check-in to see if there were any special notes, like who might need more attention or who wasn't feeling well.

"Hey, Jamal. How was your weekend?"

He looked up from the pile of magazines he was straightening. "Hey, Ben. It was okay. How about you?"

"Thanksgiving was great, but I made the mistake of going to the mall Saturday."

He laughed. "Oh man, you couldn't pay me enough to go anywhere near that place Thanksgiving weekend."

"Tell me about it," I said, nodding. "Anything special I need to know for today?"

"No, just the usual. Oh, Artie's in the bookstore. He told me to ask you to stop in when you got here."

I walked over, pausing to say hello to several people along the way. Bobby was perched on the stool near the cash register reading when I came in.

"Hey, Bobby, Jamal said you wanted to see me?"

Yeah, I wanted to thank you for getting Nick and me back together."

"You mean you guys are back together—like in really back together?"

"Well, yes, but I meant getting Nick to come here to meet with me face-to-face. If I'd just gotten the card, I'm not sure I'd have followed up and called him. It was a shock seeing him out of the blue like that, but we both needed to see each other again. And talking with him Friday was good. We...uh...spent the weekend talking."

"I'm glad it's working out for you. He seems like a nice guy."

"He is. He was always the sweetest person I ever met, and seeing him now, he still is. And Ben, I have a favor to ask."

"Sure, what can I do for you?"

"We decided we're going to live together, and we want to celebrate it—sort of like having a marriage ceremony—and we'd like you to be there."

"Are you kidding? I'd be honored. When are you planning to do it?"

"We still haven't worked out the details, but it won't be for a week or two. Nick's got to get things arranged for his fellowship at the School of the Arts. Once that's done, we'll set a date."

"Fantastic. And again, congratulations."

I went back out to the hall feeling so happy. If things could work out for Bobby and Nick after all those years, maybe Adrian and I really would be able to have a future together.

I looked around and saw Mr. Lehmann sitting at a table reading. I walked over and asked him if he knew of any books Herman might like. He mentioned a few titles, and we went to the bookstore and picked one out. When we went to pay for it and Bobby found out who it was for, he told us the center would foot the bill. We picked out a card, and the three of us signed it. Then Mr. Lehmann and I went around and got signatures from Mr. Shalit, Mr. Levine, Mr. Melnik, Mrs. Kadelburg, Melvin, Jamal, and a few others. When Rosalita signed the card, she said the hospital was on her way home, and she'd be happy to drop the book and card off after work. I envied her being there to see the look on Herman's face when he saw all those signatures.

MOM AND DAD were in the kitchen when I got home.

"Hey, where's Grandpa?"

Dad glanced at Mom.

"He's watching TV in his room," she said. "He's not feeling well today."

"I'll go keep him company until supper."

"I'm sure he'd like that. But it might be better to let him rest."

"Oh, okay."

"Doris called," Dad said. "She wanted you to give her a call as soon as you got home."

I went to my room, plopped down on the bed, and grabbed the phone.

"Hello, Mrs. Whitfield. It's Ben Carpenter. I'm returning Doris's call."

A few seconds later, Doris picked up.

"Okay, Mom. I got it—" A click told us her mother had hung up. "Ben, you're not going to believe this."

"These days, I'd believe anything."

"Hope's parents bought her a car—a Ford Probe, no less."

That news brought me to my feet.

"I don't believe it. They know she's got a drinking problem, and they actually think putting her behind the wheel of a car is a smart thing to do? How did you find out?"

"I caught up with her after school and offered to drive her home like you suggested. She was all smug and told me she didn't need a ride because her folks had gotten her a car. She said all she had to do was promise them she'd quit drinking."

"And they trust her?"

"I know. It's crazy."

"When you talked to her, was she still mad at you?"

"Well, she did talk to me, so that's something."

"Did you tell her about you and Patrick?"

"Yeah, but I don't think she believed me."

"If she sees the two of you together, maybe she'll wake up."

"Maybe."

"Hey, did I ever tell you about my friend at the senior center?"

"No."

"Okay, get this. There's this guy named Artie—actually, it's Bobby, but that's a long story. Anyway, he's gay."

"Competition for Adrian?"

"Don't be silly. This guy's ancient—like in his thirties. But listen, a guy came looking for him, and it turns out he's his long-lost boyfriend from high school. They hadn't seen each other since they were teenagers. So, they've talked things over, and they're going to live together. They're even going to have a ceremony to make it sort of like a marriage."

"That's so romantic. But why not have a real marriage ceremony?"

"I don't think that's legal for two guys in this state."

"No, I mean like a religious ceremony. I could talk to my priest. She's very open-minded. I bet she'd do it for them."

"That's an interesting idea. Next time you see her, ask her about it. In the meantime, I'll mention it to Bobby and see if that's something they might be interested in."

Chapter Fourteen

THE WEEK AFTER Thanksgiving, time seemed to speed up. With a little less than a month to go before the Christmas break, teachers began piling on the work to gear us up for end-of-semester midterms. Doris and I tried to keep an eye out for any sign Hope might still be hitting the bottle, but our chances were limited because she was serving her in-school suspension week. From what we could see though, she seemed sober enough, so we were cautiously optimistic. Unfortunately, she also showed no signs of ever getting over her anger at us.

Bringing Ted to his senses was another lost cause. He remained in complete denial about Adrian's sexual orientation and thoroughly convinced I was leading him down the primrose path of debauchery. The only good thing was he seemed to be resigned to the fact there was nothing he could do to stop Adrian from seeing me. On the other hand, given the way things were going, he didn't have much to worry about.

All the extra homework made it nearly impossible for Adrian and me to get together after school. Riding to and from school and morning break were moments we treasured, but without the chance for more intimate physical contact, that old saying about absence making the heart grow fonder was proving painfully true. By Saturday morning, I wanted Adrian so bad I didn't think I'd make it until he came over that afternoon. Flash images of the condoms in my night table drawer were popping into my head all too often, and I couldn't imagine how Bobby and Nick had survived all those years without being together.

Eliana had gone back to Dickerson before the end of Thanksgiving weekend and wouldn't be returning until late December. After our heart-to-heart talks about relationships and things, I really missed having her around. Her absence also served to amplify the family focus on Grandpa's deteriorating condition.

He'd settled into a slow but steady decline. His appetite was dwindling, and he talked less and less. He also slipped in and out of coherence. Sometimes he'd act like a weaker, wearier version of his old self. But other times, he was really out of it, not knowing where he was, or calling me Oren or Beryl. A trip to the doctor on Friday ended with the decision to have him admitted to the center on Monday. I knew it was for the best, but it upset me all the same.

While I was getting in a few extra hours on Saturday, I talked with Bobby and told him I couldn't shake the fear that if Grandpa was admitted to the seniors' home, he might fall in his room or get hurt somehow. He said it was natural to worry but assured me he and the staff would pay extra attention to him. That helped, although nothing could relieve the sadness of knowing I'd have even less time with my grandfather from now on.

I'd just gotten home when the phone rang.

"Ben, it's me," Doris said. "I talked with my priest, and she said she'd be happy to officiate if your friends want it. She said they could even do it in the church as long as there weren't any regular services scheduled."

"Hey, that's great, Doris. I'll pass it along to Bobby."

A knock on the door drew my attention. Adrian was standing there smiling.

"Doris, I've got to go," I said, breathless and waving him in. "Someone's at the door."

"Tell Adrian I said hello."

I hadn't finished hanging up the phone before Adrian threw his arms around me and kissed me.

"I've needed that all day," he said.

"Mmm, you and me both. Come on."

We padded up to my bedroom and spent a good half hour necking and cuddling. At one point, Adrian was lying on his side with his head resting on my chest while I stroked his hair.

I kissed his forehead and said, "You remember I mentioned my friend at the center?"

"Yeah."

"Okay, well I didn't tell you he's gay. So, he and his old high school sweetheart are going to move in together."

"Uh-huh."

"They're going to have a ceremony to kind of make it official, like a wedding. And Bobby—he's the guy I called Artie, turns out that's just a nickname—anyway, he asked me to attend their ceremony when they set the date. So, I was wondering, if you don't have anything else to do that day, you think you might want to go with me?"

"You mean, like, as your date?"

"Well, yeah. I mean, it'll be a gay wedding, so it ought to be okay for me to bring my boyfriend."

He held me tight and kissed me on the neck just below my ear.

"Mmm, you know that drives me crazy."

"Can't a guy show his boyfriend how much he appreciates him?"

SUNDAY WAS A day to stay indoors. It didn't get above freezing until midday. I spent part of the afternoon working on the last of my weekend homework assignments. Dad and Grandpa watched a football game while Mom went through Grandpa's things, packing for the center. After I finished my homework, I went to give her a hand.

"I'm really going to miss having Grandpa around," I said.

"Me too. But you'll be able to see him while you do your community service hours, and you can always visit him other times as well."

"Yeah, about that. I've been thinking that maybe I'll keep volunteering there after my community service is done."

"That's quite a change," she said, folding a shirt. "You didn't want to do it at all when you started."

"I know, but I've met a lot of nice people—the staff and some of the clients and residents—and it feels good to be helping out. Bobby says I've got a knack for it."

"You've always been a kind and generous person, so it doesn't surprise me. If volunteering at the center is something you want to make a regular part of your life, I say go for it."

"Actually, I've also been thinking that when I go to college, maybe I'll take some courses or maybe even make social work my major."

"I thought you wanted to be a writer."

"I could always do that on the side. And let's face it—my stuff's not that good."

"It's all in the eye of the beholder, Ben. But yes, I think you'd make a good counselor too."

We continued packing Grandpa's things.

"Do you want me to pack his prayer shawl and *tefillin*?"

"No, we'll pack them tomorrow morning. That's one thing he'll like about living at the center. He'll be able to do his prayers with the other guys."

"Yep."

I noticed an old photograph sticking out of one of the boxes and picked it up. It showed a man and woman, arm in arm, smiling at the camera. The guy's hair was cropped short and slicked back, but his eyes, nose, and mouth looked like someone had cut my face out of a picture and glued it onto him. And the woman, aside from the silly-looking bun she had her hair in, was the spitting image of Eliana, if a little plumper.

"Hey, what's this? Who are these people?"

Mom sighed. "Who do you think they are? It's Grandpa Marty and Grandma Ilana. It was taken around the time they got married, maybe a year or so before I was born."

I stared at the photo, feeling like I was looking back in time. In my mind, I could see my grandparents walking down the street in New York City after the war. The world was black-and-white then, like in the old movies, but it was cleaner, and all the men wore suits and ties, and hats with wide brims. It was a world I wanted to know so much more about. That one conversation I'd had with Grandpa wasn't nearly enough. Then I realized I didn't know how much time I still had for those or any other kind of conversation with him. A lump formed in my throat. I put the photo back in the box and tried to think of something else.

MONDAY STARTED OUT even colder than the day before, and I dreaded the thought of going to school in the subfreezing temperatures. I did have the consolation, however, of again waking up to Adrian sitting on my bed showering me with kisses. His cheeks were so chill-blushed they were rosy, and I brushed my fingers over them and kissed them to warm them up.

After I showered and dressed, we joined my parents in the kitchen. Grandpa was still in his room.

"When are you taking Grandpa to the center?" I asked, pouring cups of coffee for me and Adrian.

"We were just talking about that," Dad said. "It should be above freezing by midday, so we'll wait and take him then."

"You never did tell me how he took it when you told him he was going to live in the center from now on," I said.

Mom sighed. "I'm not sure he understands that's what's happening. We're playing it by ear."

"I'll be sure to spend time with him when I get there after school," I said. "Maybe it'll help if he feels lonesome."

Thoughts about Grandpa preoccupied me all day. Doris was sympathetic, which helped. In a way, Ted did too. His ongoing ill will was a welcome, if unintended, distraction. Our campaign to make sure Hope wasn't drinking was another. And Adrian was so wonderful. He not only hung out with me during morning break as usual, but he also skipped out of his fifth-period study hall to keep me company during lunch.

Still, three o'clock couldn't come fast enough. When the final bell rang, I raced to the car and pulled out as soon as Adrian got in.

"Just drop me off anywhere near my house," he said.

We drove in silence for a few minutes.

"If you want to talk this evening, just call the house. Let it ring once and hang up. I'll call you back. But listen—don't feel like you have to. Only call if you want to or need to."

I looked over at him and sighed. "Do you have any idea how wonderful you are?"

He squeezed my hand. "No, but I'll take your word for it. I mean, you are the king of wonderfulness after all."

I dropped him off with only a quick goodbye kiss and went straight to the center.

I had barely stepped foot in the door when Bobby caught sight of me and came over.

"Hey, Ben. Come in and get warmed up."

"How's my grandfather doing?"

"He's okay. I'll take you to his room."

"Does he know what's going on?"

"Yes. I haven't talked with him in detail, but so far, at least, he's aware of why he's here, and he's taking it in stride."

"Are my folks still here?"

"No, they left about three o'clock. We thought it might be better for him to get used to discrete visits. They were here, and they left. Now, you're here, and you can visit. Then, after you leave for the day, he'll join the others for dinner and have some time to socialize before lights-out."

In all the times I'd been helping out at the center, I'd never thought much about how different the experience must be for the residents. The clients were just visitors, and at the end of the day, they went home to their families. But for the residents, the center was their whole world.

We walked through the connector to the residents' building and went down the hall past a half dozen doors on either side. Each door had a resident's name in large bold letters. When we got to the door with Marty Blackburn emblazoned on it, Bobby stopped and smiled.

"Oh, I know you'll want to spend time with your grandfather today, but I've also got a surprise for you."

He opened the door, and a heavily accented voice greeted us.

"And watch out for that *meshugeneh* Gilder. Not only is she crazy, she cheats like nobody's business."

Grandpa was sitting in a chair with his oxygen tank, listening and nodding. Across from him, I was surprised and happy to see Herman Topolski.

"Marty," Bobby said, "you've got another visitor."

Grandpa looked up, and although watery, his eyes sparkled a little, and he smiled.

Herman leaned forward like he was passing on a secret and said, "Marty, Benjamin here is one of the few people who doesn't cheat. Confidentially, given how bad he is at backgammon, I'm surprised he doesn't try. But what can I say? He's a *mensch*, a real *mensch*."

Then he stood up and shook my hand. "Thank you for the book and the card. It made it a lot easier to stay in that torture chamber of a room."

He patted me on the shoulder. "And now, I'll leave so you and your grandfather can visit."

"Thanks, Herman. It's good to see you back," I said. "We've missed you."

"So you keep saying. The only reason Shalit and Levine are glad is because they want to try cheating me at cards again. Well, I'll show them. *Zayt gezunt*, Marty."

"*Zayt oykh gezunt*," Grandpa mumbled.

Bobby motioned for me to take Herman's chair. "I think I'll be saying goodbye too, Marty. I'm sure you and Ben have a lot to talk about."

He went out, closing the door behind him.

I looked around and said, "How do you like your room, Grandpa? Can you have a TV in here?"

He stared at me blankly.

"I'll find out, and if you can, I'll bring your TV from home tomorrow."

I stayed with him for ten minutes or so. Every now and then, he muttered a word or two, but I did most of the talking. I decided he was probably tired and didn't feel like talking, so I told him I had to go out and mingle.

"I'll pop back in before I go, so if you decide you want me to bring anything, let me know."

He nodded, and I went back to the hall and made the rounds. Herman was playing backgammon with Mr. Lehmann, eyeing each of his moves with suspicion. Mr. Lehmann, on the other hand, seemed genuinely happy to have him back.

"Annt! No cheating, Lehmann. I may be old, but I'm not blind yet."

"Topolski, you've got that right," he said, smiling. "You may not be blind, but you are old—an old grouch."

A little while later, I went to the break room for some water. Rosalita was leaving as I got to the door, and we exchanged greetings. Bobby was writing a note in a folder.

"Ah, Ben, how's Marty settling in?"

"He seems kind of tired, or maybe he's a little depressed. But I guess he'll be as contented here as anywhere."

"I hope so. I'll make a note for the night staff to keep an eye on him. They would anyway, but it never hurts to put it in writing."

"Is it all right for them to have TVs in their rooms? He's got one in his room at home, and I could bring it tomorrow."

"Sure. Ask Jamal, and he'll help you set it up right."

"Thanks."

I filled a cup with water and pulled up a chair across from him.

"Bobby, I hope you don't mind, but I was telling a very good friend of mine about you and Nick and the ceremony you're planning to have. She's very discreet."

"I'm sure your friends are trustworthy and not the kind to spread gossip."

"Not usually, no. Anyway, she suggested that if you want, her priest would be willing to officiate if you guys wanted to have a church ceremony."

"Unless the Pope's done a major about-face, I don't know too many priests who'd marry two men to each other."

"Oh, she's not Catholic. I think she's an Episcopalpalian or something. Her priest is a woman, and Doris told me she said she'd be happy to help you guys out if you wanted."

Bobby leaned back in his chair. "Marry Nick in a church.... It's an interesting idea. I'll have to talk it over with him."

"Whatever you guys decide, just let me know, and we'll take it from there."

"Thanks, Ben. You're a good man."

"It's really a self-serving idea. I might want to have a ceremony like that for Adrian and me someday."

"And when that day comes, you better invite Nick and me."

"Are you kidding? You'll be the first names on the list."

THE NEXT DAY, after I stopped off at the house to enjoy a little cuddle time with Adrian, I grabbed Grandpa's TV from his room and proceeded to the center. He was in the main hall, sitting at a table with his friends. His wheelchair and oxygen tank made it easy to spot him. After saying hello, I found Jamal, and the two of us went to his room and set the TV up on a special shelf.

The rest of the week passed without any major speed bumps. Adrian and I snuck in as much time together as we could. Doris and I continued to keep an eye on Hope, who as best we could tell was staying on the wagon. And the expression on Ted's face every time he saw me confirmed that he still blamed me for Adrian being gay. But as the days passed, a weird feeling, like when you jump out of a swing, began to build up inside me. It felt like I was being hurtled towards some dramatic and, I feared, tragic end.

Life at home felt especially strange. My parents and I had supper together just like we'd always done, and we watched TV and did all the other things people usually do at home. But the house seemed quiet and empty without Grandpa. A lonesome feeling worse than when Eliana had first gone away to college haunted me every minute I was there.

The ten or so minutes I got to spend with Grandpa every day grew more and more important to me. I had mixed emotions when I was with him. It was hard seeing his health deteriorate so quickly with each passing day. His breathing was becoming more labored, despite the oxygen, and he was getting so thin a strong breeze could have blown him away. Nevertheless, he seemed to like my company, which I found warmly satisfying.

The weekend was low key. Aside from the quality time Adrian and I spent together, we invited Doris to take in a movie with us Sunday afternoon. It gave her an opportunity to forget her troubles with Hope for a while, which she clearly appreciated, and she got to know Adrian a little better. After the movie, she pulled me aside and told me she could see why I liked him so much—that he wasn't anything at all like Ted. Before taking off, she gave me a note with her priest's name and phone number to give to Bobby.

When I got to the center on Monday, I spied him talking to Mrs. Kadelburg and stopped long enough to give him the note. He read it over and thanked me. Then Melvin asked me to referee a game of hearts between Herman and Mr. Melnik, Mr. Levine, and Mr. Shalit. As usual, Herman was convinced one or more of them were cheating, but at least he wasn't getting loud about it. In the end, he took second place, which I thought was not bad given how merciless his three opponents were.

After the match, I looked around but didn't see Grandpa, so I strolled over to the residents' hall and rapped on his door.

"Grandpa, it's me. Can I come in?"

When I peeked inside, what I saw shocked me. The difference from when I'd last seen him on Friday was so stark it frightened me. His skin was a pallid gray and his eyes were bugged out. His breath came in gasps, his lips dry and chapped.

I crept forward, my stomach queasy and my hands shaking.

"Are you all right?"

He looked my way, but his eyes were cloudy and didn't seem focused.

"I'll be right back," I said, turning to the door.

One of the nursing staff was coming out of a room a few doors down.

"Excuse me," I said, trying to keep calm. "Has anyone checked on my grandfather, Marty Blackburn, recently? He's having a hard time breathing, and I'm really worried."

She came over, looked inside his room, then briskly walked to the nurse's station and picked up the phone.

"Dr. Markov, you need to see Mr. Blackburn... His breathing is stertorous... Right."

She went inside a little room behind the desk and emerged a minute later with a tray holding medical stuff of some kind. I started to follow her into Grandpa's room, but she set the tray down on the table and held up a hand.

"You need to wait outside. I know you want to help, but it would be best for both of you if you're not in here right now."

I backed out of the room and didn't stop until I was leaning against the wall. Dr. Markov hurried down the hallway and disappeared inside. I stood there waiting with my arms crossed tight and tried to keep my hands from shaking. A mumbled conversation between Dr. Markov and the nurse was taking place just a few yards away, but I couldn't make out what they were saying. From the tone of their voices, it didn't sound encouraging.

I didn't even notice Bobby walking up to me.

"I understand Marty's not doing so well."

"He looks terrible. His eyes are bugging out, he can't catch his breath, his skin is... Is he dying?"

Bobby sighed. "From a broad view of things, yes, he's dying. He's been dying for some time. That's what things like emphysema and cancer do. But that doesn't necessarily mean he's going to die right now. He sprang back from a similar thing recently, didn't he? The night you got him home before he threw up?"

"Yeah, I guess so. It's just... I'm afraid, Bobby. I'm just getting to know him, and he's going to be gone soon. I don't want him to die."

I didn't realize how upset I was until I felt the tears running down my cheeks. I unlocked my arms to wipe them away, and he gave me a warm hug.

"You're holding up well. And it's okay to cry; the tears show how much you love him."

Then Dr. Markov came out of the room, and the look in her eyes said everything. Grandpa wasn't going to spring back from this one. The nurse followed her out and went straight to the phone at the nurse's station.

"Benjamin, your grandfather is very sick and needs more medical attention than we can give him here. I suspect he has pneumonia. We're calling the hospital."

My knees buckled, and I leaned back against the wall, afraid I was going to faint.

"Ben, come on," Bobby said, helping me up. "Let's go to the break room and call your folks."

The rest of the night unfolded like a scene from one of those doctor shows on TV. I called home. Dad said he and Mom would meet me at the emergency room. The ambulance came, and they carted Grandpa away. Bobby made me promise to drive carefully, giving me a hug before I left.

Once my parents and I got to the emergency room, there was nothing to do but wait, and we paced back and forth for hours. Finally, sometime after ten, a doctor came out to update us.

"I understand Mr. Blackburn has emphysema and cancer. The strain on his system has weakened him, and he's contracted pneumonia. We're doing what we can, but I have to tell you, it doesn't look good."

"How long does he have?" Mom asked, her voice shaky.

"It's hard to say. At most, he could linger for a couple of days, maybe a week, but given his condition, I suspect that's overly optimistic."

Then my mother did something I'd never seen her do before. She started crying. I was stunned. She'd always been so strong and stoic in emergencies. She hadn't even cried when Grandma Ilana died. And now there she was, weeping.

Dad wrapped an arm around her. There were silent tears running down his own cheeks.

Suddenly, I felt queasy and wanted to be anywhere else but there. My world seemed to be crumbling all around me. Nothing made any sense. I was a helpless child, lost and afraid. And there was nothing firm I could cling to. The man and woman whose strength I'd always depended on were as helpless as I was.

"I...I want to go home," I heard myself say and stood up.

Mom saw the tears in my eyes and hugged me. I was trembling, and all I could do was stand there in her arms.

She kissed me on the cheek. "Yes, you should go home. But are you okay to drive?"

"Yeah."

"Are you sure?"

"Yeah. I'll call when I get there."

"Okay. You drive safe and take your time. Get the number from one of the nurses and call as soon as you get there. Then I want you to eat something and go straight to bed."

"Yes, Mom."

She let go of me, and Dad gave me a hug, saying, "I'll walk you to your car."

It was a cold night with starry skies twinkling above the city glow. I'd left my jacket at the center, but I barely noticed the icy breeze stinging my cheeks.

"You've had it rough over the last few weeks," Dad said, wrapping an arm around my shoulder. "The things Grandpa Marty's going through have been hard on all of us, but I think especially hard on you. You weren't too happy about him coming to live with us as I remember, but I've seen you grow closer and closer to him as time went on. And now, soon, we're all going to lose him."

I wiped a freezing tear from my cheek. "What's the use of loving someone if you're only going to lose them?"

"Believe it or not, love, and the pain we feel when we lose someone, is part of how we know we're truly alive. We grow from the love we share with others. And Ben, the love they give us doesn't die with them. It stays with us even after they're gone."

We stopped at my car. Dad looked me over

"You sure you don't want me to drive you home?"

"Thanks, Dad, but I'll be all right. The last thing I want is to wind up in the emergency room. Mom would kill me."

He smiled. "Yeah, she probably would. So, just take your time, be careful on the road, and call us a soon as you get there."

I hugged him, got in the car, and drove home, going well below the speed limit and coming to full stops at every light. After I let myself in, I called the hospital, and Mom told me she was glad I got home safely and that there was no change in Grandpa's condition. She finished the call by telling me she loved me. I made a sandwich and ate it in the silence of the kitchen and then stopped off for a quick shower before collapsing on my bed.

I DON'T KNOW how long it took me to drift off, but the next thing I remember was the sound of Adrian rapping on my window. I waved for him to meet me at the kitchen door and let him in.

"Hey, what's going on?" he said after a quick kiss. "Where's your folks?"

"They must still be at the hospital," I said, stifling a yawn. "My grandfather's taken a turn for the worse."

"Listen, I can grab a ride with Ted today if you need to go be with them."

"No, I'm going to school. There's nothing I can do at the hospital, and besides, my mother would have my hide if I skipped, no matter what the reason."

He studied me for a second before replying.

"Well, if you're really going to school, go get your shower, and I'll make you some breakfast."

"There's no need for that. I can grab a Pop-Tart or something. I'm not even hungry, to tell you the truth."

"Don't be silly. Go shower while I scramble you some eggs."

He kissed me and then gave me a shove, popping me on the behind.

By the time I returned, showered and freshly dressed, he was setting a plate of scrambled eggs on the table. He'd also brewed a pot of coffee, made toast, and poured me a glass of orange juice.

"Aren't you going to join me?"

"After I wash the pan. I don't want to leave a mess for your folks to have to clean up. Go ahead, get started."

The breakfast was hot and hearty, and being with Adrian helped take my mind off Grandpa. I begged him to have some of the eggs, but he said he'd already eaten. Instead, he sat across from me, munching on toast and sipping coffee. The whole scene, just the two of us sharing breakfast, felt cozy and romantic. I had another vision of us living together and how nice it would be to come home to him every day.

"You know, I wish I could marry you."

He glanced at the table and blushed. "Me too."

"Who knows, maybe one day they'll actually let gay people get married."

He looked up with bashful eyes. "If they ever do, you better not marry anyone else but me."

"Have no fear. I'm like a cat. Now that you've fed me, I'm going to hang around you forever."

He sighed and tilted his head to one side. "I love you so much."

"I love you too."

After we finished eating, I let Adrian bus the table while I brushed my teeth. When time came for us to leave, I took one of Dad's old winter coats to wear, which Adrian found hilarious.

"Definitely not your style," he said, giggling.

We got in the car and spent a few minutes hugging and kissing while the engine warmed up. After we arrived at Chadham High, we shared another hug before getting out.

"Just remember. Let me know whatever you need."

"You're already doing it. Just being with you makes everything I'm dealing with easier. You're not only beautiful and kind and loving, it's like you've got this aura or something that gives me strength."

"Well, if there's anything else, just tell me. I'm here for you."

I sighed and squeezed his hand.

But the uplifted spirits Adrian had fostered in me evaporated all too quickly. Sitting in homeroom, I realized my folks hadn't called to make sure I was up for school. What worried me more was that they hadn't called to tell me what was happening with Grandpa. I could only hope that no news was good news.

Doris gave me a hug when I told her what was going on. It was a nice gesture, but it didn't make me feel any better. I couldn't get Grandpa out of my mind.

We had our midterm in U.S. Government that morning, and given how distracted I was, I was lucky it was such an easy exam. I breezed through it. But then I had the rest of the period to brood over Grandpa and wonder what was happening.

Just before the second-period bell rang, the intercom came on. As usual, our principal, Mr. Allen, began his announcement by clearing his throat.

"Benjamin Carpenter, report to the office for a message from your father."

I grabbed my things, a sinking feeling in my chest.

Doris whispered, "It's got to be good news or he wouldn't have left a message."

Buoyed by that thought, I left for the office and got there ahead of the class change. The usual morning busyness was in full swing. Three students were waiting in line to get tardy slips, while two of the secretaries were still calculating attendance statistics.

Over to one side, Mr. Allen was talking with Mrs. Beeler, the school counselor. That made me nervous. Wanting to postpone any bad news as long as possible, I waited my turn behind the three late arrivals.

"I'm Ben Carpenter," I said when it was my turn at the counter. "Mr. Allen said my father left a message for me."

To my relief, I wasn't directed to Mr. Allen and Mrs. Beeler. I was given a note.

> *Grandfather's condition is unchanged. Finish out the school day. Will touch base with you at the center this afternoon.*

It wasn't as good as a note saying Grandpa was on the mend, but on the other hand, it could have been a lot worse.

I doubled back to my locker and then on to the M-B wing. Doris met me, and I gave her the update.

"I'm glad it wasn't bad news. Stay strong," she said, hugging me.

Ted's voice startled us. "Well, this is a change."

I turned around to see him glaring at me a few feet away.

"If you're finally coming to your senses about girls, maybe you can leave my brother alone now."

Doris stamped her foot. "Charles Edmund Douglas, you are the most insufferably stupid excuse for the male sex ever born. I was hugging him because his grandfather's sick in the hospital."

"Yeah, right."

"Show him the note, Ben."

"No." I took a step towards him and lowered my voice. "Ted, I don't give a damn what you think about me, but lay off Adrian. He doesn't need to hear you running your mouth." I made sure to lock eyes with him before continuing. "And let me tell you something. Whether you like it or not, Adrian's gay. No one made him that way, it's the way he was born, and it's not going to change. And for the record, I am in love with him, and that's not going to change either. He's told you, and now *I'm* telling you. We're in love. So just shut the hell up and deal with it."

"Faggot."

"Nice. You know, when you call me that you're also calling your brother that. Real family-values man, aren't you?"

I turned on my heels and marched off to Economics.

MY ENCOUNTER WITH Ted set the tone for the rest of my day. I was totally pissed at him and didn't care if I ever spoke with him again. It didn't help things that I couldn't spend morning break with Adrian because I had to do some last minute cramming for my pre-calc exam. And worst of all, I was worried sick about Grandpa. Despite the note from my father, Grandpa was still going to die, and nobody could do anything to prevent it.

On the drive home, Adrian let me vent about my concerns over Grandpa, which helped relieve some of the stress I was feeling. Then I told him about my encounter with Ted.

His eyes lit up at the news, and he smiled broadly. "You really told him we're in love and to get over it?"

"If we hadn't been in the middle of a crowded school hallway, I'd have told him a lot more."

"I wish I'd been there to see the look on his face."

"To tell you the truth, I don't even remember how he reacted. And at this point, I don't care. And I don't care if he never wants to be my friend again."

When we got to the house, Dad's car was there parked next to Mom's. At least one of them was home.

Adrian kissed me and said, "I'm taking off. You go find out how your grandfather's doing. I'll call you later tonight."

I yelled out a hello after entering the kitchen, and my father came out from the living room. He had on fresh clothes, and he'd shaved, but the bags under his eyes betrayed the tough night he'd had at the hospital.

"How's Grandpa?"

"They've moved him to a room. Other than that, nothing's changed. They've got him sedated, they're giving him oxygen, and they've inserted an irrigation tube in his lung to drain the fluid building up there. Right now, the fluid is the real problem. It makes it hard for him to breathe, and that weakens him."

Despair washed over me. "He's not going to get any better, is he?"

"No. Basically, they're just trying to keep him comfortable."

We sat down at the table.

"How much longer does he have?"

Dad shook his head. "It's anybody's guess. There are lots of questions and no good answers."

"Will they keep him sedated until the end?"

"I don't know."

"I wish I could talk to him one more time. I don't remember the last time I told him I love him."

Dad was pensive for a moment before saying, "You know, I once read that even when someone is sedated, they can still hear the things loved ones say to them. So, the next time you visit him, why don't you tell him you love him? He knows it anyway, but I'm sure he'll appreciate hearing you say it again."

I sighed, and my arms went limp.

"Is Mom home?"

"No, she was here earlier this afternoon. We're taking turns coming home to get cleaned up. The doctors said there's no reason for us to stay there twenty-four hours, but your mother doesn't want him to be left alone."

"I should go to the hospital."

He sat back in his chair. "Ben, I won't say no, but I will say it's important for you to take care of your community service requirements. Why don't you go on to the center and stop by the hospital for a while later on?"

He was right about the credits, and I didn't want to leave Bobby and the staff shorthanded, so I drove to the center.

As soon as I walked in, Melvin and Rosalita came up to me.

Rosalita wrapped an arm around me. "How's your grandfather?"

"He's got pneumonia. They don't think he's going to make it."

"I'm so sorry," she said, pulling me in for a full hug.

"Yeah, me too, Ben," Melvin said. "Let me know if you need anything."

"Thanks. I appreciate it."

I started for the break room but was stopped several times along the way, first by Herman, then by Jamal, and next by two of Grandpa's coffee klatch buddies. It seemed like everybody wanted to know about him, and everybody offered their sympathy. They were all well meaning, but it didn't really help me any.

Bobby was writing notes in a file when I came into the break room.

"Hey, Ben. How's Marty?"

I pulled up a chair. "It doesn't look good. He's got pneumonia."

"That's too bad. How are your folks holding up?"

"They're hanging out at the hospital even though the doctors have him sedated."

"And how about you?"

"I don't know," I said, staring at the table. "It was really hard last night at the hospital, but today, I've just been feeling kind of—I don't know—numb about it."

"That's natural. Have you been able to talk to anyone about how you feel?"

"Yeah, Adrian's been there for me. He made me breakfast this morning."

Bobby broke into a lopsided smile. "You're a lucky man. When I first met Nick, he couldn't boil water."

"Yeah, I am lucky. Bobby, it makes me feel guilty, but whenever I'm with Adrian, nothing seems quite so bad—not even Grandpa dying. It's...I don't know...weird."

"I think the correct term for it is 'love.' It gives us strength and comforts us even in the worst of times."

"I definitely love Adrian."

Bobby smiled. "And he must be in love with you. I mean, he did cook you breakfast after all."

It was the first time I laughed since finding Grandpa gasping for breath in his room the day before.

Chapter Fifteen

I WENT STRAIGHT to the hospital as soon as I finished up at the center. An oxygen mask covered Grandpa's face; one arm had an IV tube stuck in it, and the tube from a plastic sack of blood dripped into the other. Another tube snaked its way out from under the covers to a kind of pump on the floor that led to a large plastic bottle filled about a third of the way with the same kind of black gunk he'd thrown up that night we first took him to the hospital. Wires from somewhere on his chest led to a heart monitor like the one Herman had. The room stank of antiseptic.

My mother was sitting in what looked to be a very uncomfortable chair. When she saw me, she got up and gave me a hug and kiss on the cheek.

"How is he?" I said, walking to the bed.

"The doctor says he's actually a little stronger now. Draining the fluids from his lungs helps him breathe easier. The problem is it also dehydrates him, so they've got to give him lots of IV fluid and blood transfusions."

"Have you eaten anything today?"

"Yes, your father and I took turns grabbing a bite earlier, and I made myself a sandwich when I went home to shower and change. He's out having something now."

"What can I do?"

"Ben, there's nothing any of us can do."

I stood by the side of the bed looking down at my grandfather. He seemed tiny and fragile with all the tubes and machines attached to him. My throat felt tight, and I swallowed.

"Grandpa, I really wish you could get better—" I let out a ragged breath. "See…I'm selfish. I want more time with you. I feel like I've barely gotten to know you… But I've learned so much from you. You taught me to be a *mensch*, even when I'm afraid sometimes… And it meant so much to me when you were okay with me being who I am. Thank you for that. I love you, Grandpa, and I'm glad you came to live with us. I'm going to miss you."

He gurgled a little, and for a second, I thought he was waking up.

Mom gave me a side hug. "Why don't you go on home? Do you want some money so you can get a burger on the way?"

"No, thanks, Mom, I'll make something when I get home. Will you and Dad be coming home tonight?"

"Your father will. He's got to go in to work in the morning. They don't know how to drive a nail if he's not there to tell them how and point where."

"Try to get some rest."

She tousled my hair. "Drive safe. I love you."

"I love you too, Mom."

THE WEEK DRAGGED on. I went through the motions of going to school, taking my midterms, and doing chores at the house, mainly the laundry and feeding myself. With each day, my time at the center took on a whole new meaning, and I began to see the old people I interacted with in a new light. They weren't creepy; they were individuals with their own unique histories. They'd lived through joys and tragedies, and they'd experienced the pain of losing loved ones. And now, they were in the twilight days of their own lives, wondering where the time had gone and pondering what was in store for them. And they still had so much to offer—a lifetime of experiences and wisdom for anyone who cared to listen. I felt privileged to have the opportunity to spend time with them.

Every day after I got off from the center, I stopped by the hospital, and each time I saw Grandpa, he looked thinner and weaker. His skin stretched over his bones. His hair and beard were matted and greasy. The doctors said he was losing the battle with pneumonia, and the emphysema and cancer were also taking their toll.

My mother was exhausted. She only came home to shower and change her clothes, and then, only when my father was able to take over the vigil. As for him, his diet was in a total shambles. The only decent food he ate was when he happened to be home to share supper with me. The rest of the time, he was grabbing whatever he could at fast-food places on the run.

Through it all, Adrian was my anchor. He was there every morning early enough to cook breakfast for me, and after I got home Thursday night, he came over and cuddled with me.

Lying there in his arms, I realized my love for him had grown even deeper. It was a bond eternity couldn't break. I'd go to college, and I'd miss him terribly. But he'd eventually graduate from Chadham High, and we would be together for life.

Sometime Friday afternoon, Eliana came home for the Christmas break. Dad dropped her off at the hospital, and she was still there that evening when I stopped by. We rode home together.

For most of the way, we were silent, no one speaking until we turned onto Franklin.

"Mom's exhausted," she said, staring at the road ahead of us.

"I know, but she doesn't want him to die without one of us being there, and it's easier for her to take time off than Dad."

"I'm going to tell her I'll stay over tomorrow night so she can get a good night's sleep."

"If she'll do it."

We turned the corner from Franklin to begin the final stretch home, drove on in silence for a few moments, and pulled up to a stoplight.

Eliana looked over and studied me.

"And how have you been holding up?"

"Me? I'm okay. I mean, it's been tough, but I'm getting through it."

"What about you and Adrian?"

"You have no idea how wonderful he's been. He's such a beautiful *boytchik*."

She laughed out loud. "*Boytchik*? Oh man, no one would ever guess you've been hanging out at the Beth Israel Community Center. I bet he's a real *mensch* too."

"He is," I said in a pseudo-Herman accent. "He's been cooking me breakfast every day. And he listens to me when I *kvetch*, and he's there for me when I get all *verklempt*. He's my *neshomeleh*."

We both laughed.

I SLEPT IN late Saturday morning. After the week I'd had, I thought I deserved the extra rest. Stumbling into the kitchen, I paused to look out the window. Dad's car was gone. I put on a pot of coffee, just in time for Eliana to make her own yawning entrance. She went to the fridge, poured herself a glass of orange juice, and pulled out a chair.

"Dad's not home," I said. "I guess he either had to go by one of the job sites, or he's at the hospital. You think we should call and check in?"

"No. I'm going to take Mom's car and go there in a bit. With any luck, I'll get her to come home and get some rest."

"Good luck with that."

The coffee was ready, so I poured us both a cup.

"It's good to have you home, sis. I've missed you."

"I've missed you too."

A light knock revealed Adrian standing outside the kitchen door. I let him in, and after I kissed him, he glanced over at Eliana with a timid expression.

"It's okay," she said. "I've seen sweethearts kiss before. Anyway, I'm going to go clean up and get dressed."

After she left the room, Adrian said, "I'll never get used to your family. But I wish mine was exactly like them."

I hugged him, and we shared another kiss.

"Have you eaten yet? I was just going to make breakfast."

"You don't have to cook anything for me."

I gave him a peck on the cheek. "It's the least I can do after you've cooked for me all week."

In the end, it was just a basic scrambled-eggs-and-toast meal, but to me, it was a feast because I was sharing it with Adrian.

We were just finishing up when I heard Dad's car pulling up outside. I got up to take my plate to the sink but stopped halfway as Mom and Dad both walked in. They looked sad, and Mom's eyes were bloodshot.

"Grandpa Marty's gone," Dad said.

I knew it was coming. I'd known it since Tuesday night. I'd been expecting it at any moment all week. But it still came as a shock, and it was as if I was all alone in the middle of some dark landscape, lost and despairing. Tears streamed down my cheeks.

"I should go," Adrian said softly. "Ben, I'm sorry for your loss. Mr. and Mrs. Carpenter, my sympathies. He seemed like a very nice man."

"Wait, don't go," I said.

"Adrian, it's okay if you want to stay," Mom said. "Ben's father and I have a lot to take care of, and I'm sure Ben would appreciate the company."

"Where's Eliana?" Dad asked.

"She's either in the bathroom or in her room getting ready. She was going to go to the hospital."

Mom went to find her while Dad poured himself a cup of coffee. Adrian gave me a hug, and the two of us went to my room where he held me and stroked my hair while I cried.

THE FUNERAL WAS held in Petersburg on Monday. Mrs. Douglas had come by to pay her respects the day before. She mentioned that Adrian had told her I wanted him to attend the funeral, and Mom assured her that it was okay since he and I had "become such good friends recently."

Dad drove, Eliana sat up front, and Adrian and I were in the backseat. Mom rode in the hearse. Dad explained that it was a custom to not leave the body alone and told us that people from Beth Israel had taken turns and stayed with Grandpa until time to leave for the funeral.

A service was held at the synagogue attended by dozens of people who had known Grandpa and Grandma over the years, the rabbi mentioned that donations could be made to the cancer society in Grandpa's honor, and after a brief service at the cemetery, we each put a shovelful of dirt in the grave.

Adrian and I were walking back to the car when I was surprised to see Ted coming towards us. Adrian furrowed his eyebrows and took my hand. Ted saw it but didn't react.

"I'm sorry about your grandfather," he said when he'd gotten closer. "It may not be like it was between you and me anymore, but I wanted you to know I'm sorry for your loss."

"Thanks, Ted, I appreciate it. And I appreciate that you drove all the way here for the funeral. You didn't have to do that."

"Yeah, well, like I said, I'm sorry for your loss."

He glanced at Adrian, turned, and walked away without speaking to him.

The drive back to Chadham was quiet. Mom and Dad sat up front. Adrian and I were in the back. He held my hand the whole way. Stacy had driven down for the funeral, and Eliana rode with her.

We all got home and took turns washing our hands from a plastic pitcher near the door before entering. I was surprised when Mom lit the mourners' candle as soon as we got inside and recited something in Hebrew that I assumed was a prayer. We all sat on low boxes for a simple meal of eggs, lentils, bread, and wine. After supper, Adrian and I went to my room.

"What's with the boxes?"

"I don't know. Maybe so if people faint they won't have too far to fall before they hit the floor."

"And the mirrors?"

"Oh, that one I know. We cover the mirrors to remind us that appearances don't matter and that we don't have to look our best when we're mourning."

We spent the next hour or so just sitting together. As always, Adrian was such a blessing. He shared the silence with me and listened when I talked about my grandfather.

"Ben?" Eliana said from the other side of the door. "A couple of your friends are here."

I didn't have a clue who it could be. Ted had already paid his respects, and while Doris was a possibility, it didn't seem likely she'd be there with Hope.

Adrian and I walked out to the living room and found Bobby and Nick talking with my parents. As soon as Bobby saw me, he came over and gave me a hug.

"Ben, I'm so sorry for your loss. I really liked Marty a lot. Nick and I came to pay our respects. We brought a tray of dried fruit and nuts for you to nibble on when you get hungry."

"Thanks, Bobby. I appreciate it."

"And forget about the center this week. You've got enough on your mind."

He paused, turned to Nick, and broke into a small smile.

"It may not be the best time for it, but I do have one thing to tell you. Nick and I spoke with Reverend Keeler at Christ Church. She's going to—" He made quotation gestures with his fingers. "—marry us Monday the twenty-eighth at eleven o'clock. We'd love for you to be there. In fact, we've got a request. We'd like both of you to serve as best men for us. We each get one. What do you say?"

I turned to Adrian, our eyes met, and he nodded.

"It would be an honor. What do we have to do?"

"Just stand on either side of us. It's going to be a simple ceremony."

JEWISH FAMILIES MOURN for a week after someone dies, and traditionally, the family stays at home and doesn't engage in any kind of celebration. Grandpa died on the eve of Hanukkah, however, so we did light candles on the menorah and took part in some of the usual holiday-related things. Adrian stayed with me day in day out, and Sunday, Eliana commented that he'd practically become as much a member of the family as Stacy, who'd spent almost as much time over the week comforting her.

Monday the twenty-eighth was cold and rainy, with bits of sleet and wet snowflakes mixed in. Adrian told his folks I'd invited him to join me for a friend's wedding, and although I gathered Mr. Douglas thought it was weird, his mother had given him permission. I drove over to pick him up at about ten o'clock. He came bounding out of the house in the same dark blue suit he'd worn for Grandpa's funeral but with a more festive tie. He looked gorgeous.

Christ Episcopal Church was on the north side of town. It was a huge stone building with stained-glass windows and a tall bell tower. We walked inside, shook the snow out of our hair, and looked around. Nick and Bobby apparently hadn't arrived yet.

A brown-haired woman in her late thirties wearing a white-collared black shirt, and black jacket and skirt greeted us.

"You must be the best men. I'm the Reverend Keeler, but you can call me Bethany. I'll be officiating."

She sat in a pew with us and walked us through what was going to happen. It really was going to be easy.

A few people began arriving. It was no surprise when Doris showed up with Patrick Frost in tow and revealed she'd be assisting Bethany in the service. Then, Dr. Markov, Jamal, Melvin, and Herman Topolski came in. When I introduced Adrian to them as my friend, Jamal smiled and winked at us, leaving us both blushing.

Presently, Nick and Bobby walked in together, wearing matching black suits with violet ties. I had to admit, for people their age, they both looked kind of hot.

Bethany had them stand before the altar, with me standing next to Bobby, and Adrian on the other side next to Nick. She launched into the ceremony, clearly taking a few liberties with the printed text.

First, she turned to Bobby and said, "Robert Duncan Warren, will you have this man to be your husband; to live together in the covenant of marriage? Will you love him, comfort him, honor and keep him, in sickness and in health; and, forsaking all others, be faithful to him as long as you both shall live?"

Bobby actually blushed while squeezing Nick's hand and said, "I will."

Then, she turned to Nick. "Nicholas Udall Horton, will you have this man to be your husband; to live together in the covenant of marriage? Will you love him, comfort him, honor and keep him, in sickness and in health; and, forsaking all others, be faithful to him as long as you both shall live?"

He grinned from ear to ear and said, "Yes, I will."

Bethany looked at Adrian and me. "Who will give these men to be married to each other?"

We answered, "We do," in unison.

She then said a prayer, and everybody sat down. She had the four of us take some chairs that were lined up to the side halfway between the altar and the pews.

Next, Bethany read something from her bible about love being patient and kind. It was a beautiful passage, and I made a mental note to get a copy of it.

There were a couple of other readings, and then she stepped over to a kind of speaker's box.

"Dear friends, I rejoiced when Doris, the young member of our congregation serving as acolyte today, asked me if I would be willing to officiate at a special wedding ceremony. She explained to me that she had a friend who had told her about two men who were planning a commitment ceremony to celebrate their decision to share their lives together. She said she knew our laws currently discriminate against gay people, not allowing them the dignity of marriage accorded to straight people, but she thought a more traditional religious service might be something they would like.

"I told her to tell them if they wanted my assistance, I would be delighted to help out. A few days later, Bobby called and told me their story. My friends, I would like to share it with you.

"Bobby and Nick met when they were fourteen years old, here in this town at Chadham High. They became friends, and as they grew more aware of their orientations, they fell in love. But in those days, they had to keep their love a secret. Then, tragically, their love became known.

"They were young and vulnerable, and they deserved all the support and encouragement of any two teenagers in love. Instead, they were condemned. Bobby was savagely beaten and left for dead in a high school restroom. Think about that for a moment. A child was brutalized for being in love. It took him months to heal, and I'm sure there are invisible scars he still suffers from to this day.

"And even more tragically, Nick's father beat him and threw him out of the house. That's right, my friends, his father beat him and disowned him. How could any parent do that to a child? Sadly, although Nick's father eventually came to realize how wrong he was, he never lived to reconcile with his son.

"So, Nick had no one to help him, and he was forced to do things no human should have to do in order to survive, least of all a child.

"But survive he did. He made his way to Toronto and sought out his brother. Raymond took him in, got him into school, and eventually, Nicholas became an artist and graphic designer.

"And as for Bobby? He toughed it out, spending the remainder of his time at Chadham High ridiculed and bullied as an outcast. And all because he had committed the great sin of falling in love. But he withstood it all, graduated, and enrolled at Dickerson where he became a psychologist and dedicated his life to helping others. Today, he serves at the Beth Israel Community Center and Seniors' Home.

"Now my friends, despite Nicholas's success as an artist and Bobby's successful career as a counselor, this story would still be a tragedy but for one thing. Nicholas came back to Chadham to search for Bobby. Bobby's brother Oscar suggested he try the senior center. Even then, it looked like fate would keep them apart because the person he spoke to there was a young man who only knew Bobby by his nickname. And yet, it did not end there. Bobby had told Benjamin here a little about his past, and when he discovered Bobby's real name, he contacted Nicholas. And so, after twenty-two years, Nicholas and Bobby found each other again and are now standing here before you, committed to spending the rest of their days together.

"As I said, we live in a society whose bigotry and ignorance will not allow gay people to marry. It's not been that long ago when engaging in acts of love could even land gay people in jail. And today, acts of violence against them are still all too common. Discrimination holds sway in far too many hearts.

"I ask you—how can we in good conscience claim the moral high ground, and yet allow hatred to fill our hearts? Who among us can deny the hypocrisy of claiming to believe in God—the God whom scripture tells us is Love itself—when we condemn two people who simply had the temerity to fall in love?

"My friends, the Commonwealth will not recognize this marriage we are celebrating today. And there are many in this very church community who would be appalled by it. But if the love Nick and Bobby share is not genuine, if the life they build together is not worthy of our encouragement and respect, if the blessings of God do not extend to them the way it does to a heterosexual couple, then *no* marriage is genuine, and all our proud swaggering about the faith is a lie.

"So let us celebrate Nick and Bobby's marriage. And let us continue to pray for that day when the hearts of haters will be turned, and the love of all people will be recognized by the state. For only then, when we have eradicated bigotry from our hearts and society, will we be able to truly call ourselves the children of God. Amen."

Bethany stepped down from the speaker's box and motioned for us to take up our positions facing the altar. Nick took Bobby's right hand in his.

"In the Name of God, I, Nick, take you, Bobby, to be my husband, to have and to hold from this day forward, for better, for worse, for richer, for poorer, in sickness and in health, to love and to cherish, until we are parted by death. This is my solemn vow."

Then Bobby took Nick's right hand in his and made the same vow to him.

Doris brought a tray holding two rings forward, and Bethany said a prayer over them. Nick and Bobby placed them on each other's fingers. Then Bethany joined their right hands together and said, "Now that Nick and Bobby have given themselves to each other by solemn vows, with the joining of hands, and the giving and receiving of rings, I pronounce that they are husband and husband, in the Name of the Father, and of the Son, and of the Holy Spirit. Those whom God has joined together let no one put asunder."

We all said Amen, and as Bobby and Nick kissed each other, I don't know who was crying harder—me, Doris, or Adrian.

After their kiss, Bobby hugged me.

"Thank you, Ben. Without you, this day might never have come."

Nick came and shook my hand. "Yes, thank you, Ben. Thank you from the bottom of my heart."

After we posed for pictures and everyone was filing out for a small reception, I looked over and saw Ted coming our way. Adrian, who was wiping away a tear and holding my hand, tightened his grip when he saw him.

"What are you doing here?" he growled.

Ted sighed and looked down. "When I heard you were going to a gay wedding with Ben, I thought it was going to be some sordid freak show. So I came here to drag you home."

Adrian rolled his eyes, but Ted continued.

"I know, I know. It was stupid to think such a thing. But then I got here, and it really was a wedding service, and, uh, the service, and the minister's sermon…it made me realize a few things. I was wrong not to accept that you really are in love with Ben. And I should have respected you enough to let you be who you are, not who I wanted you to be. So, anyway, I'm sorry. If you two want to be in love, it's none of my business." He turned to me. "Ben, I don't know if it can ever again be like it was between us, but I do hope we can at least still be friends."

"Sure," I said, shaking his hand.

"Well, I guess I should be taking off."

He turned to go, but I just couldn't let things between us end on that note.

"Ted, wait. Hang around. I'm sure Nick and Bobby won't mind. And Doris will be delighted to know you've come to your senses."

"Yeah, I guess I owe her an apology too."

"Well, between you and me, Hope is the one you owe the apology to—that's assuming you like her enough to date her."

"Yeah, of course I do. I just never thought she could like me like that. And now, after making such a fool of myself, I don't know if she'd even have me."

"You'll never know unless you try."

Doris and Patrick came walking up the aisle. She looked surprised and a little apprehensive at seeing Ted standing next to Adrian and me.

I held up my hands. "It's all right, Doris. The madness has left him."

Ted looked down and said, "Doris, I'm sorry I've been such an ass recently."

"Well, I probably ought to have just suggested that you ask Hope out. But I thought if I hinted around long enough, you'd work it out on your own."

He half smiled. "I thought you knew me better than that."

Doris laughed out loud and immediately clapped a hand over her mouth as the laughter echoed through the empty chapel.

"Come on," I said. "Let's go congratulate Nick and Bobby."

The reception was being held in a room in the parish hall. As we went in, Jamal was shaking Bobby's hand.

"Rosalita sends her congratulations," he said. "We drew straws to see who'd get to come, and she lost."

"Send her our thanks," Bobby said, positively beaming.

Ted was sipping punch, and I was filling cups for Patrick, Doris, Adrian and myself, when a guy who looked like a taller mustached version of Bobby walked over to us.

"Hi, I'm Oscar, Bobby's brother. What you kids did means a lot to him and Nick. You helped them get back together, and seeing you supporting them here today encourages us all to believe the future doesn't have to be like the past."

He smiled at us and added, "Oh, and if Mr. Ferguson still teaches physics at Chadham High, tell him I said hello. I used to teach there."

A few minutes later, while Adrian and I were chatting, Herman came over and put an arm around my shoulder.

"Benjamin, I was so sorry when they told me your grandfather Marty died. We'll all miss him."

"Thank you."

"Yes, he was a real *mensch*. And you know, when I got to know him, I saw where you got it from. So, tell me, when will you be coming back?"

I glanced away before answering. "I, uh, I don't know that I am coming back. I had thought to keep volunteering even after I finished my community service requirement, but that was before Grandpa died. Now I'm afraid going back there will just remind me of him."

"Of course, going there will remind you of your grandfather. What are you, made of stone? Of course not, you're flesh and blood, a human being. But I think I know you a little—" He wagged a finger at me. "—and I think you *will* come back, and you'll honor your grandfather by being there. Just like him, you're a real *mensch*. And besides, if you don't come back, where am I going to find another backgammon opponent—one who doesn't cheat?"

He wagged his finger at me again and walked away.

Adrian turned to me. "So, are you going back?"

"I don't know. I wouldn't want to let them all down."

"Admit it, Ben, you love working there. Do you realize half of what you talk about when we're together are things that happened at the center? It's part of what makes you so lovable."

We were in public. There were people all around us. We were in sight of Patrick Frost.

I didn't care. I pulled Adrian close and kissed him.

After seeing Nick and Bobby off for their honeymoon—personally, I didn't get the appeal of visiting New York in December—Patrick, Doris, Ted, and Adrian and I were standing under the church's front portico chatting. The skies were still cloudy, but at least the icy rain and snow had stopped.

"Hey," Ted said, "who's up for a bite to eat? My treat."

Doris's eyes went wide, and her mouth dropped open.

"You? Spend money? Ben, I thought you said he'd come to his senses. He's clearly ready for the psycho ward."

"Hey, I didn't say it would be the le Royale in The District."

I rolled my eyes. "It's not *the* le Royale, it's just *le* Royale. But since you mention The District, Adrian and I know a place there that would be perfect, especially, if old Skinflint Douglas is paying. It's not expensive, and the food is fabulous. It's called Layla's Café."

Patrick asked, "What kind of food do they serve?"

"Lebanese," Adrian said.

Patrick and Ted both looked doubtful.

"I don't know anything about Lebanese food," Patrick said.

"You'll love it," I said. "Trust me; like my father says, Jews know two things—suffering, and where to get the best ethnic food cheap."

We formed a little caravan and drove from Christ Church down to The District. Adrian and I led the way with Ted following in Baby, while Doris and Patrick brought up the rear. The streets were slippery in places, so we took our time getting there.

Finding parking places proved to be as easy on a Monday as it usually was on a Saturday, and I wondered how the businesses there survived in a world where people preferred malls and shopping centers.

As we gathered to walk down the street to the café, Adrian quipped, "Recognize the location, Ted? Layla's is where Ben and I were coming from the evening you...met us."

From the expression on Ted's face, I could tell the jab stung, but he didn't say anything. It reminded me that as mature as Adrian could seem, he was still, at heart, a fifteen-year-old boy who liked to pick on his older brother.

We all entered the café, and our usual waitress smiled, delighted that Adrian and I had brought three new customers. When she asked where we'd like to sit, I said a booth would do, and she showed us to the one Adrian and I considered ours. Adrian scooted in on one side, followed by me and Ted. Patrick slid in on the other side, with Doris next to him.

The waitress had just distributed menus when Doris sighed and turned to Patrick.

"Did I lock the car?"

"I think so. I mean I didn't notice because we were talking... but I'm sure you did."

"I don't know." She turned to Adrian and me. "Do you think it'll be all right to leave it there if it's unlocked?"

I shrugged a shoulder, "I haven't seen any wild street gangs in all the times Adrian and I have been here, but I still wouldn't want to chance it."

"I'll go and check," Patrick said.

"Hey, I'm in the aisle seat. I'll do it," Ted said, and he trotted off.

"I probably did lock up," Doris said. "It's just there have been a couple of times when I didn't, and I was just lucky."

The waitress returned with water glasses.

"Excuse me," Doris said. "Which way are the restrooms?"

"Over there," she replied in her thick Middle Eastern accent, nodding in the direction of a short hall near the counter.

Doris excused herself and disappeared.

"So," Patrick said, "you guys are, like—queer too—is that right? Like the guys that got married."

"Well, we're guys who are attracted to each other," Adrian said with a stony expression.

"Hey, it's cool," Patrick said." To each his own. You seem right for each other and happy together."

"Thank you," I said. "We are."

"Yeah, it's a funny thing," Patrick said, looking at me. "I kind of always knew you were queer. In fact, for a while there, I thought you had a thing for me. But—" He turned to Adrian. "—I wouldn't have guessed you were a fag in a million years."

Adrian's cheeks flushed, and his eyes narrowed. While neither of us appreciated Patrick's use of slurs, I was willing to overlook it as born out of his cultural ignorance—something I was sure Doris would address over time. Adrian, on the other hand, abhorred the thought of being stereotyped, and I could see he was one step away from blowing his top.

"Patrick, might I suggest you try the shawarma? It's kind of a meaty sandwich I think you'll really like. It's right there," I said, pointing to the menu.

While he read the description and looked at the picture, I gave Adrian's leg a squeeze and winked at him. His expression softened.

Ted came back and stood at the end of the table.

"Where's Doris?"

"Here I am," she said, walking up behind him. "Was it locked?"

"Nope," he said, turning around to face her. "It was totally unlocked, and—" He held up her wallet. "—you might want to start being more careful where you leave this."

"Oh, my God," she said, taking it from him. "Thank you, thank you so much."

She reached out to give him a good-natured hug, and he wrapped an arm loosely around her.

"Hmph," a familiar voice rang out. "Try to lie your way out of that one,"

Ted and Doris stepped apart and turned to the door. I leaned over and looked too.

Hope stood just inside the entrance, her hands on her hips, red-faced and scowling.

"Hope, what are you doing here?" I asked, scooting to the edge of the seat.

"Of course, I should have known you'd be here too, traitor."

"What *are* you doing here, Hope?" Doris asked more forcefully.

"I was coming back from the Cathedral, and I saw him—" She nodded at Ted, her voice becoming more emotional with each word. "—and I thought, 'Doris swears there's nothing between her and Ted,' so I decided to surprise him. Well, it looks like I surprised him all right. Looks like I surprised all three of you. And to think I thought you were my friends."

She swung around, flung the door open, and ran down the street.

For a second, all five of us looked back and forth at each other, speechless.

Then Doris punched Ted in the arm. "Don't just stand there, go after her."

He bolted for the door.

"Come on," I said to Patrick. "Hope needs to see you to know she's got things all wrong."

I gave the waitress an apologetic smile as Patrick and I took off after Ted, with Adrian and Doris right behind us. Ted was a block away. We could hear him calling after Hope to stop, but she'd already made it to her car and was jumping inside. She started it up and scratched off into the street, just missing Ted as he tried to catch up with her. The four of us stopped in place.

As the red coupe passed us, Hope was taking a big swig from a bottle.

Doris screamed, "Oh my God, she's drinking. Ben, she's drinking. How could she be so stupid? She's going to get herself killed."

The car was tearing down the street way too fast, and it weaved in the lane hitting icy spots on the pavement.

"Come on," I shouted.

We got to my car at the same time as Ted.

"Get in," I said as I unlocked the door. "We've got to stop her."

Patrick, Doris, and Ted crowded into the back seat while Adrian jumped in next to me. I slammed down on the gas pedal, and the Plymouth took off.

And then it happened.

Off in the distance, we saw the Ford Probe swerve to one side. Hope must have tried to compensate, but the car skidded out of control, completely spinning around, and slammed sidelong into a lamppost on the opposite side of the street.

All five of us gasped.

Doris shouted, "No!"

"Oh, my God," Patrick mumbled.

I brought the Plymouth to a stop a few yards away from the Ford Probe and hit the flashers. All five of us scrambled out. A few people had come out of the buildings on either side of the street and stood gawking at the wreck.

The Probe lay half wrapped around the lamppost, which was now leaning to one side. Skid marks revealed the path the out-of-control car had traveled. The passenger side was totally crushed, the windows shattered, and the hood knocked open. A blue haze drifted in the breeze from the airbag. The engine was still running, but the impact had knocked it out of gear. The air was acrid with the smell of burned rubber.

Hope was hunched over against the driver's side door. Blood coated her forehead and streaked down the window. She was so still I couldn't tell whether she was unconscious or dead.

A knot formed in my throat. Doris was shaking, and Patrick had an arm around her. Adrian stood next to me, his eyes darting from one end of the car to the other.

Ted ran to the Probe and was about to open the door when one of the men standing nearby yelled, "Don't touch her. Moving her could make any injuries worse."

All Ted could do was pound a fist on the car's roof. "Hope, Hope, are you all right?" His voice gave away his increasing panic. "Hope, wake up. Speak to me, Hope. Hope!"

Doris began weeping.

Chapter Sixteen

THE FIVE OF us sat in the emergency room waiting area. Patrick had an arm around Doris. She'd been quietly weeping off and on for hours. Ted sat with his elbows on his knees, his chin resting on his palms. He stared at the floor, his expression as remote as if he were alone on a deserted island. Adrian had his arm around my shoulders. Every now and then, he gently squeezed me.

Hope's parents sat by themselves on the other side of the waiting room. Mr. Murphy had been livid when he came in and saw us, and Mrs. Murphy confronted Doris, demanding to know what had happened. After she gave a rundown of the events leading up to the crash, Mr. Murphy tried to blame us for Hope's drinking and was about to have us thrown out, but Mrs. Murphy told him to let us stay.

An hour or so later, she came over and questioned Doris about what had been going on between her and Hope over the last couple of months. She listened without betraying her thoughts while Doris summarized her ill-fated attempt at matchmaking and how it had backfired. She also told her how we'd kept an eye on Hope since Thanksgiving in the hopes of preventing her from drinking at school again.

Mrs. Murphy leaned back in her chair for a moment.

"What you've told me fits a lot better than the little we've been able to get out of Hope. I'm sorry we blamed you. None of this is your fault. If we'd put her in St. Dominic's from the beginning, none of this would have happened. Hope should never have gone to Chadham High."

She went back to her husband, and we all continued waiting for any word on Hope's condition. As the hours went by, we made calls to our parents to tell them where we were and why. My mother told me to pass on to the Murphys that they were in her prayers—the kind of thing she'd never have said before Grandpa came to live with us.

It was past nine before the doctor came out. She went over to Mr. and Mrs. Murphy, and we all rushed over to listen.

"Well, she broke her left arm in four places. It took time to set and bandage the breaks. She also broke her right shin. That was easier to set. Now, the blow to the head is another matter. We'll need to keep her a day or so to ensure there's no complication from the concussion. But other than that, she's a very lucky girl. With time, she should fully recover."

We all breathed sighs of relief. Doris and Mrs. Murphy hugged each other and cried. The doctor told Mr. and Mrs. Murphy they could spend a couple of minutes by Hope's bedside, and they went in.

The five of us collapsed into the chairs.

"Thank God," Doris said.

Ted was silent.

She studied him for a moment.

"Ted, how are you holding up?"

"This is all my fault. You always said I was stupid, and you were right. If I hadn't got things all wrong, none of this would have happened."

Doris took his hand. "It's as much my fault as anyone's. If I'd just suggested the two of you go out, or kept my mouth shut entirely, things wouldn't have gone so wrong."

"There's enough blame to go around for all three of us," I said. "Let's just be glad she wasn't hurt worse. And when she gets better, let's straighten out this whole business and see she gets the help she needs on the drinking."

"Well," Doris said, "after totaling her car, she's sure to lose her license, so I don't think we'll have to worry about her drinking and driving again for a while."

Mr. and Mrs. Murphy stepped out from the emergency room. He went back to where they had been sitting. She beckoned to us, and we all walked over to her.

"Hope is sedated," she said. "There's nothing you can do here. We appreciate your prayers, but it's getting late, and I think you should go on home. When she comes to, I'll tell her you were all here and how worried you've been about her."

She paused and looked the five of us over.

"Doris, I know Ted and...Ben—" She always hesitated when referring to me, like I was the skunk she couldn't keep out of her garden. "—but who are these two young men?"

"Oh, I'm sorry. This is my boyfriend Patrick Frost, and this is Adrian, he's Ben's—uh, Ted's brother."

Mrs. Murphy noted that Adrian was standing very close to me while Ted was on the other side of Doris and Patrick. She cocked an eyebrow and pursed her lips, then her nostrils flared like she'd just discovered another skunk among the flowers.

"Well, like I said, I'll tell Hope you were all here."

We told her we were glad Hope was going to be all right and said goodbye.

It was running for ten o'clock as the five of us emerged from the hospital. Patrick and Doris said good night and turned to walk toward her car. Ted, Adrian, and I continued to where the Plymouth and Baby were parked next to each other. Ted took out his keys.

"Come on, Adrian. Let's go home."

"I'm staying at Ben's house tonight," he said, quickly adding. "I cleared it with Mom earlier."

Ted's eyes flashed in anger.

"Don't look at me," I said. "This is the first I've heard about it."

Adrian glared at Ted. "You said I should be who I am, not who *you* want me to be."

Ted sighed, but his face was still hard. "Ben, you'll have to watch out. He's always been a manipulative little shit."

He got in his car, backed out, and drove off.

"You know, you really might have at least run it by me before deciding to spend the night."

"I'm sorry. But after a day like this one, I just didn't want to sleep by myself. Please don't make me go home."

I shook my head in surrender. "What am I going to do with you?"

"I don't know, but if you take me home, I'm sure you'll think of something."

He took me in his arms and kissed me. I tousled his hair and unlocked the passenger's side door. We held hands the whole way home. I parked the car, and we went inside to the kitchen. The sound of the TV drifted in from the living room.

I yawned and my stomach growled in reply. "Hey, do you want something to eat before we turn in? I don't know about you, but I can't remember the last time I ate anything."

"Only if you're having something."

"Well, I'm definitely having something."

I opened the fridge and pulled out a tray of cold cuts and a bag of dinner rolls left over from sitting *shivah*. I poured us each a glass of tea, then we sat at the table and cut the rolls to make sandwiches.

We'd just taken our first bites when my father came in.

"I thought I heard mice in here. How's Hope doing?"

"She broke her arm in several places," I said through a mouthful of roast beef. "She also broke one of her legs, and her head required stitches, but they think she's going to be all right."

"Let's keep our fingers crossed," Dad said. "And how was the wedding?"

"Oh, God," I said, setting down my sandwich. "That seems like ages ago now. It was good. It was a very nice service, and they make a cute couple."

"What about you, Adrian? What did you think of it?"

"It was beautiful."

"Well, I'm glad the two of you were there. I'm sure it meant a lot to Bobby and Nick."

He said good night and turned back to the living room, leaving us to munch on our sandwiches. After a few minutes, the TV went silent, and the light from the living room grew dim as one by one the lamps were turned off.

Adrian sighed. "I wish my folks were more like your folks."

"Your mother's okay. She's always been nice to me."

"Maybe, but my father...ugh. If they ever do legalize gay marriage, he's going to be your worst nightmare—the father-in-law from Hell."

I felt my cheeks warming. "I'll put up with him. You're worth the inconvenience."

We clasped hands for a moment and stared into each other's eyes.

"Do you want to shower first?"

Adrian slipped into a lopsided grin. "Wouldn't it save water if we showered together?"

I rolled my eyes and smiled. "Not tonight, dear, I have a headache. Seriously, let's make our first time happen on a less dramatic, more romantic occasion. And I don't know about you, but I'm exhausted."

He shot me a pouty face but nodded.

We cleaned up and went to my room. I gave him a pair of my underwear and a T-shirt and told him where to find the towels and a spare toothbrush. While he was cleaning up, I switched on the receiver and must have dozed off because the next thing I knew, Adrian was in bed next to me, kissing my cheek and caressing me. He did look hot in nothing but my T-shirt and boxers. As tired as I was, the taste of his lips and the touch of his warm, moist skin made my heart race. But after a few minutes luxuriating in the sensual pleasure of it all, I finally pulled myself away for my own shower.

When I again opened my bedroom door and peeked inside, the most adorable sight greeted me. Adrian had worked so hard to arrange it so he could stay the night, and he'd tried so hard to turn me on, even after we both agreed we were exhausted and it wasn't the right time. And now, there he was on his side, snuggling a pillow, sound asleep.

I'd never seen him asleep before, and I stood there taking in the whole vision for several minutes. His face was peaceful, with an air of innocence that made him even more beautiful than I'd have thought possible. His arm, draped over the pillow, was strong and well-toned. His legs were sturdy and muscular. As tired as I was, I could have stood there mesmerized by the sight forever. Only the promise of lying next to him, feeling those legs and arms spooning me, could force me to end my vigil and climb in bed.

WAKING UP THE next morning, we spent a good hour nestled in each other's arms. Our hands roamed freely, and as Adrian touched my flesh, the sensations began stirring a fiery frenzy inside me. Entwined, we let the waves of desire rippling through us build in intensity. Clutching each other and writhing, we surrendered as the pure embodiment of our love engulfed us.

Slowly, as the sensations subsided, we reluctantly pulled ourselves away from each other, mellow and satisfied. Staring into each other's eyes, our cheeks were as flushed from the timid openness we shared as the love overflowing inside us.

"Be mine forever," he whispered. "Share your life with me, or I'll never be complete."

"With all I am, I love you," I said, stroking his cheek. "My love for you will never end, it will never die; it will rage in my heart forever."

"Really?"

"I promise."

We shared breakfast together, and I drove him home so we could spend a few extra last minutes together. The rest of the day was dreamlike and suffused with a contentment I couldn't put words to. At one point, I wondered how I'd ever thought Colby Ryder could offer me anything like what I now shared with Adrian. How could he? The feelings Adrian provoked in me were unique, pure, and absolute. There was a depth in the love we shared I could never find in any other person. I made a silent vow that day that I would be with him as long as he'd have me, and if he ever turned me away, I'd spend my life, like Bobby, never settling for anyone else.

THE WEEK FLOATED by for me. A trip to the mall Wednesday ended with me buying a Divinyls pullover for Adrian as a belated Christmas present. The next day, he gave me a gift-wrapped LP.

"I would have given it to you for Christmas, even if you don't celebrate it, but it wouldn't have been right under the circumstances. I hope you like it."

I tore open the wrapping and smiled. It was Sade's new record. I put it on, and as "No Ordinary Love" purred from the speakers, we settled down and spent the next forty-five minutes necking with abandon.

Thursday was New Year's Eve. Adrian celebrated with us, and we kissed each other when the clock struck midnight. Eliana and Stacy broke into some good-natured wolf whistling that left us blushing but didn't stop us from enjoying the moment.

I got a call from Doris on Saturday.

"Hey, Ben, Happy New Year!"

"Happy New Year. Did you have a nice time? I assume you and Patrick rang in the New Year with some major-league tongue wrestling."

"Hush. I'll have you know we had a nice time celebrating with my folks and their friends."

"So you're saying you only held hands and gave him a peck on the cheek at midnight?"

"Well, no. We snuck off by ourselves. What about you and Adrian?"

"What can I say? When that boy kissed me at midnight, corks weren't the only thing popping."

She laughed and then paused.

"I saw Hope yesterday," she said, the joy gone from her voice.

"And?"

"I wish I hadn't gone."

"What happened?"

"I took Patrick with me. Her mother let us in, reluctantly. Hope was even less happy to see us than her mother. The first thing she said was 'get out.' But her mother told her not to be rude to her guests. Ben, I told her for the umpteenth time that I'd never been interested in Ted and how my matchmaking had confused him. I also told her that when she saw me hugging him at that café, Patrick was right there in the booth. She didn't believe me until her mother told her she'd seen him with me in the emergency room that night."

"So did you two make up?"

She sighed. "Not really. She says the matchmaking was dumb, and me doing it the way I did shows that I don't respect her as a person."

"Ouch."

"Yeah, I know. I told her I was sorry. But, I don't think she'll ever forgive me. I wish I'd never started that stupid matchmaking thing."

"You can't blame yourself. She's obviously got issues that have nothing to do with us. I think it's all tied to her alcoholism—because let's be honest, that's what it is. She's an alcoholic. She didn't just start drinking recently. She used to stop off at the restroom after lunch last year too. Now that she's getting sober, maybe she needs to get away from us to evolve."

"Oh, Ben, she's been my best friend since first grade."

"I know. It sucks. But I guess we've got to give her space, and if that means she doesn't come back to us, we've got to respect it. And look, my relationship with Ted's never going to be like it was, and that has nothing to do with your matchmaking. My father always says 'a man's like a sausage; you never know what's inside.' Ted was okay with me being gay until he had to deal with Adrian being gay too. And now that he's had to face what that means, it's going to be there staring him in the face even if Adrian and I break up—God, forbid."

I paused and added, "*Oy vey*, I'm turning into my grandfather."

She broke out laughing, and I joined her.

IN FACT, HOPE never did connect with us again. She transferred to St. Dominic's at the start of the spring semester and chose a private Catholic college after she graduated the following year. Where she went from there, I never heard. Wherever it was, we all hoped she was happy. And we all missed her. For a long time, it really hurt Doris that Hope was no longer a part of her life, but having Patrick was some consolation for her.

As far as Ted and I were concerned, we made a stab at maintaining our friendship, but it didn't work, and we drifted apart. He couldn't overcome being uncomfortable with the thought of two guys really falling in love. It also came between him and Adrian, but I guess, for better or for worse, lots of things can come between siblings. Anyway, Adrian never seemed troubled by it.

Because of Hope's absence and Ted's aloofness, Doris and I grew closer. We became the kind of friends who can tell each other anything and who are always there for each other when things go wrong. I spent a lot of time with her when she and Patrick broke up during our senior year. It wasn't a particularly nasty breakup, and Patrick was already away attending college at the time, but with Hope already being gone from Doris's life, losing Patrick was harder on her than he'd ever know.

After some hesitation, and with Adrian's encouragement, I went back to the senior center. Being there did make me think about Grandpa every now and then, but Herman had been right—it didn't take me long to get back into the swing of things.

When Herman died that summer, I was devastated and thought about quitting again, but then after the funeral, I found out he had left me his prayer book, his prayer shawl, and his *tefillin*. I was going to refuse them, but then I remembered my father saying that the love we share with someone doesn't die with them, it stays with us, and gives us the ability to live and love others. So, I accepted them as a reminder of Herman and the honor it had been to know him. (Incidentally, along with the prayer shawl and *tefillin* I inherited from Grandpa Marty, they are now among my most treasured possessions.)

Bobby continued to be a good mentor and friend. He and Nick even became friends of the family and celebrated Thanksgiving with us for years. He wrote me a glowing recommendation to Dickerson that I was certain swayed any doubters about my application. And although he told me he had sworn to never set foot in Chadham High again, he and Nick joined Adrian and my folks in cheering me on at graduation.

Speaking of graduation, Doris surprised us all that night. She had decided to go to Dickerson too—to be a marriage counselor, no less. Once we'd enrolled, we studied together when we could, and we grew to depend on each other. We shared our fears, cheered each other on through tough times, and our friendship grew ever deeper. And she was a godsend when Adrian and I broke up.

Ah, Adrian... He and I had tried hard to stay together, but that first year after I graduated put too much strain on our relationship. When studying necessitated one too many canceled visits back home, he said I was taking him for granted, and I said he was being childish. Then he said maybe we needed to take a breather. And just like that, we were through, and I was certain I'd never love again.

I'd always vowed that if Adrian ever wanted to move on, I'd let him go, but when we broke up, I honestly felt like my life was over. I don't know how I'd have survived if not for Doris. She was literally the shoulder I could cry on. She was the voice of reason when I bottomed out and needed it most, spending days in my dorm room. Thanks to her, eventually, I did kind of move on, but I never got over losing him.

IT WAS A snowy day in the winter of 1998, my senior year at Dickerson University, and as I stared out my window, I remembered that day in my third year at Chadham High when I first learned about my grandfather's fall. I couldn't help but smile at how naïve I was back then. I thought I was so mature, that I knew exactly what friendship and love were all about. Love was crushing on a pretty face, friendships were immutable, parents were gods who were never shaken by anything, and old people were creepy. I had it all down, I knew where I was going in life, and my future as a writer awaited me.

Then Grandpa Marty moved in, and everything began to change. Before I knew it, I discovered that old people weren't so creepy after all, and several even became good friends. Grandpa was there as I fell in love with Adrian and started on a journey that revealed love to be something quite different from what I'd always thought it was. And his death was the first time I realized my parents were vulnerable human beings just like me. Grandpa Marty taught me so much just by being there that I owe much to him for being the man I've become.

And what had I learned from falling in love with Adrian? I learned that putting your lover's needs first is what love's all about—even if you suffer because of it. And Bobby was right; love may break our hearts sometimes, but we do need it more than the breaths we take.

Speaking of Adrian, long after we'd broken up, any time I saw a guy who vaguely looked like him, I still died a little inside. Even when I thought I was over him, I'd surprise myself by thinking about him or wake up in the middle of the night dreaming about him. Whenever I'd visit Chadham on break, I seemed to always find myself driving by the Douglas house, Whitney Huston's "I Will Always Love You" running through my mind.

During the summer of 1997, while I was working as an intern at the center, I was surprised one day to find a note stuck under one of my car's windshield wipers. It was from Doris and said I'd earned a free meal at Layla's Café in The District. We'd both been so busy that a chance to sit down over a good meal and catch up was more than a little appealing, so I called her, and we confirmed plans to meet there the next day.

As I drove to The District, I recalled the first time Adrian and I ate at Layla's. The memory made me melancholy, but I was determined to cheer up so Doris and I could have a good time.

I walked in and looked around for her. The waitress—it turned out she was Layla—welcomed me, grinning from ear to ear. I told her I was meeting someone and asked for a table. But she hustled me over to what had been Adrian's and my booth, me protesting the whole way. A lump formed in my throat as she motioned for me to have a seat.

Then I looked over and saw Adrian sitting there, as gorgeous as ever.

"Hey, Ben. Doris couldn't make it. Would you mind having lunch with me instead?"

It was awkward, but I took a seat across from him, and we ordered. While we ate, we chatted, and he asked me a lot of questions about life at Dickerson. But all the while, those eyes were casting their spell, and by the end of the meal, I was staring into them, my heart burning with the same love I'd had for him since the beginning. We were just talking, like friends, but I wanted him so bad I was afraid I'd say something wrong and spoil the moment.

As we were sipping Lebanese coffee after the meal, he leaned back and studied me.

"You know, I never thought you'd be one to break a promise."

"What promise did I ever break?"

"Well, you said, and I quote, 'With all I am, I love you. My love for you will never end, it will never die; I promise.'"

"Adrian, you were the one who said we needed a breather. I never wanted to break up."

"And one time, you said I was worth everything on earth."

"Adrian, I—"

"Ben, I was a fool to break up with you."

"As I remember, you said you were tired of me treating you like a child."

"Well, sometimes I am childish. I'm not perfect. You're not; nobody is. But, Ben, I still love you."

I took a deep breath. What I was going to say to him was the hardest thing I'd ever have to say in my life.

"We can't just pick up where we left off. There's been too much water under the bridge."

"I know, but can't we start over? You once told me about a dream you had where when I got out of Chadham High, you and I would move in together. Well, I've graduated. I can show you my diploma, pictures, everything. I'm going to Dickerson this fall, and if you'll have me, I'd like to find a place where we can be roommates."

"Roommates?" I said, chuckling. "How do you even know it would work out? It could be the worst mistake of our lives."

"Ain't I worth the risk?" he said with a smile.

I sighed and looked into those dazzling eyes, staring so deeply into mine. Damn it, he was doing it to me again, hypnotizing me and bending me to his will.

Then he straightened up. "Okay, seriously, we've got the rest of the summer. If by August we both think it might work out, we can find a place."

"Actually, I've got an apartment already."

"Do you have a roommate?"

"No. It's a one-bedroom apartment."

"All the better. If it doesn't work out for us, I can move into the dorm. But if it does...I ...want you to marry me."

I laughed out loud. "Adrian, you know as well as I do, it's illegal."

"That didn't stop Nick and Bobby, did it?"

"Well, no."

He took my hand in his. "Damn it, Ben, I'm proposing to you. And it's an open-ended proposal. You don't have to say yes right now; I'm willing to wait for you."

"What will your folks think about you moving in with Ted's queer former best friend?"

"Who cares? They knew we were close when you were still at Chadham High, and anyway, I'm enrolling under a full scholarship, so what are they going to do, cut me off?"

"You've got all the answers, don't you?"

"Not quite. I need you to have all the answers. Without you, the other answers aren't worth crap."

"Okay, but let's take things slow."

He scooted out of the bench, came around to my side, and slid in next to me.

"It's a deal." He wrapped his arms around me and pulled me close. "So what say we seal it with a nice—" He pecked me on the cheek. "—slow—" His lips brushed over mine. "—kiss?"

And then we were kissing.

All that summer, we dated and spent time together, and we realized we were as much in love as we'd ever been. But now, our love was so much deeper, perhaps because we both knew what it meant to lose each other. Late in August, my family, Nick and Bobby, Dr. Markov and several of the center staff, Doris, and Mrs. Douglas, joined us at the synagogue. There, our very forward-thinking rabbi, along with Bethany from Christ Church, performed a marriage ceremony for us. At the reception, everyone congratulated us, and Mrs. Douglas even said we were clearly made for each other. But, for me, the most meaningful compliment came from my mother. She pulled me aside and told me Grandpa Marty would have been proud that we married under a canopy.

Later, Adrian and I spent a long weekend at Virginia Beach, after which, we drove up to Dickerson and moved into my apartment together.

So there I was, staring out my window as snow coated the landscape on a cold winter's day in 1998, listening to an old Berlin song on the radio and waiting for Adrian to come home and take my breath away. Sometimes, things do work out.

Glossary of Yiddish and Hebrew Terms

Boytchik—nice boy
Bubbela—sweetheart; dear; sweetie. A term of endearment used by an older
　　person of a child

Fagalah—dDerogatory; homosexual male
Fakakta—something not working well; crap, crappy, worthless, silly,
　　ridiculous
Fershtinkiner—louse, stinker

Kibitz—offer advice as a spectator, often in an uninvited or annoying way.
Kippah—skullcap worn by observant Jewish males
Kolboynicks—know-it-alls
Kvetch—*to* complain
Kvetches—complainers

Mensch—an upstanding person (male), a man of integrity and noble values
Meshugeneh—a crazy or idiotic person
Mishegaas—silliness, lunacy, craziness, insanity

Neshomeleh—sweetheart
Nosh—to snack, munch, graze. Also, the thing snacked on.
Nudnik—pesky person

Oy vey—literally, oh woe

Shadchan—matchmaker
Shegetz—the male version of a *shiksa*
Shiksa—a non-Jewish female; the term sometimes used disparagingly of
　　one particularly alluring to Jewish males
Sitting shivah—Jewish period of mourning lasting seven days after the
　　burial
Shmendriks—idiots
Shmo/shmoes (plural)—jerk, idiot, fool, a naïve or annoying person

Shnorrer—moocher, cheapskate
Shoah—literally, catastrophe; the Holocaust

Tefillin—leather boxes containing parchments with scripture for the
    forehead and arm, used in prayer
Tuchus—ass, posterior, similar in use to "behind"

Verklempt—overwrought, emotional, upset

Yarmulke—skullcap worn by Jewish males.
Yentzer—cheater

Zayt gezunt—be healthy, be well; farewell
Zayt oykh gezunt—farewell to you too

About the Author

Huston Piner always wanted to be a writer but realized from an early age that learning to read would have to take precedence. A voracious reader, he loves nothing more than a well-told story, a glass of red, and music playing in the background. His writings focus on ordinary gay teenagers and young adults struggling with their orientation in the face of cultural prejudice and the evolving influence of LGBTQA+ rights on society. He and his partner live in a house ruled by three domineering cats in the mid-Atlantic region.

Email: hustonpiner@comcast.net

Website: www.hustonpiner.com

Facebook: www.facebook.com/huston.piner

Twitter: @HustonPiner

Other books by this author

My Life as a Myth (Seasons of Chadham High, book 1)
Conjoined at the Soul (Seasons of Chadham High, book 2)

Also Available from NineStar Press

Connect with NineStar Press

Website: NineStarPress.com

Facebook: NineStarPress

Facebook Reader Group: NineStarNiche

Twitter: @ninestarpress

Tumblr: NineStarPress